The
GREAT
HUNT

ALSO BY WENDY HIGGINS

Sweet Evil

Sweet Peril

Sweet Reckoning

Sweet Temptation

Flirting with Maybe

The Great Pursuit

The GREAT HUNT

BOOK ONE OF THE EURONA DUOLOGY

Wendy Higgins

HARPER TEEN
An Imprint of HarperCollins*Publishers*

HarperTeen is an imprint of HarperCollins Publishers.

The Great Hunt

Library of Congress Control Number: 2015943568
ISBN 978-0-06-238134-7

Typography by Carla Weise
16 17 18 19 20 PC/LSCH 10 9 8 7 6 5 4 3 2 1
❖
First paperback edition, 2017

For my daddy, Jim Hornback,
the fisherman and soldier. Hooah.
And for Mama Ilka and lil sis Lucy.

KINGDOMS OF EURONA
AND THEIR RULERS

LOCHLANACH, THE WATERLANDS,
King Charles and Queen Leighlane Lochson

ASCOMANNI, THE COLDLANDS,
King Dagur and Queen Agnetha Vikani

TORESTA, THE RIDGELANDS,
King Gavriil and Queen Lavrenty Cliftonia

ZORFINA, THE DRYLANDS,
King Addar and Queen Meira Zandbur

KALOR, THE HOTLANDS,
Prince Vito Kalieno

LOCHLANACH
ROYAL FAMILY

KING CHARLES AND
QUEEN LEIGHLANE LOCHSON

Princess Aerity (17)

Princess Vixie (15)

Prince Donubhan (10)

LORD PRESTON AND LADY ASHLEY WAVECREST
(YOUNGER SISTER TO THE KING)

Lady Wyneth (18)

Master Bowen (14)

Master Brixton (12)

Master Wyatt (9)

LORD JAMES AND LADY FAITH BAYCREEK
(YOUNGEST SISTER TO THE KING)

Master Leo (12)

Lady Caileen (8)

Lady Merity (6)

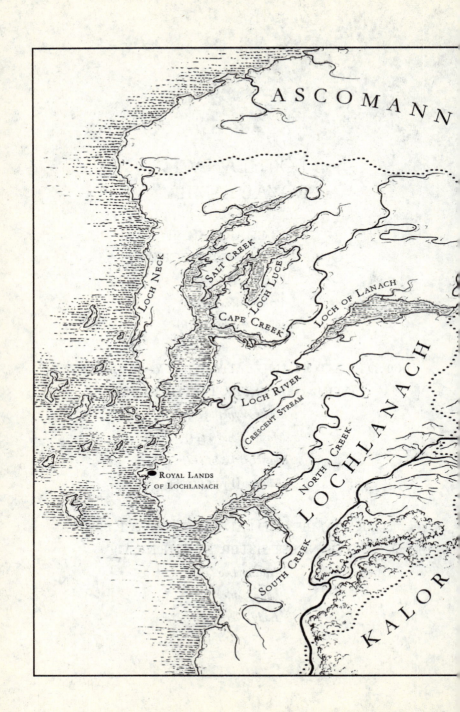

ASCOMANNI

LOCHLA·NACH

TORESTA

ZORFINA

KALOR

ROYAL LANDS OF LOCHLANACH

1   CASTLE
2   WEST COMMONS
3   RED CRAB ISLAND
4   ISLE OF LOCH
5   ROYAL DOCKS
6   ROYAL TRADE PORT
7   ROYAL SEA COMMAND
8   STABLES
9   ROYAL MARKET
10 GARDENS

The
GREAT
HUNT

Chapter
1

A late summer breeze blew warm over the deep and wide Lanach Creek. Moonlight caught the shock of Wyneth's red-orange curls as she let her fiancé, Breckon, lay her back on the end of the dock. She could scarcely see his face in the dark of night as he hovered gently above her, but she knew every angle and plane by heart.

Another breeze crested down the creek from the nearby sea, but the couple's combined heat warded them against it.

"I don't want you to leave," Wyneth whispered.

"If it were up to me, I'd stay right here with you. But it's my duty." He leaned down and kissed her gently at first, then deeper. Wyneth bent her knee, letting the silken layers of her dress fall back to expose her leg. Breckon's hand cupped

1

behind her knee, sliding up farther than she'd ever allowed him to touch before.

"Just think," Breckon said, his breaths coming faster, "in three months, I'll be back from the sea and we'll finally marry."

Wyneth moaned, not wanting his hand to stop moving. "I wish it were now."

She pulled his face to hers again, feeling brazen and greedy for his soft lips. She hated when he left for the sea; it always filled her with a pang of worry and longing. Wyneth urged Breckon closer.

A rustle sounded from the nearby dark woods. The couple stilled, listening.

The noise came again like a crackle of dead leaves and brush. Definite movement.

In a rush, they sat up, Wyneth pulling her skirts down. Breckon readied his hand over the dagger at his waist.

All was quiet except the warble of water bugs, frogs, and the splashing of tiny waves at the shore.

"Do you think someone's spying?" Wyneth whispered. She imagined her young cousin Prince Donubhan and his gang of trouble seekers, but the queen would have his hide if he sneaked out after dark.

"No." Breckon shook his head, a lock of hair falling across his worried brow. "It's most likely a deer." But to Wyneth's ear, he didn't sound so sure.

He relaxed and gave Wyneth a smile, but the mood had

been broken by thoughts of anyone witnessing their intimate time together. It was impossible to find privacy within the castle walls with the royal family, servants, and naval guards running about. The private docks at night had been their only hope without leaving royal lands.

"Perhaps we should go back," she said halfheartedly as Breckon leaned in to place a trail of warm kisses down her neck to her collarbone. "We can fetch Harrison and wake Aerity and sneak down to the wine cellars again."

Breckon chuckled. "The only matchmaking I'm interested in tonight is you and I."

"But that noise—"

"You worry too much. We're safe and alone out here, I assure you. I'd never put your safety or reputation at risk."

Or his own. As the youngest naval captain, Breckon Gillfin's actions were under constant scrutiny. Gossipmongers said he'd risen the ranks quickly because of his long engagement to the king's niece, but anyone who'd seen Breckon in action knew that wasn't the case. King Charles Lochson did not play favorites. Breckon was brave, loyal, and driven. These were all reasons her family accepted Breckon's courtship and offer of marriage when Wyneth was only sixteen. He'd waited patiently these two years since, working hard all the while, and after this next short stint at sea their long wait would at last be over. And if Wyneth had her wish, her cousin Princess Aerity would finally fall in love with Breckon's cousin Harrison, and all would be right in the world.

Another abrasive rustle from the trees caused them to break away again. This time they both stood. Something or someone was surely out there. Wyneth looked to Breckon, who scanned the trees with a scowl.

In the darkness, a large shadow moved within the mossy trees as they swayed. Wyneth grabbed Breckon's arm, and he stared intently into the trees. His dagger, which she hadn't seen him unsheathe, glinted in the moonlight.

"Who's there?" Breckon called. "Show yourself!"

The trees stilled. Even the bugs and frogs stopped their chatter. It was too quiet. Wyneth's heartbeat quickened.

"What if it's the great beast?" she asked, a tremor in her voice.

Breckon shot her a rueful smile and rubbed her hand, which was likely cutting off the circulation in his bicep. "You know the great beast is only a tale among the commoners to impose a curfew on their youth. Besides, the royal lands are protected by the stone wall and the seas. It's probably a buck. Wish I had my bow . . ."

His voice trailed off as they stared into the dark woods.

Rumors of a great beast had arisen through the waterlands of Lochlanach over the summer. Four watermen villagers had been killed, all at night, leaving behind only scraps of bodies. Tale or not, the castle maids who did their shopping beyond the royal wall said they'd never seen such fear among the people.

Just as Breckon was about to sheathe his dagger, a deep snort sounded from the trees.

4

"Oh, my lands!" Wyneth stiffened. "What was that?"

Breckon had tensed and lowered his voice. "Wild boar, perhaps?"

Wyneth had never heard of wild boars on royal lands. Only deer and small creatures.

"Stay here," Breckon ordered. "I'm going to scare it off."

"No!" She grabbed for his hand and he kissed her forehead, gently prying himself away.

Before he could take two steps from her, the dark shadow in the trees resolved itself into a gigantic creature on the sandy walkway. They both stared, not daring to move.

It was taller than any man, standing on its hind legs. Wyneth questioned her own sanity as she stared in disbelief. Its body was massive, the size of a bear, with wiry hair like nothing she'd ever seen. Its face was as ugly as a boar's. Tusks curled up around a dripping snout, sharp teeth shining. Its beady eyes eerily caught the moon's reflection. Everything about its stance and posture screamed feral. Deadly. Impossible.

The long length of the dock separated them from the thing, but it was not far enough for her. Not nearly far enough.

Wyneth couldn't breathe. Her jaw hung open, poised for a scream, but not a sound escaped. She'd never known such crippling fear. Even Breckon made no move except the heaving of his chest from jagged breaths.

The great beast was not a carefully devised tale. It was real.

"Stay behind me," Breckon whispered without moving. "If anything happens, swim for your life across the creek. Do you understand?"

For a moment Wyneth could not respond. Then her voice broke as she frantically whispered, "I can't leave you! Come with me. We'll swim together." She wanted to reach for his hand, but she was stiff with terror and feared giving the beast reason to attack. Perhaps if they stayed very still and quiet it would go away.

When Breckon turned his head to her, insistence in his eyes, that small movement was all it took. The great beast let out a roar, forcing a startled scream from Wyneth. Breckon bit out a curse. The thing charged down the dock, its steps shockingly quiet, for Wyneth had expected the thunder of hooves, not large paws. But then she felt its heaviness shake the wood beneath her feet with each landing.

"*Go!*" Breckon yelled.

At the same time, she grabbed for his arm and screamed, "*Jump!*"

But Breckon had no plans to run from the beast. He grasped Wyneth's waist and pushed her backward with all his might. She felt herself flying through the air off the dock, all breath leaving her lungs as her body submerged with a crash into the cool water. All sound muted. Disbelief struck her once again.

This could not be happening. It couldn't. It wasn't real.

But when her wet face hit the air and she gasped for breath, it took only a moment for her to turn toward the growling sounds and see the monster reach Breckon, towering over him.

Skies above! "Breck!"

"Swim!" He angled himself to avoid the beast's mouth. "Get help!" Breckon launched his strong shoulder into the beast's abdomen and they began to grapple, sounds of grunting and snorting carrying over the water.

Finally Wyneth snapped from her fear-induced stupor and the instinct of flight kicked in. She couldn't fight this thing with Breckon, but she could do what he'd commanded: get help. She turned and swam with all her might. She kicked and her arms sliced through the water as if the beast were right behind her. Indeed, she expected to hear the splash of the thing following at any moment, but it never came. Wyneth hardly heard her fiancé's strangled screams as he fought for his life on the dock behind her.

Breckon was an excellent sailor and soldier. A fearless fighter. He had his knife. The beast was only an animal—no match for her betrothed.

He'll be okay, Wyneth reassured herself with each quick stroke through the water.

After swimming nearly a hundred yards, her body was numb when she reached the dock on the other side of the creek. She pulled herself up, panting for air and cursing her wet, heavy garments. Her eyes scanned the water, but it moved at the same calm, slow speed as always. Then she allowed her eyes to seek out the dock beyond.

The great beast was nowhere in sight, and hope rose in her chest.

The dock was covered in patches of dark moisture that glinted in the moonlight against the dry wood—a sickening trail of it. All hope vanished as she comprehended what lay at the edge of the wooden planks. In the very place she'd been kissed only moments before, were the remains of her life's great love.

Paxton Seabolt sat on a wooden stool with his elbows on the beaten plank bar, sipping his ale and listening to the chatter of two excitable lasses at a table behind him. He felt their eyes on his back, but he wasn't in the mood for flirtations. His thoughts were heavily weighted by one of their own watermen, who'd been killed two nights before by the great beast.

The man had worked with his father for years, hauling in oysters and clams. Paxton recalled his husky laugh, which always seemed too deep for his gaunt face and thin body.

Other men and women from the village of Cape Creek spilled into the dim pub straight from work, bringing marshy smells of salt water, morose faces, whispering rumored details.

"It killed six others in water towns during the summer months, you know. . . ."

"Old man Pearl said he saw it with his own eyes . . . said it was a giant creature like nothing he'd ever seen before."

Paxton would doubt that statement if old man Pearl wasn't as sound and respectable as they come.

As a couple of older women bustled in, Paxton caught sight of the notice that'd been nailed to the door the day prior—an official order from the royal army to stay indoors when the sun went down. A night curfew. Apparently the beast was nocturnal.

"Did you hear?" asked one of the women to the people in the pub. "They're sayin' royal lands were attacked by the beast last night!"

"Impossible," said the barkeep. "It's fortified. Nothing can get past that wall or the navy."

"I don't know how the thing got in, but it killed one of their officers."

The barkeep grabbed a rag and scrubbed a wet spot. "Well, if that's true, perhaps they'll finally do something about it."

"Aye," Paxton agreed gruffly. "Perhaps they'll finally believe us filthy commoners."

The barkeep glanced at Paxton's nearly empty glass and filled him another without asking. "How fared the hunting today, Pax?"

Paxton shrugged, frustrated he hadn't seen any deer that day. "Only a rabbit."

"Your mother will surely make something nice with it." He set the ale in front of Paxton, then wiped his hands on his dirtied apron.

Just as Paxton lifted the full glass to his lips, someone jostled too close and bumped his arm, spilling ale down his chin and the front of his tunic. He glared at the grinning face of his younger brother, Tiern.

"Oy, got a little something there, Pax." Tiern pointed at his older brother's dripping chin. The girls behind them laughed, and Tiern rewarded them with a smile.

"Don't make me snap you, clumsy twig." Paxton wiped his chin with the back of his wrist, but Tiern was unperturbed by Paxton's dark mood. The younger Seabolt brother appeared as put together as always, with his brown hair tied back neatly, in contrast to Paxton's wavy strands hanging messily around his face.

"Everyone's right shaken up about this monster, aye?" Tiern pulled out a wobbly stool, scraping the hard dirt floor, and sat.

The barkeep peered down at Tiern's boyish face. "What're you having today?"

"Just water for him," Paxton said. When Tiern frowned, he continued. "We don't need you getting silly off one ale."

"I don't get silly."

The barkeep chuckled and poured water from a jug. "Aye, you do. You start hugging everyone and telling them all the things you love about them."

Tiern pulled a face and took his water, muttering, "It's no crime to be friendly." He abruptly set down his water. "Oh! Did you hear about Mrs. Mallory?" His face turned uncharacteristically serious.

Paxton's ears perked. "Is she in labor?"

"Already?" asked the barkeep.

"Aye, she is, and it's too early. Mum was running to their cottage to help when I left."

Paxton's stomach soured. The barkeep shook his head and looked away. It was never a surprise when pregnancies failed, yet each time felt like a blow to the village. The birthrates in Lochlanach were at an all-time low—only four children under the age of five in their entire village. It was said to be that way through all of the lands of Eurona, having declined drastically in the past hundred years, though nobody could say why. Many blamed the Lashed Ones, as if it were some sort of magical curse. Paxton knew the truth, but he could not voice his theory without being seen as a Lashed sympathizer.

At that moment the oak door to the pub flew open with a bang and Mallory's husband ran in, his face ashen and his eyes red. People made a quick path for him as he moved to the bar, peering around frantically as if lost.

"Mr. Sandbar," the barkeep said. "What do you need?"

"I . . . alcohol. To stave off infection." He looked about wildly, shoulders stooping. "There were two. Twins . . . boys.

Both gone." The entire bar gasped as a wave of sorrow passed through the room. Mr. Sandbar lifted a shaking hand to his disheveled hair. "Mallory's bleeding too much."

"Okay, man. Stay calm for her." The barkeep filled a cup with clear liquid and thrust it forward.

"I can't pay you right now. I—"

"Don't worry about that. I know you're good for it."

Before Mr. Sandbar could take the cup the door opened again and everyone went still. In the doorway stood Mr. Riverton, an ordinary-looking man in his early thirties. But to the village he wasn't ordinary at all—he was their one and only registered Lashed. He rarely came out except to pick up a bottle of mead from the bar now and again. Paxton felt himself go tense all over as his fellow villagers glared at the man. Mr. Riverton hadn't fared well in the last few years, but the Lashed never did. They seemed to age faster than normal people, dying decades sooner than they should. It didn't help that most couldn't find jobs and had to support themselves on the land or starve.

Paxton had caught his own mother sneaking food to Mr. Riverton's lean-to porch early one morning, but he'd never told her he saw.

Mallory's husband began breathing fast and ragged as he took in the sight of the Lashed man.

Mr. Riverton looked about at the staring faces, landing on Mr. Sandbar's. "S-sorry, I was only picking up something to go . . . I'll just . . ." His hand fumbled for the door handle to exit, but Mr. Sandbar flew across the room in a rage, brandishing a knife from his pocket that he shoved to the Lashed man's throat, pressing him against the wall. Everyone crushed forward to see. Paxton and Tiern leaped from their stools, pushing through the crowd.

"What did you do to her?!" Mr. Sandbar shouted.

Mr. Riverton kept his hands up, his eyes closed. "I didn't do anything, I swear!"

"I saw you look at her two days ago. You stared at her stomach! What did you do?"

"I was glad to see how well she was progressing—that's all!"

"Lies!" Mr. Sandbar pressed forward, denting the Lashed man's throat, causing a trickle of blood to flow. "You're a filthy murderer! Just like your hero, Rocato!"

Mr. Riverton's panicked eyes shot open. "Rocato was a madman! I'm nothing like him—"

"More lies!" Mr. Sandbar's shout came out a sob as tears began to seep from his angry eyes. "You took my boys, just by looking at her!"

"Mr. Sandbar!" Paxton shouted. He grabbed the mourning man by the shoulder. "He can't hurt her with his eyes. You know this. He has to touch with his hands to work magic, and I'm certain he's never gotten that close. Am I right?"

Paxton looked at Mr. Riverton, who whispered hoarsely with his hands held high, "Aye. I never touched her."

"Come on," Paxton said. "Let's get you back to Mallory." He gave the man a gentle tug to pry him away from the frightened, cornered Lashed.

Tiern, who'd had the good foresight to grab the cup of alcohol, took the hand of Mallory's husband and pressed the cup into it. His knife arm dropped and his eyes cleared, seeming to remember why he'd come.

"I'll go with you," Tiern said. He led the stricken man out of the bar.

The people continued to glare at Mr. Riverton, who lowered a shaking hand to his bloodied neck. He took one last glance around at the hostile faces before turning and rushing out, not bothering to get what he'd come for.

"Good riddance," a woman whispered. "Their kind shouldn't be allowed in here."

Paxton clenched his teeth as a roar of familiar anger clawed inside him. He pushed his way back through the people and slid two copper coins across the bar. "This should cover Mr. Sandbar's bill and my drink. Keep the rest." The barkeep nodded, pale faced, and took the payment.

When Paxton turned to leave, the two lasses stood in his path, pretty in long braids and cotton skirts. He knew them to be sixteen, a year younger than Tiern.

"That was generous of you to pay his debt," one of them said, tilting her head demurely up at him. "The poor man."

When he looked at the girl, all he saw was future heartache and loss—the same fate that awaited all who wished to start families—not the kind of future he wanted for himself. Paxton didn't plan to remain in Cape Creek forever.

"Get yourselves home before nightfall," Paxton said.

He sidled past the girls and left the suffocating pub behind him.

Chapter
3

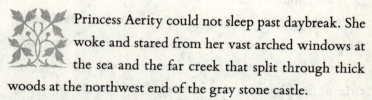Princess Aerity could not sleep past daybreak. She woke and stared from her vast arched windows at the sea and the far creek that split through thick woods at the northwest end of the gray stone castle.

In all of her seventeen years, Aerity had never seen her father, King Charles, so focused on a foe. The entire castle was on edge. And for good reason.

The great beast was real.

Her cousin and dearest friend, Lady Wyneth, had seen it with her own eyes mere days ago, and the kingdom had lost one of its best and brightest naval officers. Breckon had been the pride and future of Lochlanach.

Since that attack, the entire castle seemed to be covered in a suffocating blanket of grief and fear.

Her maid knocked once gently, and entered her chambers with an armful of clean laundry. The girl set Aerity's pale dresses, petticoats, chemises, and corsets across the dressing table and began putting the items in their proper places.

Staring back out the window, Aerity asked her maid, "Are you well this morning, Caitrin?"

"Aye, Princess. Thank you."

"Any happenings during the night?" Aerity's stomach clenched in anticipation of bad news.

"No beast sightings, Your Highness." Her maid hung up the last dress of light green silk, and then ran her hands down her apron. The girl's cheeks were pink from exertion. "But there are rumors. . . ."

Aerity raised her eyebrows. She wasn't allowed to wander the grounds on her own since Breckon's death, so she relied on her maid to carry news to her from the royal market, where citizens from local towns came to sell and trade their wares.

"What sort of rumors?"

Caitrin glanced around the room, as if making certain they were alone, then lowered her voice to a whisper. "People are saying the great beast is a monster created by the Lashed."

Aerity felt her brow tighten. "That's preposterous. They can do many things, but not something of this magnitude."

Caitrin gave a small shrug. "Would you like a fire in the hearth, Princess?"

"No, thank you." It was chilly, but not cold. Her shawl was enough for now.

"Breakfast is nearly ready in the informal dining room." Her maid gave a curtsy and turned to leave.

"Caitrin," Aerity called, and the girl stopped. "Please don't pay any mind to the Lashed rumors. They're unfounded."

The maid gave a smile and nod before leaving her.

Aerity sighed and leaned against the window. The Lashed were always blamed when something went awry in Lochlanach, even though it'd been more than a century since they were permitted to openly use their magic. Lashed had once been revered like royalty for the amazing things they could do with their hands. They could cure illness and heal minor wounds, even cause a living being to sleep and plants to grow or die. But Lashed Ones also had the ability to kill by paralyzing the heart.

All it took was one wayward Lashed, the now infamous Rodolpho Rocato of the hotlands, to change all that. He'd killed the king of Kalor over a hundred years ago in an attempt to take over the kingdom. And he hadn't been alone. A handful of power-hungry Lashed from each kingdom followed his lead, rising up and attempting to overthrow the thrones throughout Eurona.

Aerity shivered when she thought of the old tales. It must have been a horrid time to have lived. So much war and death. Lashed from all five kingdoms, innocent or not, were rounded up and killed—men, women, and children—anyone who bore the telltale signs of magical use under their fingernails. Each time a Lashed One used their power, the magic manifested as a horizontal purple line under their nail. Like a bruise. A lashing.

Were they capable of creating something like this? She shook her head against the notion and went to her wardrobe to retrieve a drab, gray gown. She would mourn the loss of her cousin's fiancé until Wyneth was up and about again. Only then would Aerity don dresses in soft colors.

Before the great beast, breakfasts in the informal dining room were warm and filled with laughter. Now, even the bright tapestries and colorful foreign rugs seemed as dull as the wooden tables. Her father sat next to her mother, Queen Leighlane, and absently stroked her hand with his thumb. Aerity recognized their lost-in-thought expressions, their plates still full. Even under duress their love was palpable.

She adored the story of her parents. As a young king, Charles ignored his adviser's warnings and married the commoner girl he'd fallen in love with. Leighlane was the daughter of traveling acrobats who'd come to entertain the Lochlan royalty. After only a week at the castle, at the young king's urging, Leighlane stayed behind while her parents took to the road again. Three months later they were married. The oft-repeated tale of their love was a steadfast comfort.

Since the death of Breckon, the king's face was lined with the pain of guilt, robbing some of the confident light from his eyes. As much as her father respected his queen, he still scoffed at commoners' superstitions. Many of them were silly, meant to frighten children into good behavior. But these recent mysterious attacks had left mutilated bodies in their wake.

Before Breckon was killed, her father and his advisers had tried to reason these away as the attacks of a madman, or a resurgence of wild wolves that had once roamed the waterlands before being chased into the ridgelands by floods decades ago. Their explanations weren't perfect, but the holes in their reasoning were easier to deal with than the existence of a monstrous predator.

They'd been wrong on this one, and they had chosen to do nothing. All the royals had had their doubts about the tales, though deep down Aerity had known something strange was happening in Lochlanach. Something that couldn't be so easily explained away. Caitrin had appeared more shaken each morning as she relayed information to Aerity about the great beast's attacks.

Now there was no denying its existence.

Soldiers and castle commanders were running about, shouting orders of a massive hunt, and a royal decree had been issued for people to remain inside with doors bolted at night.

The princess hoped they caught and killed the great beast soon, because this was no way for anyone to live. Since Breckon had been killed three days ago, they hadn't been allowed out of the castle, day or night, and she hadn't seen her cousin Wyneth or her dear friend Harrison. Breckon had been buried at sea, a sailor's ritual, with his family aboard the mourning ship.

Aerity's father stood and silently left the dining room with her mother at his side. Aerity shared an awkward moment of quiet glances with her aunts and uncles before they all stood to retreat to their quarters of the castle as well. It was strange not to receive a good-bye or well wish for the day from the king and queen.

Aerity didn't want to return to her chambers. She decided instead to visit someone in the castle she hadn't seen in a while. Heading toward the east halls, she spun around when she heard light footsteps on the stone behind her.

Vixie stood there, holding up her navy blue skirts, and watching her older sister with wide, hopeful eyes. Aerity sighed. Vixie's hair was a wild state of dark red curls. It was a sign of their mother's preoccupied thoughts that she hadn't insisted Vixie have her hair tamed. In Aerity's opinion it would do well for her sister to start acting like more of a young woman and less of a child.

"Where are you going, Aer? May I join you?" The fifteen-year-old lass sidled up to Aerity.

"I'm visiting Mrs. Rathbrook. You'll be bored to tears."

"Do you think she'll work a bit of magic for us?"

Aerity started forward again, and Vixie rushed to keep up. "Mrs. Rathbrook's magic is not for your entertainment. How long has it been since you had your hair brushed?"

Vixie frowned. "It hurts when Valora does it." Valora was their mother's maid, who had no patience for anyone other than the queen.

"It's probably time you had your own maid. Until then, you need to learn to do it yourself. I'll send Caitrin over to teach you. She's gentle, and she works wonders with a warm comb and touch of oil."

Vixie scoffed. "As if you need it."

True. Aerity's hair lacked the bright curls of Vixie's. She'd inherited her father's nearly straight, strawberry blond strands. She often felt left out as the only royal child without the trait. Even their younger brother, Donubhan, had a mop of glorious dark red waves. At least she shared the same hazel eyes as her siblings and father. Her mother's were gray and striking against her cabernet curls.

They rounded the corner at the end of the hall and took a set of stone steps that spiraled upward to the south tower. It'd been too long since Aerity had visited the royal Lashed One, and the woman rarely left her chambers. Mrs. Rathbrook had healed a cut on Aerity's finger eighteen months ago after her arrow lodged too deeply in a tree's trunk, and she'd yanked it out in earnest. She hadn't seen her since.

At the top of the stairs, a tall, older officer named Vest stood at attention before the large door. Officer Vest was a retired navy guard whose sole job now was to watch over Mrs. Rathbrook. He accompanied her everywhere.

"Good morning," Aerity said. "We're here to see Mrs. Rathbrook, if she's willing."

The officer nodded and rapped twice on the door.

Mrs. Rathbrook opened the door, smiling, a long gray braid lying over her shoulder. "I thought I heard voices. These ears are still good after all. Please, come in, Princesses. Seas alive, how you've both grown!" The woman glanced up at the guard, who gave her a nod before closing the door behind them.

The girls entered the dim chambers, breathing in the powdery-scented incense.

"Hello, Mrs. Rathbrook," Aerity said.

"Yes, hello, Mistress," Vixie added.

The shorter woman looked them both over, clasping her hands together. "You appear well. Are you in need of healing?"

"No," Aerity told her. "We've come to visit. I hope that's all right. But if you're busy—"

"Nonsense!" The woman smiled, seeming delighted at the idea of a visit, and Aerity felt a stab of guilt that she rarely gave the healer a passing thought these days.

Mrs. Rathbrook led them to her seating area of old chairs and offered tea.

"No, thank you. We've just come from breakfast."

"What brings you?" She eyed the princesses with curiosity, resting her frail, wrinkled hands in the brown skirts at her lap. Her nails were trimmed neatly, and Aerity couldn't help but stare at her nails, which were nearly all purple. She felt no fear, but was awed nonetheless at the knowledge that those hands could kill as easily as they could heal.

Aerity shifted. "This morning I heard of rumors . . . ridiculous rumors. I suppose it just made me wonder how you were faring. I know father's been keeping you busy with the injured men."

"Ah, yes." Mrs. Rathbrook nodded. "I've saved a few who made it to me in time, but not all. And some refuse my help, of course." A shadow cast across her face. "Their poor families. I imagine these rumors you've heard are about the Lashed Ones, aye? Folks saying we're responsible for this beast?"

"I know it's not possible—" Aerity began.

"Perhaps not, my dear," Mrs. Rathbrook said in an ominous voice. "But the need to place blame is human nature."

"But the Lashed are not evil," Vixie said, sitting forward. "Why are people such idiots? We know your grandson saved father's life with magic."

"Vixie!" Aerity gasped with embarrassment and leveled a glare at her sister. Under her breath she ground out, "A bit of tact, please." Mrs. Rathbrook's grandson was not something the royal family spoke of. Vixie stared back as if to say, "What?"

But the old woman lifted a hand. "No, dear. I don't mind. We are safe here."

"Will you tell us the story?" Vixie asked eagerly.

"Vix . . ." Aerity hissed. She was regretting allowing her

25

pushy sister to come, but Mrs. Rathbrook only smiled and settled back.

"Really, I don't mind. As you know, when your grandfather King Leon reigned, his closest adviser was my son-in-law, General Marsh. The general did not know he'd married a woman with Lashed blood, because my daughter was not Lashed and I was careful to never use my power. My grandson, Sean, grew up with your father. They were best friends from the time they were wee lads." Mrs. Rathbrook's damp eyes shone as she remembered the boys. "Your father, a prince at the time, adored running with the royal hounds. He was often scolded for letting them out of their pens to wrestle and play." She chuckled, remembering.

"Well, in the summer of their eleventh year, one of the dogs was bitten by a rabid raccoon and became ill. The dog attacked your father—had his bloodied leg between its teeth and wouldn't let go. Sean grabbed hold of the dog without thought, and the animal dropped. It was the first time he'd ever used his powers. Sean didn't understand what had happened until he saw the marks under his nails. He'd killed the animal with his sheer willpower to save his friend. Charles lost so much blood that he passed out, until Sean healed his wound."

The girls were quiet and still as the woman continued. It wasn't the first time Aerity had heard the story, but it never ceased to give her chills.

"Sean ran straight home. My son-in-law feared repercussion against his family, so he packed up the lot of us and moved us during the night, abandoning his high position. When King Leon learned what had happened, he let us be. He couldn't afford to be seen as a Lashed sympathizer. But when your grandfather died and your father became king, he sought us out. By that time the general was past his prime and could no longer work for the navy. And Sean, poor Sean, had taken his own life. When your father asked if I was Lashed, I decided to be honest. Out of honor to his childhood friend who'd saved his life, King Charles asked me to work for him as the royal Lashed healer and I agreed."

The three of them were quiet for a respectful moment.

"I don't understand why people think Lashed are evil just because of one man," Vixie said.

The woman nodded. "Like regular folk, most of us are not evil. But you can be sure, young princess, there are evil Lashed Ones. More than one. History has taught us as much. Greed and magical power are a potent combination."

Vixie frowned and crossed her arms. "It's still not fair."

Mrs. Rathbrook let out a sigh.

Since Rocato's attempt to take over Kalor more than a century ago, magic use had been outlawed everywhere in Eurona, with the exception of a few trusted Lashed who worked for the royalty in all five kingdoms, for their personal healing. All Lashed were required to be registered as soon as their capabilities became known, usually around the age of seven. Periodically the royal guard would do rounds, and any Lashed found with the markings were hung without question.

It saddened Aerity to think of the lost potential, those tortured for their talents, and she especially abhorred stories of people bullying children who'd just discovered their magical capabilities. Magic was inherited, but it was rare. There seemed to be no pattern, simply random chance.

Now the Lashed were seen as worse than criminals or diseased. They were outcasts.

Mrs. Rathbrook spoke quietly. "Your father the king is only upholding the laws that have been passed down to him for the safety of the kingdom. He cannot allow that kind of power to threaten us again. And it's not his fault that his people act out of ignorance and fear. Perhaps someday my kind will be better understood." Her voice carried an undercurrent of both sadness and hope.

Still, it pained Aerity to think that the innocent Lashed throughout the kingdom were being suspected of this recent madness.

"There's no way a Lashed One created this monster," Aerity said.

Mrs. Rathbrook shook her head. "I cannot think of how our power could be used in such a way, but there are many far more powerful than me."

An icy sting ratcheted up Aerity's spine. The Lashed could not wave their hands and create a monster from nothing.

Their magic didn't work that way. She refused to believe the Lashed had anything to do with the great beast.

Mrs. Rathbrook appeared tired after so much talking.

"Can I get you anything?" Aerity asked her.

"No, no, dear. My maid takes good care of me. In a few moments I'll walk the roof gardens with Officer Vest."

"Is Mr. Vest your lover lad?" Vixie asked, blinking her wide eyes.

Aerity nearly choked on her own tongue. "High seas, Vixie! That's none of your concern!" Aerity had always wondered herself if there was romance between them, but she'd never dare ask.

Vixie's cheeks reddened and she muttered an apology. Aerity realized her sister had probably repeated something she'd heard, not even realizing how improper it was.

Aerity was still in a state of mortification when Mrs. Rathbrook began laughing.

"Don't hold your tongue on my account," the woman said. "Officer Vest is very dear to me. I trust him with my life each day." She gave the girls a wink and made to stand. Aerity helped her, though the woman seemed quite capable.

"Thank you so very much for visiting. Please come again soon." Mrs. Rathbrook put a hand on Aerity's arm, and the princess bent to kiss her cheek.

"It was my pleasure. I promise to return."

Vixie was still blushing when she leaned forward to kiss the woman's cheek, and then rushed from the chambers, nearly tripping on her skirts.

They'd barely made it to the bottom of the steps when Vixie whispered, "What's wrong with lover lad?"

"Vixie . . ." Aerity shook her head and silently cursed their mother for not talking with the girls about important things. They learned far too much from the lips of maids. "When someone has a lover it means they have . . . a romantic relationship. Like married people."

Aerity headed in the direction of High Hall.

"You mean kissing and the like?" Vixie asked.

"Yes, Vix. And it's impolite to ask people about such private matters. Understand?"

"Have you ever kissed anyone? Or is that too private for me to ask, even of my sister?"

Aerity sighed. She wanted to shush her sister, but Vixie didn't have the blessing of a cousin her age or a friend to speak of such things with. Her best friend was her horse.

"I've kissed one lad." On several occasions. She felt Vixie's big eyes on her.

"Is he your lover, then?"

"No! Stop saying that word."

"Who was the lad?"

"Breckon's cousin, the lieutenant." Her heart gave a squeeze.

"You mean Harrison Gillfin? But he's twenty! Three years your senior!" Vixie pulled a sour face, as if he were an old man.

Aerity laughed.

"Are you going to marry him?" her sister asked.

This gave Aerity pause. She loved Harrison, but not in that way. They'd tried many a time to force something romantic, but their friendship overrode those notions. Their kisses had lacked passion and often ended in laughter. But during the summer gala when Aerity, Harrison, Breckon, and Wyneth had sneaked down to the castle's wine cellars and shared several bottles of mead, Aerity and Harrison had made a fuzzy-minded pact as they snuggled together between two crates, giving their cousins privacy.

"What if I never find a lad to marry, Harrison? What if I never find a good match or fall in love, like my parents did? What will the people say if I rule alone?"

She'd been leaning back between Harrison's legs, and he kissed her hair.

"You will rule well on your own or otherwise. But if you feel you must take a husband, I will marry you in a heartbeat."

She'd turned to peer up at his smooth-shaven face. A face she trusted. "You will find a wife long before that."

He'd stared past her, his eyes going blurry for a moment in thought, then he took a long drink from his bottle. "I don't think so, Aer. I will always be here for you."

But it hadn't been a confession of love. Of that she felt certain.

"I don't know, Vixie," Aerity finally answered. "I'm not sure I'll ever marry."

"Me either!" Vixie said.

Aerity pushed open the doors of High Hall and let out a relieved breath at the sight of their little brother and cousins running about. She pushed heavy thoughts from her mind.

Already the lot of them were at one another's throats with boredom, whining and shouting, and it had been only three days since they'd been confined to the castle. Princess Aerity had volunteered to entertain the children during the day while studies were suspended, distracting them and keeping them away from the adults, in exchange for having her acrobatic silks brought up from the practice room, a space which was too small for all of them to play in.

Her youngest cousins, Caileen and Merity, were playing with the silks, running through them, letting the light fabric flow over their heads. Six-year-old Merity grabbed hold of the bottom of the red silk, which hung from the tall ceiling. She tried to climb, but it slipped through her fingers.

"Here," said Caileen, much wiser and able at eight years of age. "Let me show you." The girl took hold of the silks as high as she could reach with both hands, and attempted to circle her leg around the bottom. She made a frustrated sound when the fabric wouldn't catch against her foot, repeatedly sliding through.

Aerity giggled, and the girls turned. Their faces brightened.

"Aer! Show us!" Caileen begged.

The princess obliged. "You've got to get it nice and tight around your foot, like a band, to the point where it nearly stings." She grabbed hold up high with both hands, wound her ankle about the fabric with a downward thrust to tighten, and then placed her other foot securely on top of the silks to leverage it, stepping up. Aerity swung lightly above the ground, her legs locked, muscles tight. She explained each step as she went, then hopped down to let the girls try. "One at a time, youngest first." Caileen pouted as Merity cheered.

The other six children were loud behind them. Aerity clapped her hands. "Let's line up and have a race!" Her voice echoed off the slick marble floors, tall stone walls, and massive windows. The room was large enough for grand balls, but it was a poor substitution for running through grasses, climbing trees, and swimming.

"No cheating, Donubhan," Aerity warned.

Her ten-year-old brother grinned up at her, mischief in his eyes, too adorable with all that thick hair.

Vixie stood with the younger lads and lasses, hiking up her skirts to run, stuck at the age where she still wanted to play yet also wanted to be treated as a grown woman when the mood struck.

Aerity lifted her arm and lowered it, shouting, "Go!"

Redheads of every shade dashed across High Hall and Aerity couldn't help but smile. Her two siblings and seven cousins were safe and exuberant, despite the chaos outside their doors.

All the royal children were present except Wyneth, the oldest. She was still in her chamber. Daggers stabbed at

Aerity's heart to imagine what Wyneth had been through. The horrors. She couldn't fathom the deranged animal her cousin had seen.

Where had such an atrocity come from?

The princess turned to the grand window and stared out at the castle lands. High Hall was the tallest point of the castle besides the towers, with windows adorning all four sides. Marksmen would be on the roofs above them at that moment with their bows strung tight, scouting. Below, the only people about were soldiers, both naval and royal, bustling on their missions. The edginess never left Aerity, even as she tried to hide it from the curious children.

From this western window she could see the commons area and the seas past it with the trade port. Merchant and fishing boats were always going in and out. From the north window was forest and the royal docks along Lanach Creek. From the east window she could see hundreds of acres of lush land, rolling and green. Beyond that, out of sight, was the fortified stone wall that went from Lochlanach Bay above to Oyster Bay below. The south window looked out over the royal markets, where people came from all over to buy, sell, and trade goods.

Looking out at the waterlands kingdom of Lochlanach, the princess was reminded how much they had to lose. The people who worked so hard. The peace her father and his father before him had worked to bring about after years of war.

Now a single creature threatened all that, and it made

Aerity wish she were a warrior princess who could kill the thing herself. But, alas, she had no talents other than acrobatics, swimming, and simple archery. Nothing useful.

The children screamed and laughed behind her, but she hardly heard them. She stared from the giant window at the crashing waves beyond. At sea were naval ships of all sizes. Water, water everywhere. Aerity couldn't imagine it any other way.

There were the bays and all their wide creeks stretching out like fingers from a palm to touch everything in sight, feeding into rivers, streams, and lakes. Vast fields of vegetation and crops lined forests that backed up to streams and lakes, both saltwater and fresh. At sea were miles of uninhabited barrier islands and tropical islands farther out, which held coveted spices and vegetation used in valuable trades with other kingdoms—all of it in peril.

When her mother arrived in High Hall with a maid bearing a tray of cinnamon sweetcakes, Princesses Aerity and Vixie rushed to her side. The children abandoned their race and bombarded the maid.

"Mother, may I visit the stables now?" Vixie begged. "The horses have never gone this long without me."

"I know, dear," said the queen. "But your father still doesn't want you to leave the castle. The horses are being tended."

While Vixie pouted, Aerity stepped up.

"Mother, may I see Wyneth?" Aerity asked. "Please."

The queen pressed her lips together. Her eyes dropped.

"She is not well, love. She won't speak."

Aerity swallowed hard at the thought of joy-filled Wyneth gone silent.

"I won't bother her. I swear." It was killing her to be kept away.

Queen Leighlane thought about it, and Aerity's spirits soared when she finally nodded. "Perhaps seeing you would be best for her. But don't be offended if she wants you to leave. Don't press her. Understand?"

"Aye."

"And be gentle with your aunt Ashley. She's not herself either."

Aerity nodded, sad to hear it.

Her mother's maid stayed to watch over the children while Aerity rushed to her cousin's chambers. Wyneth's mother, the oldest of the king's younger sisters, sat on a cushioned bench in the hall, a handkerchief held loosely in her hand as she stared at the wall.

It hurt to see this strong woman appear lost and broken. Lady Ashley's usually pristine dress was slightly crumpled. More faded hairs than ever streaked her red locks. Princess Aerity knelt with her hands on her aunt's knees and lowered her head in respect.

"I'm sorry for your loss, Aunt Ashley."

Everyone knew she'd loved her future son-in-law. They'd all loved Breckon.

Lady Ashley softly patted Aerity's shoulder but said

nothing. The princess stood silently and went to Wyneth's room. She knocked twice and pushed the heavy wooden door open. The curtains had been drawn, and no lamps were lit, blanketing the room in darkness. Aerity's first instinct was to brighten the space, but she didn't want to shock her cousin's eyes.

Wyneth lay curled in the middle of the bed, a grievous sight. The princess rarely found reason to cry, but she feared she might now. She climbed onto the bed and curled herself around Wyneth, swallowing back the burn of moisture. Aerity pressed her cheek to the back of her cousin's head and rested her palm against her arm.

"I'm so sorry." Aerity's voice shook.

Her cousin's words came out garbled and nearly unrecognizable. "It can't be real, Aer. Tell me it's not real."

"Oh, sweet Wyn . . ." The princess's heart swelled with grief.

An anguished moan rose from Wyneth, and her whole body rattled, making Aerity break out into gooseflesh at the mournful sound. Wyneth fumbled weakly for Aerity's fingers. The princess reached out and grabbed her cousin's searching hand, lifting it to her cheek.

Together, they held tight to each other and cried.

Chapter

4

Breakfast in the formal dining room was a drab affair. The room felt stifled by the dead air, and the heavily embroidered curtains hung limp without the sea breeze. Aerity doubted that opening the castle windows during the day would lure the beast, but her father and his men weren't taking any chances.

Princess Aerity glanced around at the somber faces of her parents, aunts, and uncles. Everyone but Wyneth was present. Her young cousins seemed to have caught the grim mood of the room, which further plummeted as a messenger arrived and whispered in the king's ear.

Her father's face fell into stern lines as he sent the messenger away. His jaw muscles tightened. The adults and Aerity set their utensils down while the children continued to fuss among themselves, pushing their food around.

"What's happened now?" whispered Queen Leighlane.

Fury burned underneath the king's response. "Two of the royal guards were killed during their night hunt."

Aerity's stomach constricted. She thought of Harrison and was glad he was part of the navy and not the guard.

The queen and Aerity's two aunts shared troubled glances, and her uncles pushed away their plates. Breakfast was over.

❧

Rumors flew through the castle all day.

Princess Aerity didn't know either of the victims or their families, but it still grieved her. Panic rose as the restless energy around the castle grew. Aerity eavesdropped on the adult conversations, wishing her parents would include her. She was seventeen, after all, and she'd be queen someday.

She heard one of the guards had still been alive when they found him, but not for long. His injuries had been too grave for the royal doctors. Even Mrs. Rathbrook could not repair a body when its internal organs had been haphazardly ripped out.

Aerity wished she hadn't sought out the gruesome details.

How had the great beast gotten past the castle wall to attack? The wall was incredibly tall. If it somehow climbed over, it would have surely been spotted by the myriad of guards stationed at the perimeter. The only other way in or out was to swim the waterways, which were deep and wide, with powerful currents.

The thought of the great beast being able to swim sent a shiver zinging across Aerity's skin.

Even worse, what if there was more than one beast? Animals didn't simply appear from nowhere as lone entities.

Her breakfast churned in her stomach. She stood and motioned Vixie to accompany her to High Hall while the others finished.

In the echoing High Hall, with the doors shut, Aerity stepped out of her layered skirts, wearing only her overblouse and leggings. She coated her hands in powdered rosin from a bowl. Vixie sat on the floor cross-legged and watched as Aerity ran her hands down the flowing red silks. She bundled each of the two strands in her hands. This was where she could clear her mind, letting her body and the silks work together as one. She'd been working on a routine all summer in preparation for the fall gala, and though plans had been stopped, Aerity continued to practice.

She used the curves of her body and her limbs, twining the silks like ropes about her, testing the strength of each move with gentle tugs to make sure she was prepared to move to the next position. Aerity climbed as high as she could, the silks wound tightly around her feet, then leaned back and spun a bit to circle the fabric around her waist. She heard Vixie gasp as she let go with her hands and leaned back, glorifying in the stretch of her arched back, grabbing hold of her pointed foot.

"You're so high. . . ." Vixie's fearful whisper filled the room.

Aerity smiled to herself and moved to hang upside down fully, suspended with the cloths pinching her thighs and hips securely. She grasped the hanging silks and waved them at her sister below. Ironically, they were both frightened of the other's talents—Vixie was afraid of heights, and Aerity couldn't imagine performing on the back of a moving horse.

"Come up and get me," Aerity teased.

"Not on your life. Come down here and be my horse. I miss riding."

Aerity swiveled, repositioning, and rolled downward at top speed, stopping herself just before the bottom, tensing all her muscles as she hung perpendicular to the floor.

"Show-off." Vixie, the master of showing off, leaped forward in a handspring, then dived again and walked on her hands in a circle around the dangling Aerity. "Come on, Sister. I need a horse."

Aerity let go of the silks and gracefully stood. "You're too tall for us to do that now."

"Oh, let's just try. Please?"

Aerity sighed and went to her hands and knees. Vixie giggled and landed on her feet, quickly straddling her sister's back. They laughed as Aerity moved sluggishly forward, Vixie clinging.

"Come on, then. You're as slow as an old mule." She swatted Aerity's bottom, making the older princess squeal.

"I'll buck you off!" She laughed.

Aerity picked up speed as Vixie moved, light and agile,

resting her knees on Aerity's lower back, and her palms on Aerity's shoulder blades.

"Nice and easy," Vixie said. Aerity tensed as she felt her sister's weight change, all the pressure going to her upper back as Vixie moved into a handstand.

Aerity was holding her breath. She had stopped.

"Keep moving, you naughty horsie," Vixie breathed from her handstand.

Aerity tried to go forward, but couldn't keep her back tight enough, and the two sisters toppled into a heap, Vixie landing on Aerity with a thud. They laughed together as they hadn't done in a long time.

Outside they heard hushed, serious voices passing, and the girls stilled. They looked at each other.

"I'm worried about Mama and Papa," Vixie said. "And Wyneth."

"I know," Aerity whispered. "Papa will figure something out, though. Things will be back to normal soon." She gave her sister a small smile, and Vixie smiled back, seeming relieved.

<hr>

Yet the following morning proved Aerity's words to be worthless. A villager had gone missing in the night. They found his leather boot by the canal near his house, his foot still inside.

When Aerity saw the fierce look of determination on her father's face as he sped down the halls, spouting orders to his men, she felt her first spark of hope—it seemed he'd finally had enough. She flattened herself against the wall as the men passed, so focused they never glanced her way.

". . . respond with force," she heard her father say. Yes! He spoke of sending out thousands of soldiers across the kingdom, on both royal and common lands. So much manpower and expertise. They would have to kill the beast.

Her mother, who'd been steps behind the men, saw Aerity and took her by the hand. "It will be all right now. Keep to your rooms so you don't get trampled. And be on the lookout for Donubhan. I can't keep track of that child." The queen kissed Aerity on the temple and left to catch up.

Aerity sighed. She checked in on a sleeping Wyneth before heading to her own chambers, wishing she could venture outdoors. In the corridor she spotted a slight movement in the wall curtains and marched over, yanking the curtain back. Donubhan let out a holler of surprise and Aerity bit back a smile.

"What in Eurona are you doing, Donny?"

He exhaled and smacked his hands to his thighs. "Nobody will tell me anything!"

"They won't tell me anything either," Aerity said. "Come on. Let's find Vixie and visit the indoor archery range together. I'll challenge you both to best out of five."

"You're on!" He ran ahead, dark red locks flopping around his head.

Everything was going to be okay. Forces would be dispatched this very day to try to catch the nocturnal beast where it slumbered. They would hunt through the night if necessary. By the next day, this madness could be over.

⁂

Princess Aerity awoke to the hope of celebration, but when she tiptoed out of her chambers for an update, she was met with eerie silence. She found Donubhan, Vixie, and the younger cousins eating with the maids in the informal dining room. She rushed past before they spotted her. Following low voices coming from the end of the long hallway, she found her parents, aunts, uncles, and the king's advisers inside his office. She slipped in behind the standing bodies. When all eyes turned to her she stood straighter, clasping her hands behind her back and lifting her chin as if daring them to make her leave.

Her father only sighed. "Continue," he told one of the commanders.

Aerity felt a moment of proud glee.

The commander looked ragged, as if he hadn't slept. "Your Majesty, the men were stationed throughout the kingdom— in trees, at the edges of the water, anywhere we could think. The beast attacked from behind along the east inlet—one of the places it's never been spotted before. My men say the beast felled ten men within minutes. Their weapons were useless. They say it has tough skin, thick tusks, and sharp claws. It roared loud enough to pierce their eardrums, and . . . the few surviving soldiers ran."

The commander sounded ashamed to admit this as the king grimaced. His soldiers ran. For some reason this shocked

44

Aerity more than any other fact. Grown, trained men had run because the beast was that frightening. The room seemed to grow colder.

"Your Majesty," began Lord Preston Wavecrest. "Perhaps we should round up a few Lashed to try and kill it with their powers—" The king adamantly shook his head, and her uncle hurried on. "With all due respect, now's not the time to have a bleeding heart. A Lashed One could kill the beast with a single touch!"

Aerity's father slammed a fist against his oak desk, making it rattle. "I will not force civilians to face the beast against their will, Lashed or not. Would you have women, children, and elderly out there when our own soldiers run from it?"

"There are men on the Lashed records. Not many, but—"

"I said no."

Lord Preston gritted his teeth. Aerity could see the desperation on her uncle's face. He'd already lost his future son-in-law, and his daughter had withdrawn to a dark place in her mind, gone from them as well.

"Lord Preston," the king's adviser said. "From what I know of the Lashed, they must be able to lay hands on a living being and concentrate. Our men are being flung ten feet from the beast with barely a shrug of its arms. If we could somehow trap it and hold it down, a Lashed One would be valuable, but we have not yet discovered a way to do so."

Lord Preston gave a nod and looked away in defeat. Lady Ashley took his hand.

"Tonight, the soldiers go again," the king said. "Any who are willing. I will offer a healthy financial reward to the one who kills the beast or injures it enough to take it captive."

From that day on, Aerity was allowed into the adult conversations without question. She desperately wanted to drag her grieving cousin along with her, since they'd always done everything together, but the last thing Wyneth needed was to hear talk of the beast.

Aerity rushed straight to her father's office for news the next morning, but it was empty. The castle was strangely silent. Aerity neared High Hall, where a guard stood at attention outside the doors. He allowed her to pass without hesitation. She saw movement through the crack of the door, and she opened it enough to peek in at the mostly empty room.

Aerity held her breath at the sight of her mother climbing the hanging silks. She hadn't seen her mother perform, even casually, in years. Aerity recalled how weightless her mother had always seemed in her silk acts, but today there was a heaviness about her ascent. Queen Leighlane's cabernet-colored curls were pulled up tightly and she wore a close-fitting tunic and leggings. She was halfway to the ceiling when she stopped, resting her cheek against the fabric as she swayed.

The sight filled Aerity with sadness. What was going on in her strong mother's mind? Was all hope lost? She refused to believe it.

Queen Leighlane seemed to come back to herself. She

reclined into a lean and pulled her knees up, repositioning her feet with a glide of the cloth. Her body wound and slid into position with the silks around her waist. Aerity recognized the position of a drop roll. Her mother began to soar downward, and the princess quickly saw that her mother was not stopping the roll soon enough. Queen Leighlane reached up wildly to grab at the silks, but tumbled to the ground with a thump.

"Mama!" Aerity ran into the hall, the guard at her heels, and fell to her mother's side.

The queen sat up, pressing a hand against her hip.

"Your Highness!" The guard crouched beside her.

"I'm fine," she whispered, closing her eyes.

"Shall I fetch Mrs. Rathbrook?" he asked.

"No. It's only bruising. You may leave us."

He hesitated before standing. "I'll be just outside the door if you need anything, Your Highness."

The queen reached for Aerity's hand and they clasped, moving closer.

Aerity helped her sit up. "Are you certain you're okay?"

"I've had worse falls." The queen managed a small smile, which quickly faltered as she met her daughter's eyes. The woman's chin trembled.

"What is it, Mama? What happened last night?"

"Your father . . ." She sniffed and composed herself. "He's at his wit's end, love. The men refused to hunt last night. Hundreds of them. Even after your father offered a larger reward.

We cannot stretch the kingdom's finances further. They're asking for higher-powered weapons, more versatile versions of the cannons they use at sea, but it could take months, years, to develop and produce something like that."

"Seas alive," Aerity whispered.

Her mother's eyes cleared as she looked at her. "I'm sorry. I shouldn't put this burden on your shoulders—"

"No." Aerity's voice was resolute. "I need to know what is going on. The kingdom's burdens are mine as well as yours."

The queen's eyes watered. "This beast. It's too strong, too vicious. The men say their war cries only taunt it. My girl . . . I'm frightened for what's to come."

Aerity shivered and pulled her mother against her. She needed her mother to stay strong, for all of them. She'd never seen her like this. "Everything will be all right, Mama. Father will figure something out."

She hoped if she kept saying it, it would become truth.

⤚⧽⤙

Aerity held hands with her mother as news was issued in the king's office.

"Three fishermen were reported missing. Traces of their remains were found at daybreak at the sea's edge. They were . . ." The adviser swallowed hard. "Their bodies were spread over a vast area, as if the beast had dragged them about."

Nausea filled Aerity.

Lady Ashley clung to her husband's elbow and leaned her face against his arm. "It has to stop," she whispered.

Aerity agreed. The tales were unbearable. Everything around her felt fragile.

The king leaned his knuckles against his desk, his eyes shut tightly.

"Your Majesty." One of his commanders stepped forward. "The number of men willing to enter the forest to fight the beast has dwindled to nearly nothing. Wives of soldiers are lined at the castle walls during daylight hours, begging for mercy for their husbands, pleading for them not to be forced into the woods." The man sounded desperate, almost frantic. "The kingdom is petrified with fear. Businesses are shutting down because some fear leaving their homes, even during the day. Some have taken the opportunity to loot. Many are fleeing to the coldlands of Ascomanni or the mountains of Toresta."

"Enough," the king said in a growl. "Everyone leave me. I need to think." He pushed up and went to the window-lined wall, staring out as the others filed away in silence. Aerity's mother squeezed her hand before taking her leave. When the room cleared, Princess Aerity walked to her father's side and placed a hand on his shoulder.

"Father . . ."

He continued to stare out the window, his anxiety obvious. Without looking at her he reached up and gave her hand a single pat.

"While I've been busy, you've grown into a young woman. You call me father now, not papa."

Aerity's heart softened. How long had it been since they'd spoken one-on-one?

"I thought I was prepared for anything. I prided myself on defending this kingdom against rebels and uprisings and foreign invasion. To be bested by a single creature . . . to see my people in despair . . ."

Her grip tightened on his shoulder. "You've not been bested. There is hope. You're doing all you can, Father."

"Am I?" He looked at her now, his watery eyes scanning her face. He ran a hand through his hair, overgrown strands of light red. He was a man in his prime, and Aerity didn't like seeing his strength frayed.

"I don't like being pushed to desperate measures," he whispered, almost to himself.

Aerity swallowed back her emotions enough to speak. "Any who know you do not doubt that you act out of love for the kingdom. Always. Do what you must."

He stared back out the window until Aerity's hand fell away from him.

"Seas forgive me," he whispered. Princess Aerity left her father to think, having no idea how her own words would come to affect her.

Chapter 5

The castle windows remained tightly locked, denying the rooms and halls of their usual scented breeze, stifling the royal living spaces. That evening when Vixie and Donubhan feigned nightmares, Aerity let them cram into her bed. It left Aerity tired in the morning after being kicked and nudged and snored at all night, but she was glad to be able to comfort them. And their nearness was a comfort to her as well.

Something had to be done. The entire kingdom of Lochlanach was exhausted. Frazzled. On the verge of self-destruction. If the beast wasn't caught and killed soon, fear would overtake the lands.

Fear was a dangerous, unpredictable weapon.

Princess Aerity wasn't surprised when her father called a royal family meeting the following day. She wondered what extreme measures he had decided upon, and hoped the people of the kingdom would come to understand and support him. One thing Aerity had learned from being the daughter of a king is that sometimes sacrifices had to be made for the greater good.

They filed into High Hall—even cousin Wyneth, who left her bed for the first time since Breckon's death. Aerity was proud of her for coming. She forced herself not to pounce on her cousin with affection, instead holding Wyneth's hand tightly as the older women doted on her, smoothing her curls and flooding her with greetings.

In order to show her hope for the kingdom, Aerity wore a pale shade of periwinkle blue, her first colorful garment in days, while Wyneth still donned gray.

The king and queen sat at the head of the long table in their tall oak chairs lined with crushed blue velvet. As a child, Aerity could remember running her fingers along the carved grooves of the chairs where generations of kings and queens had sat before them.

King Charles's younger sisters flanked the king and queen on either side with their husbands—the Wavecrests on one side, the Baycreeks on the other. The king was the eldest child and only son. He'd always been close to his sisters and brothers-in-law, and welcomed their counsel.

Princess Aerity sat beside Wyneth, who still held her hand. Wyneth preserved her tough exterior, but Aerity felt the truth in the slight tremble of her cousin's fingers.

On Aerity's other side was a fidgety Vixie. Across from them were two of Wyneth's three younger brothers, fourteen-year-old Bowen, and Brixton at twelve. Wyneth's youngest brother, Wyatt, ran about the expansive space of the hall with Donubhan and their cousin Leo, while Caileen and Merity sat with sketchbooks and fine chalks.

The clearing of the king's throat was loud enough to draw everyone's attention. His face had taken on an ashen pallor, the skin drooping under his hazel eyes. It was alarming for Princess Aerity to see her father in such a state. He set his elbows heavily on the table before him.

"Never in my reign have I experienced such desperation."

Aerity's heart sank like an anchor to hear the truth in those words.

"I've spoken countless hours with my advisers and officers," he continued. "I've notified the other kingdoms of our predicament, and thankfully no other lands of Eurona suffer such a beast as ours. We've no idea where it came from, or if there are more than one, but it must be stopped. If it continues, or, seas forbid, multiplies . . ." A shiver seemed to ricochet through him. "My men are not hunters. They are soldiers and sailors and watermen. I cannot allow my men to continue being slaughtered and terrified. If I don't act, the people will act on my behalf. They've already begun."

Revolt? Aerity's innards shook at the idea of an uprising. Chaos.

Lord James sat forward, stiffening. "What do you mean, they've already begun?"

The king's lips pursed. "In the north village, where one of the murdered fishermen lived, the townspeople went door to door as a mob, looking for Lashed. They found a man with fresh markings . . ."

"Seas alive, no," Lady Faith whispered. Aerity's stomach turned.

"The Lashed man was ill, could hardly walk. He told them he'd healed a baby bird that fell from a tree, but they were beyond sympathy, beyond reason. They stoned him to death."

The queen dragged in a sobbing breath and covered her mouth. Aerity tasted bile as her own emotions rose.

"He should not have used his magic, aye, but I cannot have people taking the law into their own hands," the king said with a pained inflection. "I cannot allow senseless killings of innocents in my land."

"Have you any ideas what we can do?" Lord Preston asked.

"One." Aerity's father spoke the word in a near whisper. Then he looked straight at her, his eldest daughter.

Goose bumps rippled in a cold wave across the princess's skin.

Aerity's mother grabbed the king's forearm in a hard grip and turned toward him, besieging him with a whisper. "Charles, perhaps we should tell her without an audience."

Her father eyed her mother. His gaze held something Aerity had never seen before. Something utterly unsettling. Something hardened.

"You speak of me?" Aerity whispered.

"Aye," her father whispered in return.

"Shall we leave?" Her uncle Preston began to stand.

"No," Aerity said. They all turned to her, as if surprised by her strong tone. "Please stay. We've always been as one. Whatever he has to say to me can be said in front of all of you."

Truth be told, she was frightened and took comfort in being surrounded by family. She'd no clue what this meeting had to do with her, but they were all in this together. Everyone settled again, but not one of them appeared comfortable.

"They call me the liberal king," her father continued in that same ominous, quiet tone. "The romantic." He looked at his wife, who gave an encouraging nod. "Because I believe in marrying for love, not lands or money or family name, the way it was for centuries before me. I promised my daughters they could choose their future husbands, just so long as the lads met our general approval."

Everyone around the table nodded. They all knew this, and had agreed. The king had even fought his parents for his sisters to be able to marry of their own choosing. But Princess Aerity could not nod along with them. A horrible sense of trepidation had taken root inside her.

Why was he bringing up marriage? He wouldn't even

allow young men to court her until she turned eighteen next year.

"But these are desperate times," he whispered.

Heavy sea snakes slithered in the pit of Aerity's stomach.

"What are you saying, Charles?" Lady Ashley asked.

Again, her father looked directly at Aerity. "I must ask something of you that I never wanted. I never expected. As your father, it pains me. As your king, it is necessary."

Her eyes burned, but she could only nod at his sincerity. Next to her, cousin Wyneth's fingers flexed against Aerity's, her first signs of life.

"Aerity . . ." Her father paused. "I must ask you to sacrifice the promise of love for the sake of our kingdom."

He stared at her hard. She tried to swallow, but she could only stare back, frozen.

"I will be issuing a king's proclamation to all five kingdoms of Eurona to send their best hunters, but I must make their journeys worthwhile. I must ensure that the strongest will be willing to face this foe. A monetary prize is not enough, and as you all know, most of the kingdom's excess funds are wrapped up in my son's land and youngest daughter's dowry. Therefore, I have only one thing left to offer the man who kills this beast. I offer the hand of my oldest daughter in marriage."

No. Spirits of the seas, no.

Princess Aerity felt heavy, unable to move or take air into her lungs. On one side of her, Vixie made a high-pitched sound. On the other, Wyneth gasped. Her aunts and uncles gaped at him.

The queen leaned forward to garner Aerity's attention, that same desperation in her eyes that the king had, her voice thick. "Please, darling, don't think of it as sacrificing love. Who's to say you won't fall in love with him? I imagine he'll be brave and . . ."

The queen had to stop and cover her mouth against the mounting emotions. Aerity felt as if she might be sick. All around the table were the shocked faces of her family, but none of their horror matched the turmoil within her. She knew she should say something, but words . . . there were no words. Her life, as she knew it, was over. Her future, and the freedom she'd imagined, was dead.

Vixie began swiping tears from her cheeks. "This isn't fair for Aerity, Papa," she said.

"Truly, Charles," said Lady Ashley. "There must be another way."

The king's jaw set. "You don't think I've thought this through? You think I came to this decision on a careless whim, Sister?"

"I think we could have discussed options as a family—"

His voice rose. "I've spent countless hours speaking with every able-minded adviser in the kingdom. I've nothing left to give! Our lands had two years of drought and two years of rotting rain. Trades are down. All land in Lochlanach is owned by commoners or claimed for our royal lines. Would you have me break off pieces of your lands as reward?" The king pushed back in his chair; the queen placed a steadying hand on his forearm.

"There's no need to raise your voice at her," Lord Preston said.

"I believe there bloody well *is* reason when I'm being accused of tossing my daughter away without a care!" He looked at Lady Ashley. "You of all people should want this beast killed."

"Of course I want it killed!" she shouted back at him. "But this is unprecedented."

"It cheapens the royal line," Lord Preston added.

"How so?" the queen asked. "Because hunters are mostly villagers?" She raised her eyebrows in challenge.

"You know I have no prejudice against you or commoners, Leighlane," Lord Preston scoffed.

"Charles, please," Lady Faith spoke. "We know you're under pressure. We know you wouldn't make this decision without a care. It's just that we're all a bit . . . surprised. You do realize a proclamation like this could invite any vagabond, brutish, scoundrel to have a lucky shot at the beast and live out the rest of his life in the castle, don't you? And with your daughter, no less."

The queen sucked in a breath. "Don't be crude."

"It's only the truth," Lady Faith said. "We need to discuss the reality of this situation."

"The reality is that we're facing a beast that we struggle to beat," the king snapped.

"I agree," Lord James said. He sent his wife an apologetic look for opposing her. "I think this is a worthy sacrifice. Arranged marriages were the way for many years until our generation. Aerity will survive."

As they argued, Aerity imagined the kind, handsome face of Harrison, but the comfort he brought her was suddenly beyond reach.

"Papa, please," Vixie pleaded. "Use my dowry instead."

Oh, sweet Vixie. Aerity's heart cracked.

The queen shook her head. "Vix, you will need that, trust me."

"I don't want it!"

"You're too young to understand the importance, love."

"I'm old enough to know this is wrong!" Vixie was crying in earnest now.

Lord James shook his head. "This generation of royal children doesn't understand the obligation we have to the people. These kids have lived indulgent lives with no responsibilities, playing and doing circus tricks all day."

Queen Leighlane glared. "Exercise and agility is nothing to frown upon."

Lady Faith waved a dismissive hand at her husband. "They learn of hardship through their studies. No need for them to actually *experience* it." At this, Lord James rolled his eyes, and the arguing commenced.

Vixie's wails became background noise to the entire family fighting, emotions rising along with their voices. Aerity's queasy stomach continued to spin, making her dizzy. While the adults quarreled, Wyneth's worried eyes met Aerity's.

Am I selfish to want to refuse? Aerity silently asked. Wyneth tightened her grip on her cousin's hand under the table, and Aerity knew that even though Wyneth would do anything to avenge Breckon's death, she would not hold it against Aerity if she defied her father in this.

Lord James stood, his chair flying back, knocking over a water glass as he pointed at Lord Preston. Others rose to their feet as well. Their voices echoed in Aerity's ears, the words mashing together without meaning, making her head pound.

Thirty men had been slaughtered this week. Thirty women were grieving for the men they loved, and one of those women was her cousin. Thirty mothers had to live with images of their sons' strong bodies being ripped apart. Now her family was at odds.

Could this proclamation end their suffering?

She forced herself to sit straighter, grasping at fleeting strands of confidence.

"Father." The single word was lost amid a myriad of loud voices. Frustration and desperation painted her loved ones' faces. She yelled over them, "Father!"

The room silenced. All heads turned to her.

"I will do as I must." Her words were strong, forceful, even though she felt nothing of the sort. She looked at her father's red face. "I do not fault you for making this difficult decision. Send out your proclamation. Let the hunt begin as soon as possible."

His eyes lit in pride and gratitude. When his chin trembled, the chin of a man who never backed down and never showed weakness, Princess Aerity had to release herself from Wyneth's grip.

The truth of everything began to soak into her, like rain, each drop speaking to her. . . .

A stranger.

A hunter.

Your husband.

Overwhelmed, she turned and gathered her skirts, forcing her chin to remain up as she walked steadily from High Hall.

Chapter

6

 Aerity did not want to speak to a soul. She sat on the edge of her bed, numb. For the first time in her life she felt an understanding of what it truly meant to be royal—a kinship with generations before her. When a soft knock sounded at her bedchamber door, she called, "Leave me be."

The door opened a crack and Aerity saw a tangle of red curls around a tearstained face. Vixie. All at once, her sister's offer to use her dowry and her cries on Aerity's behalf was like a river of sentiment through her.

"Oh, Vixie, come here, love."

Her sister came straight to her bed and climbed up into her arms, clinging to her. Aerity swallowed hard, trying to hold it together.

"I'm so mad at him, Aer." Vixie pulled back, her pretty lips pursed. "I refuse to call him papa anymore."

This wounded Aerity more than anything so far. She didn't want this kind of divide in the family. Aerity rubbed Vixie's arm. She understood her sister's refusal to call him papa. Tonight, she'd felt like a king's subject, not a king's daughter, but she had to get past that feeling.

"Hush now, Vix. I'm sure he's doing what he thinks is best. . . ." The words felt vile on her tongue, though she remembered their discussion of honor and sacrifice. Those things had seemed simple in theory, when it hadn't been her own freedom on the line.

"You cannot seriously be all right with this!" Vixie pulled her arm away.

Aerity was torn between what her heart felt and what her mind knew. All her life she'd been taught to put the kingdom first. This was the first time she'd have to see that duty in action. Never did she imagine it would be like this.

"I will have to make difficult decisions when I am queen—"

"You will never make decisions that hurt your children!"

Aerity's breaths were shaky. She hoped to the seas she'd never be faced with something like this when she had to rule. Could she ever sacrifice one of her children's happiness for the kingdom? If not, would that make her a weak ruler?

She swallowed hard.

"Thank you for what you said in there, Vixie. You don't

know what it means to me."

"I know you're trying to be strong, and all of that queenly nonsense, but I am angry enough for both of us. I refuse to speak to him."

Aerity choked back a laugh and took her passionate sister in her arms again. "Please don't hold on to your anger too long."

Vixie sniffed and looked up. "You really will do it, won't you? You'll marry a complete stranger."

Aerity's stomach turned like a rough gale. She shut her eyes. "I don't want to," she admitted. "But, aye. I will. I want this beast dead. I have to hope for the best, Vix."

When Aerity opened her eyes she found Vixie studying her.

"You will make a good queen someday," the girl said softly.

This was the thing that finally brought Aerity's emotions to the surface, causing her to fight for breath. She didn't feel like a future queen, and definitely not a future wife. She felt like a girl who had just lost something important. "Will you stay with me tonight?"

"Aye. Anything for you."

Chapter 7

Most males in Lochlanach focused on fishing, crabbing, and harvesting shellfish. Brothers Paxton and Tiern Seabolt were two of the few who focused on land animals. Hunting. The lands of Lochlanach were best for growing crops, not raising livestock, so meat such as poultry, pork, and beef were in low supply at any given time. Only the wealthiest merchants could afford to raise animals for personal consumption.

In winter months when meat was scarce, the village turned to the Seabolt brothers. They kept a lean-to in the nearby forest with freshly salted venison and sold it as cheaply as they could, barely making a profit, not wanting anyone to go hungry.

Even though they themselves were nearly always hungry.

It didn't used to be that way. Before their father's knees went out two years ago, he'd been a successful deep sea fisherman. They'd lived comfortably on an acre with a stream, eating fish as thick and meaty as beefsteaks. Now they were without a boat, crammed within one of the row houses of the village, lucky to salvage bits of leftover venison jerky.

Seventeen-year-old Tiern took their family's fall in stride, as good-natured as ever. But Paxton, two years his senior, had turned even angrier and more withdrawn than usual. Tiern suspected there was more to Paxton's issues, secrets that Tiern had been sheltered from and reasons his older brother seemed to carry the weight of the world. But Pax was a private person, even among the ones he loved.

The fall morning was crisp as Tiern and Paxton made their way through the wooded brush with stealth, bows at the ready. For tall boys wading through fallen leaves, they scarcely made a sound. Paxton could go hours without talking—hours of listening to sounds of the forest, staring through leaves and branches for signs of movement.

Tiern could do it as well, but he didn't relish it the way Paxton seemed to. Inside, Tiern was bored and restless. He wished a bloody deer would show itself already so they could skin it, drain it, hang it, and have their feet up in front of the fire before the curfew. He hated the cold evenings. Why couldn't it be summer year-round?

They found a ridge of decaying logs and nestled themselves

side by side, one brother facing each direction. And they waited.

After a while with no sign of anything but songbirds flying south, Tiern glanced at Paxton from the corner of his eye. Pax was eyeing the forest in earnest.

Paxton's brown hair was wild with waves, and almost long enough to tie back with a strip of leather. Tiern didn't know how he could stand to have it in his face like that. His own hair was the same dark brown shade, but straight. He kept it pulled back neatly at the nape of his neck. More rugged. More muscular. More mysterious. That was Pax.

Tiern could make girls laugh, and flattered them with compliments. They felt comfortable in his presence. Ironically, they flocked to Paxton for just the opposite reason. His abrasiveness seemed to be a challenge that kept girls on edge. Paxton never took the time to notice anything, but a single moment of eye contact with a girl could make her cheeks flush. No words necessary. Tiern wanted to laugh at the backwardness, at how blushing lasses gravitated toward his older brother who couldn't be arsed to give them a lick of his attention.

Tiern saw movement and tore his gaze from his brother. His eyes met the trees just in time. A brown blur moved twenty yards away. All of Tiern's fidgeting and boredom dissolved. For one shade of a second he wondered if it might be the great beast, but he knew it never came out during daylight hours. No, the animal's form materialized into a gentle beast, nothing to fear.

Never taking his eyes from the deer, he gently nudged Paxton before ever so slowly nocking his arrow to his bow and lifting it. Aiming. Waiting for the perfect shot.

He could feel his brother's silent anticipation next to him.

They were different in so many ways, but in these moments they were the same—joined by the thrill of the hunt.

Tiern's heart pumped hard and the whoosh, whoosh, whoosh through his ears became a soothing mantra. This feeling. This rush made the boredom of waiting worthwhile.

Just as the doe stepped into the clearing, making for a perfect shot, Paxton's fingers tightened on Tiern's shoulder and his eyes flicked to the side.

Tiern's heart sank.

An older fawn, still sporting its fading spots, came bounding out beside its mother.

"Bucking seas," Tiern cursed. The brothers had a rule about not killing does while they were raising babes. Once the fawns were older, losing their spots, their mothers were fair game.

Tiern lowered his bow, disappointment washing through him. But seconds later Paxton's fingers gripped him again. He followed his brother's gaze, and was hit with elation at the sight before them.

A giant buck with an eight-point rack stood between the trees, gazing toward the doe. A deer that size could feed half their village this week.

"Take it," Paxton said, so low Tiern almost couldn't hear.

Technically the buck was on Paxton's side, but he must have felt bad about the doe, so he was giving his little brother the go. Tiern turned himself, achingly slow, and nocked his arrow to the bow once again, pulling it rigid.

Come on, big lad, he thought. *Give me a good shot.*

He didn't have to wait long. The unsuspecting buck, focused solely on the doe, stepped out.

Tiern didn't hesitate. He let his arrow fly and it found its mark beneath the ribs. He released a huge breath of relief as the beautiful animal faltered and fell. The doe and fawn dashed away.

Paxton leaped to his feet and ran to their prey. Tiern always let him take care of this part. His brother unsheathed a dagger from his waist and squatted at the animal's side.

"There now," Paxton soothed. He reached out slowly, with care, and pressed a hand to the buck's head. The animal was still alive, breathing hard. "Go, be at peace. Your life will not be wasted."

Those words, spoken at every kill, never ceased to bring a chill of awe to Tiern. He watched as his brother raised the dagger and ended the creature's suffering. If only the lasses in town could see Paxton here in his element—see how capable their handsome brute was of gentleness, even as he killed. They'd likely be elbowing one another out of the way and racing to see who could lift their skirts for him the quickest.

Aside from their father, Tiern was the only person who knew this side of Paxton. He felt honored, as if witnessing something private and intimate.

When Paxton was ready, they got to work.

⤖

It was stew for dinner that night. Maryn Seabolt cooked a small portion of the fresh venison in a pot with potatoes, carrots, and the last of the thick-skinned tomatoes from their summer garden. She hummed a folk song as she bustled about. When everything was ready, she made heaping bowls for her two boys and brought their suppers to them in front of the fire. They ate like kings on the night of a big kill.

If only it happened more often.

"Thank you, Mum," Tiern said.

"No, thank you, laddie." She kissed his forehead.

"Thanks," Paxton said. Their mother rumpled his mess of hair before turning away, humming again.

The front door swung open with a rickety creak and their father lumbered in, his cane clanking against hard, dirt floors. His body looked as pained and burdensome as always, but his eyes shone. He sniffed the air.

"I heard you got a big one, aye?"

"Aye, Father," Paxton said, his voice deep with pride. "Tiern took it."

The corner of Tiern's mouth quirked up and his cheeks shaded.

Their father rumbled a laugh and gave his youngest boy

70

a punch on his lean shoulder before falling into his chair with an *oof*. Their mother was at his side the next moment holding a steaming bowl.

"Grab a bowl and join us, Maryn," he told her. "There's news. Big news."

Her hand flew to her heart. "Not another killing?"

"Nae, nae. But it does have to do with the great beast. Our king has issued a proclamation."

Her eyebrows rose, and the boys traded looks of interest.

"We didn't hear about any proclamation when we were in the market," Tiern said.

"It was just issued. Hurry yourself." Mr. Seabolt gave his wife a smack on the bottom.

She rushed off with an uncharacteristic giggle and Paxton shook his head at his grinning brother, turning his attention back to the stew.

"So the king finally believes there's a beast and plans to do something about it?" Paxton asked. "Now that his own men have been killed and not just peasants?"

"It would seem so," his father said with a frown.

Paxton grumbled.

Tiern and his father ignored Paxton's gibe and tone. They were accustomed to his negativity toward the king, and toward everything in general.

When the four of them were gathered around the fire, Mr. Seabolt set down his empty bowl and placed his large palms on his knees. All attention turned to him.

"The king's proclamation states that the best hunters from all of Eurona are invited to Lochlanach for a massive hunt. Whoever kills the great beast will get the most valuable reward the king can offer . . ." He paused and the room was thick with expectancy. "The hand of Princess Aerity."

Mrs. Seabolt gasped, nearly toppling her bowl.

"No shite?" Tiern breathed. His mother must have been in shock because she didn't even swat him for his language.

"Aye," their father said.

Tiern and Paxton stared at each other, their eyes distant as their minds swirled with possibility.

Killing the great beast would turn a regular man—a mere hunter, a commoner—into royalty. He would marry a princess, thereby earning himself the most gorgeous of waterway lands with abundant crops, enclosed within the safety of the legendary stone wall. Their family would be comfortable for generations. Beyond comfortable.

"Get it out of your minds. It's too dangerous," Mrs. Seabolt whispered, panicked. "Even soldiers cannot kill it!"

"The boys are smart," their father said. "The king's soldiers have become lazy due to our blessed lack of war, and they train primarily for sea battles and defensive attacks, not tracking. Our boys know the forests. They have common sense and a world of skill. I think they should both enter. Someone has to kill this beast. It may as well be them. They'd be heroes, and think of the prize!"

Mrs. Seabolt pursed her lips at him.

"I'd be out hunting the beast anyhow if it weren't for the bloody curfew threatening to arrest everyone," Paxton said.

His mother propped a hand on her hip. "Pfft! I don't think so, young man!" But they all knew she wouldn't have been able to stop him.

Tiern and his brother became lost in visions of the ultimate hunt.

Their mother absently fiddled with her apron, twisting it and then smoothing it, a nervous habit. "This is absurd. I think . . ."

Their father's eyebrows drew together. "What, dear?"

"It's just that . . ." Her eyes slid to Tiern with worry and he sat up straighter.

"He can rival any hunter, Mother," Paxton told her.

"Aye, but he's young still." She swallowed and shook her head.

Tiern ground his teeth. When would she stop viewing him as a wee lad? He knew how children were valued in their society, but he hated to be coddled and sheltered. He shot her a pleading expression.

"I'm seventeen, Mother. Not a child."

Her eyes scanned his lean frame as if he were still five. "I know, dear." She barely got the words out before tears were escaping. "But this beast . . ."

"Now, now." Mr. Seabolt sighed and reached for his wife's hand. "Fear not. The boys will look out for each other—"

"You're not frightened at all?" she asked, louder now. "I

don't care about the riches! I care about my boys. You can stop them! Forbid them."

Both sons turned to their father. Indeed, Tiern could see there was reluctance, and something darker, in the man's face. Maybe fear. But he knew their father could see the hunt for what it was: an honor and the opportunity of a lifetime.

"The boys do not have to go, Maryn, but if they choose to participate, I will not stop them."

"Mother." Paxton's voice was firm, his eyes like strong mahogany as he held her gaze. "I vow not to let harm come to Tiern. One of us will kill this beast and we will both return home safely. We will make you proud. Please, let us go with your blessing." He spoke with absolute conviction, and Tiern wondered if he'd ever be able to talk like that and be taken as seriously as his older brother.

Their mother covered her mouth and squeezed her eyes shut. After a long pause, she finally nodded, letting out a whimper. Their father patted her knee, beaming at his boys.

Tiern and Paxton met gazes, the older brother giving him a nod, solidifying their partnership in this adventure. Tiern's chest swelled with pride and excitement. The ultimate hunt. The hand of a princess. What could be better?

Chapter
8

Princess Aerity held her skirts in her fists as she ran down the stone hall of the royal quarters and burst into Lady Wyneth's bedroom. She knew she could not face what was happening in the royal streets of castle Lochlanach without her cousin.

Lads. Men. Over a hundred of them. All potential husbands.

Aerity found her sitting in a chair in another gray gown, staring at the wall. Wyneth was fully dressed and her hair had been brushed.

"Wyn?"

Her cousin startled at the sound of her name. It broke Aerity's heart all over again to see the vibrant girl so washed out. Aerity slid into a crouch beside her.

"How do you feel?" Aerity asked.

Wyneth gave a weak shrug, and Aerity suddenly felt bad for bothering her. The princess dropped her eyes, fidgeting with nerves.

Wyneth sat up straighter. "They're not here already, are they? The proclamation just went out."

"It's been over a week. . . ." She swallowed.

"A week already?" Wyneth's eyes cleared as they looked at each other. "Oh, Aer. Are there many?"

Aerity tried to stay calm, but all the fear and nervousness tangled together to make her voice shaky and high. "There are hundreds of them."

"Where are they? Can we spy?" These words from Wyneth filled Aerity with relief. They'd always faced things together, practically joined at the hip.

"Aye, Cousin. I don't think I can do this without you."

Wyneth stood and took both Aerity's hands in hers. "We go together."

A grateful smile graced Aerity's lips, the first real one since she'd agreed to this madness.

"Well, let's go scout the lads then," Wyneth said. Her grip on Aerity's hand tightened. "Don't be afraid. I'm certain one of them will be perfect for you."

Aerity's chest tightened. She wasn't certain of that at all, but she appreciated the sureness in her cousin's voice.

"I'm sure they'll all be in love with you before the hunt

ends," Wyneth said with false cheeriness. Aerity let out a breathy laugh, but her stomach turned at the thought of how many deaths could be wrought through this hunt.

Hand in hand, they headed toward the south covered parapet walk along the edge of the castle that overlooked the royal market. They sneaked quietly out the doors. Wyneth's hand shielded her eyes and she let out a small sound of discomfort as they exited the arched doorway into the fresh air. With a pang, Aerity realized this was Wyneth's first time outdoors since Breckon had died. She hooked her arm through Wyneth's and pulled her close.

"Thank you for doing this, Wyn."

"Always," her cousin whispered.

As they neared the edge and peered through one of the tall embrasures, Wyneth exclaimed, "Great seas . . ."

The streets were crammed and the atmosphere was exuberant. People were smiling for the first time in months. Men of differing statures, ages, and appearances were milling about, sharpening blades and tightening bowstrings. And it seemed that everyone from Lochlanach had come to see. Aerity's heart punched the inside of her chest as her eyes raked the people.

Somewhere in that huge crowd was the hope of their kingdom . . . and her future mate.

She noticed beards and smooth faces, dark skin and light, local clothing among styles of fur and bright colors from distant lands, voices rising in foreign languages. Some of the men looked like brutes with oversized muscles and grimy outfits. Aerity closed her eyes and tried to breathe. The idea of giving herself to some surly stranger made her ill with fright.

"Brave men." Wyneth kept her voice quiet. She hadn't let go of Aerity's arm. When the princess looked at her, she saw eyes haunted by memories. Wyneth would know firsthand what those brave men would be facing. She hadn't spoken of the beast to Aerity, but it clearly tormented her thoughts.

"Indeed," Aerity said.

They leaned on the stone opening for several minutes before one of the town's women caught sight of them from a booth of scarves. Aerity heard the joyous sound of murmurs from below, whispers of "Look! It's Princess Aerity and Lady Wyneth!" Both girls stopped as hundreds of eyes turned up to them. They were accustomed to this, but today it felt different. Today, many of the eyes in the crowd were gazing up at their possible future prize. Swallowing hard and forcing a smile, Aerity raised her hand and waved. Townspeople waved back with excitement, but the strange men only stared, some grinning, some nudging each other.

When a respectable amount of time had passed, Aerity gently pulled her cousin from the ledge, out of sight. She leaned against the wall and closed her eyes, feeling Wyneth's hands on her shoulders.

"Are you all right, Aerity?"

The princess was shaking, but she nodded. "I'll be fine."

"You're a blessing to this kingdom, you know." Wyneth

pulled her into a hug, their heads resting perfectly on each other's shoulders. "I would have likely fought the king's decision. I admire your dedication." Wyneth had always been strong and lively—it felt good to see a glimpse of that returning and to be able to lean on her cousin once again.

"Oh, look." Wyneth peered down over Aerity's shoulder. "Is that Mrs. Rathbrook?"

Aerity turned to see the woman at one of the market tables that sold herbal leaves and powders. Officer Vest stood nearby, scanning the people. Aerity was just about to remark how it was nice to see Mrs. Rathbrook out, when she noticed the space around the woman. The market was crowded, but nobody was near her. In fact, people were casting her furtive, even aghast, glances, ushering their children away.

Each time Mrs. Rathbrook moved a step, the crowd shifted.

"By the seas." Aerity scowled as she strained to watch from the distance. "Look at that."

Mrs. Rathbrook slid her payment on the table and the unsmiling clerk tossed copper coins in front of her, yanking her hand back. The Lashed woman seemed not to notice, saying something with a kind smile and retreating with her bag. Mrs. Rathbrook walked stoically through the people, who stared as they cleared a path for her, crushing together to keep out of arm's reach.

"Awful," Wyneth whispered.

Aerity's jaw was set in anger. Even the guards and military

personnel gave Mrs. Rathbrook a wide berth as she made her way through the booths. No wonder the woman kept to her own chambers most of the time.

"Pardon me, Princess and Lady."

Aerity pulled back at the sound of one of the king's errand boys standing in the arched doorway.

"Princess Aerity, his majesty would like a word."

"Of course. Thank you."

He rushed off and Aerity took Wyneth's hand again, not wanting to be alone. She made her poor cousin accompany her to her father's study, where he spoke in hushed tones to one of his military advisers.

"Ah, Aerity," he said when he caught sight of her. He rose from his grand chair and came around, nodding at Wyneth. "It's good to see you about again, Lady Wyn."

Wyneth gave a small curtsy. "It's good to be about, Your Majesty."

His adviser shut the door, and the four of them remained standing. Her father still showed signs of exhaustion, but his eyes gleamed with the same hope of the townspeople in the market.

"I hate to ask more of you, Aerity. . . ."

She braced herself. "What do you need, Father?"

He cleared his throat. "As you've surely gathered, hunters have begun arriving. We fear once the hunt begins there will be many who want to flee after they see . . ." His voice trailed off as his sights shifted to his niece, who dropped her eyes. "We would like to keep up their morale as best as possible. We'll be gathering the hunters in the west commons area so they may practice their skills and have a place to rest in peace after the hunt each day." He paused, hesitating. Aerity thought he could probably face down other kings with more confidence than he had facing down his own daughter.

He continued. "It might be difficult or uncomfortable, but I was hoping you'd be willing to visit the west commons area daily. You would of course have guards, and you're never to be alone with any of the men. Our hope is that seeing you will . . . lift the spirits of the hunters."

And remind them of their prize.

She tried to breathe steadily, feeling embarrassed and used, reminding herself this was all for the best. She was one life among tens of thousands. Still, no matter how she reasoned with herself, her gut still churned.

She wasn't accustomed to speaking to males outside of their family and the Gillfins. Her nerves bunched into tight bundles, making Aerity light-headed, but she managed a nod. "Of course, Father." She knew this was not easy for him. He sounded just as afraid as she was about what kind of man she'd end up with—what kind of man they'd be welcoming into the royal family. But regardless of who he was or where he hailed from, if he killed the beast, they would owe him respect and gratitude.

"I've got servants setting up tents and tables and shooting ranges in the west commons area now. If you could make an appearance during the dinner hour I'd be appreciative."

"I'll be there."

"Good." The king's adviser bustled to the desk, turning the king's attention back to work. Aerity swallowed her emotions, and the girls slipped from the room. Wyneth shot one questioning look at Aerity, as if to gauge her thoughts.

"I'm okay," Aerity said, letting out a long breath. "Not every girl is lucky enough to have hundreds of suitors, aye?"

Wyneth huffed a mild laugh through her nose. Then she got quiet and looked at the princess. "You don't have to act brave on my account, you know."

Aerity swallowed. "I know." She had to stay brave for her own self. They stopped when they reached her bedroom door.

"You'll come with me tonight to the west commons, won't you, Cousin?"

Wyneth ran her fingers down a strand of Aerity's long hair, smoothing it. "I won't leave you. I promise."

Aerity smiled. She could do this. With Wyneth at her side, she could resist the urge to escape her fate, to flee somewhere far away where her life and choices were her own. She'd agreed to this, and the wheels were set in motion. Running from her responsibility wasn't an option. She would have to make the best of it.

Chapter

9

Mrs. Rathbrook was glad to feel the sunlight on her skin for the first time in months. She needed to restock a few herbs in her cabinets. It was a fine day to be in the markets. Busy. Festive. Hunters of all nationalities filled the royal plaza, taking some of the attention off her. But not all. She could still sense the stares, though she no longer let it bother her. Years of stares had toughened her. Officer Vest remained close behind, a constant refuge.

Mrs. Rathbrook couldn't help but glance around at the nearby men in their strange furs and head wraps, wondering which one of them might kill the beast and marry the princess. A shock of heartache filled her on princess Aerity's behalf. The king's decision seemed hypocritical to her, seeing as how he refused his late parents' wish for him to marry a princess of Toresta. Though she would never voice her opinion aloud.

As she browsed the selection of fresh, dried, and powdered herbs, someone sidled close to her side. Much closer than usual. Mrs. Rathbrook caught a flash of orange fabric from the corner of her eye.

"Good day, royal Lashed One." The smooth, husky female voice was not Lochlan.

Mrs. Rathbrook turned her head up to the stranger, and sucked in a breath at the sight of her. Shining black hair against light brown skin. Eyes of crystal blue. A brown cloak over a silken, orange dress. The woman gave her a smile, but something about it felt . . . off. Disingenuous.

"Hello," Mrs. Rathbrook said.

The woman glanced down at Mrs. Rathbrook's hands, which held a satchel of coins.

"Your hands are very beautiful."

Mrs. Rathbrook's heart sped up. Nobody spoke openly of her lashes, or her ability in general. She withdrew her hands, hiding them within her pockets. The woman gave her that ominous smile again.

Officer Vest stepped closer, but the woman ignored him. She only had eyes for the royal Lashed One, and she obviously had something to say. Mrs. Rathbrook could not help her curiosity.

She kept her eyes on the woman as she gave a nod and said, "It's all right, Officer Vest."

He stepped back, giving them space.

"Your own guard," the woman drawled. "How charming."

Mrs. Rathbrook narrowed her eyes. "Who are you?"

"My name is Rozaria. I hail from the hotlands of Kalor."

The name meant nothing to Mrs. Rathbrook. This woman must have accompanied the Kalorian hunters.

"How does it feel to be a slave to the Lochsons?" The pleasant look never left the woman's face, even as she spoke abrasive words.

Mrs. Rathbrook went still. She'd never been to Kalor. Perhaps open rudeness was acceptable there, but she did not appreciate it. She lowered her voice and responded curtly.

"King Charles and his family treat me very well, thank you." She turned back to the herbs, hoping the woman would take the hint and leave her be. No such luck.

"A comfortable room in a lavish castle, while others of your kind suffer throughout the land."

Mrs. Rathbrook stood tall and faced the woman again. Her words had cut deep. She often thought about her own comfort compared to the despair of other Lashed, but she felt powerless to do anything about it.

"What would you have me do, Miss?" Then she remembered that Rocato, the root of prejudice against Lashed, had been from Kalor. "Perhaps if the Lashed in your land had not pursued their greed and hatred, these issues would not be upon us."

The woman's eyes hardened with anger.

Officer Vest stepped forward. "I'm going to have to ask you to move along, Miss."

The woman, Rozaria, ignored him. "You know nothing," she hissed at Mrs. Rathbrook. "But you will soon learn."

"And just what is that supposed to mean?"

The woman's sneer transformed her beautiful face into something frightening. Then she briskly turned and walked from the stand, keeping her hands deep in her cloak pockets, disappearing into the multitude of bodies. Mrs. Rathbrook noticed people quickly turning their heads away when they saw her looking.

"Are you all right, Mrs. Rathbrook?" Officer Vest asked. The crinkles around his eyes were further deepened with worry. "Did she threaten you?"

Mrs. Rathbrook shook her head. She wasn't quite sure what had just happened, but it had left her weary. "I think I've got all I need for now." She kept her head down as Officer Vest walked her back to the castle, her heart burdened with the woman's words.

Chapter
10

Paxton could immediately tell the true hunters from the ones motivated only by the king's promised reward. He couldn't help glaring at the gentlemen with their pretty bows and pristine arrows as they took their time aiming at the wooden targets. No doubt they'd never had to raise a bow for protection or a meal. He'd be happy when the hunt began and the impostors cleared out, wetting their fancy trousers in fright.

Aye, being on royal lands put him in a fine mood.

The west commons area was surrounded by a stone wall, a miniature version of the wall protecting the royal lands. The area's single entry had two iron gates that swung inward, covered in vines. At the far side were long tables for eating.

Against the wall by the tables were sets of stone and wood steps, likely used for spectator seating at events. The middle area of the commons consisted of fine grass where the men gathered for target practice and exercise. Tents had been erected at the southern end.

Next to Paxton, Tiern shifted from foot to foot, unable to stay still. "When do you think these idiots will finish? They've been at the targets forever."

Paxton peered at the current archer and grimaced as his arrow missed the target completely, wobbling to the side and clanking into the wall. The archer frowned at his bow and grumbled, as if the bow were the problem. The man next to him commented about the gust of wind that likely took the arrow off course.

Paxton could take it no longer. He ran a hand through his unruly waves to get the locks out of his eyes as he walked over to the shooters.

"Oy, there. Time to rotate." He didn't bother with niceties. Paxton wasn't there to make friends, but he nearly smiled in amusement at their startled expressions.

"We're allowed five shots each," one of them protested.

"Then get a move on. There's a bloody line forming."

The polished young men looked like they wanted to argue, likely unaccustomed to being spoken to in such a way, especially by a townsperson. Paxton stepped back and crossed his arms. He saw Tiern press his lips together to keep back a grin. The men, appearing rattled, turned back toward the targets and fired off their last shots.

Soon after, Tiern was up.

"Don't show off," Paxton warned Tiern, who sighed with disappointment.

The brothers made quick work of their time at the target, angling their bodies from different positions for each shot, and hitting within the middle circle each time. Paxton heard whispers from the handful of wealthy men surrounding them, but didn't care to gauge their reactions.

After they'd retrieved their arrows, Paxton sat with Tiern on the stone seats by the wall, eyeing the crowd of hunters. Tiern rambled on about each of them, telling Paxton snippets of things he'd overheard, mostly braggarts boasting of their kills.

"That one there hunts lions down in the Kalor hotlands," Tiern whispered excitedly, pointing to a man with what appeared to be lion hair around the sleeves of his shirt. "He had to wrestle one and kill it with his bare hands!"

Paxton almost laughed. "Don't believe everything you hear from these hotheads. They'll try to intimidate."

"That's a good idea. . . ." Tiern thought. "I could start a rumor about how we had to take down a twelve-point buck on a rampage with only our daggers."

Paxton chuckled. "How about we ignore the ridiculous politics of the hunt and just kill the grizzly boar, aye?"

"Fine. Rob all the fun from it, won't you," Tiern said with a smile.

In a way, Paxton agreed with his mother, and wished his brother hadn't wanted to participate. Tiern was a good hunter, but he was still naive in so many ways. Paxton understood his mother's fear for the lad, though he would never crush Tiern's confidence by saying so. From what he'd heard of this beast, it was strong beyond belief and its skin was hard to penetrate. The last thing Paxton wanted was to be distracted by worry over his brother while they were facing down the monster. But he knew Tiern was capable of being serious when necessary.

"High seas!" Tiern shouted as he jumped to his feet and pointed. "It's the king!"

Paxton shielded his eyes against the angle of the sun, and, sure enough, the king was walking along the balcony, with its ornate pillars of stone, that overlooked the west commons area. He was flanked by several heavily armed men. All through the commons, Paxton saw guards dispersing themselves through the crowd, eyeing the hunters.

"Brave hunters of Eurona!" called one of the king's advisers from the ledge above. "I respectfully ask that you lower all weapons to the ground while His Majesty King Charles Lochson speaks."

Paxton reluctantly obeyed. The king stepped forward, the sun glinting off his gold crown.

Paxton had been expecting an arrogant man with cruelty in his eyes, but he saw none of that. This man appeared to hunch with fatigue. His eyes, lined with dark circles, glistened with emotion. It somewhat annoyed Paxton, who didn't care for surprises. He had his reasons for not liking royalty, or many other people for that matter. Reasons he wouldn't share with anyone.

Reasons only his late grandmother understood.

"Welcome, each of you, to the kingdom of Lochlanach," King Charles said in a powerful voice. Paxton and the other men squinted in the midday sun above the king. "I am honored and grateful that so many brave men have responded to my proclamation. Our kingdom is in dire need of your expertise. Throughout the day my men who have faced the great beast will be among your ranks to share their experiences and provide insight. Maps of the land are available. You will each be fed and housed here in these quarters until the waterlands are freed of the beast. I have no doubt that one of you will achieve this feat of greatness and reap the rewards."

A roar tore from the crowd. Tiern punched the sky and hollered his own war cry. Paxton never took his eyes from the king.

"And to the one who does . . ." King Charles paused, and turned to gesture behind him, as Paxton felt the breath he was drawing stop short. "I would like to introduce you to my daughter Princess Aerity . . . whose hand you will have in marriage."

Was it Paxton's imagination, or did the king's voice falter?

A hush fell over the hunters as a shocking beauty walked gracefully to the king's side. He put an arm around her slender shoulders, and she moved close, fitting her own arm around her father's waist before eyeing the crowd somewhat shyly. She certainly didn't look as if she hated her father for being willing to give her away.

"High seas," Tiern whispered.

Paxton stared at the girl. Like her father, she was devoid of the haughtiness he expected to see from someone who lived a life of privilege. Around her head she wore a small golden circlet, which held a sapphire in the center of her forehead that sparkled like the sea. Her arm seemed to cling to her father with nervousness, though her face appeared assured and resolved. The princess's act of kindness was well played.

A breeze lifted her strawberry blond strands, which fell gently back against her waist. Tiern whispered something else, but it was lost in the wind. Princess Aerity was the very image desires were made of. Her silken cream dress was cinched at her waist, accentuating her femininity.

"You don't live with the looks," his mother had always told him. *"You live with the personality, so try and be pleasant. And choose a girl with a loving heart."*

Paxton wasn't here for the girl anyhow. He was here to kill the beast that terrorized his people. Despite whatever show the king and princess were putting on for them, he had no doubt she was a spoiled lass, probably incapable of passion for anything other than herself. Paxton would not be fooled. He would do as he must to keep his family healthy and at peace.

But, seas alive, she was sweet on the eyes. He unabashedly took his fill.

As the king turned to escort his daughter from the balcony, Paxton caught his brother's starstruck eyes.

"I think I'm in love, Pax."

He grabbed his younger brother around the neck and ground a knuckle into his head, pulling hair from his perfect ponytail.

"Gerrof me! Not the hair!"

Paxton chuckled, but let out a grunt when Tiern put a fist in his stomach. Tiern was smiling as Paxton released him. The boy's hair stuck out everywhere.

"You always were a fool for a pretty face," Paxton told him.

"And gorgeous hair," Tiern added. "And perfect curves. Don't forget those." He pulled the leather strap from his hair and smoothed the strands back again.

Paxton shook his head, trying not to smile. "She's probably as cold as the far seas."

"Don't speak that way of my future wife," Tiern said.

Beside them, a group of older men in fur-lined vests and dark trousers were passing. They had beards of differing lengths, and hair of dark blond past their shoulders, some balding on top.

"Only in your dreams, little boy," one of the men said to Tiern, making the others laugh. The man was squat and wide, like a hairy boulder. "You probably wouldn't even know what to do with a lass like that." More raucous laughter.

Tiern's joking demeanor shed, and his spine straightened.

Paxton stepped closer to his brother, making his loyalties known. When their eyes raked over him, their laughter quieted a fraction, but the man who'd spoken only smirked. With a jerk of the man's head, the foreign hunters walked away, talking loudly once again.

"Ascomannians," Paxton murmured of the coldlands natives. "Best not to engage them when they provoke."

"Aye," Tiern agreed. Paxton could see the tremble of anger in his brother's chest. "That big one is called Volgan. I've deemed him Volgan the vulgar."

Paxton chuckled. "You'll earn their respect in time, Brother."

Tiern gave a stiff nod.

In the meantime, Paxton would have to remember not to put his brother in any more headlocks or do anything to undermine his right to be there hunting.

Paxton was there to kill the great beast, not to brawl with big-headed men who thought to pick on his brother. Although he'd been known to do the latter plenty of times.

Two Lochlan men approached then, one obviously a peasant with his threadbare tunic and mess of brown curls, the other dressed sharply in thick trousers with a military-style haircut, short on the sides, longer in front.

"I'm Samuel Gullet of Loch Neck," said the peasant. They shook hands, Paxton and Tiern introducing themselves in turn.

"Lieutenant Harrison Gillfin," the other man said.

"Gillfin?" asked Tiern. "As in, related to Captain Breckon Gillfin?"

A shadow passed over the young man's face. "Aye. The very one."

Tiern swallowed and glanced at Paxton to save him.

"We're sorry for your loss," Paxton said.

Samuel clapped the lieutenant on the shoulder. "He's become something of a legend, your cousin. The way he took on the beast single-handedly."

Harrison nodded, grim.

At that moment royal soldiers came into the commons area, carrying oversized rolled papers. Maps of Lochlanach. Hunters flocked around the tables as soldiers pointed out marked areas where the beast had been spotted, places where people had been killed, and lands where the beast's paw prints had been found. It didn't take long before voices were raised, tension spanning like bands between the bodies as men shouted out the areas they wished to claim.

"Here!" Paxton had worked his way to the front and laid a solid finger on the strip of Oyster Bay where the beast had been spotted most. "We should all stake these miles right here. Every one of us. Our numbers can overpower it."

The thick Ascomannian who'd arsed with Tiern earlier let out a sharp laugh. "All of us, you say? But what if the beast shows here?" Volgan stabbed a stubby finger at a northern waterway on the map. "Or here?" Now he poked a southern route.

"You're called Volgan, correct?" Paxton asked the man, trying to keep calm.

The bearded man from the coldlands puffed out his wide chest and stomach, like a preening bird. "Aye, I am. And I say we break into groups and each scout different areas of the kingdom." A few of his men grunted behind him in support. "What say you?" he shouted to the masses.

Some nodded their agreement.

"Volgan," Paxton said, "if you insist on spreading out in smaller groups, I suggest that each group takes a few of the Lochlan hunters—"

"Oh, you'd like that, wouldn't you?" Volgan bellowed. "To have your hands in each slice of the pie and take all the glory!"

Fool. Paxton bit back his irritation. "We know these waterways and the lands, the best places to lie in wait—"

"We don't need your help! Men of the coldlands can read a map and hunt better than any in Eurona. You offend every man here by assuming otherwise." He waved a hand over the crowd as if Paxton had purposely disrespected the lot of them. "If you waterlands men are so valuable, then why haven't you killed the beast before now, eh? You had to call upon us to help, so leave off and let us work!"

Anger boiled within Paxton, his fists tingling for rough contact.

In Paxton's stewing silence, Tiern spoke up. "There was a curfew instated."

"There was a curfew. . . ." Volgan mocked him in a high voice, and the Ascomannian men laughed. Bright red spots bloomed on Tiern's cheeks.

The soldier Harrison spoke up. "Some of us here have lost loved ones to this beast already. This is not about glory for us but the safety of our lands and people."

"So you say," Volgan muttered, scowling.

Harrison glowered back at him. "My own cousin battled the beast and lost his life. I am here to avenge him."

"And bed the princess, no doubt." Volgan's mirth was cut short when Harrison swiftly moved forward with his blade and sliced off the tip of the coldlander's beard. Volgan watched it flutter to the ground in shock.

Pointing the blade at the man's face, Harrison muttered. "Do not disrespect the princess."

Volgan's face was murderous. His fellow hunters moved in closer.

"Enough." Paxton leveled Volgan with a hard glare. As much as he enjoyed seeing the Ascomannian bested by the Lochlan lieutenant, they needed to move forward with the hunting plans. "Have it your way, Volgan." The foreign hunters would learn soon enough what they'd be battling.

He shouldered his way out of the crowd with Tiern at his heels. When they were out of earshot, Paxton muttered, "There's no reasoning with that load of idiots. And the rest are sure to follow him because he's the loudest."

Behind him, Paxton heard arguments breaking out over

which areas the groups would take.

"Perhaps he'll be eaten tonight," Tiern said.

Paxton grinned mirthlessly at his brother's dark humor. "Come on. Let's find a tent and rest before dinner."

In truth, Paxton didn't care for resting or eating. What he really wanted to do was hunt.

Chapter
11

As Princess Aerity and Lady Wyneth took the cobbled path from the castle to the west commons gates, Aerity squeezed her cousin's hand to quiet the shaking inside of her. Thankfully Wyneth held tight in return, not seeming to mind the princess's sweating palm.

Aerity still felt a bit guilty after Vixie had begged and pleaded to come see the hunters, swearing she'd keep quiet despite her feelings over the situation. Aerity adamantly refused. She was too nervous to handle Vixie's excitable, unpredictable personality at that moment. Ultimately their mother had to intervene, pulling the incensed Vixie away.

Aerity had taken off her jeweled circlet. It made her feel like a spectacle when she wore it outside of royal galas. The girls pushed their windblown hair back over their shoulders as a breeze came up from the sea, swirling the bottoms of their skirts. The late afternoon was gorgeous—warm and clear—as if Mother Nature were trying to make up for the abominable beast she'd created.

You'll have to do better than that, Aerity thought.

Behind her, she heard the clank of swords and armor as royal guards flanked them. Perhaps Aerity was naive, but she doubted the guards were necessary. She couldn't imagine any of the hunters trying to hurt her. And besides, the balcony overlooking the commons area was lined with armed guards.

Her stomach flipped end over end as they gauged the sight of the long tables filled with men taking their meal. They grouped together based on nationality. Aerity took in their differences—the furs and beards of the Ascomannians, the draping head coverings of the dark-skinned Zorfinans, the shaved heads and narrow eyes of the Torestans, and what appeared to be lion manes around the sleeves of the tanned Kalorians.

For a group who was about to face a fabled, vicious beast, they were lively and loud. Aerity pulled Wyneth to a stop, apprehension and nervousness halting her feet and threatening to make her turn away. When the first man spotted her, he nudged the hunter at his side, and eyes began to turn Aerity's way. She found herself standing taller under hundreds of hushed gazes.

"Right, then." She cleared her throat. "On we go."

Wyneth gave her hand a last squeeze of reassurance and then released her, but she never left her side as they approached the first table.

Aerity wondered for a moment if she should keep her hands to herself. It would be the smart, safe, proper thing to do. But as she came eye to eye with the first young man at the end of the table she found herself reaching out her hand.

"Thank you for coming, brave sir."

His eyes widened and he abruptly dropped the turkey leg, wiping his hand on his brown breeches. The man's skin was shades darker than Aerity's, his round eyes brown and his black curls slicked back. His hand shook as he reached out to embrace hers.

"*Princesca* . . ." She recognized the vowel pronunciations of his accent.

"You hail from Kalor?" she asked.

It took him a moment to ponder and translate her words before he answered, "Jes." Yes. The hotlands. He'd traveled up from the southernmost hemisphere, a land of rain forests and smoldering humidity from what she'd learned in geography lessons. The princess smiled at him and switched languages, speaking now in Kalorian.

"Long trip. I wish you blessings on your hunt."

His eyes crinkled in awe at hearing his native tongue come from a foreign princess's mouth. Languages were her favorite subject of study. Ascomanii, Lochlanach, and most of

Toresta spoke Euronan with individual dialects, but Zorfina and Kalor had their own languages. She released his hand and moved to the next man, making her way down the table.

And so it went. For an hour she went through the rows, meeting each man, fumbling through introductions when particularly strong accents arose, or a hunter spoke too quickly in excitement. She'd never been more thankful for her language tutoring.

Some of the men, like the first, were filled with quiet wonder, while other prideful men boasted of their accomplishments. Most were young, ranging from late teens to late twenties, though a few seemed older. Widowers, perhaps. Some were handsome, and some were not, but she found herself grateful for each one of them and their willingness to be there. She ignored the quake of unease in her gut each time she thought of marriage and all it would entail.

The sun was preparing to set as she neared the end of the last table. Only ten men remained, all Lochlans. As she scanned a row, her eyes stuck like sap to the man at the very end. His brown hair shielded a portion of his face, but what she could see was so pleasing that she felt herself warm. His dark brown eyes met hers and her breath stuttered. He didn't smile. Nor did he nod or show any reaction. He merely watched her.

Aerity felt her hand going up and down as the man in front of her shook it. Tearing her gaze away from the handsome lad at the end, she gave the man from Toresta her attention. He bowed his smooth head, smiling up at her with his narrow, brown eyes. She smiled back and thanked him for coming down from the ridgelands.

She felt guilty, because all she wanted to do now was hurry through the next nine hunters so she could get to the last. But as she moved down the line and looked toward the end again, she found that the gorgeous man was no longer there.

Confusion and disappointment rose as she searched the area. She felt Wyneth sidle up close and whisper into her ear.

"Are you looking for the skirt raiser?"

Aerity tried not to snort at her cousin's phrase for good-looking lads, and gave a shrug.

"He's by the stone risers, gearing up. Must be in a hurry to hunt."

Aerity wouldn't look yet. The last few men were waiting.

As they moved down the line, she felt Wyneth's hand reach out and tighten around her arm. Her cousin suddenly stepped forward, asking, "What are you doing here, Harrison?"

Aerity gasped in surprise. Breckon's cousin, the lieutenant, raised his chin at Wyneth. He appeared as poised as ever with his brown sailor's haircut. His eyes went from Wyneth to Aerity, and the princess fought the urge to run into his arms and beg him to steal her away from all this. Her handsome friend.

His face remained stoic. "I'm here to hunt, of course."

Aerity's stomach plummeted. The hunt. No wonder he hadn't responded to her couriered message that week. If anything happened to Harrison . . .

"What about the navy?" Wyneth sounded ready to panic.

"They've temporarily discharged me with honor to hunt."

"But Harrison, you—"

"Don't worry, my lady," Harrison said gently. Aerity noticed that he looked upon Wyneth with an underlying pain in his eyes that seemed to match hers.

Aerity gently pulled Wyneth back a step, stopping her cousin from saying anything else in front of the other hunters and causing a scene. Wyneth's eyes were already glazing over, and she dropped her head, seeming to retreat into her memories.

"Thank you so much for coming out, Lieutenant Gillfin," the princess said, for the sake of those watching.

He looked as if he were holding back a smirk at her properness toward him.

"There was never any doubt when I received the proclamation, Your Highness," he said, matching her in politeness.

Aerity swallowed her fears and spoke quietly so only he could hear. "Please be safe, Harrison. I don't think your family could handle losing another." She didn't need to add that she could not handle losing him either.

"I know." Harrison's eyes were grave. "But I must hunt, Aer. I must try."

Wyneth pressed her lips together. As frightened as Aerity was for him, for all of them, she respected Harrison's need to hunt. Aerity took Harrison's hand and held on for a moment, conveying her understanding. His returned gaze was grateful.

"Let me introduce you to Samuel from Loch Neck." Harrison gestured to the curly-haired man at his side, who appeared a few years older with small lines creasing his eyes.

"Hello, Samuel," Aerity said. "Do you have many family members in Loch Neck?"

"Only my parents, Your Highness. My wife . . . she died in childbirth two years past."

Aerity's heart sank. "I'm so sorry to hear that. You are brave to join the hunt, and you're in good company with Lieutenant Gillfin here."

Samuel nodded, shifting his weight. "Aye, Princess. Many thanks."

Harrison gave Aerity a rueful wink as she stepped away and made it down the row to the last lad. He appeared to be one of the youngest in attendance, and she couldn't help but smile when he beamed up at her with his white teeth and a boyish cleft in his chin. He bowed his head.

"Princess Aerity. This is such an honor. My name is Tiern Seabolt."

"Seabolt. A strong Lochlan name." She smiled when he placed a gentle kiss to her fingertips. "How old are you, Tiern Seabolt?"

"Seventeen, Your Highness." Older than she'd thought. Such a baby face. "Same as you, I believe, Princess?"

"You believe correctly. Thank you for coming. I wish you well in tonight's hunt."

"It is my honor. Thank you, Princess."

He bowed his head, and Aerity now allowed herself to turn and look toward the stone wall. The handsome lad was strapping a bow across his back. And a fine, broad back it was. He checked each arrow thoroughly from tip to end before slipping it into the quiver. Aerity looked at Wyneth with questions in her eyes. Should she approach him? Why hadn't he stayed at the table to meet her?

Wyneth shrugged a shoulder in silent response.

His back was to them. He seemed focused and determined. Perhaps he didn't wish to be distracted from the task at hand. Aerity knew she should probably let him be, but curiosity burned through her. Besides, he'd obviously known she was headed to meet him at the table before he left, and she wasn't accustomed to being ignored.

She grabbed her skirts, lifted her chin in forced confidence, and moved toward the risers. Wyneth was a step behind, and the guards several more behind her. She wished the guards wouldn't follow so closely.

The young man's body stilled and stiffened, as if sensing their approach.

"Pardon me, sir?" Princess Aerity was surprised at the nervous tremble in her voice.

He didn't turn right away. He continued to run his finger down the last of the arrow's feathers before shoving it into the quiver and turning to face her. She was standing a decent distance from him, but still she stepped back, surprised by the fierceness in his eyes.

She didn't know what she expected. Well, that's not true. She expected a bow of his head or some other sort of respectful acknowledgment, but he gave none. The princess felt her mouth open and stay that way for far too long. The lad's eyes flicked past Wyneth to the guards behind them, and then back to the princess.

"Forgive me . . ." she found herself saying. "I didn't have a chance to meet you at the tables."

High seas, her mouth had gone dry. No man had ever made her nervous like this. Why did he appear so angry? And why did every detail of his appearance appeal to her on such a base level? She felt sweat beading along her neck and spine as she made a concerted effort not to stare at the way he wore his dark tunic and breeches so well.

"I'm Princess Aerity . . ."

A small huff blew from his nose and his mouth quirked. "Yes, Princess, I'm aware of who you are."

Lands and seas . . . his voice. Wait—was that sarcasm? Next to her she heard an intake of surprise from Wyneth. Aerity blinked, shaken.

A lad jogged up beside them and patted the baffling, handsome hunter on the shoulder. Aerity recognized the young man Tiern smiling at her once again.

"You've met my older brother, Your Highness?" Tiern asked.

"Not officially," Princess Aerity said. Now that the shock of their meeting began to wear off, she felt a pang of offense at the older lad's demeanor.

"This is my brother, Paxton Seabolt." He gave Paxton another hard pat, smiling with pride. "He's nineteen."

The princess held out her hand as she had to every other man, but a horrible realization dawned on her that he might refuse to take it. The very idea made her frown and stand taller.

To her utter relief he took her hand in his rough, warm one. Paxton then did something that none of the other tables full of men had dared to do. Still holding her hand, he dropped his gaze down to the swell of fabric at her chest, and kept it there too long, his hand tightening and seeming even hotter around hers. Another shocked sound left Wyneth, this one high-pitched. Aerity's chest sizzled under the hunter's heated attention, and she dropped his hand.

In unison, the guards behind her stepped closer, one of them clearing his throat. When Paxton Seabolt's eyes drifted lower across her waist, Princess Aerity refused to cower. She was torn between offense and flattery at the intimate way he took her in with his eyes, perusing at his leisure until Tiern discreetly bumped him with his shoulder.

When Paxton looked at her face again, he stepped back. Aerity's blood flooded her system in a hot rush as they held eyes.

"I," she began, "thank you for coming. Blessings to you both as you hunt."

The princess nearly tripped over her own feet as she stooped to grasp her skirts and turn, bustling through the line of guards. She heard Tiern hiss, "What's wrong with you?" but she didn't dare turn to catch Paxton's response.

She halted and turned when a young guard caught up and called, "Shall I have him removed for his insolence, Princess?"

"What? No, of course not." Her skin was still flushed from the feel of Paxton Seabolt's eyes. "He's a hunter. We knew some of them would be . . . rough by nature."

The guard frowned. "Your Highness, he was blatantly disrespectful—"

"Enough. Gentleman or not, he's putting his life on the line. Let him be. I don't plan to get close enough to allow another moment of indecency again."

The guard pursed his lips, and Princess Aerity turned to walk once more, catching a look on Wyneth's face she couldn't decipher. Perhaps a mix of astonishment and humor. They walked faster, putting some space between themselves and the guards.

Wyneth whispered under her breath, "I'm willing to bet you wouldn't be so quick to take up for him if it'd been one of the other men who ate you up with his starving eyes."

"Let's not make something of nothing."

"Truly, Aer. I thought at first you were going to smack him, and then just as quickly it looked as if you might kiss the lad!"

"Hush, you." Princess Aerity smashed her lips together so as not to smile in her embarrassment.

As they neared the venue gates, voices rose behind them.

Aerity turned to see men pointing out at the bay. The late day sky matched the water.

"Oh, my skies above," Wyneth breathed.

An extraordinary Ascomannian ship was making its way to the docks. Princess Aerity had only seen such a sight in books. Its wooden hull was raised high and curved at the end like the grandest of vessels. Several light-haired men jumped from the ship to tie it, but one man with a silver breastplate stood tall, surveying the land before him. His shoulder-length blond hair caught the breeze and he raised his sights to the hunters now standing at the entrance to the commons. His blond beard was cropped short, neat in comparison to the other rugged Ascomannians.

"It's Lord Lief Alvi!" One of the Ascomannian men yelled. Men from the coldlands erupted in cheers.

A lord? Was he joining the hunt or simply here to support his men?

As Lord Alvi made his way up the dock, Princess Aerity couldn't help but stare. Like many of the Ascomannians she'd met that day, he wore less clothing than men from other kingdoms—ironic since the temperatures in their lands were much lower. They must have been numb to the elements. He wore a leather kilt to his knees, fur-lined leather boots, and a sleeveless tunic with a burnished breastplate over it.

His arms . . . seas almighty. His arms were all muscle, bulging without even flexing. Same with his calves. And his face was chiseled as in the coldlands tales of old.

Wyneth grasped the princess's hand as they stared.

Several guards and one of the king's primary advisers met Lord Lief Alvi at the edge of the docks. They conversed for a moment, shook hands, and then led the man straight toward the princess. She and Wyneth straightened.

The king's adviser brandished a hand toward the girls and opened his mouth to make introductions, but before he could, Lord Alvi bent to one knee and lowered his head. Now that was how a gentleman greeted royalty—with civility and grace. This was the type of male Aerity was accustomed to meeting . . . minus the kilt and breathtaking Ascomannian beauty.

Given all of that, the princess was surprised she did not feel the same heat course through her that she'd felt for the rude commoner moments before.

Lord Alvi stood and his crystal blue eyes went straight to Wyneth. He reached for her hands and her eyes bulged.

"Princess Aerity," he crooned in a low voice.

Whoops.

Aerity bit the inside of her lip to hide a giggle as her cousin's cheeks reddened.

"No, kind sir. I am Lady Wyneth Wavecrest. This is my cousin Princess Aerity herself." Her eyes were still huge as she turned to gesture toward the princess.

Was it Aerity's imagination, or had he appeared momentarily crestfallen as his eyes changed course toward her? He stepped over and gave another bow, taking Aerity's hand.

When his gaze rose to her, full of brazen confidence and an easy smile, she thought she must have imagined his initial disappointment.

"Forgive me," he said in a deep rumble of northern accent. "I was told the princess had hair like fire."

Aerity smiled. Compared to Wyneth's vibrant curls, her own hair was a sorry excuse for fire. But his eyes were far too kind to take offense.

"Nothing to forgive, Lord Alvi," the princess said, giving a small curtsy in return.

"Please, Princess. Call me Lief. I'm told it's not too late to join the hunt."

"You're hunting?" Wyneth asked. Her face paled and she placed her fingers at her lips when she realized she'd spoken.

"With great joy," Lief told her in all seriousness. "I've come to slay the beast."

Princess Aerity's heart tightened while she watched her cousin swallow hard, an ill look passing over her face.

"Be safe," Aerity whispered.

"Aye," Wyneth said. "Blessings of the seas be with you."

The lord nodded his head in thanks, but no fear showed on his face.

"Princess and lady," the king's adviser said, stepping forward. He gestured worriedly toward the darkening skies. "Night beckons. We must get you both inside."

A reminder of the dangers hidden in the dark caused the girls to sidle closer.

Princess Aerity turned to the hoard of brave men at her back and raised a hand to wish them well. They returned her gesture, appearing as a solemn but determined bunch, and a lump of emotion lodged in her throat. Would one of these daring hunters kill the beast? Would one of these men wed her? Take her to his bed? She tried to shake away the thought, but now it was her reality. She had to face it.

She caught sight of Harrison through the myriad of faces. He stood naturally as if at attention, giving her a small smile and quick mock-salute that filled her with tenderness.

Her eyes then scanned the crowd until she found the other man she was looking for—the one who lacked respect, and yet . . . his attraction, at the very least, seemed to match her own. It wasn't ideal. It definitely wasn't anything to base a relationship on, but her body sought him out all the same.

Paxton Seabolt leaned lazily against the stone wall, lean, muscled arms crossed over his chest, his bow jutting out behind him. When their eyes met he didn't look away or move, causing a strange fire to zing straight into her abdomen. He'd been watching her. She sucked in a ragged breath and turned away.

Aerity took Wyneth's hand and headed down the path for the castle, wishing with all her might that the beast would be killed that night once and for all. Preferably by Harrison . . . or perhaps the brazen Paxton Seabolt. If it was wrong to have preferences, then seas forgive her. It wasn't as if her choices would be taken into account anyhow.

She felt selfish for having such petty thoughts. Her only consideration should be for their safety.

She sent an amended wish along the salty breeze that the man she was fated for would kill the beast, and that no hunter's blood would be shed in the process.

Chapter

12

Darkness engulfed the hunters soon after the princess left. Torches were lit along the insides of the commons' walls.

Paxton knew his behavior had been inappropriate, but it was her own fault. He hadn't wanted to meet her. He'd chosen to leave the table because he knew he couldn't act as the others had—trying to win her approval like groveling chumps. And still, she'd sought him out, taking him by surprise and causing him to act on impulse.

He raised his eyes to the skies in frustration. It would take more than a blushing princess with hair of rose gold to make him forget the teachings of his grandmother, of the injustices instated by the princess's ancestors, still blindly carried out by her own father.

Oh, how civilization forgets.

He wished he hadn't given the princess the satisfaction of an eye caress. He'd surely inflated her ego even further. Not to mention he'd raised the notice of the guards, who seemed unappreciative of his behavior with the royal lass.

So be it.

The naval lieutenant sidled up next to him, wiping his long daggar to a sheen before sheathing it at his waist. "You'd do well not to insult the princess again."

Paxton's defenses went up. He didn't deal well with royal arse-kissers. "Didn't look to me as if she minded."

Harrison faced him. "She's a friend of mine. She's trained not to react. You've no clue what she's going through."

Paxton crossed his arms. "Aye, poor lass. Forgive me if I don't pity a royal."

Harrison's face contorted in frustration as he looked away, and Paxton felt an unusual stab of guilt. This man had lost his cousin. He'd left his duties to hunt. He didn't deserve Paxton's disrespect.

He forced out the words, "My apologies, Lieutenant Gillfin."

The man stuck out his hand. "Just Harrison." They shook, and an easy silent agreement was made between them. Paxton would be careful to keep his opinions to himself from then on.

Night awaited. It was time to put everything else out of his thoughts.

All day the hunters had been at odds before finally deciding where they each would hunt.

But that had been before supper. Before the princess had graced them with her presence and turned the men to mush, intensifying their competitiveness. Before Lord Lief Alvi showed—seemingly the only Ascomannian with any sense. Paxton had smiled sardonically to himself when he heard the blond lord ask his ranks, "Why are we splitting off from the other men? Have you not heard the tales of our prey?"

Their stuttered responses were cut off by the sound of a drum coming from the other side of the tents. Paxton and Tiern made their way over to the far side of the commons where a fire pit had been lit, surrounded by Kalorians who'd painted their faces like the night. Stripes of the mud paint went down their necks and arms. One of them kept beat on a lap drum, and the other Kalorians fell into step, circling the fire.

Paxton had heard tale of Kalorian prehunting ritual dances. Now, chills covered him, the beat of the drum sinking beneath his skin, into his bloodstream. He watched with the other hunters in silence as the Kalorians performed their orchestrated tribal dance. Together they stomped and squatted, thrusting out their spears with sharp shouts. Paxton could imagine this scene in the jungles of the hotlands. The men finished, stabbing the sky with their spear tips. A respectful hush filled the air until the Kalorians turned, ready to hunt.

"Amazing," Tiern said under his breath.

Samuel chuckled. "Aye. I'm ready to kill something."

Roughly twenty men from each kingdom set out, over a hundred in all. The largest group, the Ascomannians, insisted on hunting the area Paxton had pointed out as the beast's past stomping grounds. Paxton clenched his jaw in annoyance, but since they had the most men he wouldn't fight it. It was smart.

Sadly, the group of Lochlans fared the lowest numbers. A mere thirteen of them had come, from all waterways, and four of their ranks were wealthy men for whom archery was only a hobby—not actual hunters. He supposed it made sense that their numbers were lower, considering many of their land's bravest men had already faced this foe or given up hope.

They left royal lands through the southern gates, passing the massive wall that hundreds of workers were diligently fortifying against the beast during the daytime, building it even higher. Pulley systems lifted heavy stones to men on ladders. Vines, a cursed burden battled by all Lochlans, covered stretches of the wall as far as the eye could see.

"Beautiful," Tiern muttered. Paxton looked to where Tiern was gazing over his shoulder, at the castle beyond—lit by hundreds of torches along its parapets, walls, and in the windows of High Hall atop, light gray stones of the towers stretching high into the night sky.

Paxton turned back to the path, saying nothing.

They hiked over five miles through trees and marshland

to the southern creek, where the beast had most recently killed the fisherman. Two of the younger lads, sixteen years old each, climbed into trees overlooking the land and creek. Paxton and Tiern found a half-rotted log and brush pile and they sat back to back. Their entire group was in earshot of one another. All at once they silenced and the sky blackened. Moonlight cast shadows through the trees. Sounds of the creek and night creatures lulled them through their wait.

Paxton's entire body was on high alert, and he felt Tiern rigid behind him. At one point a particularly large fish jumped in the creek, and Samuel stood with a holler, shooting an arrow blindly toward the water. All of the men stood, on instinct, only to chuckle at their own reactions. Harrison gave Samuel a joking shove and they moved back to their places. Paxton caught Tiern's nervous grin just before they hunkered down again.

The four wealthy men began to talk among themselves, but Harrison hushed them.

Hours passed and Paxton carefully shifted as temperatures dropped. His damned arse was asleep, and his feet were cold. Tiern took his lead and shifted himself, too. The brothers leaned more heavily on each other, garnering body heat.

Where was the beast? It'd been hours. He hoped his body could quickly adjust to the change of schedule. He'd be staying up during the nights until the beast was dead.

Or until he was.

At one point Paxton felt Tiern drift to the side and heard

his light snoring. Paxton elbowed him none too gently and Tiern grunted awake.

More time passed with no sign of the beast. When that first slice of soft light buttered the horizon, Paxton's gut sank with disappointment. The men stood, stretching their stiff limbs with groans and rubbing their faces. The two lads jumped nimbly down from the trees and cracked their necks.

"That was bloody brutal," Tiern grumbled. A few men chuckled. The wealthy men looked miserable with their wrinkled trousers and muddied boots.

They trudged back to the royal lands, tension hanging in the air between them. Paxton peered around at the woods, not trusting their surroundings. Day or not, the beast could be hiding, watching, waiting. It'd never attacked during daylight, but Paxton didn't count anything out at this point.

"Keep watch for tracks or skat," Paxton said. All the men combed the ground with their eyes as they hiked, but saw nothing out of the ordinary.

They picked up their pace as spires from the distant castle came into view. Paxton knew they were all as anxious as he was to find out what, if anything, had happened with the other groups of hunters. They entered royal lands through the heavily guarded south gates behind a line of traders with carts of goods, stating their names and homelands to the guards each and every time they went in or out.

As they headed up the cobbled path toward the castle and market, it quickly became apparent that something was wrong. Ahead, Paxton could see the shining heads of Torestan men with their packs stuffed full, rushing down the path as fast as they could go. Their faces were scrunched with alarm, eyes narrower than usual. As Paxton and the other Lochlan men neared, Paxton gently grabbed one lad by the shoulder to stop him.

"Why are you leaving? What's happened?"

The lad's eyes were wild. "It kill many! We shoot with arrow, but no work. We try dagger, but the beast—" He stopped, struggling for words, curling his fingers to show them, like claws. "Too strong. Too big. To fight is no use. No man can kill. We must go."

Paxton could hardly make out the strongly accented rambling, but his insides tightened as the young man's words became clear.

Samuel stepped up. "Was there any weakness shown by the beast? Anything you can tell us?"

He shook his head fast, waving his arms side to side. "No. No use. It never die. Never. We go home." Wrenching himself from Paxton's grasp, the lad ran from the Lochlan hunters to catch up to the other Torestan men, fleeing back to their mountain homes. *There go a fifth of the hunters*, Paxton thought darkly.

"It must have a weakness," Samuel mumbled, shaking his head of matted curls. "Nobody's discovered it yet, but every living thing can be destroyed somehow."

Paxton nodded. He caught sight of Tiern's pale face as he

watched the Torestan hunters hurrying away.

"Come," Paxton said. "Let's fill our stomachs and talk with the other men, then we'll rest. Later we can scout the lands to try and find where the beast keeps during daylight."

Tiern, appearing young and forlorn with his shoulders slumped, dragged himself down the path behind Paxton.

Raised voices issued from hunters inside the west commons as they approached. Paxton readied himself for the tense scene ahead—hungry, tired, proud, and alarmed was not a good combination.

The thirteen of them pushed their way into the large group surrounding one long table. Hunters from Zorfina with their loose clothing and head scarves came in behind the Lochlans, the last group to arrive. They began questioning what had happened. Voices lifted, everyone attempting to speak at once.

Castle guards had entered the west commons and spread out, eyeing their harried groups with caution. More guards lined themselves across the balcony.

"Enough!" Paxton shouted.

Lord Lief Alvi jumped on the table, muddied boots and all, causing all eighty men to shut up when he bellowed, "Quiet!"

Lief was most definitely the only Ascomannian Paxton could stomach.

"Here is what we know!" Lief began. "Four Torestan hunters were killed by the beast in the night, and one is in dire condition. They were posted farthest north of royal lands in a spot where, until now, the beast had never been spotted. I think it's safe to say we cannot predict where the beast will show. Nor should we underestimate it. Every account says that arrows cannot break its natural armor. Its brute strength can fling away any man who attempts to wrestle it. We need to overpower it with sheer numbers. Wear it down and overwhelm it with a nonstop onslaught."

Paxton felt half his mouth lift in a grin as Lief unknowingly voiced the idea Paxton had raised to the men the prior day. He ignored the glare Volgan shot him.

"What say you?" Lief asked.

The vast majority nodded their heads.

"Very well," the blond lord said. He hopped down and bent over the map. "Men of Lochlanach, if you'd be so kind as to point us to the areas where our numbers could be best concealed."

Paxton, Tiern, Harrison, and Samuel stepped to his side, the rest of their men close behind them. They pointed out the heavily forested areas that edged waterways.

"Lord Alvi," Volgan said gruffly, "do you think it's wise to bunch all of our ranks so closely in one area of the kingdom? What if the beast is somewhere else?"

"The beast goes where there's warm blood to be easily had," Paxton answered for him. "It will find us."

Paxton and Lief locked eyes as the lord nodded, an

understanding and respect forming between the two men.

Volgan ran a hand over his scraggly dark blond hair and grunted.

Their discussion ended just as palace maids bustled onto the grass carrying covered platters. Tables were filled with fruits and pastries and steaming piles of eggs and sausages. Paxton was more concerned with sleep than food at that moment, but he needed to keep his strength. He walked to his spot at the end of the table. Before he sat he glanced up at the balcony and paused, his heart giving a sudden bang.

The princess, locked hand in hand with her lady cousin, were looking down upon them, appearing worried. Her hair was damp and freshly combed, heavy about her body. Both girls wore dresses that appeared simple, the princess in yellow and the lady in gray, but their fabric and stitching was far finer than anything a commoner wore. Shawls with pastel rainbow beading draped over their shoulders against the morning chill.

The princess's eyes darted across the men's faces until they landed on Paxton. The brightened relief that crossed her face was like a punch to his gut, followed by something pleasant and warm, a feeling that appealed to him on a deep, masculine level.

Seas be damned, Paxton thought with near amusement. Princess Aerity was glad to see him alive. She wore her emotions freely across her face, unguarded. She continued to surprise him, which he didn't care for.

Her expression of relief was followed closely by dark shadows in her eyes at the sight of the empty seats. Her gaze moved along and halted once again. A small smile graced her lips. Paxton saw Harrison send a nod up to her, and something soured within him. Harrison said he and Princess Aerity were friends, but perhaps she fancied herself in love with him? Wouldn't that be the rub for the poor princess?

A cool breeze blew through. The princess dropped her head, clutching her shawl against the chill. She turned and nodded at her cousin. Together, they left the men to break their fast.

A wide fire pit was lit on the tent side of the commons. The hunters from the remaining four lands found themselves around it after their meal, unable to rest just yet.

Chapter
13

Princess Aerity had a splendid view of the west commons from the sitting room window of her chambers above the balcony. Alone, she peered down upon the field area where the hunters exercised their skills, and the tables where the men were finishing their breakfasts. She hadn't realized how nervous she'd been for Harrison and the Seabolt brothers until she saw them alive and well this morning and experienced a current of relief. Now she found herself staring unabashedly from her window at Paxton Seabolt, wishing she had a seaman's scope so she could peer closer.

His movements were thought out and steady. Unhurried. Nothing wasted. Next to Paxton, his brother Tiern seemed like a bolt of energy, moving about, turning his head this way and that as if keeping an eye on everything at once. The contrast between them amused Aerity.

Something interesting she noticed about the men as a whole was how they naturally broke into groups based on their lands of origin. She understood the comfort level of similar culture and language, but it seemed a shame that the men rarely interacted except to fuss over that blasted map. She imagined they could learn a lot from one another, but what did she know? Men were strange creatures.

The cloudless sky was bright blue and Aerity longed to be out in the autumn breeze, feeling the sun on her skin. Trees beyond the commons were beginning to turn shades of yellow, orange, and maroon.

From the corner of her eye she noticed movement along the northern corner of the commons wall. Panic welled inside her as she leaned to the window and stared at the place where a lone spruce tree was shifting against the wall. Behind it was movement again, then something dropped down into the commons area. She jumped to her feet in panic, although this creature seemed too small to be threatening. Then she caught a flash of red curls.

"Donubhan!" Aerity gathered up her yellow skirts and raced to her chamber door, quickly changing from her house slippers into leather walking shoes. She rushed down the main corridor to the exit where two guards stood.

"Donny's sneaked into the west commons," Aerity

informed them. The two men shared looks of frustration. Donubhan was a master escape artist.

Aerity moved between them. One guard stayed behind at the door while the other followed her. By the time they burst through the gate, startling the guards there, Donubhan was entertaining the crowd with his stunts. Aerity rolled her eyes.

The men laughed and clapped as the prince did a front flip, keeping his bow tucked tight in his arms. As he landed, he shot off an arrow, which lodged in the farthest circle of the target. She wanted to ring his little neck. It wasn't safe for him to be wandering about the royal lands, and he shouldn't be distracting the hunters. Perhaps she could embarrass him into learning this lesson.

Aerity squeezed in among the group and put a hand on her hip. "Still not taking time to aim for the center, Donny?"

At the sound of her voice, the men turned their heads in surprise. Aerity pretended not to notice how Paxton stood with his arms crossed and Tiern grinned next to him, nudging his brother, who watched her closely. The group of men chuckled at her teasing. Donubhan's face paled to a point that made his freckles stand out more.

"How'd you find me already, then?"

"It's hard to hide that head of yours." Again, the surrounding men laughed. Aerity grinned and moved forward, ruffling his hair. "Back to the castle. You know it's not safe to roam."

Donubhan threw his head back dramatically and groaned his protest.

"Argh, scallywag," Harrison said, crouching menacingly in front of Donubhan, who grinned. The boy attempted darting aside, but Harrison caught him and tossed him easily over his shoulder.

The guards were already surrounding the prince, prepared to take him by force. They were accustomed to his antics.

Donubhan saw the guards from his high place on Harrison's shoulder and began to grasp for an excuse to stay. "Wait! First show the hunters how well you can do the trick!" He pointed at the princess. Harrison swung around to face her.

Aerity's mouth dropped open and her face flamed as every man turned to her with raised brows. She released a breathy laugh. "I think not."

"Yeah, Princess!" said Harrison, lowering the prince, but holding his shoulders. "Show us!" Aerity shot him a pleading glare which only made him grin.

The widower Samuel and the handsome lad Tiern nodded.

This could not be happening. There's no way she'd flip for a crowd of men.

"I'm in skirts. . . ." she muttered lamely. "It's not proper. Come along, Donny."

Lord Alvi gave a loud laugh, flashing his white teeth at her. "Ah, I don't believe she can do it!" His men chuckled. Aerity knew he was only being playful, but the heat crept further up her face.

The Ascomannians began to chant, "Show us! Show us!" and soon the other men joined in. Aerity wanted to crawl over the wall and hide. She'd only done that silly trick in front of her siblings and cousins during the many hours they spent cooped up in the castle together. But the hunters' smiling faces were filled with the hope of a moment's entertainment to take their minds off the recent day's disappointments.

Perhaps she could do it. Just once.

A tight smile pushed its way upward, despite her humiliation. "Fine! But I must change. Lieutenant Gillfin, don't let that little fox out of your sight." She pointed to her brother.

Harrison patted the boy's shoulders. Everyone cheered as Aerity huffed a breath and turned to leave, shaking her head in disbelief at what she was about to do. Her blood thrummed in nervous anticipation.

Ten minutes later she found herself peeking around the gate, partially hidden by the myriad of vines woven through the metal bars. She hoped to find that the men had forgotten her silly agreement and gone back to their own business.

No such luck.

They were standing in the sunshine, in the exact same places, many of them with their arms crossed. Waiting. Expectant. Chatting contentedly among themselves.

Blast that Donny! She ought to whack him with a whale bone.

Behind her, Aerity heard quick, light footfalls and panting

breaths. The princess turned to see her sister and cousin, their faces pink from running. Wyneth wore her gray skirts, but Vixie wore trousers like Aerity and held her bow.

My, word travels fast, Aerity thought.

"Do Mama and Papa know you're out here?" Aerity asked her sister.

Vixie lifted her chin. "I don't care what the king says. But no. They don't know."

Aerity fought back a smile. Their parents would know soon enough. Aerity was still nervous about having Vixie near the hunters, for several reasons, but she realized allowing Vixie to participate would take a fraction of the attention off herself. "All right, then."

"Well, you'd best hurry," Wyneth said. "If the queen finds out her children are flipping through the air with arrows at the ready in front of all these hunters, we're all in trouble!"

With a deep breath Aerity led the way into the commons and the men cheered. She felt foolish, like a performing monkey from her grandparents' former circus days, improperly dressed no less, but it was too late to back out now.

With all three royal children in the west commons, guards poured in, lining the crowd. Aerity spotted marksmen from the castle rooftops and balconies, moving to get a better look at the spectacle below.

Fantastic.

She refused to look around and see if the man Paxton was watching. If he wasn't, then he was the only one. It would be her luck to fall on her face in front of everyone.

"Let's get this over with," she muttered to herself. Louder, she said to her siblings, "Line up beside me facing your targets. We go on my count."

The sun was high in the sky, surrounded by wisps of cottony clouds. Despite the cool fall breeze, Aerity was warm enough to break a sweat.

Men shuffled around them as the two princesses and the prince stood in a row with Aerity in the middle, their quivers with single arrows fit tightly over their backs. Aerity did not look toward the crowd, though she felt their eyes on her. She'd taken many years of calisthenics and archery, but was not accustomed to having a large audience.

Aerity focused her sights on the target and took a deep breath, relaxing her muscles. She felt the light weight of the quiver on her back, and gripped her bow tighter, tucking it at an angle across her body. Then she took ten steps back, her brother and sister doing the same. In her peripheral view she could see them smiling as they watched her.

"Ready . . ." Aerity began. "And go."

They sprinted forward, gaining quick momentum, and at the same time all three of them launched themselves into forward flips, tucking their legs. As she felt her body completing its arc, Aerity reached back and snatched the arrow. She had it lined up, and her bowstring pulled back as her feet smacked the earth. Her eye met the target in a blur as her knees bent, and she loosed the arrow. She heard the slaps of feet and pings of arrows beside her. In a rush all three arrows hit the targets with synchronized *thwats*. Donubhan's wobbled in the outer ring. Vixie and Aerity's both hit the inner ring, but not the bull's-eye.

Still, the men raised a great cheer and Aerity laughed in relief. Vixie jumped up next to her.

"Nice one, Vix," Aerity said.

A few men from Kalor stepped up with smiles and motioned to the targets.

"We try?"

"Oh yes, please." Aerity and Vixie moved out of the way. Donubhan was more than happy to assist the dark-haired men.

When Harrison walked over to inquire of Wyneth's well-being, Aerity stepped away with Vixie to let them talk.

"Very impressive, princesses," said a jovial voice behind them.

Aerity and Vixie turned to find Tiern standing there. Aerity returned his smile and glanced past him to see Paxton walking slowly to join them, as if forced.

"Vixie, this is Tiern Seabolt, a local lad," Aerity said.

Tiern gave her a friendly nod. "You're as full of spunk as they say."

High seas, Vixie's eyes grew and her face turned a dark shade of pink, reminding Aerity that her demure sister was less than two years younger than them, and quickly maturing.

Aerity intervened on her sister's sputtering behalf. "I'm

sure you could do that stunt with your eyes closed, aye, Tiern?"

He laughed.

"He doesn't have time for playful antics. Some of us have to work for a living." Once again, Paxton's words and tone struck an uncomfortable chord. Aerity eyed him, trying to figure him out. He looked her over in return, causing her heart to dance against her ribs as if the two of them were alone. She wanted to level him with a witty quip, but her mouth felt glued shut.

"We spend most of the day with dreadful tutors," Vixie said, seeming oblivious to Paxton's cutting remark. "The king says schooling is our job at the moment." Aerity wished her sister would hush, but she kept on. "I just wish he'd fully lift this daytime curfew so we could visit the stables again."

In truth, the curfew on the royal children was ridiculous, and Aerity intended to speak to her father about it at once. They'd already begun lessons again. It was time to get back to normal as much as possible.

"You like to ride?" Tiern turned his eyes to Aerity.

"Aer's afraid of horses," Vixie answered for her, causing Aerity to grit her teeth.

"I'm not afraid of them."

"Only when they go fast." Vixie bumped her hip to Aerity's, and the older princess wanted to strangle her.

"I thought you royal lot were supposed to be as lively as dolphins, doing tricks of all manners," Paxton said. Unlike when Tiern spoke, Paxton's words felt like accusations and judgments. He stared at her with laughing eyes. If he wanted a reaction from her, he was out of luck.

"You should see Aer on the silks," Vixie said. "She's dazzling!"

"Enough, Vix." Aerity was feeling uncharacteristically embarrassed, but she refused to appear rattled. "I'm sure these hunters are not interested in our pastimes." She cleared her throat and forced her eyes to Tiern. "Lochlanach is lucky to have hardworking lads such as yourselves."

His eyes and smile became soft and dreamy as he gazed at the older princess. "And the kingdom is lucky to have a kind, smart, talented princess such as yourself."

Paxton crossed his arms, looking away.

Vixie abruptly piped up. "Do you plan to kill the great beast and marry my sister, then?" The girl watched Tiern with a curious expression. Tiern swallowed, his eyes darting over to Aerity. Paxton chuckled without humor.

Oh, seas. . . .

"Vixie . . ." Aerity whispered. The rest of the words eluded her. It was time to go.

A hush settled over the entire commons and men began to raise their heads to the balcony, shielding their eyes against the bright sun. Aerity's father stood there, flanked by guards as he stared down at his three children. He found Aerity and with two fingers beckoned her to him. He appeared unamused.

"Good day to you," Aerity said to the Seabolt brothers. She

grabbed her brother and sister, looking around for Wyneth.

She found her cousin standing over by a table talking to none other than Lord Lief Alvi. They kept a respectable distance, Lief full of grinning confidence and Wyneth smiling shyly. Harrison stood with them, his arms crossed in silence as he watched the two of them converse. Wyneth's eyes met Aerity's and she said good-bye to the Ascomannian lord and Harrison before gathering her skirts and rushing to meet her cousins at the gates. Aerity sent a wave to Harrison, who only nodded. He seemed in a strange mood all of a sudden.

Donubhan and Vixie walked ahead of them, following two guards. Aerity sidled close to her cousin and they synchronized their steps.

"What were you and Lord Alvi chatting about?" Aerity whispered.

Wyneth kept her eyes on the stone walkway. "Nothing of importance. He was asking if I could do the trick as well. I had to explain that I'm not inclined toward physical talents."

Wyneth's primary talents were the arts, something Aerity wished she could do.

"And what about Harrison? He seemed off."

Wyneth's eyebrows scrunched. "Aye. He didn't say much, but I had the distinct feeling he doesn't much care for Lord Alvi."

"I wonder why?"

"Protective of me, maybe. Bit of a flirt, that coldman."

"Indeed. Lord Alvi seems . . . keen," Aerity murmured.

She wondered if the man knew Wyneth had just lost her beloved to the very beast he was hunting.

"He's agreeable for an Ascomannian," Wyneth said diplomatically.

Under other circumstances Aerity would have probed for more, even joked about the man's "agreeable" muscled arms, but it was simply too soon to speak of other men to Wyneth, even in jest. And given that Lief was in the running for Aerity's hand in marriage it seemed uncouth.

Aerity wondered if the days of comfortable, easy conversation would ever return.

"Do you think Uncle Charles is angry?" Wyneth asked.

"Who cares?" Vixie scoffed.

"I'm sure he wasn't happy seeing Vixie and Donny out there," Aerity answered. "Probably thinks they're being a nuisance and bothering the men. Doesn't want anyone making jesters of the kingdom."

"I'm not a nuisance!" Vixie's scoffing continued.

Aerity recalled the conversation they'd just had with the hunters, and her sister's unfiltered questions. "You have to be careful what you say to these men, Vixie. It's all very . . . touchy. And personal." To her, as well.

Vixie rolled her eyes. "You know I'm not one to hold my tongue."

"Aye, I know." Aerity sighed.

"Well, all three of you were well received, I thought," Wyneth said. "The men needed a break."

"Agreed." Aerity linked her arm with her cousin, then her sister. "You'll join us so you can tell him that yourself?"

Wyneth sighed. "Oh, fine. I'm not afraid of Uncle Charles. Your mother, on the other hand . . ."

The girls giggled quietly as they entered the castle.

Chapter 14

"Must you always have something snide to say in the princess's company?" Tiern asked as he followed his brother to the sharpening post.

"I don't know what you're talking about." Paxton removed his quiver and began taking out his arrows, examining the head of each.

Tiern stopped in front of him. "You needn't be so gruff with her. It's embarrassing."

"Deep seas, Tiern," Paxton muttered. "Men don't embarrass."

"*You* don't embarrass, Pax. Sometimes I wonder if you feel anything at all." Tiern dropped his quiver with a clatter and sat, draping his arms across his bent knees.

Paxton ran his thumb over the tip of an arrow. Just a fraction more pressure and it would cut through the tough pad of skin. Tiern knew nothing of what he felt, and he planned to keep it that way.

"All I'm saying is that it wouldn't kill you to show a bit of kindness to Princess Aerity. She's been nothing but pleasant to us."

"It's all an act." Paxton slid the sharpened arrow back into the quiver.

"Must you always be so cynical? Can you not acknowledge genuine kindness and beauty when it's right in front of you?"

Paxton grunted. He didn't want to think about her. Aerity.

How she'd controlled her body so fluidly as she'd flipped and landed with complete grace, her hair fanning out like a sunset.

Or that she'd focused on the target and owned it—an action that spoke to Paxton in a language he could understand.

He'd never in all his days seen a lass do something like that. It made him wish he could dive into the deep, dark ocean afar to cool himself. He longed to rid his mind of these unwelcome thoughts.

Again, Paxton grunted.

The royal children clearly had too much time on their hands. And despite what his brother thought, he believed every person needed to be put in their place from time to time. Especially the wealthy ones.

"Here." Paxton tossed the sharpening block to Tiern. "Hurry up and tend to your arrows so we can rest before dinner. Focus on the hunt, not the lasses."

Perhaps he should take that advice himself.

From his spot on the ground, Tiern's eyes widened. Paxton turned to see what he was gaping at. Lord Lief Alvi had approached them with a rolled map in hand. Paxton admired the man's vest of fine rabbit fur.

"You're locals, correct?" Lief asked.

"Aye." Paxton stood and his brother followed. "From Cape Creek, a village fifteen miles northeast of here."

Lief nodded, unrolling his map. "My men are adamant about hunting on our own for now, and since the total numbers of hunters are great enough I have agreed." The lord sounded reluctant, but Paxton knew part of what made a great leader was compromise. So they would keep to their original groups. Lief needn't state the obvious—that his men wanted the glory of the kill and the prize of the foreign princess to themselves—things Lief could surely appreciate, even if the methods of his men weren't the smartest.

Harrison and Samuel approached, nodding their greeting as they joined the conversation.

Together, the men plotted the best areas for each of the four groups to scout that evening. They decided to hunt in a slightly closer range, rather than spreading out as they had the night before. This would give them an opportunity to give chase to the beast, from group to group, possibly keeping it in their sights.

Once everything was decided, they called over the leaders of the Zorfinan and Kalorian groups and explained the plan. All were in agreement. With that, Paxton and Tiern retired to their small tent in the corner of the commons and slept deeply, garnering energy for what was to come.

⁂

Raised voices of their fellow hunters woke the brothers. They jumped from their cots, running out to see what was happening. The men were grouped, surrounded by guards, and as the brothers got nearer, Paxton noticed four new hunters standing in the middle, tall and proud in fitted black outerwear with black head scarves wound about their faces. Wicked bows made of animal's antlers were slung across their backs.

". . . not hunting with women," Paxton heard Volgan grumble loudly. His eyes went back to the newcomers, to their high cheekbones and long lashes against dark skin.

In a flash, one of the women stepped forward and whipped out her bow, nocking her arrow and stretching it back just inches from Volgan's nose. Her stance was strong. Paxton felt his eyes go as wide as Volgan's, who had lifted his palms in surrender. That man hadn't made any friends on this hunt. A hush ran through the hunters.

"Zandalee hunt," the woman said in a thick accent.

"Whoa," Tiern whispered, matching Paxton's astonishment.

The Zandalee women were famous throughout Eurona but were spoken of as if mythical—a matriarchal tribe in southern Zorfina between the desert and the sea, bordering Kalor. A tribe where the women ruled. When Lochlan women were feisty, the men often joked that they were going Zandalee. But these women were nothing to joke about. They looked as if they could snap a man's neck with their bare hands.

"Easy now," said one of the guards. "Lower your weapon."

The woman grunted out a word Paxton couldn't understand. Then, slowly, she took her bow from Volgan's pale face, scowling at him.

"Everyone step back so we can figure this out." The guards pushed their way in and faced the four women. The main guard hesitated, as if he didn't quite know what to say. Then he lamely asked, "Eh, what can we do for you?"

"Zandalee hunt," the woman repeated in a solid voice.

"Zandalee?" asked the guard. "Are you saying *you* are a Zandalee? And you want to hunt?"

"Speak Zorfina." She rolled the *r* harshly, making her sound even tougher.

The guard massaged the back of his neck and looked toward the male Zorfinan hunters. They shook their heads and stepped back as if they wanted nothing to do with the Zandalee women. The guard spoke to another guard over his shoulder. "Go to the castle and find someone who can interpret Zorfinan."

Awkward minutes passed in which the male hunters stared down the female hunters, some whispering, as the women stared back with challenge in their eyes. Tiern gave Paxton an awestruck look as if enjoying the show.

Moments later, Paxton was surprised to see Princess Aerity return with an older officer at her side, flanked by guards. Her eyes went to the women with curiosity.

"Eh, Princess," said the guard. "These women . . . I believe they wish to join the hunt, but . . ."

Aerity's eyebrows went up as she moved forward. Guards pressed around her, forcing the male hunters to step away. Aerity spoke to the women in Zorfinan, accentuating the inflections, surprising Paxton with her level of fluency. She looked so petite standing there, conversing with an upward tilt of her head. A smile of admiration split her face and she turned back to the officer.

"These are women of the Zandalee, truly! They've sent their strongest hunters—isn't this brilliant?" The man's eyebrows shot up as he eyed the women in disbelief.

After several minutes of conversing, the princess nodded and turned to the hunters. "Right." She cleared her throat. "The Zandalee will join the hunt. If one of them kills the beast, the brother of their head huntress, Zandora"—she motioned toward the woman she spoke with—"will collect the . . . reward on her behalf." Once again the princess cleared her throat. Hunters muttered to one another under their breath.

"Wait just a moment." The officer frowned. "Your Highness, I think we should discuss this with your father—"

"There is nothing to discuss," Aerity snapped. "They are brave enough to join the hunt, so they shall hunt. I have accepted their terms. It is done, and I will alert the king." She lifted her skirts in her fists and shared a nod with the Zandalee huntress, then kept her eyes firmly ahead as she marched away. The guards quickly followed, leaving the hunters gaping in shock. Paxton grudgingly admired the princess's open acceptance of the unorthodox agreement.

Zandora's gaze scouted the males as they all slowly retreated into their respective tented areas, whispering their dismay and casting backward looks.

Paxton, Tiern, Samuel, and Harrison stood there glancing around at one another before moving forward to the women. The Lochlan men stood eye to eye with the Zandalee women, who were a strange mix of feminine features and rough edges. They wore a stretchy sort of black cloth belted around their narrow waists, with head coverings that hid their hair and necks. They appeared as warriors, in contrast to the male hunters from other tribes of Zorfina who wore browns and tans to blend with desert sands. Their eyes were differing pale shades.

Harrison was the first to give a small bow of his head. "Welcome to Lochlanach."

Paxton wasn't sure if the woman understood, but she inclined her head as well, and the rest of them did the same, showing their respect.

"I can't believe you're here," Tiern said, and Paxton sensed a babble coming on. "We've grown up hearing about the Zandalee, but we didn't know if you were real. High seas, you're amazing! You're—"

"Tiern," Paxton cut in. "That's enough."

Tiern, unperturbed, turned his awestruck eyes back to the girl before him, who appeared to be the youngest. She reached up and grabbed his chin, giving it a pinch in her fingertips. Zandora chuckled.

"*Khoshteep*," she purred in Zorfinan, and the women gave mischievous laughs.

Tiern let out a nervous laugh of his own as the women sized him up. Paxton coughed into his hand to hide his mirth.

"Join us for a meal?" Harrison asked, pointing to the tables, which were currently being laden with food. Other hunters were beginning to make their way over again.

As the Lochlan men turned to lead their group to the table, the younger Zandalee squeezed Tiern on the bottom, making him yelp, his eyes going round. The women kept walking, and Paxton could not hold back a chuckle at the scandalized look on his brother's face. Thankfully none of the other hunters seemed to have noticed.

"By the tides," Tiern hissed. "I feel like a piece of meat!" He didn't sound particularly upset about it, though.

"Aye." Samuel chuckled under his breath. "I think someone wanted a slice of Tiern for supper."

Tiern couldn't stop smiling, unlike the other hunters, who were all still frowning and stewing about this newest development.

The Zandalee didn't back down from anyone. They met the stares head on, throwing off airs of confrontation. Paxton was enjoying the addition of the huntresses more and more, especially as they sat down to eat with their weathered hands, grubbing with the best of them. When one of the Zorfinan hunters stared at them from under his head wrap, a snarl of contempt on his face, Zandora held up two curved fingers, like snake fangs, and hissed at him. He pursed his lips and dropped his eyes. The women laughed.

Paxton wondered what the story there was. Zorfina, like most of Eurona, was patriarchal. Were the men from other tribes ashamed of this matriarchal tribe in their midst? Kingdom politics were a funny thing. To each his own.

The Seabolt brothers grabbed turkey legs and slices of hearty bread before gearing up for the night's hunt. The sun had already dipped low over the sea, casting shadows within the west commons, as lingering sunlight sparkled off the far waters of the ocean. The beat of the Kalorian drum rose up. Sounds of the hotlands ritual filled every space of the commons as the men and women prepared.

Anticipation filled the space between the hunters. As a whole, they kept their voices down, speaking only as needed. Quivers and bows were donned, long daggers sheathed, and leather boots tied. In a moment of surprised unity, men and women of all the nationalities nodded in respect as their eyes met.

The hunters raised their gazes to people filling the balcony above. In front was the entire royal family, come to see them off. The woman standing next to Lady Wyneth dabbed at her eyes with a handkerchief. All around them were servants and guards. Nobody spoke, but an understanding stretched along the autumn winds.

Paxton spared his last look for Princess Aerity. Even from afar she seemed to be looking right at him. She brought her slender fingertips to her lips and left them there, as if her hand could keep her emotions from escaping.

Paxton heard Tiern sigh. The sap.

In silence, the hunters grouped together, the Zandalee joining the Lochlans without question as they set out. Paxton did not look up again.

Chapter

15

The Lochlan and Zandalee hunters exited royal lands through the south hold and followed along the North Creek, keeping an eye out for animal tracks. Now and then someone would point to deer prints, but nothing of major interest. The rich men walked loudly through the dry leaves, leading with hard heels. Zandora turned with pinched eyebrows to see who was making all the noise, and though the men looked momentarily frightened at her pointed attention, they didn't seem to understand why she was throwing hostile looks their way.

When Paxton gritted his teeth in annoyance, Tiern back-tracked to the men and began showing them how to walk light-footed. They were surprisingly open to the suggestions and made progress, quieting a fraction as they became more aware of their bodies and the earth beneath them. The way a hunter should.

Paxton breathed easier, admiring his brother's gentle way with people. It's good there were men like Tiern alive, or there'd be no peace in all Eurona.

The night was blessedly warm. Paxton and Tiern found a large half-hollowed log and hunkered behind it, back to back, pulling their quivers to the side. The Zandalee refused to sit, opting to lean against trees so they could see in different directions.

Paxton's eyes adjusted when darkness descended, his hearing heightening as sounds of night came to life.

He settled into his body's awareness of his surroundings, muscles tense and ready to move at a moment's notice. But like last time, all was still for many hours. The Zandalee never sat or moved. Their determination and stamina was unmatched by any of the men, who often fidgeted or grunted quietly.

In the deep recesses of night, when his frame became heavy and his legs went numb, a noise rang out. At his back, he felt Tiern stiffen. The sound had been faint, like a distant shout. Paxton held his breath as he listened intently.

There it was again! Zandora lifted her arm as some kind of signal to the other Zandalee.

A shout from afar came louder this time, followed closely by others. The hunters jumped to their feet.

"It's coming from the east," Harrison said.

"The Kalorians," Paxton added.

Without discussion, they sprinted into the dense trees, away from the water and toward the sounds where the Kalorians were stationed eastward. As he ran, Paxton pushed through jagged branches that whipped against his face. He cursed and kept running, too wild to feel any of it.

It seemed like only minutes later when a low, inhuman sound filled his ears. Paxton slowed his steps, and Tiern grabbed his shoulders from behind to avoid colliding into his back. Together they peered into the trees, moonlight casting shadows through the leaves.

"Listen," Paxton whispered. The other hunters stopped, as well. Above their panting breaths were more yells from men, closer now, and an unmistakable roar, feral and vicious. The hairs on Paxton's arms stood on end as Tiern's fingers dug into his shoulder. Zandora hissed low.

The great beast was near.

One of the wealthy men shook his head and stepped back. "Seas alive!" He sounded ill, his eyes wide in the moonlight.

"We have to help them!" Paxton tore into the trees once more, sheer determination overpowering his fear. As the Lochlan men and the Zandalee crashed through the underbrush, sounds of the Kalorian men became clearer, yelling war cries. They were herding the beast straight for them.

"It's coming!" Tiern shouted from behind him.

The two youngest Lochlan lads climbed hurriedly into the nearest trees with their bows. Two of the wealthy men fled to the south. Paxton, Tiern, Harrison, and Samuel found shelter behind trees, some standing, some kneeling, all with weapons at the ready. Paxton caught the glint of Zandora's long, sharp arrow, where she knelt within bushes.

He peeked around the tree trunk and watched slivers of the wood exposed by moonlight. Tiern sidled close to him, watching from the other side.

He'd heard descriptions of the beast. Pictured it many times in his mind. But as it burst through the brush, nothing could prepare him for the infamous creature. It was unlike any animal he'd ever seen. A mixture of scales and coarse dark fur, beady black eyes and tusks that curled to the side around a mouthful of sharp teeth. Massive paws with oversized claws.

The people hadn't exaggerated its size. Paxton's jaw clenched in horror as it barreled toward them on all fours. A barrage of arrows bounced off its thick body. The beast stood and gave a great roar, shaking the ground, and Paxton thought he saw dark fur glistening under the beast's squatty neck. Blood? Paxton broke from his shocked trance and sent an arrow flying at the beast's mouth. As if sensing the approaching danger, it lowered its head and the arrow pinged off its skull, falling to the ground like a mere gnat.

Paxton swore.

All at once, a group of ferocious Kalorian men broke through the trees behind it. The next moment was chaos. Paxton didn't dare shoot while so many men surrounded the beast.

"Stay here!" he told Tiern as he rushed forward.

"I don't think so, Brother," Tiern responded from behind him in a shaking voice.

Paxton wanted to argue, but there was no time. The great beast spun and crouched, preparing for the Kalorian attack. When the men got within reach, the beast swung its arm in a flash, throwing three men into nearby trees. It slashed its claws through another man's belly. Paxton wrenched his dagger from his waist. At once, he, Harrison, and Zandora leaped high onto its back. The beast was nearly wide enough for all three of them, and smelled pungently of wet decay.

Before Paxton could get a grip, he felt himself soaring haphazardly, high into the air, until his body smacked the ground hard, knocking the wind from his lungs. Through his wide eyes he saw the beast running straight at him, staring him down. He raised an arm to shield his face. The creature never stopped. It kicked him in the ribs as it ran past, its claw ripping the skin of his arm, sending him tumbling in pain. He lost his knife somewhere in the brush.

"Pax!" Tiern crouched over him as he fought for breath, his eyes frantic. "You're alive—thank the seas. Here's your dagger." Tiern leaned over him and shoved the knife back in his sheathe with shaking hands just as a bloodcurdling yell sounded from a man behind them. Pax tried to sit up and hollered at the jabs of pain searing through his body.

"Don't move, Brother. You're hurt. You need to put pressure on your arm."

Pax absently grabbed his bleeding arm and lay there in dismay, watching as the great beast tore through hunters with no effort at all. And yet, it didn't seem as if it wanted to fight. It seemed as if it wanted to get away, as if the people were a nuisance in its path. Tiern sat up on his knees and shot an arrow just as the beast raised its head. It nicked the side of its neck and the great beast roared, stumbling as it swatted at the spot.

"You hit it!" Pax said. The effort to speak sent agony through his ribs.

One of the wealthy men somehow ended up in the beast's fleeing path.

"Get out of its way!" Paxton yelled hoarsely, grimacing.

The man stared up at the monster in sheer, stunned terror and let loose a horrible high-pitched scream. Paxton wanted to cover his ears against it. The youngest Zandalee woman jumped in front of the man with a wild shout, brandishing a hooked dagger. To Paxton's confusion, the beast paused, sniffed the air, and then whacked her aside with the back of its paw. She cartwheeled, airborne. Paxton could see how she was about to land and the angle of her knife, but there was nothing anyone could do. Her dagger pierced straight through her gut as she fell. The Zandalee girl seized for a moment before going still.

The monster grabbed the screaming man with both massive paws and shoved his waist into its gaping mouth. It held the man between its teeth as it bounded away on all fours, into the dark woods. The bloodcurdling cries lessened and became fainter, but never stopped, echoing through the forest.

Paxton numbed himself to the revulsion of it, forcing himself to think straight. He ignored Tiern's objections and stood, his torso banded by bruises already. "We have to follow it."

"You're not well enough," Tiern said. "Stay here."

"Wait!" Panic flooded Paxton's body as he watched his brother sprint into the trees with Harrison, Samuel, Zandora, and a Kalorian. He followed at a pathetic pace, and made it a quarter of a mile before he fell panting against a tree, holding his ribs. When he caught his breath he moved again, this time only at a jogging pace. He'd never felt so worthless, but he couldn't stop. Not while Tiern was out there with the beast.

As sounds of the rushing nearby river became apparent, Paxton heard voices. Tiern and the three others came running into his sight and stopped when they saw him, except for Zandora, who rushed on to tend to the injured huntress.

"By the depths, Paxton, are you mad?" Tiern said with a scowl of disbelief. "You shouldn't have followed! Look at you, bleeding everywhere!"

"Where is the beast?" he asked.

"It ran into the river and submerged itself," Harrison said, shaking his head. "The beast dived in like a bear and we never saw it come back up. It took the man with it."

He cringed. What an awful way to go.

"So, the beast can swim," Paxton mused. Prints they'd

found by the water had led him to believe it was a possibility, but he'd hoped the beast was land dwelling only. Now he knew why it was so hard to find and trap.

"Come on," Tiern said. He lifted Paxton's arm across his shoulder, making him wince. "Let's get you back to the castle."

"Daylight is coming." Harrison nodded up at the lightening sky.

Samuel and the Kalorian ran ahead to inform the others of what had happened and help the injured back to royal lands.

"The beast has a weakness," Paxton said. Ignoring his pains, he walked as quickly as he could, clutching his arm.

Harrison and Tiern both nodded and said, in sync, "Its neck."

Problem was, the beast's head was like a boar's—it hardly had a neck to speak of. Its head slumped down to its shoulders and only raised slightly when it roared.

"One of the Kalorian men said they'd slashed across its throat when they first attacked it," Harrison explained. "That's why it was running. It'd been injured."

"Good," Pax said. The beast was stronger than he could have possibly imagined, but at least it had a weakness.

That, at least, was a start.

Chapter 16

Eight-year-old Stephon had learned to be the first one out of the schoolhouse each day, and to run like the wind through the soybean fields, all the way to their lean-to hidden in the forest. As the son of a registered Lashed in Rambling Brook of Lochlanach, it was never a good idea to dawdle. But this day he'd had to stay behind at his teacher's request.

Her lips were pursed as they stood before the class's small aquarium where baby rainbow trout floated belly-up. "Did you kill the fish, Stephon?"

The boy shook his matted head insistently. "No, ma'am."

"You know the rules. You are not to touch any living

thing in this class. Your gloves are to stay on at all times in this room."

"I understand, miss. I promise I didn't touch it. And . . . I'm not Lashed."

Her lips pursed tighter. "So you and your mother say."

The boy's chest filled with the heat of shame and frustration. He dropped his head and mumbled. "I saw the other boys poking it with a stick."

"It is not proper to tell lies and blame innocent people when you choose not to take responsibility for your actions. The other children told me they saw *you*." Her voice filled with a scary sort of satisfaction. "Take off your gloves, Stephon."

He knew what she wanted. She wanted to see lash marks. He slowly pulled off the threadbare gloves and held out his hands. His teacher backed away to a safe distance, then bent slightly to get a closer look. She frowned at the sight of his clean, unmarked nails, and stood tall again. "Leave. And stay away from the fish tanks from now on."

Stephon pulled his gloves back on and grabbed his bag, rushing from the room. A quick glance around the schoolhouse showed that the other children had gone home. He ran through the long grass until he hit the village's main path, which would lead to the soybean fields by his house. As he turned a corner at the Reefpoole farm, he slid in the gravel, almost crashing into two women in his path.

"Whoa, dear one, careful now." The woman wore a light hooded covering that hid most of her face, and she talked funny.

Stephon scrambled to his feet and was set to keep running when a voice rang out from the rickety steps of the nearby house. Seas, no, the last thing Stephon wanted was to attract the attention of Farmer Reefpoole.

"Watch out, ladies, don't let that boy touch you!"

The two women and Stephon both turned their faces up to the man on the steps, boots covered in dirt and face red from the sun. A boy from Stephon's school was at the man's side, scowling down at him. "His mama's Lashed, and he's trouble."

The women's heads snapped to Stephon, and he felt pierced by the icy blue eyes of the one who'd spoken. Her hood had fallen back a little to reveal shining black hair and the prettiest face Stephon had ever seen. But those eyes . . . they seemed to dissect him.

"Is that right?" the woman crooned in that strange accent. "Are you dangerous, boy?"

It took him a moment to register her words, then he shook his head. Half a second later he felt a sting as something sharp bashed into his arm. The woman gasped and looked up at the steps. The farmer's son threw another rock, this time hitting Stephon in the chest. He grabbed his rib in pain.

"Get away from those ladies!" the boy yelled. His father smirked.

Stephon stumbled as he spun and then ran, not looking back.

After watching Stephon disappear into the fields, the woman stared up at the man, a small smile gracing her lips.

"Thank you for . . . saving us."

The man tipped his chin down. "Our pleasure. You don't sound like you're from around here."

The women moved closer, to the bottom of the steps. One still kept her face hidden under her cloak's hood.

"We are traveling through from the lands of Kalor, looking to trade spices."

"Ah." The farmer nodded in appreciation. Trading was his livelihood. "Never been to Kalor. Heard they haven't fared well since the wars of Eurona."

The woman eyed the farmer's shanty house. "It seems most lands have not fared well, sadly. Rocato left quite a lot of damage in his path."

The man growled at the name Rocato, crossing his arms. "That he did."

"We have many tales where I'm from." The woman slowly made her way up the steps, pulling her hood back to reveal her full beauty. The man and his son stared, relaxing their stances as she neared, as if enchanted by her voice. "They say if Rocato had had a better plan, and had not been so impulsive, he would have succeeded in taking over the kingdom."

"Well," the man breathed, mesmerized by her eyes. "That's a frightening tale."

She continued. "And they say Rocato had a son who few knew of, that he has descendants who have been carefully planning how to succeed in all the ways he failed. For the Lashed to have power and respect once again." She smiled in amusement. "Can you believe such tales?"

"More like nightmares!" The boy sneered.

The woman bent and patted his cheek, smiling. "Indeed." She stood. "Thank you again for saving me from that horrible boy. I don't know how helpless people like me could survive without capable people like you."

Neither the man nor boy objected when the beautiful foreign woman reached out to grasp their hands in apparent thanks. Yet three short beats later, both fell to the porch in a pile, limbs limp with death. The woman stared down at her fingers, her heart accelerating in thrill as she watched a new line rise beneath her nails to join the many others with scarcely a space between them.

"We will burn this disgusting hovel." She glanced down the steps at her companion, who hadn't moved during any of this. "Make certain no one's coming."

"Yes, Rozaria," the girl said. She pulled back her hood, revealing a jagged scar across the side of her olive-skinned face. The two women looked up and down the empty path before bending and taking hold of the wood beams of the porch with their hands.

❦

That afternoon, young Stephon watched as flames rose to touch the sky from the other end of the vast soybean fields. An acrid breeze blew past. His mother lay a bony hand on his shoulder.

"That looks like Mr. Reefpoole's house."

Stephon nodded, but he didn't understand. He'd been there twenty minutes before, and there'd been no sign of fire.

"He's not a nice man, but I wouldn't wish that upon anyone," his mother murmured. Again, Stephon only nodded.

"Good day, Lashed One."

Stephon jumped and his mother let out a startled noise at the sound of the foreign woman's voice. She must have come through the forest, rather than the fields, staying hidden. The other traveling woman remained a short distance away, her face shrouded behind a draping hood.

Sudden trepidation filled Stephon. His mother shoved him behind her, voice shaking. "We don't want any trouble. I'm clean. Look." She held up a trembling hand to show her unmarked nails.

"What a pity." The foreign woman moved closer, running her ice blue eyes over Stephon's mother. Even though the woman seemed nice enough, something about her felt strange to Stephon. He picked up a stick and held it up, ready to use it.

The woman cocked her head at him and gave a low laugh.

"Stephon!" His mother snatched the stick away, but kept it in her own hand at her side.

The woman ignored the stick and focused on Stephon's mother's face. "You should be using your magic. You should be living in a proper home and have meat on your bones. Your son should have the honor of his peers, not their judgment."

Who was this woman and why was she saying these

dangerous things to his mother? Stephon peeked up at his mother's gaunt face. Her mouth hung open wordlessly.

"You are like so many I have encountered," the foreign woman continued, her eyes sad yet fierce. "Frightened into shameful submission. This is not a life, my dear."

The woman walked to the dead garden beside their house, the vegetables that rotted in an overabundance of rain. She crouched beside a wilted squash vine and took a stem in her hand. Stephon watched in wonder as a trail of green moved from her hand up and down the stem, down into the ground where the roots lived and into the large, spiky leaves. Bright yellow flowers budded, then bloomed, falling off as the flesh of a yellow squash pushed outward, oblong and perfect. In minutes, she'd grown food with a simple touch. It was the most beautiful thing the boy had ever witnessed. Stephon's mother raised a trembling hand to her mouth.

"See what you could have?" asked the woman. "What you *should* be enjoying? Your magic can defy seasons and weather. It can defy disease and poverty."

Another breeze danced across their skin, bringing choking scents from the fire. The woman stood and put her hand out to touch the wisp of smoke. "Can you feel the winds of change? Will you grasp it, as I have?" She closed her hand around the air and smiled. The fervor in her eyes sent a jolt down Stephon's back. And then he noticed her purpled fingernails. His mouth and eyes gaped open, his heart hammering in fear at her nearness.

"I—I'm sorry, miss," his mother stuttered. "I can't. . . . I don't know what you mean."

"Soon, you will." The woman continued to give his mother a knowing smile. "Be ready."

Stephon's mother pulled him close as the strange women turned, walking into the path of smoke.

Chapter

17

Paxton was taken straight into the infirmary wing of the castle, along with four other men. Several refused magical treatment. Eight had been killed that night. Six Kalorians, one Lochlan, and the youngest Zandalee. Paxton considered himself lucky, though his injuries were worse than he'd first assumed.

The gash on his arm gaped, filled with dirt. A path of now-dried blood had run down to his hand, soaking his tan tunic, so he removed it. His back, chest, and stomach were bruised. And on his left side he had cracked ribs and several severe scratches where the beast had kicked him.

But he was alive.

He leaned against the wall on the cot in the infirmary

room where the guards had left him alone. The room was small and clean with only a cot, a side table, and a chair. He'd cleaned his wounds and now sat waiting.

Without a knock, the wooden door opened and an old woman stepped in pushing a cart with a covered plate. She had a long, gray braid across her shoulder. Her eyes were wise as she approached Paxton. Perhaps it was in his imagination, but he could have sworn he felt static in the air. Energy. Immediately, he knew the woman was Lashed and he felt a strange feeling of peace and tenderness—something he hadn't felt since childhood.

She came to his side without smiling. "Don't be afraid, Paxton Seabolt. My name is Mrs. Rathbrook. With your permission, I will heal you."

"I don't fear you," he said. His voice sounded reverent to his own ears. Paxton openly stared at the woman. He had expected the royal Lashed to be much younger. He'd never seen a Lashed person of her age, or one in such good health. Mrs. Rathbrook had to be in her sixties.

Emotions he hadn't allowed himself to feel for many years rose up and overflowed his system. The words poured out against his will. "My grandmother was Lashed."

He'd never said those words out loud. A pang of fear for his family tightened inside his chest, until Mrs. Rathbrook took his mangled hand in her own. Looking down at his injury, she said, "I know. I knew Margaret Seabolt well."

Paxton's heart kicked. "You . . . you knew her?"

166

"Sh. Let me work." The woman held his hand, touching his skin around the injury on his arm without brushing the torn flesh. "You'll feel heat. It will be uncomfortable for a moment. Stay still."

Paxton nodded and the woman closed her eyes. His heart went erratic . . . but it had nothing to do with the magic pouring into him.

She knew his grandmother.

He became so engrossed in his thoughts that he hardly noticed the intense heat rushing through his veins, straight to his hand where the magic flamed, stitching his skin and muscle back together. He watched in awe as purple lines fused in the tiny space of white at the bottom of her nails. Her entire fingernails were purple with the exception of two paper-thin white lines near the top. Mrs. Rathbrook let out a hum of satisfaction.

Her cool hands moved across his chest. He closed his eyes as she worked, and allowed himself to fully remember his grandmother for the first time in so long. Her tiny cottage on the ocean where she lived by herself after his grandfather's passing at sea. While Tiern ran about in the sand, picking up shells and terrorizing crabs, Paxton gravitated to his grandmother's side. He'd known she was special before he knew she was Lashed. He experienced that same static energy in her presence.

Their grandmother Seabolt had looked after the boys during the day while their father fished and their mother haggled with vendors.

He recalled the summer morning when he was eight and a woman round with pregnancy came bursting into his grandmother's cottage.

"It's not moving! Something is wrong—I can sense it. Please, help me, miss!"

Paxton had been confused by the woman's frantic pleading. He couldn't understand what his grandmother could possibly do to help.

His grandmother had gone an ashen shade of gray. "I cannot help you. I'm so very sorry."

"Please!" The woman had begged, her shaking hands splayed across her belly. "I know you're Lashed! My own mother told me. I know you can feel for its heart and . . . and . . ." She began crying. "This is my sixth pregnancy. None have lasted this long. Please . . ."

Paxton had hated the sad feeling that overtook him at the woman's desperate sobbing, and the way his grandmother's eyes filled with tears.

"If I help you, I will be killed when they do the census. I have grandsons to care for. I cannot risk it. Please . . . you must go."

Paxton's eyes burned as the memory faded and a hot bout of flame overtook the skin at his waist. He hissed and watched in awe as the bloodied claw marks sealed themselves between the woman's splayed fingers. Mrs. Rathbrook's creased forehead relaxed and she opened her eyes.

"There now. Good as new."

"Thank you." He slowly pushed himself up, marveling at the lack of pain. But the woman placed a hand on his shoulder and urged him to lie back.

"Magic can take a toll on the body. You'll need to rest for

a bit and eat something." She pushed a cart to his side filled with sliced fruit, bread, juice, and dark coffee, a delicacy imported from the forests of Kalor.

"Thank you," he said again.

Mrs. Rathbrook gave him a small smile and pushed his hair out of his face. When she turned to go, he called out, "Wait."

She faced him again, her head tilting.

"She wasn't very old when she died," Paxton said. He felt like a child, unable to hold back the words, remembering. "Her health declined so quickly."

"Aye." Mrs. Rathbrook nodded solemnly. "As do all Lashed who do not use their powers."

Paxton sat up, wincing, and the woman gently pushed him back down. "Easy now."

He propped up on his elbows to see her face better. "So the two *are* linked? A Lashed One's health to their magic?"

"Aye. How do you think I've lived this long?" Indeed. It was just as he'd feared.

"I thought perhaps Lashed had shorter lifespans by nature, or that some were sickly from a lack of nutrition. I hoped it was coincidence." He felt like a fool for not acknowledging the truth of it sooner. He lay back, staring at the ceiling. "I miss her." Deep seas . . . he hadn't spoken of her in years. He expected to feel weak after vocalizing his feelings, but he didn't. He felt only loss and regret.

"I'm sure you do," the Lashed woman murmured in

return. She gave his cheek a fond pat. "I hope you'll visit me whenever you're in the castle, Paxton Seabolt."

And with that, the woman with magic hands left him, and Paxton fell back, rubbing his eyes, chest burning with familiar anger. His grandmother could have lived longer had she used her magic. He could still have her today if it weren't for the law of the land.

Chapter

18

Princess Aerity woke with a start as she remembered the hunters leaving for last night's hunt. She untangled her long nightgown from the covers and ran to the window, heart racing as she threw aside the thick curtains. Her eyes squinted against the bright morning sky as she scanned the people below.

Her stomach turned, realizing there were definitely fewer hunters, and they didn't seem to be celebratory. Some were milling about, taking off their weapons. Others were clustered in small groups, slumped as they spoke. She recognized three of the Zandalee in all black, facing the wall on their knees, as if praying. Had they lost one? Aerity's stomach dropped in sadness.

She scanned the crowd, and found fewer dark-haired men. There was Harrison's short hair—thank the seas! He seemed well, and her stomach began to right itself. She spotted Tiern Seabolt next. Her eyes circled all around him, but didn't find his brother at his side.

Where was Paxton Seabolt? The brothers were always together. Air moved faster into her lungs, pressed out in short spurts. She shouldn't care this much. He'd never even been civil to her. Still, concern ate at her.

She jumped from the window seat and snatched her robe from the hook, throwing it over her arms. Aerity yanked open the door and found her maid standing there with a tray. Caitrin jumped and let out a small squeal.

"I'll be right back!" Aerity ran past her.

"But, miss! Your Highness, your shoes!"

It wasn't proper to be seen outside her chambers in night-clothes, and it was even more uncivilized to be seen barefoot. Aerity didn't care, driven by some frantic fear for a complete stranger. She ignored the open stares from servants as she passed, and she barely noticed the guards following as she burst from the castle doors and ran down the path to the west commons area. It wasn't until she neared the vine-covered gates and men came into view that she began to worry about her state.

Based on the gawking of the guards at the gates, she must have looked a fright, tangled hair and all. She stopped and peeked through the end of the gate until she found Tiern again. He appeared stern as he cleaned his boots, but not heartbroken. Aerity hastily ran her finger through her hair and twisted it over her shoulder.

She then moved forward, speaking to the closest guard. "Excuse me. Can you please fetch that lad, Tiern Seabolt? I wish to ask him about the hunt." He glanced at her bare feet and blinked before obeying. Aerity wiggled her toes against the cool stones, feeling foolish and nervous as guards watched her.

Tiern ventured out of the commons, and stopped in his tracks at the sight of her. She resisted the urge to smooth her hair back again.

"I apologize for my appearance. I was eager to hear how last night went . . . ?"

Tiern's face darkened as he recalled it.

"Is your brother all right?" she blurted before he'd had a chance to speak.

His eyebrows rose. "Er, aye. He's in the castle for his injuries, but he'll heal."

Aerity let out a breath, embarrassed. "What happened, then? Did you see the beast? Has it been killed?" Her blood pumped rapidly, only slowing when Tiern gave a regretful shake of his head.

"It still lives."

The princess was torn between disappointment that the beast would live another day, and relief that the fate of her future marriage was not yet sealed.

"What happened out there?"

Tiern retold the night's events, each detail making Aerity's skin crawl.

Aerity considered calling Harrison over to discuss it all, but hot shame filled her at the thought of him seeing her like this. He'd only laugh and tease her, but he knew her well enough to know she had to have been out of sorts to leave her room in such a state. She thanked Tiern and rushed back into the castle before one of her parents or aunts caught sight of her.

⁂

Twenty minutes later she bustled down the infirmary hall wearing her favorite pale pink gown cinched extrafirm at her waist and dipping a bit lower at the top than her other dresses. She told herself she'd grabbed it from her wardrobe at random, but she knew it was a lie.

Aerity stopped a nurse her age. The girl's eyes widened and she dipped into a curtsy. "Your Highness."

"Hello, miss. Can you please tell me where the hunter Paxton Seabolt might be?"

"Certainly, Princess. Last door to your left."

Aerity rushed to the closed door and paused, hesitating with a hand pressed to her nervous stomach. She only wanted to see him, to see for herself that his injuries weren't too grave, and then she would leave. She knocked softly, but heard nothing. After a few seconds she slowly pushed the door open and peeked inside. A gas lamp dimly lit the room. Aerity held her breath as she beheld a sleeping Paxton on the cot, one arm curved over his head and the other draped across his middle. He lay shirtless, his brown trousers slung low. Muddied leather boots were splayed on the floor.

She stared openly from the doorway at his body. It was the most skin she'd ever seen on a grown man. He had a small, brown trail of hair down his taut stomach. Aerity found herself holding her breath as the air around her closed in.

She wondered how it would feel to touch him, this lad she hardly knew who intrigued her so.

High seas, why did her skin feel so prickly and her blood so . . . heavy?

He was obviously well. She needed to close the door and leave before someone caught her staring. But then Paxton inhaled a ragged breath and sat up, as if waking from a dream. His eyes were alert and untrusting as they darted around the room, landing on the princess. Aerity gripped the door, caught.

"I'm sorry," she said. "I didn't mean to wake you. I only wanted to see how you fared. You look . . . healthy." She swallowed and backed up. "I'll leave you to rest."

"Wait." He slung his legs over the side of the cot and gripped the edge. "Have you seen my brother?"

Aerity stopped and nodded. "He told me what happened last night. I can't believe it can swim."

Paxton dragged a hand through his dirty hair and grimaced. "Aye. That complicates things indeed." He was speaking to her in a civil manner. Aerity hid her surprise.

The hunter looked down at his abdomen and then back up at the princess. He rubbed a hand down his stomach. "I'm not sure where my tunic's gone . . . it was bloodied."

Aerity waved off his comment with a shaking hand and said, "It's all right." As if she were used to being in the presence of half-naked, attractive men.

Do not look at his chest . . . or his stomach. . . .

"Only a few Kalorians remain to hunt," Paxton said. "They were extraordinary last night. They attacked it and gave chase."

He was being awfully chatty. Perhaps a near-death experience would do that to a person.

"Tiern said you did the very same thing, attacked it without fear."

Paxton shook his head and paused as he looked down at his hands. "It wasn't enough. I was like a rag doll against its power."

Ah, so Paxton Seabolt had been humbled. His hair was a mess, and she wanted to brush it from his face.

"But it won't be so next time," he said, his voice lowering. "I know the beast's weakness now, and I will kill it."

Paxton's eyes bored into hers. His words echoed in her mind.

He wanted to kill the beast. And if he did . . . he would become her husband.

Aerity felt a heady rush of bravery. She glanced over her

shoulder at the empty hall and then let the door slide closed behind her. She swallowed hard and leaned against it. Oh, lands below, what had she done? She'd just closed herself in a room with him! Her mother would die if she found out. Gossip would fly.

"I didn't want our conversation to upset anyone," Aerity explained lamely.

Paxton crossed his arms, examining her, scrutinizing. "If you knew anything about us villager lads, you'd know better than to shut yourself in with one of us." His eyebrow rose and fell provocatively.

Her mouth dropped open. This had been a bad idea. Very bad, indeed. Paxton might be a brave hunter, but she didn't know this man at all. And he was right; the kind of flirting banter popular among commoners was seen as inappropriate among royalty, though he made no move to come near her.

"You're a cheeky one," Aerity managed to say, trying and failing to cover her embarrassment. Paxton's mouth pulled to the side in a smirk that made her stomach flip.

"You've no idea, Princess."

She'd only wanted to continue talking in private. Instead, she'd made things horribly awkward. At a loss, the princess blurted, "My cousin saw the beast. She . . . it killed her fiancé." The words made her light-headed.

Paxton's face dropped. "Lady Wyneth . . . aye. I'd heard the captain was engaged to the king's niece, but I never put it together." He stared past her shoulder, in thought. Then his eyes slid back to hers with newfound intensity. "It will die. Your cousin and all the others will be avenged."

"Good." Aerity cleared her throat against the dry croak that had invaded, made worse by Paxton Seabolt's intrusive searching of her face.

"Why is it that you've come here, Aerity?" There was an edge to his voice. "You want me to kill the great beast?"

Her breath caught. Aerity. Not *princess*. No formal title. Only familiarity, which they hadn't yet earned. Still it warmed her to her core.

She stammered, "Of course I want the beast to be killed."

Paxton walked slowly to the small table, examining the cup. He turned his head enough to gaze warmly at her through strands of his hair. "But do you want *me* to be the one to kill it? Is that why you're here? To persuade me?" His words were spoken in a low voice, sending Aerity's thoughts into a whirlpool of confusion.

"No. I mean . . . I . . ." She tried to sort out any hidden meaning in his words, but he was difficult to read.

If he killed the beast, she would get to touch him. Run her hands over him. He might not like Aerity for whatever reason, but from the heat in his gaze she knew he'd welcome her hands on him. He'd probably welcome any lass's hands on him. That thought darkened Aerity's musings. He half smiled.

"Or is it Harrison you want? Do you still think you have a say in who marries you?" he asked. "Even after your father's proclamation?"

And with that, Aerity felt her wits returning as she returned his steely stare. Did he think she was some girl to be toyed with? How dare he make light of her situation?

"If you're looking to have your ego stroked, Paxton Seabolt, you've asked the wrong lass. I would prefer my future husband to love me, if you must know. This arrangement does not please me, but the safety of the kingdom is more important than what I wish for. So don't speak lightly of my circumstances."

And why had he mentioned Harrison? Had that been a twinge of jealousy in his voice?

His eyes roamed her face as if searching for cracks in her words. He appeared unapologetic for any disrespect he might have meant. Aerity could not understand this bold man or how he perceived her.

As they stared, Aerity felt a sudden nudge at her back from the opening door. The princess jumped and saw Mrs. Rathbrook. Paxton stood straight. Aerity's cheeks heated and she pressed a hand to her chest. This must have looked bad, but the woman smiled at them both with apparent delight.

"My apologies, Mrs. Rathbrook," Aerity said. "I heard Mr. Seabolt was injured so I came to check on him, but he's already in perfect condition, thanks to you. I was just leaving."

Mrs. Rathbrook reached out and took Aerity's clammy hand, squeezing it as if to calm her. In the woman's other hand was a man's tunic. Paxton looked back and forth between the woman and girl, seeming almost confused or surprised about something. The older woman tossed the shirt at his face and he caught it.

"It's not proper to go around shirtless in front of a royal lass," she gently admonished, "no matter how beautiful she might be."

She winked at Aerity, who blushed all over again.

"Please don't tell my father or mother," Aerity began, but the woman only chuckled and shook her head.

"There is nothing to tell. Two people talking."

Aerity, beyond thankful, embraced the woman and kissed her cheek.

She felt Paxton watching her with a keen awareness, but she refused to acknowledge him or say good-bye. She peered around the door and slipped into the empty infirmary hall, gulping breaths of cool air. Her hands shook and she curled her fingers into tight fists to fight the trembling.

She didn't doubt that Paxton had felt her attraction. It's surely what gave him the confidence to be as forward as he pleased. But she couldn't allow another moment like that to happen between them. In his eyes lived something deep, dark, and untold. Something that frightened her.

But it didn't scare her enough to make her want to stay away from him. Not nearly enough.

Chapter

19

Lady Wyneth stood at the gates of the west commons, peering through at the quiet hunters milling about. Most of them appeared to be finishing their morning meals and heading toward the tents for rest. No sign of her cousin anywhere.

Wyneth turned and strode along the cobblestones back to the castle. She wondered where Aerity could be. She'd caught wind of the night's events from two castle maids, and wondered if the princess had heard about Paxton Seabolt's injury.

As the lady rounded the corner she heard low male voices and nearly crashed into several men.

"Whoa there!" Harrison took her by the forearms to

181

steady her, chuckling. The other men walked around them, except Lord Alvi, who stopped.

"So sorry, Har— um, Lieutenant. I was looking for Aerity."

"Haven't seen her. We've just returned from scouting for signs of the beast. No luck."

Wyneth nodded. She hoped with all her heart that Harrison would kill the thing to avenge Breckon and marry her cousin. She'd always wanted him and Aerity together . . . though the princess seemed to have taken an interest in the daring skirt raiser, Paxton. She supposed she couldn't fault her, though Harrison would be the safer bet.

Harrison watched her with fondness in his light brown eyes. "I'd better go wash up."

"Good to see you, Lieutenant," she said.

Harrison began to leave her, but Lord Alvi remained. When Harrison stopped, the Ascomannian lord waved him on with a smile. "I'll be along momentarily." Harrison's face hardened, and he made no move to exit. He looked to Wyneth, who felt unease at the awkwardness.

Wanting to defuse the tension, she said, "It's fine, Lieutenant. I shall see you this afternoon." He hesitated, looking displeased before he finally strode away.

"Walk with me?" Lord Alvi held out his elbow, and Wyneth took it, letting him lead her off the path and into a nearby grassy area with a smattering of trees. "How are you this morning, Lady?"

His voice was as low as the deep blue sea. Wyneth swallowed hard. Something about this man was disarming. He made her incredibly nervous. His attention was flattering, but Wyneth did not take it to heart. They stopped behind a wide tree, and he turned to face her. His dominating presence was flustering.

"I'm well," Wyneth said. Her eyes darted this way and that, attempting not to look into the cool arctic blue of his. "How goes the hunt?"

He peered out at the glistening ocean beyond. "The beast still eludes us in the day. They watched it enter the water, but we can't find where it might've come back out."

Wyneth's clutched the gray fabric at her chest. "The beast took to the water?" Sudden fear gripped her like fingers of icicles, and she felt dizzy.

Lief moved closer, took both her elbows. "You look faint."

"I'm all right," she whispered. He slowly let her go.

She blinked, eyes burning. She hadn't cried in two whole days. But hearing that the beast could swim—that it could have followed her into the creek that night . . .

Wyneth covered her mouth, breathing deeply through her nose as she closed her eyes. How easily she could have been killed. Just like Breckon.

Breckon.

Lady Wyneth was hardly aware as Lord Alvi led her farther into a shroud of evergreens, out of sight. He took her face in his hands and swiped the tears as they fell. His face was a mixture of confusion and alarm.

High seas, she was crying in front of a hunter. A stranger. A foreign lord.

"I—I'm sorry." Wyneth stepped back, out of his grasp, and his bare arms fell to his sides. She had no idea why she felt the sudden urge to tell him everything. Perhaps his kindness. Perhaps to kill his interest in her. What man would find interest in a woman with a shattered heart?

"The beast killed my betrothed." Her voice was thick. She wiped the last bit of moisture from her eyes and stood taller. "I saw it attack. We were together on the docks. I fled, swimming across the creek. I—I left him."

Lief's handsome face slackened. "That was you? You were engaged to the captain?"

No more tears. Wyneth tightened her jaw and nodded.

Understanding crossed his face. "So you've seen the beast?"

A flash of teeth and claws and blood flashed through Wyneth's mind's eye and she rocked back on her heels.

"Of course . . ." He moved toward her, and she stepped back, causing him to tilt his head to the side. "I can't begin to imagine what you've been through."

She swallowed. "Why didn't it come for me in the water? It could have killed us both."

There were times, especially during the first couple weeks, when she wished she were dead too. She thought death might have been better than to feel the heartache anew each morn when she woke. Breckon had been her life and her future. He'd been there as her mind-set changed from that of a girl to a woman, and he'd loved her every minute, patiently.

"There are many things we don't understand about the beast and its motives," Lief said quietly. "But the fates kept you alive for a reason. You have a life to live still, Lady Wyneth."

Wyneth allowed herself a look at him.

Breckon had been polished. Lean. His hair had been short, and he was polite to a fault. Lord Lief Alvi was a contrast to all of that. A rogue. Wild waves of blond hair rested on his shoulders. A vest of fur fitted against his massive chest, his shoulders and arms of muscle jutting out.

It felt wrong, wrong, to look upon another man this way. Especially a man who was in the running for her cousin's hand in marriage. Surely she was losing her mind.

"I must go."

In a move like a dance, Wyneth turned away, only to feel the warmth of his grip around her wrist, spinning her back around, pulling her with a silent command right into that solid chest and those strong arms she'd just been admiring. Without a single word, Lord Alvi took Wyneth's mouth with his own, practically lifting her off her feet as his hands circled her waist and tugged her body against his.

She heard herself make a noise of surprise which morphed into a moan at the closeness and warmth, the scent of clean masculinity. For a long moment she shut off her mind, letting her senses have full control. Lief's hunger for her lips was like nothing she'd ever felt. He was not careful, nor did he bother with niceties as she was accustomed to. He took complete ownership, crushing her body to his in a way that made her long for more.

All at once, the two names closest to her heart were shouted inside her mind.

Breckon! Aerity!

Lady Wyneth pushed against his wide chest, and he let her go. She struggled for air. He wiped the corner of his mouth with his thumb and smiled.

"You—we can never do that again," Wyneth said. Her voice was a shaky jumble of want and need and regret.

"Why not?" His head cocked in that curious way again.

"Why not?" she repeated back at him in disbelief.

"I've wanted to do that since I first laid eyes on you."

Wyneth's blood raced at the flattery of hearing that from a man like him. But it wasn't as simple as he was making it out to be. "I only just finished telling you I've lost the man I was to marry. My heart . . . still aches."

He appeared crestfallen. "I'm sorry, Lady Wyneth. I thought it might help."

Oh, the logic of a man, Wyneth thought. "What's more, Lord Alvi, if you kill the beast you'll be granted the hand of my cousin. My best friend!"

Wyneth was still in shock that he'd kissed her, this man she scarcely knew, and that she'd been so completely willing.

Being so near him, she felt the lingering lust burning under her skin, and the churn of guilt in her gut. It was the worst kind of situation. Couldn't he see that?

Apparently not, based on his easy smile. "Life is for living, Lady Wyneth. You needn't feel guilty or worried. Fate will intervene to make things right, when necessary. I hope to see you this evening before the hunt." He brought a massive hand to her hair and let his palm and fingers stroke a lone curl.

Her chest was still heaving as he walked away.

Blasted "fate." Outlandish notions.

Wyneth grasped her gray skirts and marched back to the castle through crunching leaves and dry pine needles, overrun by a maelstrom of thoughts. She was quite certain that kissing one of her cousin's suitors mere months after the death of her fiancé was not fate. It was simply one man acting on an inappropriate urge. She was ashamed that her first reaction had been to welcome his touch instead of thwarting it.

She felt utterly alone. Wyneth could never tell Aerity. She could never tell anyone.

As she burst into the castle, a gust of wind at her back, she could still feel Lord Lief Alvi's firm lips against hers. She avoided the eyes of the guards as she passed, bringing a hand to her mouth to hold on to the feel of Lief's kiss for a moment longer.

Just a moment more, and then she'd put him from her mind.

Chapter

20

 After her studies, Aerity donned her leotard and a
soft pullover tunic. Another day had passed, and
the beast was still at large. The only good thing
to happen was that the king was feeling a bit more comfortable about letting his children out of the castle during daylight
to places other than just the commons. The hunters' presence
seemed to make everyone feel safer. The beast had never
attacked or been seen during the day, and it hadn't set foot on
royal lands since the night it took Breckon's life.

At least not that they knew.

Vixie had sprinted from the doors toward the stables,
her guards racing to keep up. Donubhan and several of their
young cousins were accompanied by maids and guards down

to the royal beach where they could dig for sandcrabs and enjoy the autumn sun a bit before winter began to show its face.

Flanked by several guards, Aerity headed the back way to the side of the castle, avoiding the entrance of the commons. The giant oak tree loomed, awaiting her company, with magenta silks hanging from a high, thick branch. The guards kept their distance, making a square around the tree. She hardly registered their quiet presence anymore. She gave the silks a tug to be sure everything was sturdy before taking off her tunic and dropping it to the ground.

This was Aerity's favorite silk. Rather than two separate strands, this one was connected, making a U at the bottom like a hammock. Aerity held the silks up high and lifted her knees, sliding her pointed feet through the gap, feeling the burn of her abdominal muscles. She hung upside down a moment by her knees, letting the tips of her hair drag along the ground, twisting side to side to warm up and stretch. Then she lifted herself until she was sitting in the silks, like a swing.

A breeze blew and Aerity looked up at the rays of sunshine shooting through the canopy of yellow and orange leaves. In that moment, there seemed to be peace in the land, but an ache deep in Aerity's gut reminded her that all was not well— that all might never be truly well for her again, even after this monster was killed. She pulled herself to standing, the silks pressing into the bare arches of her feet. Then she let her body take over in a series of climbs and wraps, twisting and stretching, leaning her body in unnatural ways that pushed her flexibility to the limits. She split her legs and struck an upside-down pose, where she hung by her hips, her whole body tight to keep balanced. With a twist of her waist, she spun, her arms and legs out, hair flying.

Nearby cheers sounded, causing Aerity's core to momentarily loosen and make her wobble. She reached up and pulled herself quickly to sitting, turning her head to see her audience—nearly all the hunters had climbed the side wall where the wooden risers were, and were sitting on top of the stones, watching her. She became acutely aware of her tight leggings and leotard.

"Don't stop on account of us, Princess!" Tiern yelled.

Her face flushed as men of all nationalities smiled up at her, clapping. The Zandalee women cupped their hands around their mouths and let out keening sounds. She gave them all a small wave, feeling exposed.

Then Aerity's eyes caught the still form of Paxton on the end beside Tiern. He leaned his elbows on his knees, watching her with his unreadable stare. Those dark eyes made her feel more than exposed. She felt naked.

Despite their protests, Aerity slid down from the silks and grabbed her tunic. She walked quickly toward the castle, giving a polite smile in their general direction before she disappeared.

"Deep seas, she's something, isn't she?" Tiern raved. "Did you see her, Pax? And when she walked off, all bashful like? Adorable! Did you see?"

"Aye, I've got eyes, don't I?" Paxton had seen, all right. And he'd heard every word the bloody Ascomannians had muttered in lewd laughter out of earshot of the guards. He thought there'd be a fight between Harrison and one of the men when the lieutenant told him to shut his mouth, but Lief had defused the situation, making them all laugh with a story about a coldlands woman who'd dumped her ale over the man's head when he'd commented on her bottom.

Paxton didn't move a muscle, even after the other hunters climbed down and went about their business. The Zandalee three jumped from their high perches into the field with the oak tree, landing in impressive crouches. He stared absently as they took turns on that fabric thing. Judging by the way they struggled and grunted, it must have been harder than it looked.

Aerity had made it look easy. He thought about that morning in the infirmary, the way she'd hugged Mrs. Rathbrook and kissed the woman's cheek. It was one thing to be polite to a Lashed, which few were, but to show that level of affection? It had taken him completely by surprise. Aerity was the future of this kingdom—she'd someday be queen. She could change these lands for the better. Was there hope to be had after all? Paxton gave his head a shake.

He turned and hung his feet over, facing the commons area, and dropped to the rows of seating below.

Lord Lief Alvi was waiting for him at the bottom. They clasped hands when Paxton reached him.

"Quite the prize, is she not?" the coldland lord said, nodding in the direction of the tree on the other side of the wall.

Paxton shrugged, sort of wanting to silence Lief with a punch to the throat at that moment. "If you fancy the circus life."

Lord Lief Alvi gave a loud laugh. "If only marriage were as entertaining as a circus. But at least that one would bring a bit of fire to the arrangement. Not all royal lassies are so . . . interesting."

Paxton said nothing, unsure if Lief was baiting him for his stance on royals. He sometimes forgot the hunter was royalty in Ascomanni.

"Your man Harrison, though. He's got a history with the princess, aye?"

Paxton shrugged. "They know each other. Friends, supposedly."

Lief's eyebrows went up and down, and he chuckled. "The lad's in love, I'd say. This hunt's a dual purpose for him—vengeance and love."

This turned Paxton's stomach for some reason, and he found himself saying, "I believe there is only friendship between them."

At this, Lief laughed and slapped Paxton's arm. "He's after her hand, just like you and I."

"I don't fancy the idea of marriage," Paxton stated.

"Aye. I probably wouldn't either if it wasn't expected of me."

Paxton supposed each man and woman had their struggles to overcome, but he was glad not to be a royal with all the ridiculous things expected of them.

"I daresay you will fancy the idea of marriage a bit more if you kill the beast and earn a plump bed inside that castle." Lief elbowed Paxton in the upper ribs, making him grunt.

Paxton grumbled, and the Ascomannian lord chuckled, walking away.

Chapter
21

 The next morning, after the night's silent hunt and silent breakfast, Paxton and Tiern sat with the other hunters around the fire pit to discuss. Though it was daylight, the fire was good for keeping them warm against gusts coming up from the sea. The Zandalee were the last to join, one of the women shamelessly rubbing her hip against the back of Tiern's head as she passed. His mouth froze midsentence. Samuel and Harrison choked back their laughter.

"I agree, Tiern," Lief said from across the fire, not having seen. "It seems to set out at random. There's no pattern to where it chooses."

"*Jes*," said the Kalorian man who'd seemed to have a

leadership role among his men, and one of the few who spoke Euronan. His hair was shaved along the sides, a strip of black slicked down the middle. "This is like no animal I have hunted. I cannot predict."

Paxton and the others nodded.

"*Auda*," Zandora said in a low voice from where she sat behind him. Paxton nodded. He recognized the Zorfinan word for water.

A hissing sound was made from across the fire. Paxton was surprised to see the Zorfinan men staring at the Zandalee with contempt. When Zandora made a gesture with her fingers, they all looked away.

"Why do you think they hate each other?" Tiern asked Paxton.

"They say our tribe is cursed," Zandora murmured from behind them. "They are fools."

Paxton, Tiern, Samuel, and Harrison all swung their heads around.

"You speak Euronan?!" Tiern said.

Zandora gave a shrug. "When it suits me." Her accent was strong.

"Why am I not surprised?" Samuel chuckled, shaking his curly head.

The three Zandalee looked smug in their black head scarves wrapped securely around their dark faces and necks. They each sat on the grass lazily, two leaning back, Zandora in the center with an elbow on her raised knee.

"My sisters speak only Zorfinan."

"They're your sisters?" Tiern nodded to the other girls.

"*Jes*. I am the oldest. Some call me queen of our tribe."

"So, the girl you lost," Paxton said respectfully, "she was your sister, also?"

Zandora kissed her fingers and touched her shoulder in some kind of tribal sign. "*Jes*. Our youngest. She brings our tribe much pride with her bravery."

The men nodded. After a quiet moment, Tiern asked, "What is the story with you and them, then?" He nodded across the fire to the other Zorfinan hunters. "I mean, if it suits you to tell me."

Zandora threw back her head and gave a rich laugh. "I like you, Tiern Seabolt. My sisters enjoy you even more."

"Oh, erm." Tiern rubbed his neck and gave a nervous laugh as the sisters watched him like prowling cats. "Thanks . . . ?"

"Why do they think you're cursed?" Harrison asked. "Because women rule your tribe?"

"No. It is because the Zandalee allow magic. We do not give census keepers permission to enter our lands. If they try, we kill them."

Paxton's heart thrummed erratically. The other men raised their brows. Samuel said, "You mean, you allow your Lashed to work freely?"

She gave him a fierce look. "Is that a problem for you?"

"No." Samuel raised his hands. "I have no problem with the Lashed."

Paxton tried to keep his voice steady. "I didn't know there was any place in Eurona where it wasn't outlawed."

To this, she shrugged. "Zandalee do not care for laws of Eurona. Or Zorfina. We make our own. In this way, our people flourish."

The men nodded, eyebrows still raised. None of them dared say anything against this.

"Do you have children of your own, then?" Tiern asked.

This brought a smile to Zandora's face. "A son and daughter for me. A son for my sister." She motioned to the older of the two, then the younger. "This one married just this summer."

"So many children . . ." Samuel's words trailed off and his eyes glazed as he stared off.

A clang echoed from the commons gates, and they turned their heads toward the sound of running. A military commander from the castle burst through the tents to the fire pit, out of breath. Paxton jumped up with the other hunters to hear the news.

The man's forehead was creased in remorse. "A fishing village in the north was attacked during the night. Doors ripped from the hinges, men were devoured while their wives and children watched helplessly." He stopped, swallowing.

Curses. It was breaking into homes? Why couldn't the beast have shown itself where any hunters had been instead of a helpless village? The hunters shared horrified expressions.

"Perhaps we can station hunters in the sea towns with horns, so they can alert us if the beast comes," said Samuel.

Paxton shook his head. "We don't have the numbers for that. But we can send word to towns to have their own men with horns at the ready. Each town could come up with their own system of alert, stationing their people at different intervals, maybe in trees—"

"But there are curfews throughout the kingdom," the officer said.

"Blast the curfews!" Paxton shouted. He closed his eyes to calm himself.

Harrison stepped forward. "With all due respect, sir, if people are willing to help, I think they should be allowed."

The officer set his jaw. "I will speak with the king's commanders. If they agree, we'll send mounted messengers to towns to set the plan in motion."

The hunters nodded, and the officer left them to prepare for that night's hunt.

They hunkered over the maps.

"Our greatest success was the night we were all close enough to hear one another's calls," Paxton reminded them. "If they approve the horns, we can afford to spread a bit farther, but it'll be at least two days until we know." He ran his finger along a length of the waterway.

"But the beast has moved north," Volgan argued, pointing closer to the ridgelands.

"That's the last place it attacked," Harrison said. "But the beast has attacked many places with no rhyme or reason. Always along the waterways."

"Then you can stay down there by the creeks, and we'll follow the beast north along Eurona River," Volgan argued, chest puffed.

"It's a swift swimmer, and it knows it's being hunted," Lord Alvi told them. "I say each group takes one of the major waterway veins—North Creek, South Creek, Eurona River, even up around the bay. My men and I will take midriver. We'll be too spread out to help one another, but if we have no luck, we'll go back to grouping closer again tomorrow night. Agreed?"

Paxton gritted his teeth in annoyance. He knew Lief was trying to appease his men, but Paxton wanted to stick to a plan where he felt their odds of killing the beast were much better. He was sick of wasting time and lives for the sake of stroking the pride of a few.

⚡

After another silent night of hunting, the Zandalee were irritable on their return to royal lands at daybreak. They kept snapping at one another in Zorfinan, and the men moved further away, steering clear. Samuel suggested cutting through the nearby town to get them back quicker.

Families filtered out of their homes, women sweeping their steps, men off to work. The Zandalee watched the women with interest. Their few children approached with caution, curious, watched closely by their mothers.

"How goes the hunt?" one woman called, a hand on her hip.

Harrison shook his head. "No sign of it last night. We'll get it, though, miss. Soon."

The woman, probably his mother's age, stepped into the street and kissed Harrison's cheek. She beamed grateful smiles at the other Lochlan men, and then stared openly at the huntresses.

"These are the Zandalee," Tiern explained. "They've joined the hunt."

The Lochlan woman's mouth dropped open. A crowd began to form around them.

"You mean . . . ? The real Zandalee?"

Tiern nodded. Whispers about the foreign huntresses spread all around them, faces lighting up with excitement, people shuffling and standing on their tiptoes to see. The Zandalee took it all in stride, looking around at the pale faces, but not smiling. One brave Lochlan woman stepped forward and took the hand of Zandora, who stood in front. She patted her hand, beaming.

"Thank you!"

Zandora stared down at her, and Tiern laughed nervously, stepping up. "They are women of few words."

A toddler scrambled down from his mother's arms and went to Zandora's legs, touching the strange material.

"Grayson, no!" The mother rushed forward, stopping when she saw Zandora give the child a smile, her earlier irritation seeming to vanish. His mother relaxed, but remained close.

When Zandora patted his head, the town's few children rushed at the Zandalee, wanting to touch their clothes. The presence of the children seemed to cheer the huntresses, who were glad to squat down and let the little ones touch them. After a few minutes Harrison called out to the people.

"Thank you for your kindness, but we must be getting back."

The Zandalee were in far better moods after that. They all were, until they reached the commons. A set of military men was leaving, their faces grim. The Ascomannians and Zorfinans stood in separate groups, talking, but they came together when they saw the Lochlans and Zandalee approach.

Lief spoke. "The beast attacked the Kalorians. They were all found dead."

"Curses." Samuel rubbed his face.

Paxton's jaw flexed as he ground his teeth in anger. Having fought the beast alongside those men, it made him furious to know they hadn't had backup. He wanted to keep his composure, but his jaw was so tense he could only speak through gritted teeth. "This was avoidable. We should have hunted closer together."

Volgan's lip rose in a sneer. Paxton turned on his heels for the tents, afraid of what he'd do and say if he remained a moment longer.

He collapsed onto his cot in the small tent, pressing his fingers to his temples. Tiern came in behind him, but knew not to bother him when he got like this.

After a few minutes, Tiern mumbled, "Bloody seas," and fell asleep.

⤛⤜

A steady rain began. As the day went on, the rain progressed into a thundering storm, which settled into more rain. The land turned to mud. Accounts of flooding waterways came to them from castle messengers in high boots. Even the path outside the commons area had been covered over by a stream of mud. With regret, they decided to call off the hunt for that night.

Since water had seeped under the tents, High Hall was turned into the hunters' quarters. The men sat around playing cards and drinking tankards of ale. The Zandalee had been allowed guest quarters of their own. They had looked exhausted when Paxton saw them trudge away.

Paxton knew he should take the opportunity to relax, but he was too frustrated about the prior night's losses and tonight's hunt being called off for weather. He turned his back to the others and lay on his cot in silence, wondering how close Aerity's chambers were to the hall. Wondering what she was thinking and doing within those same walls that very moment.

Chapter
22

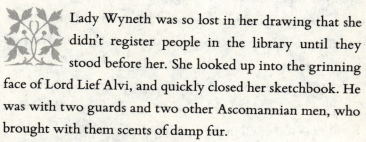Lady Wyneth was so lost in her drawing that she didn't register people in the library until they stood before her. She looked up into the grinning face of Lord Lief Alvi, and quickly closed her sketchbook. He was with two guards and two other Ascomannian men, who brought with them scents of damp fur.

"Hello, my lady," Lord Alvi said.

"Er, hello." Wyneth's head was murky with creativity, lines still moving about in her mind, begging to be drawn. She pulled her feet out from under herself, smoothing down her gray skirts. Sounds came back to her now, muffled rain against the tall windows.

"We're giving a tour of the castle, Lady Wyneth," a guard

said. "Sorry to disturb you."

She shook her head and forced a polite smile, feeling Lord Alvi's warm gaze on her all the while. "No problem at all."

"So, this is the royal library." The guard motioned his hand around at shelves stretching to the high ceilings, and cozy nooks with leather chairs and woven rugs. The other Ascomannians grunted, making a quick scan, looking bored.

"Where is the indoor archery range?" the hairiest man asked.

"Down this hall, past the stairs." The men set to leave, looking back at Lord Alvi.

"Go ahead without me. I wish to see the ancient texts."

The larger, hairier man from the coldlands lifted an eyebrow high and then shrugged before leaving. Wyneth's insides bounced and spun as Lord Alvi's presence surrounded her. She moved her eyes slowly up to him as he turned toward her sketchbook.

"What were you working on?"

Lady Wyneth placed her palms on the cover. "Honestly, nothing of interest. I make drawings for my siblings and cousins, to entertain them."

He grinned and sat in the chair beside her, pulling it closer. Great seas, he was large. And he didn't smell musty like the other men. He smelled almost . . . salty.

"I would love to see."

Wyneth felt her face warming. "No, really, Lord Alvi—"

"Please. Call me Lief. And let me see your sketches."

Oh, fine. What did it matter what he thought? She handed the book over, her heart beating too fast. He opened it, giving his full attention to the drawings.

"'Crocket's Race,'" he murmured. "And Crocket is a crocodile?"

"Mm-hm. You see, Prince Donubhan is a bit . . . competitive," Wyneth explained. "He likes to cheat, and pouts if he doesn't win. So Princess Aerity and I came up with a story about a crocodile that cheated so much in his river races that the other crocs no longer wanted to play with him."

Lord Alvi flipped through all the pages and chuckled at the end. "Remarkable."

Wyneth went hot, resisting the urge to fan herself as she watched his strong hands skimming across her drawings. Then he plucked her pencil from the binding pouch, and did something that shocked her—he began to sketch, the pencil scratching with ease in his oversized hand.

Wyneth giggled as the form of a bird began to take shape on Crocket's shoulder.

Lord Alvi spoke low. "Each time the little croc tries to cheat, the bird gives him a peck. Like his conscience."

"That's quite good." Wyneth had never seen a man draw so well.

"Let's keep this our secret, aye?" He set down the pencil and gave her a bashful grin, softening her all over.

"My lady." He reached for her hand, but she swiftly pulled it to her lap. She could not allow a repeat of their last encounter, even though she thought of it often enough. Too often.

"My lord," she said. "We cannot."

Their eyes met, filling her with pain and longing that she couldn't comprehend.

"Lord Alvi," called a deep voice from the doorway, echoing. Wyneth jumped and Lord Alvi wrenched his head around. "Care to visit the indoor range with us?"

The Ascomannian lord gave him a nod. "Aye."

Before he could say another word, Wyneth reached over and took the sketchbook from his hand, standing.

"Good evening to you all." She nodded at the men, avoiding Lord Alvi's eyes, rushing from the library.

Emotions welled inside her. She wanted to get to her chambers before she exploded. As she turned the corner she ran smack into somebody.

"Lady Wyneth!" Harrison gave her a friendly grin. "How nice to see you."

Her throat constricted and her eyes burned.

Harrison's eyes narrowed. "What's wrong?"

Seas, he reminded her so much of Breckon: polished, handsome, polite. Even their bodies were of similar stature, the lean muscles and tapered waists.

"I don't feel well." Laughter from the Ascomannians sounded from down the hall as the men headed toward the archery room. Harrison narrowed his eyes at the sound.

"Did Lief do something to you?" Harrison took her by

the shoulders. "Did he touch you?" When she didn't answer fast enough, he said, "Tell me!"

"No, Harrison," she said in a rush.

He stared deep into her eyes until he seemed assured she was telling the truth. Then he took a deep breath and removed his hands. "I'm sorry. I don't like the way he pursues you. It's disrespectful to you and Aerity. To Breckon. Keep your distance from him, Wyn. I saw—"

"What?" Her eyes snapped up.

"I shouldn't have spied, but I had a feeling his motives were not honorable when he asked you to walk with him. I saw him kiss you in the trees. You were right to run from him."

Wyneth swallowed, her stomach churning with shame. "I have to go."

She rushed past him, covering her mouth, trying to keep it all inside long enough to burst through her chamber doors and shut them tight behind her.

Wyneth paced a minute, and then sat in a cushioned chair, breathing hard. She opened her sketchbook and ran a slender fingertip across the animated bird on the crocodile's shoulder. A dry sob choked her as she slammed the book shut and closed her eyes. Tears burned inside her eyelids, and an irrational bout of resentment bubbled up from deep inside her.

"Why, Breckon?" she whispered. "Why did you have to be so bloody brave?"

The sketchbook slid to the floor with a clatter as Wyneth

bent, her elbows on her knees and her face in her hands. Her shame was like a living, growing thing inside her.

If only Breckon had dived into the water with her. They might've escaped together. What had he been trying to prove by fighting that monster? Why did he have to go and get himself killed? If he were here, none of this would be happening with Lord Alvi, she knew that for a fact. If Breckon were here, her heart would have never wandered to one of Aerity's suitors.

"Breckon, you stupid, stupid man. Why?" Wyneth railed in absolute anger, an emotion she hadn't allowed herself to release until that moment. She let herself be overcome with rage at the unfairness of it all. She screamed, and when her maid opened the door, peeking in with worry, Wyneth threw a pillow at the door and shouted, "Leave me alone!" She then began to throw everything in sight, breaking a canvas against the wall. Looking down at the drab, gray gown, she grasped the neckline and yanked until it tore at the seams. She screamed at the top of her lungs, kicking her bedpost until her feet throbbed, punching her mattress until her hands stung.

"How much longer, Breck?" Wyneth sobbed, her face against the bed. "How much longer will it hurt like this?" She clenched the sheets.

Wyneth wept until her strength was gone, and then she feebly crawled into the abused bed and slept like the dead.

23

Aerity couldn't sleep. The wind seemed to grab hold of her windows and shake them with fury. Lightning flashed eerily through her chamber, followed closely by the rumbling boom of thunder. She didn't mind storms, actually found them soothing. It wasn't the gale that kept her awake with anxious excitement but the knowledge that the hunters were inside the castle at that very moment.

She slipped from bed and wrapped a dressing robe over her nightgown, sliding her feet into soft shoes. A peek out her door found quiet, empty halls, flames flickering from massive wall sconces. The princess walked the halls in silence, her arms crossed over her chest. It was a testament to her father's trust of the hunters that the halls weren't crawling with guards. She did see one when she rounded the corner to High Hall—a lad not much older than she was. He was leaning against a tapestry and straightened when he saw her.

"Princess," he said with a nod. "Everything all right?"

She nodded in return. "I can't sleep."

"Aye, the storm," he said. His eyes flicked up and down the wide hallway to be sure Aerity was safe before he seemed to relax.

"I think I'll visit the library." She walked on before he could respond. One of the doors to High Hall was ajar. As she neared the darkened room, she glanced back at the guard, who watched dutifully. Aerity walked slowly, and just as she came close to the doorway a flash of lightning lit up the vast room within. Men were laid out on cots and floor bundles, snores resounding upward in mock harmony. But one man was sitting against the wall, his arms draped over bent knees, face shrouded in waves of brown hair. Their eyes met just as the lightning flashed, and their gazes remained connected afterward in the dim streak of sconce flame. Aerity sucked in a breath as the thunder hit, shaking the castle. She could still feel Paxton's eyes as she continued forward, out of his sight. By the tides, how could a simple look make her tremble so?

She glanced back at the guard, who was still watching, forcing her not to linger.

Beyond the entrance to the Great Hall were steps down to the lower wing—the library to the right and a training facility with Aerity's silks and an indoor archery range to the left. She was still shaking a bit as she stepped lightly down and rounded the corner to the library. Then she heard the murmur of male voices behind her at High Hall and retreated back to the corner to listen.

"Aye, it's a nasty one." The young guard's voice reverberated down the stone hallway. "The archery range is down the steps to the left if you're looking to pass time until the storm ends."

"Very well, but my bow is in my tent." It was Paxton's voice.

Aerity's heart skipped with glee—had he followed her? The men were discussing the availability of practice bows when she peeked around the corner. Neither were looking her way. In a moment of spontaneity, Aerity slipped behind the tapestry against the open wall and rushed past, running quietly the rest of the way to the training room.

Please follow me, she thought, and then nearly laughed. He wasn't the type to follow a lass like a lovesick pup. He was a mystery, that one. A mystery she planned to solve. But time alone with him was hard to obtain.

Her nerves were alight, causing beads of sweat to break out across her skin when she heard his footsteps moving down the hall.

He's coming! she thought excitedly. Then her limbs prickled again with nervous anticipation and she realized how foolish she appeared just standing there. She hurried to her silks and grabbed hold with slick palms, twisting her ankle sloppily and hoisting herself up with a bit too much force. She swung wild and high, jerking her head toward the doorway at the sound of a throat clearing. Her face flamed.

Paxton's hair was disheveled. His dark eyes took in the sight of her swaying on the silks and he turned to glance down the hall behind him before staring at her again.

"I was told that you would be at the library and was ordered to keep my distance."

"I, um . . ." Aerity unwound one foot and reached her toe down to the floor to stop her movement. She felt utterly stupid, realizing how she must look in her night robes, swinging away like a child, her hair loose and probably a tangled mess. "I changed my mind." He didn't move from the doorway. The two of them locked eyes and forged a sort of silent battle.

"Like I said," he told her in a low voice, "I was told to keep my distance."

"Do you always follow rules so well?" It came out like a challenge. She held the silks tightly to steady herself, one foot still wound in the fabric and the other on the floor.

"Actually, no." Without looking away from her, Paxton's foot kicked the wooden doorstop, and he walked forward, letting the door creak closed behind him. "I saw the tapestry move . . ."

He knew she'd be here. He *had* followed her! Aerity had never felt more nervous in her life as he made his slow approach. She wasn't accustomed to feeling this way, her body out of sorts, her thoughts scattered. She was glad to have the silks to cling to.

Paxton took his time. Aerity thought she should say something, perhaps a witty quip, but she was afraid she'd sound breathless. She didn't want him to know how he affected her. He walked a circle around her, moving nearer, his eyes scrutinizing every element in that curious way of his. Aerity kept very still. No lad other than Harrison had dared to get this close. He stopped in front of her and looked skyward. His eyes trailed the silks to the ceiling, and he reached up, his fingers and palm wrapping around the smooth fabric, feeling his way down. When he got to her hand he let go, never touching her.

"I wonder," he said quietly. His eyes roamed over her hair and face, her robe cinched at the waist. If he thought she looked silly he didn't show it.

"You wonder what?" She was horrified to hear that she indeed sounded as breathless as she was. Curses.

Paxton's hand drifted over the hair at her shoulder, his fingers gathering a mass of light red strands and winding them gently about his palm until her long tresses were a loose knot around his strong hand. She could feel the slight tug at her scalp as his fist slightly tightened. Her chest fluttered at the sight of his thumb running back and forth over the taut hair there. She suddenly wished she could feel that caress.

"I wonder what sort of queen you'll be."

The seriousness in his eyes and meaning of his words

ratcheted up Aerity's spine, bringing her back to her senses in a heady rush. She let go of the silks and stood before him on her own two feet. Taking her cue that the mood had shifted, he let her hair slide from his hand.

Why would he ask such a thing? Exactly what aspect of her personality made him question the type of ruler she'd be? Did he think her immature and incapable? Could she blame him after she'd acted so transparently foolish just now? Aerity lifted her chin.

"I hope to be fair and just."

His face bent a fraction closer, as if hungry for anything she might say.

"To whom?" he asked.

To whom? What sort of question is that?

"To *all*, of course." She realized her hands had gone to her hips and she forced them back down to her sides. A rumble of distant thunder sounded.

Paxton's impassioned eyes narrowed and bore into her. There was something desperately needy in his gaze, and Aerity found herself wanting to fulfill that mysterious need. He opened his mouth to speak just as sounds of footsteps echoed down the hall. Aerity's eyes widened.

"Grab a bow!" she whispered urgently. "Look as if you're practicing!"

Paxton moved swiftly across the room, snatching a practice bow from the wall and facing a target. Aerity grasped the silks and wound her feet quickly, climbing a few feet in the air. The door creaked open, and she looked to see one of the higher-ranking night guards standing there. His eyes rounded as he stepped into the room.

"Princess Aerity! Are you . . . ?" His eyes moved to Paxton and his whole demeanor hardened. "How dare you close yourself in a room with the princess, hunter?"

Paxton hung the bow back on the wall before turning. "I assure you, sir, Her Highness has not been compromised in any way."

"This is highly inappropriate!" The guard appeared enraged on her behalf. Aerity quickly climbed down and moved forward.

"Mister Seabolt has done nothing wrong. I invited him in to practice—"

"Princess, with all due respect"—the guard lowered his voice—"the door was *closed*."

"Was it?" she said, feigning ignorance, waving a hand as if it were nothing. "The jamb must have come loose. I didn't even notice."

The guard glanced at Paxton, scowling. The hunter's face remained void of guilt or regret.

"Look." Aerity folded her hands in front of herself, and her voice took on a diplomatic tone. "The hunter couldn't sleep. Neither could I. I should have gone to the library and let him have this room, but I suppose I'm tired and not thinking straight. I know how this appears, but I assure you it was quite innocent. And now I'll be returning to my chambers."

She gave a yawn for good measure, covering her mouth.

The guard's face softened a fraction. "That's probably best, Your Highness. I shall accompany you."

She nearly told him not to bother, but a true wave of fatigue hit her and she nodded.

The guard cast a pointed look at Paxton that seemed to say, *Get back where you belong.* Paxton, face still blank, slid his gaze to Aerity one last time. She could have sworn she saw gratitude in his eyes mingling with amusement on his lips before he moved to walk ahead of them from the room.

Aerity silently followed, watching Paxton's strong back and the strides of his long legs as he entered High Hall for the remainder of the night. When she climbed back into bed and stilled, her scalp felt sensitive with the memory of his gentle tug. What would he have said and done next if they hadn't been interrupted? Aerity felt a bout of frustration rise; she was no closer to solving the mystery of Paxton Seabolt. In fact, his questioning words echoed through her mind long after the thunder ceased to roll.

Caitrin's mouth was set in a straight line of worry the next morning as she carried Aerity's freshly ironed dresses into the princess's chambers. Aerity sat up in bed, groggy from tossing and turning after her late-night encounter with Paxton.

"What's wrong?" she asked her maid. Then her stomach clenched. "Did the beast attack?"

"No, Your Highness." Caitrin shook her head. "It's the

poor Zandalee women. When a maid went to their chambers this morning, she found them all ill with fevers."

Aerity leaped from the bed, grabbed her beaded shawl, and threw it around her shoulders. "I've got to tell Mrs. Rathbrook!"

"She's already been called," Caitrin assured her.

"Good." She relaxed a fraction. "I want to check on them."

"Come, let me help you dress first, my lady," Caitrin called, but Aerity left her, hurrying to the guest quarters barefoot.

She halted at the corner when she saw her mother standing there, conversing with a guard at the door. They both looked at her, from her nightgown down to her feet, and her mother's mouth pinched with displeasure. Aerity took a deep breath and moved forward.

"Is anyone else sick?" Aerity asked, coming to a stop before them.

"No, thank the seas," the queen said. "The Lochlan hunters took the Zandalee through a town yesterday where they came in contact with commoners. We believe that is how they contracted the fever."

Aerity ducked her head into the darkened room. Mrs. Rathbrook was working over Zandora, who lay still on the four-poster bed. She wiped her forehead gingerly, and applied ointment to her lips. The other two huntresses were curled up on cots, shivering. Aerity moved forward.

"You can't go in there, Princess," warned the guard.

Aerity felt a prickle of frustration. She closed her eyes and leaned her forehead against the doorframe. Pain pulsed in her chest. An awful, heavy feeling had taken up residence there over the past several weeks from stress. She looked into the room again and Mrs. Rathbrook saw her. The woman bustled over.

"Don't worry yourself, Princess. They're not so far gone that they can't be healed. Illnesses such as this are different from injuries, though. It takes more time to filter magic through the blood. They won't be happy with me, but I've given them sleeping draughts. If they try to rise without enough rest, the disease can return even stronger. I suggest they do not hunt tonight."

Aerity nodded, and the woman went back into the darkened room.

The queen gently pulled Aerity's hair over her shoulder. "She's right, dear girl. You shouldn't worry yourself. Now go back to your room and make yourself presentable."

Aerity did as she was told. Her feet were cold and numb by the time she reached her bedchamber again. Caitrin led her to the plush stool, setting to work on her hair. The princess stared out the window. The rain had finally stopped. Now a dense fog hung over the land and sea.

"I've been thinking, Princess, about the Zandalee. Are you truly all right with marrying the leader's brother if she slays the beast? A man you've never seen?"

"Nay, Caitrin," Aerity said with sadness. "But if one of the Zandalee takes the beast, I have to."

"You'll go all the way to the desert?"

Aerity shook her head. "That is part of our deal. The brother will move here, but a portion of royal riches will be sent to his homeland." Her stomach cramped at the idea of marriage.

"I'm sorry, miss." Caitrin placed her hands on Aerity's shoulders. "You've got enough on your mind without my prying questions. Come on. Let's find you a pretty gown for the day."

Aerity let her maid choose the dress, too tired to care.

Chapter 24

Paxton exited the castle with the other men into the foggy morning. When they turned toward the commons, he took the path straight toward the trade port, needing time to himself. He ended up down by the water on one of the older, empty docks at the end of the port that appeared abandoned. He could barely see five feet in front of himself through the mist.

He sat on the end of the weathered wood. The water was three feet below him, splashing lightly against the pillars of the dock.

To his right, through trees beyond, he knew there to be a private royal beach and docks along Lanach Creek where Captain Gillfin was killed. On his other side were cargo ships and fishing boats. Past that would be the naval port with its vast vessels. He could hear men's voices in the distance, busy with their trades, carrying carts of bait and catch to and fro. He watched as time passed, and the sun made its way overhead, burning off a small bit of cloud cover. All he wanted was to lie back and sleep where he was.

He felt the soft thumps of footsteps on the dock behind him and turned. The princess stopped midstep when she caught his gaze and looked at him questioningly, as if for an invitation. Paxton's pulse set into a jog as he gave her a nod. In the mist behind her, a guard stood at the edge of the dock, allowing the princess to walk to Paxton, but not taking his eyes off them.

Remembering his last interaction with Princess Aerity caused a fire to light within him. He'd been out of line with what he'd asked her, but couldn't bring himself to regret it. Something about the princess made him bold. He was curious about her motives, and about how she'd react to him, in all ways. He couldn't seem to help himself.

Paxton turned toward her without standing. "I'm surprised your guard didn't follow you down the dock." The royal guard's outline was visible through the fog, but he was too far away to hear their conversation.

Aerity gave a small sigh. "Aye. I am, as well."

A quiet lull passed as Aerity fidgeted.

"I came to see if you're feeling ill like the Zandalee after going through that town," she said, interrupting his thoughts.

"The Zandalee are ill?" Paxton asked.

A breeze picked up, whipping her hair across her face, but she peeled it away, pushing it over her shoulder.

"All three of them." She let out a sigh. "Mrs. Rathbrook is healing them, but they won't be able to hunt tonight."

"Bucking seas," Paxton muttered. They were down to only the Ascomannian and Lochlan hunters for tonight, with only a handful of Zorfinans left.

Aerity sat down right next to him at the edge of the dock, as if she were a regular girl in a cotton frock, and not the princess of the kingdom, in satin and scented oils of berries and coconut, likely imported from Kalor or one of Lochlanach's distant islands.

In truth, he was surprised to see her. He thought perhaps he'd finally scared her away. Apparently not.

She wound her hair over her shoulder and twisted it to keep it from blowing. The fog was slowly drifting out to sea. As his hair slung down over his eyes, she reached out and pushed it away for him. He felt his whole body go stiff at the feel of her soft fingertips.

"You could wear it back like Tiern. To keep it out of your face."

"Would you like that?" Paxton asked. "For me to look more like Tiern?"

Her cheeks reddened, but she didn't look away. "Nay, I meant . . . it might be easier for you."

Again, Paxton looked at the water. He shrugged. "I can't

be arsed to tie one of those bothersome leather strips."

Aerity giggled, and he found himself grinning. Just a bit. "You think that's funny?" he asked.

"I think it's funny that there's something you're not good at. It obviously irks you, though it's a small thing."

"Tying a hair strip is hardly a valuable skill."

"Here. I keep one in case it gets windy." Aerity reached into a hidden pocket in her skirt and pulled out a thin, soft-looking leather. "Let me." She moved behind him, on her knees, and Paxton held his breath.

His mother and grandmother used to tie his hair back as a lad, but it had been years since anyone had cared for him in that basic way. Now, feeling her small, warm hands fingering through his hair and smoothing it back, brushing against his skin, a chill of gratification and desire rippled through him. His hair felt tight as she knotted the strip at his nape. He let himself enjoy it.

"There," she said. Her breath skated over his neck. She was close. Closer than she ought to be, just as he'd been last night, and it sent a thrill into his bloodstream. He could smell her on the breeze as she moved nearer to his ear and whispered, "What if I said I do want you to kill the beast, Paxton Seabolt? What if I want it to be you?"

Each word punctured into his skin, tiny needles that would mark him forever.

Did she know what she was saying? Did she know how it sent a deep thrill of satisfaction to his core? He slowly turned.

The princess sat back on her heels with her hands in her lap. Her eyes were filled with rebellion. Nervousness. Maybe even a touch of desperation. This future queen, at his mercy.

He knew enough about her now to know she had a good heart, despite the evils of her ancestry. But if she knew . . . if she really knew everything there was to know about Paxton, he believed she'd surely shun him. He was of Lashed blood. No woman, especially of high breeding, would want that possibility for her children. It didn't matter that she hugged Mrs. Rathbrook and seemed to genuinely care for others. When it came down to it, she would not want Paxton if she knew the truth.

And if he killed the beast and she found out after their marriage, she'd forever resent him. That had been a price he'd been willing to pay to keep his family secure, but now he wasn't as certain.

His need to protect himself outweighed his attraction and any other useless feelings he'd allowed himself to entertain. Next to her, he was nothing but a brute with dirty blood. He felt a cruel urge to remind the princess just what kind of man he was. The thought of marrying her, of feeling unworthy of her on a daily basis, sickened him.

In that moment, decision settled over him.

When it came down to the hunt, he'd do his part to track and capture the beast, but he'd let another man strike the killing blow. Then the land could be free, and he could wash his hands of this royal lass. His family would be fine—he'd continue to provide for them. These strange feelings for the princess were a complication he hadn't expected. It was time to remedy that for the both of them.

Still facing her, Paxton said, "Are you familiar with the ways of a villager marriage in Cape Creek, Princess?"

Her dainty eyebrows drew together. "What do you mean?"

Paxton's mind reeled with mischievous ideas of ways to frighten her. "What I mean, is that I am a traditionalist, and I plan to follow the ways of marriage as it's been done for centuries by the people of my village."

"Oh . . . ?" She was beginning to seem slightly confused and curious.

"In our village the man is the ruler and the woman is expected to obey, without question, in all things." Paxton fought back a smile, forcing himself to be as serious as possible, even as he imagined the strong-willed women in his village who would knock their husbands in the noggin for spouting such a thing.

Aerity swallowed, gullibility shining in her eyes, and Paxton went in for the kill.

"Any wife who's not completely obedient is subject to punishment from her husband."

"Punishment?" She sat taller. Ah, there was the indignation he'd been waiting for. Paxton found himself wanting to see how far he could take it. How deeply he could make her blush. What began as a way to scare her away was now feeling like a bit of fun.

"That's right. Punishment. We're a bit old-fashioned. We find that a good smack on the arse works wonders on disobedient women."

Aerity's chest heaved sharply with a silent gasp and her eyes went so wide that Paxton almost gave himself away with a laugh.

"Hitting is not a proper form of discipline."

"For children," Paxton deadpanned. Whipping children was practically unheard of in the kingdom, with wee ones being of such value. Parents had to find other creative ways to discipline the babes so they wouldn't become tyrants. "And don't think of it as hitting"—he made a fist and lightly punched the inside of his other hand—"so much as a series of good smacks." He opened that same fist and gave his other palm several sharp *thwacks*, then grinned, feeling devilish.

"I—" Her pretty mouth gaped and she practically stuttered to find words. "Have you ever considered conversing rather than resorting to . . . to . . ."

"Spanking?" He shrugged, pushed up his sleeves, and crossed his arms. "You seem like a very good lass, though, Princess. I'm sure you have nothing to worry about. And from what I hear, some of the wives quite enjoy—"

The princess let out a growl like an adorably angry cub, jumping swiftly to her feet. Paxton couldn't hold it in any longer.

He began to laugh, something he hadn't done in ages.

Aerity's eyes bulged. "What is so funny?"

Deep seas, she was angry. Her tiny hands were in fists and her cheeks were apple red. It made him laugh even harder. He could only shake his head as he clutched his side.

"You— Did you make that up?" She put her hands on her hips. "Are you teasing me?"

It was too much. He could scarcely breathe. The princess let out an exasperated grunt.

"You are a complete *cad*, and you should be ashamed of yourself!" A mottled shade of pink had worked its way down her neck, onto the smooth skin over her collarbones, and down the few inches of her chest before the material of her dress ruined the view. He wondered just how far that blush reached.

He fell back on the dock and sent his chuckles up to the sky as Princess Aerity stomped away in her soft leather boots.

Good, he thought. Go live your perfect life. He hadn't planned on turning it into a joke, yet it still had the desired result.

As he lay there, the laughter eventually replaced by fatigue, he found himself wondering which man would have that final blow at the beast. Which man would get to feel Aerity's hands through his hair. He wondered which of the men, if any, could make her blush as he had.

His stomach soured, and he suddenly felt no satisfaction.

Chapter

25

 Aerity, flushed and angry, poked her head into every room as she passed, searching for her cousin.

"There you are, Princess!" Caitrin said when she caught sight of Aerity bustling down the hall. "I've a message for you."

The maid rushed to keep up when the princess didn't stop.

"Have you seen Lady Wyneth?" Aerity asked.

"Er, no, Your Highness. But I'm to tell you the royal family is to sup together this afternoon in the formal dining room."

At this, Aerity halted, causing the bright tapestry beside her to stir. "Is everything all right?"

"As far as I know. Other than the Zandalee being ill."

"Yes, of course." Both girls stood in solemn silence for a moment.

Caitrin touched the princess's arm. "Are you well, my lady?"

"Oh . . . aye." Aerity forced a quick smile.

"May I brush out your hair before the early supper?" Caitrin eyed the tangles caused by wind. Aerity absently nodded and followed her maid to her chambers. To her surprise, Lady Wyneth was sitting on Aerity's window seat with a book open on the gray skirts of her lap, looking out over the west commons.

"Cousin!" Aerity rushed over and slid onto the window seat with her, grasping her hands. "I've been searching for you. You'll never believe what has just happened."

Wyneth's eyes narrowed with interest. "Why are your cheeks so red?"

"Well, partly because I've run from the docks all through the castle searching for you. And partly because of that rogue Paxton Seabolt!"

"Ooh . . ." Wyneth straightened. The light from the window brought out her soft freckles. "What did that scoundrel do?"

Aerity huffed, relishing her cousin's full attention. Behind her, Caitrin set to work brushing out her hair, starting at the bottom and working her way up.

"It's more of what he said." Aerity rehashed the

conversation, eliciting all sorts of gasping and tutting and mouth covering from her cousin. She left out the bit about telling Paxton she wanted him to kill the beast, because that was simply humiliating in hindsight. At the end, both Wyneth and Caitrin broke into fits of giggles.

Aerity gaped at them. "Must everyone laugh at my expense today?"

"I'm sorry," Wyneth told her, pulling her in for a quick hug. Aerity caught sight of her cousin's red knuckles.

"What happened to your hands?"

Wyneth's eyebrows scrunched as she pulled her hands back. "Nothing. Just chapped."

"You're too trusting, Princess," said Caitrin, shifting Aerity's attention off her cousin. "And Paxton Seabolt is likely not accustomed to sweet lasses such as yourself. His reputation precedes him."

The princess nearly gave herself whiplash turning to her maid. "You've heard of him? What is his reputation?"

Caitrin's eyes sparkled with gossip. "Well, it's said that he's known in Cape Creek for being the most eligible bachelor, but to everyone's dismay he's sworn off marriage."

Had he? Curiosity and reservation swirled inside Aerity.

"Whatever for?" asked Wyneth.

Caitrin shrugged. "Nobody knows. He's simply not the marrying type. The women he's been known to fraternize with are . . . well . . ." She looked back and forth between the royal girls' waiting faces. "Not exactly innocents. An unsavory crowd of friends, you might say. And yet, he and his family are well respected."

She had figured this about Paxton, but hearing it for certain gave her a swoop of sickening dizziness.

Aerity felt herself frowning. She wondered how Paxton viewed her in comparison with the women he was accustomed to. Did he think of her as some naive child? Embarrassment consumed her all over again, followed closely by jealousy at the thought of those other women. Would he tell everyone in Cape Creek how he'd tricked her? She'd be the laughingstock of Lochlanach.

"There, there," Caitrin said, turning Aerity by the shoulders to continue brushing. "Jesting is the way of commoners. And men don't tease women they don't like. I assure you. He was flirting in his own way."

Aerity didn't know if she believed that. It felt more like he was making a fool of her for his own mysterious reasons.

"But why would he be here if he doesn't want to marry?" she asked.

Caitrin blinked at her as if it were obvious. "Marrying a princess is something different altogether." The maid gave the princess's hand a brief, consoling pat, and left her to put away the brush.

"Hm." Aerity looked out of the window, suddenly sad.

Together the cousins stared down at the men in the commons, tending to their weapons and bending over maps. When Paxton entered through the gates, Aerity held her breath. He still wore the leather strap in his hair, but some shorter strands had escaped and now framed his face. She felt Wyneth look up at her, but she kept her eyes on the man below—a stranger by all accounts. How could he cause so many emotions to tumble through her?

"I know Paxton is your first choice," Wyneth said. "But what of the others? Have any of the other men caught your fancy?" The question felt somehow . . . loaded.

Aerity watched Paxton walk toward the tents, out of sight, and she relaxed. "No."

"None of them at all?" Wyneth prodded.

"No," she said again. "None like Paxton." She felt a fool. She really should not let herself grow attached to the idea of one of these men. If another killed the beast, it would make her future marriage all the harder.

Wyneth chewed her lip. Aerity would have brought up the fact that she suspected one of the hunters fancied Wyneth, but mentioning Lord Lief Alvi could become awkward. Aerity didn't think Wyneth was ready to consider other men, anyhow. The princess shifted uncomfortably at the idea of marrying a man who liked her cousin better, regardless of whether Wyneth returned the man's sentiments or not. She couldn't fathom having that sort of strain in her life.

"I find the younger Seabolt to be quite pleasing to the eye," Caitrin said. "The two of you would have the sweetest wee ones ever born."

Aerity smiled a little, but it was fleeting. "Tiern is kind and handsome."

"And, of course, Harrison," Wyneth said with a wicked smile.

Aerity gently swatted her knee and sighed. "Yes, he's a fine man. Perhaps he will kill the beast and your wish will come true for us to be together."

Wyneth's smiling face turned serious. "My wish now is only for your happiness, Aer. For a good match."

Aerity stared down at her hands. She'd prefer to feel passionate about Tiern or Harrison, someone good for her, but apparently life did not work that way. At least not for her. And what did it matter who she fancied? She would not get to choose.

The great beast had stolen that privilege from her.

Chapter

26

A late autumn sun beamed down on the hunters as they peered at the map. All traces of fog and rain had burned away, leaving behind mud and dampness everywhere. Paxton wiped a drip of sweat from his brow and bit his tongue for the umpteenth time as Volgan mentioned separating from Paxton and his men.

"We're down to only six Lochlans," Lieutenant Harrison began.

"Not our fault your men bowed out like cowards!" Volgan bellowed. "Your lot can join forces with the few remaining Zorfinans."

Their arguing voices were interrupted by the sounds of shuffling feet and murmuring voices drifting from the gates.

Lief Alvi and Paxton met eyes and the lord quieted his men with a raised hand. Together they looked toward the gates.

A group of men stood there, Lochlan fishermen, based on their cotton tunics and hair of browns and reds, some with leather aprons to protect them while scaling and gutting. In their hands they held gaffing hooks, rough boards, and large sticks. Two guards shook their heads, as if forbidding entrance to the men. Paxton moved forward with Tiern close on his heels.

"What's going on?" he asked a guard through the iron bars and vines.

"These men wish to have a word with you lot, but they're armed."

"To protect ourselves against the beast!" one of the fishermen yelled. "Not to use against the hunters."

"We're here to help!" another shouted.

Paxton felt his eyebrows go up. "You wish to help?"

A man with great girth and a filthy apron pushed his way to the front and grabbed the bars with both hands, pressing his face to the opening. "We've heard the beast can take to the water. We can help you trap the thing. We'll line the waterways with our boats. Maybe it'll deter it. Maybe it won't, but we're tired of hiding. We got the message and we've come. Our older boys and some of our wives will take to high trees with horns."

"The curfew has only been lifted for men," began one of the guards. "It's still instated for youth, women, and children—" began another guard, but a villager cut him off.

"The beast killed my wife's brother! It's attacking us in our own homes and we won't stand it any longer!"

The men let out a roar of cries, raising their makeshift weapons.

"This could be brilliant," Tiern whispered behind him.

Paxton nodded. Lord Alvi stepped up beside him and spoke to the guards. "Let them in, and send one of your men to oversee the conversation. Take news to the king that some townspeople and their youth will not be adhering to the curfew." Paxton nearly laughed at the looks of shock the guards gave one another. He wondered if they would dare to argue with the Ascomannian lord. In the end, Lief did not give them the chance. He simply cocked his blond head toward the maps and barreled on. "Come, we have much to discuss before tonight's hunt."

<hr/>

They set off at dusk, Paxton and his three fellow Lochlans, seven Zorfinans, and twenty-odd Ascomannians. The wealthy Lochlan hunters had pulled out of the hunt after their friend was carried off in the beast's mouth, and the parents of the two younger lads came to cart them back home to relative safety, much against their wishes.

Tonight, the men spread their ranks along the Eurona River, where townspeople and watermen would line their boats offshore. The river would take them farther into Lochlanach than they'd hunted before. It wasn't an area where the beast had attacked in the past, but it gave them the best hunting advantages—brush and trees were less dense along the riverside, and their voices could carry farther to one another if a sighting was made.

In attempts to draw the beast out, the hunters felled two fat squirrels and dabbed their exposed skin and clothing with its fresh blood. Not a single hunter had washed that day, hoping their natural scents would lure their prey.

As they walked several miles in the waning sun, they spotted older lads, lasses, and women scattered about high in trees along the way, camouflaged and holding horns and bows. Tiern grinned and Paxton nodded.

The day had been unseasonably warm, but the moment the sun dropped, all heat seemed to siphon from the air, sending a prickle of chill across Paxton's bare forearms. He should have brought along his overcoat. Autumn in Lochlanach was temperamental. No matter. Paxton prided himself on having thick skin.

The brothers took the southernmost tip of the hunt. Hours passed, with Paxton hunched against a pine tree and Tiern's still form in the distance, sitting with his knees pulled to his chest. A three-quarter moon was barely visible through the mist of quickly moving clouds. The rushing tinkle of river water was the only background noise. Even the crickets were quiet.

They waited. Paxton knew the beast was unpredictable, but he wasn't looking forward to listening to the gripes of

Volgan and his men if the monster didn't come to them, or if it attacked elsewhere. If tonight didn't work, he'd have to concede to Volgan's idea to spread their numbers sparingly over the land.

He was still contemplating the sight of Volgan's gloating face when, at the sound of a horn some distance away, Paxton went rigid. The beast had been spotted.

Paxton eyed Tiern, and ever so slowly, the brothers nocked arrows to their bows and turned in crouching positions to stare into the darkened woods. The clouds had thickened as the evening wore on, obscuring details of the land. Paxton's eyes darted about for any sign of movement in the dark, while his body remained motionless.

Another horn sounded from the south, and another, getting closer.

"Should we go to it?" Tiern whispered.

"No. It's heading this way." He knew other hunters were nearby, just north of them, and he didn't want to move from their range of hearing.

Several quiet minutes passed, but Paxton remained silent with expectation. Then he saw something—at first he thought the creature crouching in a tree on all fours was a bear that had ventured down from the mountains. But then he heard a snuffle and snorted grunt.

Blood thrummed through Paxton's body to his fingertips where he held the bowstring taut as he aimed. But he couldn't yet shoot—the beast was still sniffing at the ground, head swiveling side to side. It appeared agitated, probably from the sound of the horns.

Paxton had to hit the neck or nothing. If he shot now, it would only alert the beast of their presence. He had to wait it out.

He saw Tiern move in his peripheral vision. His brother had picked up a small rock and shot him a questioning look. Ah . . . he wanted to throw it, to get the beast to raise its head. It could either work brilliantly or cause the beast to run. Paxton stared at the rooting beast a moment longer before giving Tiern a nod.

Tiern slipped behind his tree where the beast couldn't see him and threw the rock up into the treetops. Paxton never took his eye from the beast. It snorted loudly and looked up, revealing a patch of furry neck as the rock hit high and began tumbling down.

Gotcha.

Paxton let his arrow fly. The beast began to lower its head just as the arrow hit the side of its neck and stuck there. It let out a howl and rose on its back legs, smacking the protruding object from its neck.

"Yes!" Tiern hissed in excitement.

Paxton's next arrow was already soaring, but it merely skimmed the side of the beast's neck this time, serving to further enrage the creature. When it roared, voices sounded nearby. The other hunters had heard.

From out of nowhere, Samuel appeared, sliding onto

the ground before the beast and pointing his arrow straight upward—a perfect shot. Before he could release, the beast kicked out, lifting Samuel's body like a rag doll. The man slammed into a tree, collapsing, his neck hanging at a severe angle. Paxton cursed loudly.

"Samuel!" Tiern shouted, but the man did not move. The beast snorted and took several sideways steps, as if woozy. Harrison slipped out from behind a nearby tree and crouched at Samuel's side. He checked the man's pulse and shook his head.

The beast righted itself and scratched at the ground, gouging deep marks.

Their next arrows were ready, and the brothers shot together, but it was no use. The beast now protected its soft spot. Their fast-moving arrows merely pinged off its upper chest like gnats. It set its sights on Paxton, and giving its tusks a shake, flinging thick saliva, the beast charged.

Paxton wasn't fool enough to think he could take the beast on his own, and he knew Tiern wouldn't sit back and watch without attempting to fight alongside him. That left him with one option.

"Run!" Paxton shouted. The brothers and Harrison sprinted north through the brush, bows in hand, leaping bushes and fallen logs. The beast's paws pounded the ground, and it grunted with each running step.

"Incoming!" Tiern shouted.

Footsteps pounded the ground as hunters seemed to

appear out of nowhere, Ascomannians and Zorfinans getting their first wide-eyed glimpse of the beast. Once they were a sizable group, Paxton and Tiern turned, dropped to the dirt, and aimed their bows upward. All around them men were yelling and arrows were flying.

What in the . . . ? The beast was no longer charging them. It had taken an abrupt turn.

"It's going to the water!" Harrison called.

Paxton should have known—just like last time the beast was injured, it wanted to flee. He jumped to his feet and ran with the others toward the river. A jarring boom and splash sounded from the river, and the beast roared. Far-off voices of rivermen were crying out from boats, throwing rocks and lighting small black powder bombs to toss into the water. The far side of the river was lined with even more townspeople, thrusting fiery torches in the air and screaming curses at the beast that were muffled by the distance.

The beast ran up the riverside, northward, zigzagging back and forth between the water's edge and the forest, where hunters shot arrows and emerged from the trees with shouts. Any who came near were batted away by the massive, clawed paws, but it never stopped to fight.

It proved to be faster than the men, but Paxton and the other breathless hunters ran on with fervent desperation. Paxton felt a horrible now-or-never urgency in his gut. He'd been the one to injure the beast and he wanted to be sure the job was finished by someone this very night. Watching the beast put distance between them filled him with a sinking sensation.

We can't fail tonight. We can't.

Some of the men had to stop, bending and grabbing their knees to catch their breaths. Paxton could hear Tiern's panting breaths just behind him. To his right were Lord Alvi and Volgan. To his left were Harrison and two hooded Zorfinans.

The beast veered toward the woods again, and this time disappeared into the trees. The hunters followed. As a mile turned to two, the terrain became rockier and steeper.

"It's heading for the ridgelands," Tiern said, breathless. They peered at the jagged landscape through the dark. Paxton nodded and Lief gave a grunt.

They ran on until a shroud of complete darkness fell and they could no longer see or hear the beast, which had been moving upward, away from the water. It became difficult to discern tracks in the sliver of moonlight. When the group of men stopped to catch their breaths and drink from their pouches, Paxton realized how cold it'd become.

Tiern jutted his chin toward the sky. "Look." The word came out as a mist of steam in the cool air as he rubbed his hands up and down his arms. Hulking gray clouds rolled above them.

"It will pass," Paxton said. Annoyance gripped him. He didn't have time for weather issues. The beast was at their mercy. It was out there, injured, nearby, and it would need to stop and tend to itself soon. Paxton was itching to turn and leave the others, give chase on his own.

They looked around at the silhouettes of one another. Lief's voice rang out. "Daybreak is in a few hours. We can track it thoroughly in the light, but we'll be wasting precious time. And if rain comes, all will be lost."

Paxton did not want to stop. Volgan glanced his way and seemed to read his mind, lifting his chin haughtily. "I say we continue on, my lord."

"A storm comes. We have no supplies," one of the Zorfinans pointed out in a broken accent.

"Then run back home where you're safe and sound," Volgan spat.

Paxton stopped the glowering Zorfinan from moving forward.

"It is suicide to go in ridgelands in cold," the Zorfinan said to Paxton. The man was shivering already, accustomed to the dry heat of the Zorfina deserts, his clothing and head scarf too lightweight for these temperatures.

Volgan chuckled under his breath, and Paxton could no longer stomach it. He stepped close to the hairy man and spoke through clenched teeth.

"Shut your mouth or I'll shut it for you, once and for all."

Volgan's eyes widened at Paxton's threat, his hairy face sneering, but Lief stepped between them and gave his man a push backward. "Our fight is not with one another. I was going to suggest some of the men stay here anyway, in case the beast comes back down."

The seven Zorfinans gave tight nods of agreement. Paxton turned to Tiern, who was slightly shivering, too. He spoke to his brother under his breath.

"You should stay here."

"No," Tiern ground out, standing taller. He'd always been lean, which gave him no protection against the cold. Paxton quietly sighed.

Harrison stepped up and clasped both brothers on the shoulders. "I'm going."

None of the Ascomannians volunteered to remain. They seemed immune to the cold and would do anything to impress Lord Alvi. So be it.

Just a few hours until the sun would be up and warmth returned, Paxton told himself as they set off into the cold night.

Chapter

27

Rozaria clutched her cloak tightly against the bitter wind, cursing the Lochlanach climate. She missed the constant heat of Kalor, but her mission was too important to let personal comfort hinder her. She dug a pair of leather gloves from her deep pockets and slid her frozen hands inside—all the better to hide her nails. Gloves were frowned upon throughout Eurona for that very reason, but few would question it in this weather.

She knew the hunters had come this way. Hundreds of townspeople lined the Eurona River with bonfires, celebrating how they'd helped the hunters give chase. Fools. The beast could not be so easily killed.

Into the trees she went, with her silent company of one.

For an hour they trudged as cold rain fell and the grounds began to slope upward. Rozaria was not prepared to enter the mountains of Toresta. She was about to turn and go back when she heard murmured voices ahead in the darkness. She stilled, and her companion followed suit.

Slowly, the two women crept forward until they spotted seven men huddled together for warmth. She recognized the head wraps of the drylands, and she held back a chuckle. These men knew even less about how to handle themselves in the freezing rain than she did. At least she could start a fire with her hands if needed. What pathetic excuses for hunters.

"Stay hidden for now," Rozaria said to the girl at her side, "unless I need you."

The girl nodded from the depths of her dripping hood.

Rozaria made her way around a thick tree and pulled back her hood just enough to show her face to the men. They stood when they saw her, several grabbing their weapons. Rozaria smiled.

"Hunters?" she asked in Zorfinan. This made them glance around at one another. Finally, one stepped forward.

"*Jes*. It is not safe here, miss. The beast could return down the mountain."

"The beast went into the mountains? Why have you stayed down here?" She cocked her head, as if asking out of innocent inquisitiveness.

The men exchanged guilty glances. "We stay in case the beast comes back."

"Ah. Good. But what a shame that the other hunters have a better chance at tonight's glory. At least you are safe."

Now the men dropped their eyes completely. Hiding her glee at their shame, Rozaria forced a fearful look. "Is it as awful as they say? This creature?"

The leader's head snapped up. He wiped rain from his face. "It is more terrible than the tales."

"Where do you think it came from?" she asked.

The men began to murmur, "Curse of the Lashed," gesticulating with their ridiculous signs to ward off evils.

"I see." Rozaria's heart began to race, a slice of satisfaction spreading through her. "I will leave you to hunt your cursed foe. I was traveling through when I heard there were brave hunters in this area. I have brought oat cakes. I'm sorry I do not have more to offer." She pulled a sack of small cakes from her pocket. The man took them, nodding his appreciation. They reached in, snatching the bag from one another and shoving the pastries into their mouths.

Rozaria could not hold back the smile that fought to show. The cakes were made with a special Kalorian ingredient: deadly jungle seeds.

The first man to sputter and cough fell to his knees. Then a second. Now a third. The final man who'd taken a cake looked at Rozaria with dread in his eyes, having figured out the truth. He went for his dagger, rushing at her, but suddenly gasped and looked down at a small hand around his ankle. Rozaria's hooded companion had moved from her hidden spot behind a tree to grasp him. The man tipped like a stiff tree and landed, dead.

A few of the men still shuddered, convulsing, as the hooded girl stood and moved to Rozaria's side.

"I will write their final words. Grab one of their daggers and stab each of them through. Hurry, while their blood is still warm."

The girl obeyed. Rozaria took parchment and a piece of chalk from her cloak pocket, crouching over to block the rain. Her plan was working even better than she could have imagined. Soon, it would be time.

Chapter

28

 At the moment, Tiern couldn't help but wonder why he wasn't more like Paxton. They had the same parents, the same bloodline, the same job and pastimes. So why was Paxton broad with muscle and tough as steel, while he was thin, chattering his teeth against the cold like a child?

These were Tiern's musings as he followed Paxton, trying to think about anything but the cold, and not able to keep up with the findings of their trackings. He should have listened to Pax when he told him to stay. They'd only been hiking uphill a couple hours and it was obvious Tiern was a worthless tagalong. He did his best to keep up and stay out of the way, silently.

Every so often they detoured when someone spotted tracks or broken debris. Tiern kept to the side. A hearty gust of frozen wind broke through the trees, sending pine needles shooting down at the men. Tiern stumbled and felt his boot sink into something soft. He immediately recognized the squelch of scat underfoot. He shook off his boot and peered down in the dark. It was the largest pile of animal excrement he'd ever seen, and he had to cover his nose against the vile smell.

"Pax . . ."

His brother and Harrison turned. The three of them squatted over the spot and the Ascomannians stopped to watch.

Paxton's palm hovered over the pile. "Still warm on the inside." He then poked it with a stick and raised it to his nose. "Has the smell and texture of a carnivore. Too large to be a bear's."

Harrison clapped Tiern on the back, nearly toppling him. "Well done!"

Yes, well done stepping in shite, Tiern thought to himself.

Paxton stood and looked to the men from the coldlands. "We're on the right track."

Lief grinned. At that precise moment the sky gave an ominous rumble and another gust of wind ripped through the trees.

"Sky's about to blow," muttered Harrison.

Lief cursed. "Let's hope not. It'll cover the beast's tracks."

It got darker and colder. Tiny thunks began from afar,

moving closer through the woods, and something pelletlike hit Tiern on top of his head. One landed on his shoulder and he plucked it off—a ball of ice.

"High seas, it's hailing," Tiern said. They got hail very rarely, maybe once a year during the winter in his seaside town. To see it in the fall was strange. But then again, he was many miles from home and at a much higher elevation.

"We keep moving," Lief told his men.

Paxton leveled Tiern with a questioning look, not moving.

"I'm fine. Let's go." Indeed, Tiern felt renewed after discovering the beast's scat, and was almost numb to the elements now.

They marched on for ten minutes, faces lowered. The stinging pellets began to let up, becoming something worse. Something wetter. Freezing rain.

Within minutes it was pouring, a mix of ice and rain that soaked them through.

"Curse it all," Paxton muttered. He glanced at Tiern, brown hair stuck to his face. "Do you need to stop?"

"No!" Tiern shouted. He was sick of Paxton assuming he needed babying. Tiern hated that his brother could so easily sense his weakness. Tiern surged past, hitting Pax with his numb shoulder. The Ascomannians were already a fair distance ahead. Tiern picked up his pace, thankful for the burst of angry energy.

They moved briskly through the mud, keeping their heads down. At this point, no signs of the beast could be found on the ground. Every ten feet or so, Tiern raised his head to peer around at the foliage and trees for broken limbs or trampled bushes. The incline gradually steepened, becoming rockier. To their left, through a cluster of trees, Tiern could see the rise of cliffs.

A cry sounded from behind him. Tiern spun, his heart in his throat, expecting to see the beast. But it was Harrison, slumped over.

Paxton knelt beside him. "Is it your ankle?"

Harrison nodded, sucking air through his teeth. "Twisted it. Slipped on a cursed rock." Harrison tried to stand and winced as he put weight on the leg.

Paxton glanced up the hill where the Ascomannians were disappearing into the dark, freezing rain.

"Leave me," Harrison said. "I'll be fine. They won't wait."

"No." Paxton's face was tight with resignation. "It's useless to track in this weather." He got under one of Harrison's arms and Tiern automatically moved to support his other side. "We'll find some semblance of shelter until daylight." They'd been hiking half the night, but were still barely into the ridgelands.

Tiern pointed toward the rockier area. "Perhaps through there."

Paxton nodded, and off they went. Walking with an invalid in the freezing cold was neither quick nor simple. They maneuvered clumsily through the trees and over debris and rocks. A thin layer of ice had accumulated over everything, and Tiern found himself shivering once again. His teeth chattered against his will, and Harrison's joined his. After an agonizing hour they found a high rock that jutted out with an overhanging tree, providing a few feet of meager shelter.

"Let Tiern be in the middle," Harrison said. The brothers lowered him to the edge of the dry patch and Tiern practically fell beside him. The three of them huddled together, not moving for the first time in hours, and soon Tiern's body completely overtook his mind. Next to him, Harrison's head slumped in immediate sleep. Together they shivered, but Tiern's body quaked violently after having run and hiked for hours in the cold. He looked down at his hands and was somewhat amused to find that he couldn't bend his fingers. His toes wouldn't move inside his boots either. He laughed aloud, or maybe it was in his mind. Tiern vaguely noticed Paxton staring at him. Such a worrier, that one.

The world went in and out of focus.

". . . need a bloody fire," he heard Paxton muttering to himself, turning out his pockets and cursing once again. He wanted to laugh at the sight of Paxton on his knees, gathering a pile of soaking, icy twigs. Paxton glanced up at Tiern, who could feel his own head tilt to the side, leaning against Harrison's. He couldn't read Paxton's expression at first, but when it hit him, it fractured something inside him.

His brother was afraid. But . . . Paxton wasn't afraid of anything.

Tiern's body quaked, and his eyes fluttered. He stared at

Paxton, who watched him fight to stay awake. Tiern failed, his eyes shutting, but he struggled against the complete over-taking of sleep, too shaken by the look in his brother's eyes. He heard an ongoing hiss, then a crackle. Tiern's eyes cracked open and he slowly understood how dire his situation was.

He was hallucinating. He blinked, but the strange sight was still there, Paxton hunkered down, his fists tight around a handful of twigs, and smoke seeping from the ends. Each angle of his brother's face was stern with concentration. It looked as if Paxton were drying the sticks. And then, one by one, he lit them aflame.

With his hands.

Sudden warmth hit Tiern's skin, causing his body to jolt in reaction. So this is what it feels like to go mad. . . . His eyes rolled back as he passed out.

Chapter

29

"Please!" The woman's shaking hands were splayed across her swollen belly as she begged Paxton's grandmother. "I know you're Lashed! My own mother told me. I know you can feel for its heart and . . . and . . ." The woman began crying. "This is my sixth pregnancy. None have lasted this long. Please . . ."

His grandmother's face was fearsome. "If I help you, I will be killed when they do the census. I have grandsons to care for. I cannot risk it. Please . . . you must go."

The women hadn't noticed young Paxton sidling closer, watching their interaction and soaking in their shared desperation. The answer seemed simple in his mind. This woman needed help. Who could fault someone for helping?

Paxton had never seen a pregnant stomach before. He found

255

himself face-to-face with the intriguing bulge, and without thought, he gently placed both his hands on it. Immediately he felt a natural heat flow through his body, pounding inside his hands, emanating from him. The woman gave a giant gasp, which was followed by his grandmother's own intake of air.

"Pax!"

"Don't touch him!" The woman screamed, covering Paxton's small hands with her own. His grandmother covered her mouth, her eyes watering. Paxton closed his eyes, lost to the sensation. It was as if he were searching for something through a dark maze, using only this internal sense, seeking around inside this mass in front of him, and when he found it, like a star of waning energy, his hands heated again, infusing something into this woman, into the small body that lay curled in her womb. Her stomach jumped under his fingers, and his hands cooled. A rush of energy buzzed inside him. He lowered his arms and watched as the woman ran her hands across her rounded belly. The laugh she let out, and the beaming smile she gave him, was like a gift.

"Thank you." The woman bent and took Paxton's head, kissing him repeatedly on his brown mop of hair. "Thank you, boy, seas bless thee."

But before she could even stand again, Paxton's grandmother took the woman by the throat, pushing her against the table, putting her face close. The woman grabbed his grandmother's wrist, her eyes bulging.

"Grandmother!"

She ignored Paxton, staring hard at the woman. "If you speak a word of this to another living soul, even your husband, I shall take the

256

life of you and your babe just as easily as my grandson has given it. Do you understand?"

"Yes! I swear it! I will take this to the grave. Please. You've no idea how grateful I am. I would never endanger either of you." She began to cry in earnest. "I swear it."

Paxton's grandmother released the woman, who clutched her stomach and sobbed.

His grandmother spoke again, but with much more gentleness this time. "Pull yourself together and go live your life. Never come here again."

The woman wiped her eyes and nodded, touching her throat. Then she clutched the door handle and left them.

Paxton was so confused. He felt as if he'd done something good. He'd never felt more alive. . . . Nothing had ever been so right. So why were tears streaming down his grandmother's face?

"What have I done wrong, Grandmother? I didn't mean to upset you. I . . . I couldn't help myself."

"I know, dear. I know all too well. That urge to mend what's broken." She sat on her wooden stool and pulled him to her knees, taking his face in her wizened hands. "Oh, Paxton. I had so hoped the lineage would die with me."

Tiern rushed in at that moment, covered in sand with salt water in his hair. "Come see my best sand castle ever, Grandmama!"

"I'll be right there, sweet boy. Run along."

Tiern rushed out and she turned to Paxton again. She raised his small hands and looked at his fingertips. Paxton stared, confused. Strange purple lines ran along the bottom of his nails. "What is that?"

He pulled his hands away and rubbed his thumbnail. "Why won't it come off?" A sickening sensation filled his gut as his grandmother stared at him with pity.

"The mark will move up and disappear as your nails grow out. You shall stay with me until those lines go away. I have much to tell you and it must remain our secret. Not even your mum, your papa, or little Tiern can know. I'm sorry you must bear this curse, precious boy. So terribly sorry . . ."

As dawn finally broke, a fat squirrel poked its face out of the crevasse of a nearby tree, nose twitching at the silent morning. Paxton moved with slow patience, drawing his bow, watching the animal creep its way onto the slippery branch. Before it could retreat back into its warm hole, Paxton shot. The squirrel let out a small bark and fell to the ground.

Paxton leaped to his feet and retrieved their breakfast. Back at their makeshift shelter, he skinned the small creature, all the while silently thanking it for giving its life to sustain them, by choice or not. He made a crisscross of larger, slower burning sticks on top of the fire to cook their meal. At the sizzle of meat, Tiern gave a cough and Harrison moaned beside him. They'd both been restless the past couple hours, but never opened their eyes.

Tiern rubbed his face and looked down at his hands, slowly closing them and stretching them open again. He cracked his neck, then twisted side to side to crack his back.

"By the seas, Pax." Tiern's voice was brittle. "Did we

truly wander into the ridgelands last night?"

"Aye." He gave the squirrel a quarter turn over the flames with a stick.

"You made a fire?" Harrison asked, coming to life at the end of their row. He leaned down to poke at his ankle, grimacing.

Paxton cleared his throat, hoping his brother couldn't read his lies. "I had flint. Found some dry wood sheltered by a fallen log that way." He jerked his head to the side, ignoring Tiern's questioning eyes narrowed on him.

Paxton glanced down at his dirty hands, at the fingertips he'd muddied hours ago after building the fire. He crossed his arms, shoving his hands into hiding.

"I had the strangest imaginings. . . ." Tiern stared down at the fire.

"I'm sure you did," Paxton said. "Only dreams. You were laughing to yourself like a nutter, completely frozen, and then you fell fast asleep."

Harrison chuckled, giving his ankle a gingerly turn.

"How's it feel now?" Tiern asked him.

"Better. Still tender, but I think the cold was actually good for it." He stood carefully, and nodded. "I'll make it back today, perhaps at the speed of a turtle."

Slow suited Paxton. He was ill of mind that morning. First, it felt as though he'd let the beast slip through his fingers, simply handing it to the Ascomannians, and then . . . then he'd done the unthinkable—the thing he'd promised his grandmother he'd never do—the thing that could get him killed. But he'd kept his brother and the lieutenant alive. That was what mattered. The only thing he regretted was the fact that he lived in an age with ridiculous laws and prejudices.

Paxton stood, suddenly angry all over again. He could feel Tiern watching him as he paced over frosted leaves and icy twigs. He squatted to turn the squirrel on the fire, and looked out at the forest around them, dipping downward at a slope. As the sun rose, it made the ice glitter on the trees, and slowly the sounds of droplets hitting the forest floor began as melting temperatures set in.

He didn't want to return to Lochlanach. He didn't want to face the people who'd rather see his brother freeze to death than to be kept warm by the use of magic. He didn't want to hear the land's uproar of hysteria if they found out one of the hunters was Lashed, and they were bound to find out if he didn't stay in hiding for as long as it would take his nails to grow out. Lochlans, even the fishermen and farmers, prided themselves on keeping clean hands in the off hours for that very reason.

To prove they weren't like him.

"You all right?" Harrison asked. Paxton realized his hands were in his hair, grasping at the long strands that had fallen out of the tie.

"Fine," he said, dropping his hands. He nodded at the squirrel, which was browned now. "It's ready to eat."

Tiern set to work on their breakfast, dividing the small

amount of meat and innards. He tried to hand some to Paxton, who shook his head.

"You've got to eat," Tiern told him.

"I'm fine for now." He couldn't explain to his brother the buzz of clean energy that surged through him since he'd worked magic—as if years had been added to his life. He felt like a much younger lad, and it made him realize that he, too, would age quickly, just as his grandmother and other Lashed did when they didn't use their powers.

Paxton set to pacing again, breathing fast, trying to control his raging emotions.

When they finished eating, they began the slow trek back down the mountainside. It would take a good part of the day, which was fine, because Paxton had a lot to think about. He needed to decide what to do. He wished they hadn't had to sell his grandmother's seaside cottage when she passed. It was the perfect home, away from others, where one could live out their life in solitude. Because that's what Paxton needed to seek now. Solitude.

He would have to decide whether or not to tell his family, or to let them believe he was abandoning them. Tiern should probably know, given the chance that his own children could be burdened with this curse someday.

A pang of hunger hit Paxton around high noon and he kept his eyes peeled for prey. After half a mile, when the grade in the ground's tilt began to lessen, Paxton thought he spied a nut tree with a small clearing under its canopy. He cut a path through the brush until they reached it.

Large green orbs hung limply from branches, and the ground was littered with them.

"Walnuts!" Harrison exclaimed.

The men set to crushing the tough green outer shells underfoot and peeling them off. The inner shells had to be pried open with their knives. When Paxton finally got his first one open and poured its broken contents into his mouth, his stomach gave a loud growl.

"Pax, your hands are filthy," Tiern pointed out.

Paxton dropped his hands to his sides too quickly. "I'm not going to waste valuable water cleaning my hands."

He turned to pick another nut, putting his back to them.

"River's probably less than a mile east," Harrison said. "We can detour there to wash up if you'd like."

Paxton responded without turning. "No. I'd prefer to get back sooner if it's all the same to you."

"Yeah," Tiern said, kicking a rotted nut. "I want to find out if the Ascomannians found the beast. Seas alive, I'll die if that Volgan barbarian killed it."

Harrison let out a dry laugh. "Can you imagine the princess married to the likes of him? Sad day for our kingdom."

The bitter nut on Paxton's tongue became so dry, he nearly choked. He took a glug of water, the hunger pains suddenly turning to a burning sensation of rising bile.

"Can I ask you something?" Tiern said to Harrison. The lieutenant raised his chin. "You and Princess Aerity . . .

you're . . ." Tiern shook his head and looked away. "Never mind. It's not my business. Sorry."

Paxton's heart kicked, and he eyed Harrison, who had gone still.

"No, it's all right," Harrison said. "We've known each other since we were young. I care for her a great deal."

The three of them were quiet a few moments as they cracked into the next round of nuts. Paxton felt hyperaware of the lieutenant as curiosity burned through him.

"So," Tiern went on, casually prying at a shell. "You have a past with her, then?"

Harrison stopped and faced him, a meek grin on his face. "Is there something you'd like to ask me directly, Tiern?"

Tiern cleared his throat. "I suppose I just wonder . . . if the two of you . . ."

Paxton felt as if he should intervene to make his brother stop, but he was shamefully interested in what else Harrison might reveal. Jealousy sensitized his skin.

The naval officer moved toward Tiern, his smile disappearing. "The princess is an honorable girl, and I am an honorable man."

"Of course," said Tiern, faltering. "I didn't mean that. I just meant, are you in love?"

This gave Harrison pause. He stared down at the walnut in his hand for a long while. "Like I said, we care for each other." At that, he turned away, reaching up to pluck another nut with his free hand.

A sense of mild relief washed through Paxton, and Tiern finally shut up. The fate of the princess was not Paxton's concern, and he'd do well to put her from his mind altogether.

He crushed the next walnut under the heel of his boot so hard the entire thing went to bits, insides and all.

Chapter
30

Princess Aerity waited none too patiently outside her father's office with Lady Wyneth. When the door opened, she pushed her way inside, nearly knocking aside a naval commander.

"What news?" Aerity asked, rushing to his desk.

The king stood, his face as tightly drawn as ever. "One hunter was killed by the beast. The others gave chase to the north and have not returned."

Aerity rocked back on her heels, light-headed as the blood drained from her face.

"Who?" It came out barely a whisper.

"I'm sorry, what?" the king said.

Wyneth stepped forward, paler than ever. "Uncle . . . who was killed?"

"Samuel Gullet. A Lochlan widower from Loch Nech."

Both the girls closed their eyes. Aerity felt a rush of relief followed closely by remorse.

The door to the king's office burst open, startling them all. An officer took off his felt hat and moved before the king.

"Your Majesty, the seven remaining Zorfinans were found just after daylight at the foot of the ridgelands . . . all dead."

Aerity gasped in horror, and Wyneth grabbed her hand. The queen closed her eyes.

"How?" King Charles demanded. "Attacked?"

His adviser shook his head, his face pinched. "It was rather strange, Your Majesty. Each was stabbed through the heart with a dagger. And there was a note." He handed it to the king, who read aloud.

"We are cowards. We must die or live in shame. Change is coming." He peered across at his adviser. "An honor killing?"

"Aye. I assume because they did not go into the hills with the other hunters."

"But what does that mean, about change coming?"

His adviser shook his head. "We don't know, sir. The whole thing is bizarre."

The king gripped the note in his hand, his anger surging, and brought his fist down on his desk. The *bang* echoed through the room.

"And the others? The Lochlans and Ascomannians?" asked Aerity. Wyneth's hand tightened around hers.

"We assume they're still on the Torestan border, Your Highness," answered the adviser. "There is concern for them due to bad weather in the low ridges last night."

The king rubbed his forehead. "We must find them. Send out a search party. Leave as soon as possible."

"Should I send word to the Torestan government, Your Majesty? To seek permission to enter their lands, if necessary?"

The king waved this off. "There's no time to ask permission, but we'll send news so they can be on the lookout. I'll deal with King Cliftonia. He knows we're fighting a creature of severe magnitude. He won't be happy it's on his lands, but perhaps it is time the rest of Eurona took a greater interest in what's happening here. They are not immune to this beast. This will open their eyes. Go. Search." His adviser nodded and left quickly.

"I want to go," Aerity said, letting go of Wyneth's hand to grab her skirts. Her father stepped out from behind the oak desk to face her.

"It's half a day's ride to the bottom of the hills, child. We don't know how far they made it in."

"I'm not a child, father. You above all should know that."

At this, he took her by the arm. She was itching to leave, scared to be left behind, but she didn't dare pull from her father's grasp.

His face was tight. "My men will find them—"

"I need to go."

The king cocked his head and leveled a gaze at his daughter. She answered his thoughts before he had time to ask.

"Breckon's cousin is out there, father. And I've also spoken with the other Lochlan lads. I feel I've come to know them. I only want to show my support. . . ."

She couldn't meet his eye, certain he would see through her words to the truth underneath—that she'd developed feelings for one of the hunters, mutual or not.

"I will accompany her, Uncle," Wyneth promised.

"As will I," said a voice from the doorway.

They turned to find Vixie in a lavender dress, her mane of red hair pulled back. She marched in and faced their father, making him drop Aerity's arm. It was the first time Aerity had seen Vixie acknowledge him since the proclamation was made. Aerity turned back to her father with pleading eyes.

"I'm not comfortable with this," he said.

The three girls stood shoulder to shoulder, Aerity speaking for them. "Father, we haven't been off royal lands in months. We're drowning here. The beast has never been seen in daylight and it has never attacked in daylight. We'll ride with the entourage along Eurona River to the bottom of the hills and return before nightfall."

"It's the least you can offer," Vixie said.

The king stared Vixie down, not appreciating her tone. He then turned to the queen, whose face was unreadable until she sighed.

"Charles, they'll be surrounded by our men, and the lands are safe during the day. Nobody will hurt them."

"It's foolish to take chances," he said.

The queen's eyes flashed. "With all Aerity is willing to give, with all the maturity they've shown in the face of the kingdom's troubles, Vixie is right. The least we can do is give them a bit of freedom to live."

King Charles stared at his wife a moment longer, his jaw working. The girls waited, holding their breaths until he spoke gruffly. "So be it." He turned to Aerity. "I will add additional riders to accompany the three of you on two conditions."

Aerity looked up into his eyes, which were obscured with worry.

"You will not leave the lands of Lochlanach." Aerity nodded her compliance. "And you will return before sundown, alongside your accompaniment, with or without the hunters. You ride straight there and straight back, or, so help me, you'll be chained to this castle until marriage. Am I clear?"

"Yes, Father." She dashed from the room before he could change his mind.

The three of them rushed down to the stables, not bothering to stop and change into riding clothes. They'd have to make do in their dresses.

"That was brilliant!" Vixie was practically glowing when they reached the stables.

Soldiers were rounding their steeds when a messenger

jogged up with a message from the king. The sergeant in charge looked toward the three royal girls and nodded without complaint. "We'll set off in ten minutes."

"We'll be ready," Vixie guaranteed him. She was always her most assured self at the stables, having spent time here nearly every day since she could walk.

Vixie gave orders to the stable boys to saddle up their three. They passed a large stall with three shining black gypsy steeds, deep chested and strong. "When did we get those?" Aerity asked. "They're gorgeous."

"They belong to the Zandalee."

Ah. Fitting. Aerity opened her stall door and spoke softly to her dapple gray. "Hello there, beautiful." The horse let Aerity pet the stretch of white hair between its nose and eyes, but when it caught sight of Vixie, it raised its head and let out a light whinny of happiness.

"Hello, Doll." Vixie gave her a scratch under the ear, and Aerity couldn't bring herself to be jealous. She was glad Vix gave the horses personal attention, though Aerity herself only came once a month during her required lesson time. She enjoyed leisurely riding. Aerity moved aside as a stable hand bustled by with Doll's saddle and harness. Next to them Wyneth was snuggling Mosby, her bay with a tan coat and black mane and tail.

Vixie saddled Ruspin herself, rivaling the quick movements of the stable boys. Ruspin was Vixie's fourteenth birthday gift—a solid white horse with lovely pink skin and blue eyes. She was a gorgeous, intense beast who didn't care much for Aerity. Vixie said it could sense Aerity's nervousness, so the older girl kept her distance.

Once saddled, the two princesses and Wyneth mounted their horses, hiking their loose skirts up, and set off behind the soldiers, flanked by guards. Their pace was clipped. Aerity swallowed down her fear and held on tightly. She'd have sore thighs by the end of this day, but she didn't care. She couldn't sit around the castle waiting.

They'd been riding less than two hours between the river and trees when they saw a group of burly men in the distance.

One of the guards shouted, "Oy! Hunters!" They rode faster.

As they got closer, Aerity saw they all had light hair, and were wearing furs with their knees on display over tall, rugged boots.

"Ascomannians," Vixie whispered.

Aerity scanned them. Definitely not Lochlans. Lord Lief Alvi moved to the forefront of the hunters and crossed his arms as the head officer dismounted.

"What say you?" asked the officer. "Any sign of the beast? The other hunters?"

Lord Alvi did not look pleased. "We lost its tracks when the weather turned. And we lost the Lochlan men."

Aerity's heart quickened to a gallop.

"You haven't seen them?" the officer asked.

He shook his blond head, hair about his face. "Not since

the dead of night when the storm hit."

"Thank you. We shall ride ahead. Here are some rations for your men." The officer took a bag from the side of his horse and handed it to Lord Alvi before mounting again.

Aerity watched Lord Alvi, waiting to catch his eye so she could acknowledge him, but his eyes stuck to Wyneth until they rode out of sight. Aerity peered across at her cousin, who was looking straight ahead with rather mottled cheeks.

High seas. It wasn't in her imagination. Lief had definitely found interest in her cousin, and by the looks of Wyneth's spotted blush, she was quite aware of it. Never in her life had Aerity been one to shy away from teasing her cousin and talking about boys, or men in this case, but this did not lend itself to their usual banter. Wyneth did not look happy about Lief's affections. And why would she be when she still wore the gray mourning color for the love she'd lost months before? And when this new man was a suitor in the hunt? The circumstances made Aerity feel like a fist was tightening around her gut. She cursed this terrible situation where her cousin couldn't seek happiness, even as it was staring her down, quite literally. She would gladly tell the Ascomannian lord to drop out of the hunt to seek her cousin, but she knew a man of honor would not consider quitting a cause for his own desires.

Wyneth must have caught the look of anguish on Aerity's face, because she spoke loudly against the wind and clomp of hooves, her voice breaking. "Don't worry, Aer. We will find them. I'm certain they're okay. . . ."

Aerity blinked and nodded, looking straight ahead again. On her other side she could see in her peripheral vision Vixie's perfect forward lean, her hair flying back, in her element. The cool fall air whipped against her cheeks, turning them peach.

Hours later, just as the path took them away from the river and the land began to slant upward, she heard the soldiers raise their voices. Aerity squinted and spotted men walking through the trees up ahead. Her heart hammered as her eyes scanned. There were three!

"It's them!" Vixie shouted.

Aerity nudged Doll harder, picking up speed to match her pulse. She even passed two of the closest soldiers. As they got closer, Aerity's sight honed in on the one whose brown waves sheltered the sides of his face. Paxton looked weary and worn, as did the other two. She reared back on Doll and hiked her leg over the horse's back, sliding down to her feet so quickly she nearly fell.

The soldiers let Aerity run through them to get to the hunters. Harrison was first. He walked with a slight limp and gave a bashful grin. She threw her arms around him before remembering their audience and quickly letting him go. "Thank the seas! Are you hurt?" A smudge of mud ran across his cheekbone.

"Just my ankle."

Aerity looked toward the medical soldier and called him

273

forward. If there had been time, she would have thought to ask Mrs. Rathbrook to accompany them.

As a soldier trained in healing tended to Harrison, Aerity took the hand of the next lad, Tiern. He gave a tired grin. His hair was still pulled back, as if he'd recently taken care of it. Before she could speak a word she saw Paxton walk straight past, not so much as glancing her way. Her head turned to follow as he stopped at the soldiers.

"Who killed it?" he asked in a low, dry voice. "Which Ascomannian?"

The soldiers exchanged glances and one spoke up. "The beast? Nobody yet . . ."

Aerity watched the back of Paxton's shoulders relax. He turned slightly and caught Aerity's eye, holding it for a flash of a moment that made Aerity's stomach swoop, before facing the soldier again.

"All the Ascomannians and Zorfinans made it back, then?" Paxton asked.

"Oh." The soldier's face fell. "I'm sorry, but the Zorfinans are gone."

"Gone?" Paxton tilted his head as if he'd heard him wrong. "They left?"

"No . . . they're dead. Honor killing."

Paxton stared at him incredulously and Tiern spoke up. "Honor killing? But why? Because they were ashamed of not going into the ridgelands in an ice storm? They were the bloody smart ones!"

Paxton fumed and pushed ahead through the soldiers. Wyneth frowned at Aerity.

"The beast still lives," Tiern whispered. "We were so close." Aerity's head snapped back to him, then to Harrison, who gave a saddened shake of his head.

Despite her inner warnings, Aerity's eyes found Paxton again. He walked on, alone.

"He'll be all right once he's had a good meal and a rest," Tiern told her. Aerity flushed at having been caught staring. She could feel Harrison's questioning eyes on her, but she focused on the younger brother, fearing Harrison could read her too well.

"Are you all right then, Tiern Seabolt?" she asked.

"Right as rain, Your Highness." His brown eyes weren't as bright as usual. Vixie jogged up, practically beaming. She appeared older to Aerity in that moment, with her wind-blown hair and her eyes taking in Tiern's weary appearance.

"The medic brought one spare horse. They'd like Harrison to use it," she said breathlessly.

Harrison nodded. "Thanks." As he passed Aerity, they made eye contact, and she felt the heavy weight of inquisitive concern in his eyes. She looked away, feeling guilty at the thought that he might have sensed her interest in Paxton.

Vixie pulled her hair over her shoulder. "You can share my horse if you'd like, Tiern. They've brought food rations you can eat on the way."

Tiern looked at Aerity, as if asking permission, and she

nodded. The two of them headed for Vixie's horse, and Aerity could hear the faded voice of Tiern complimenting the mare as they went. She gritted her teeth as she turned and saw the stubborn stance of Paxton Seabolt ahead, walking back on his own. Wyneth gave her a nod in that direction. The soldiers moved to their steeds, feeding them before setting off again.

Aerity rushed forward at a jog, hearing a guard close behind her.

"Mr. Seabolt," the princess called. His whole body tightened, but he did not turn or stop. Aerity wanted to scream. What had happened last night? Why wouldn't he take a moment to stop and rest, to eat?

Aerity went to her horse and opened the saddle pouch, pulling out a hunk of bread stuffed with cheese and salted ham. She jogged until she got to Paxton's side, her guard close behind.

"You must be tired, Paxton," she said.

"I'm fine."

She looked him over, and he seemed to tense as she absorbed the dried mud covering much of him, even his hands. Tiern and Harrison were not nearly as dirty. Seas, he was tense. She wanted to touch him and soothe him.

"Stop a moment, please," she begged. When he wouldn't, she took hold of his firm forearm.

"Your Highness," warned her guard from behind them, but she ignored him.

Paxton came to a stop and stared down at her. She swallowed hard, scared by the swirl of emotion in his dark brown eyes.

"Please," she whispered. "Ride with me."

"Thank you, but no." He attempted to move, but she kept her hand hooked around his arm.

"At least take this."

He peered down at her offering of food for a few beats before finally taking it. When she let go of his arm, he set back on his walk alone. What had happened to him?

"Come along, Princess," the guard said. She turned to the older man and sighed, joining him where he held her horse's reins.

When the return journey began, Princess Aerity could not bring herself to pass Paxton, like the others did. One of the soldiers offered him his horse, but Paxton politely refused. Aerity had never felt more irritated. Wyneth shook her head at Aerity, as if he were a lost cause.

Tiern and Vixie trotted beside him for a moment.

"You could ride with my cousin or sister, you know," Vixie told him. "It would be completely acceptable."

"I'd prefer to walk."

"Pax," began Tiern, but Paxton cut him off.

"A bit of time alone would do me wonders at the moment, Brother."

Tiern merely sighed and shrugged at Vixie, motioning for her to go on as he sat behind her. They trotted ahead, and moments later they were laughing together.

Aerity and Wyneth kept a slow pace behind Paxton with two guards behind them.

This was ridiculous. She looked at her cousin. "Go on, then. I'll be along soon."

Wyneth shot a look at Paxton's back, and then gave her horse a gentle kick forward. Aerity slid down from Doll and kept her reins in her hand, sidling up next to Paxton. He kept up his pace without looking her way but there was a buzz of energy between them.

The princess worked up her nerve and whispered, "Ride with me."

His response was swift. "I won't."

Aerity felt as if she'd been kicked in the gut, but the pain was followed by an exasperated anger that fired her tongue. "Of all the insolent, childish, stubborn things, Paxton Seabolt! You're obviously weary. I don't know what happened last night, but there is no good reason for you to refuse help except your own foolish pride!"

She watched the joint of his strong jaw clamp and release.

"I accepted your food, thank you, and now I'm feeling much better to walk."

Unfortunately for him, his stubbornness was matched by her own. "If you shall walk, then I shall walk."

The guard gave a low rumble of disapproval behind her.

Paxton lifted his eyes to the sky and spoke in a low whisper for her ears only. "Is it so hard to believe I'd prefer to be alone? I'm certain every eligible man in the kingdom would fall over his boot strings for a chance to ride behind your royal arse, but I am not one of them."

Aerity sucked in a breath of shock. She saw him take in the rise of her chest from the corner of his eye before looking ahead again.

Well, that settled it, the swine. Now Aerity would walk at his side for the simple pleasure of not giving him what he wanted. If he thought he could frighten her away with his words and intimidate her, he was wrong. She'd never wanted to bombard anyone with a series of smacks so badly, but she refused to show him how coarsely he affected her.

Aerity stood taller and looked straight ahead, walking as casually as he. She fought back a smile when, after five minutes passed, he turned his head to stare at her incredulously. When she didn't acknowledge him in any way, he shook his head and looked forward again.

Her guard had taken to trotting his horse from side to side, making a twenty- to thirty-foot zag behind them.

After half an hour, Paxton finally said, "You're truly not going to leave me alone?"

"Truly." She was quite chipper.

"You won't ride unless I ride with you?"

"Exactly."

He let out a growling huff and mumbled, "This will be the longest day of my life if I have to continue like this." He stopped and jutted his chin up at Doll. "Get on the damned horse."

Aerity bristled and gave a tight smile. "Well, since you asked so charmingly."

She hooked a foot in the stirrup and pulled herself up, positioning her skirts higher around her thighs so her legs could hang down comfortably. Then she scooted up and looked at Paxton's handsome, albeit dirty, face near her knee. He glowered up at her and she patted the spot behind her.

Aerity could not have prepared herself for the feel of Paxton's solid, male body as he easily settled his weight behind her. She was momentarily stunned into inaction, the air halting in her lungs as her body reacted. Her skin had never felt more sensitive—her torso, bottom, and thighs heating to nearly unbearable temperatures. Even the folds of fabric around her hips seemed to caress her in a sensuous way. Aerity had ridden horseback many times with others, but this could not be compared. Their bodies were forced together, him being heavier, naturally pushing her up so she was practically in his lap.

When she made no move, Paxton's rugged arms came around her waist and took the reins. Her lungs came alive again, sputtering in shallow bursts.

What in Eurona's name was wrong with her? *My lands above* . . . Aerity hoped her sister wasn't experiencing this same sensation.

Paxton's stubbed cheek scratched up against her softer one as he whispered in her ear. "I assume you want to return to royal lands sometime today. Allow me."

His voice jolted her back into reality as his hands tightened on the reins. She cleared her throat. Paxton hitched his heels into Doll's sides and they took off with the guard behind them. Aerity urged the horse faster to make good on her promise to get home before dark. The princess felt the solid mass of Paxton behind her, pressing against her back as he leaned them both forward to gain speed. For once, she felt no fear about the galloping animal beneath her, welcoming the wind on her face.

At one point she felt his nose against her neck, and when she pulled to the side to peer at him, his head jerked up, and he stared straight ahead.

"You . . . smell nice," he said with seeming reluctance. The princess faced ahead again so he wouldn't see her smile.

Despite the breeze that cooled as the day wore on, Aerity found herself warm the entire ride back. When they finally arrived at the commons, Paxton slid deftly off Doll's back. He strode away from her without a word, leaving her abruptly cold in the dusk air. Aerity frowned at his retreating form, wondering why he hated her, and why she couldn't bring herself to hate him back.

Chapter
31

 Paxton's mind was in a dark place as he returned to the commons. Last night changed everything. He could no longer pretend to be normal. He could no longer ignore reality. He could no longer blend in.

When he got to his tent he began shoving his belongings into his bag. His mind reeled as he packed, images of the beast and Lash marks morphing into the supple body of the princess pressed against him on horseback. So, it was a bit jarring when the tent flap opened and he saw his mother's face.

"Pax!" She rushed in and threw her arms around his middle, squeezing him tightly. His eyes closed for two beats as he held her, and then pulled back to see her comforting eyes, her brown hair pulled into a bun. His father ambled in and shook his hand. A mixture of surprise and worry filled Paxton.

"What are you doing here?" he asked. "Is everything all right?"

"We heard from villagers who'd visited the royal market that the hunt was moving northwest, so we brought your cold weather gear," his father said.

Paxton nodded his thanks, noticing the pile of items and coats, and feeling a pang of regret. He may very well need them wherever he ventured next. He felt an urge to laugh at the irony that his parents would show today of all days. He hadn't decided on whether he would tell them, or if it would be safer to leave without a good-bye visit. Seeing them now filled him with guilt. If he disappeared without a word, it would kill his parents. But it was better than them finding out the truth.

All through his childhood, rumors had flown about his grandmother being Lashed. His father had always vehemently denied it, even in their own home. "She's eccentric, introverted." People saw what they wanted to see, ignored what they refused to believe, loved ones or not.

Paxton rubbed his brow. "Have you seen Tiern? He should have returned before me."

"We're told he's still at the stables," his mother replied. Her eyes searched him as if gaining sustenance from the sight of his well-being. Paxton let out a small sigh.

"I need to speak with you both," he said quietly.

"It's Tiern, isn't it?" His mother asked. "He's not faring well in the hunt?"

"It's nothing to do with him." Paxton ushered them both to sit, his stomach tightening. They took a seat on Tiern's neatly made cot and Paxton slumped onto his messy one. He ran his fingers through his hair and saw his mother frown at the sight of his hands. He lifted them in haste to see if the lines were visible, but they weren't. They were just filthy. His mother leaned forward and rested a hand on his knee.

"I can't imagine what you've been through, Pax. The things we've been hearing . . . we wake every morning and run into town for news. If it's this frightening for us, I can't imagine . . ."

She looked to her husband, who patted her knee.

"We're proud of you both," Paxton's father said. "You've made it this far when so many others haven't. One of you is bound to win."

Paxton looked straight into his father's eyes. "It'll have to be Tiern."

His father's eyes narrowed in confusion. "And why is that?"

He broke eye contact, staring down at his hands with their dried, crusted appearance. "I'm leaving the hunt."

"What?"

"Oh, thank the seas." His mother leaned her head back. "Yes, come home, Paxton."

"I'm not coming home, Mum. I'm leaving to be on my own for a while."

They both stared at him as if he'd gone mad.

The clomp of feet running on damp grass sounded outside the tent, and then Tiern burst in. "Pax, bloody hell, that Vixie is—" He stopped and his eyes bulged. "Mum! Papa, what are you doing here?"

Their parents stood and embraced Tiern.

"We brought your cold weather gear," their father said in a thick voice.

Their mother patted Tiern's cheek. Paxton could see she was holding back tears, putting on a strong face. "That wouldn't be young Princess Vixie you were referring to, now would it?"

"Er . . ." Tiern's eyes shot to Pax. "Aye. She's got quite nice riding skills."

"Don't go falling for the younger sister of the one you might have to marry." She gave a fake smile and Paxton wanted to punch something. He was tired of all the pretending.

"No. Course not," said Tiern. "Princess Aerity, she's like a dream. Princess Vixie, she's just mad fun."

Paxton would have rolled his eyes if his stomach weren't churning at the thought of Tiern and Aerity married. A deep growl surged up in his chest, and he coughed to cover it.

"Ah, for the love of Eurona, Pax," Tiern said. "You couldn't even wash up for Mum? Look at you!" He made a grab for Paxton's hand and Pax pulled away on instinct.

"What's your problem, Brother?"

Paxton was tired of lying. Tired of feeling afraid and ashamed. He turned back to his bags, pushing in the last of his belongings. "I'm leaving, Tiern." He stood, pulling the pack over his shoulder. "The hunt is yours."

Tiern blinked. "You're joking."

"Do I ever joke?"

Again, Tiern stared, unmoving. "This is about last night, isn't it? The fire—"

In the blink of an eye Paxton had dropped his bag and pinned Tiern against the pole in the center of the tent. The entire structure shook. Their mother screamed.

"Shut your mouth," Paxton warned. The brothers locked eyes, Paxton's fierce and Tiern's stubborn.

"I knew it!" Tiern started.

Paxton bashed him against the pole again. "You don't know what you're talking about!"

"Boys!" Their father wrenched them apart with his strong hands, nearly toppling over on his bad knees.

A clear warning lived in Paxton's eyes as he stared at Tiern: *do not tell them.*

"Fine," Tiern grumbled, straightening his tunic.

"What in Eurona is going on here?" their father asked. "What happened last night?"

Paxton's fists were ready to shut his brother's mouth if he opened it. His voice was like stone. "We nearly froze to death until I managed to build a fire."

"I knew we should have brought your gear sooner," their mother said.

"We survived." Paxton bent and picked up his pack. "You should stay in our tent tonight. Don't travel back in the dark."

His father let out a breath, at a loss. "I don't understand why you're leaving."

And you never will, Papa.

"It's been a bit more than I expected." Paxton said. He couldn't even look at his father. "I need time to myself."

His father let out a huff of exasperated breath. "You can't just run when you're faced with difficult challenges, Son. I thought I'd taught you better than that."

"Leave him alone." His mother faced his father, bolder than he'd ever seen her. "Only the seas know what he's been through these weeks! Don't shame him for leaving this forsaken hunt."

His father gritted his teeth. "The people will call him a coward, Maryn."

"I don't care what they say!"

Tiern took his mother's hand and she looked down, covering her mouth as tears filled her eyes. "Where will you go?" Tiern asked him.

"I don't know. I'll travel."

"Will you come back?" His mother stepped forward. "Our home will always be your home, Son. You know that." In a quieter voice, she said, "Papa will move past this."

He nodded, though he had no plans to return. He would never endanger his family. "Perhaps someday, Mum."

She hugged him tightly. Over her shoulder he saw his father's chin quiver, though his eyes were still set in disappointment. When his mother released him, he faced his father, his throat tight. "I'm sorry, Papa. I know it's not what you want, but I swear this is what's best right now."

His father swallowed, shaking his head.

Paxton pushed through the tent flap. He could hear his mother's muffled cries and knew if he looked back he would see Tiern watching him in stunned dismay. He would not turn back.

It didn't take long before Tiern jogged up beside him. Paxton kept on. "Let me be, Tiern."

"This is my fault. If I hadn't been so weak in the mountains. If I'd been as strong as you, you wouldn't have needed to—"

"No." Paxton stopped and grasped the side of Tiern's neck. "You are strong in every way that counts. This is not your fault." He turned away from the hurt in Tiern's eyes, walking on.

"You can still hunt. Nobody has to know."

He didn't have time for this. He had to get far away from royal lands before it was too dark. Paxton stopped again and spoke in low tones. "Don't be a bloody fool, Tiern. I have lines on my nails. I can't keep them dirtied forever! They'll see them and kill me."

"Not if you kill the beast!"

Paxton inched closer, annoyed by his brother's naiveté. While Paxton had hung on to every word of Lashed news over the years, each of those stories had gone over Tiern's head. He had no idea what it was like. "They would never let me marry into the royal line, even if I brought them the beast's head on a platter."

"That's not fair."

"Nothing is fair for us, Brother, and you need to come to terms with it. This is in your blood, too. Your children could be one of us. You must prepare yourself to be on the lookout once your child turns seven, to teach them to hide it."

"I've no clue how to teach someone that!" Tiern appeared petrified.

"If you—" Paxton swallowed down a dry lump with great effort. "If you kill the beast and marry the princess, you can take your child to Mrs. Rathbrook, the royal Lashed woman. She will help you."

Tiern followed closely as Paxton began walking again. "But . . . that line will go away and you can come back. I feel like there's more to this— What are you running from?"

Paxton turned on him, his heart pounding with the grave truth of his brother's question. "I run from nothing," he gritted out. But it felt like the largest lie he'd ever told. He'd long ago mentally prepared himself for the possibility of leaving his family someday, and he'd kept his heart hardened against the girls in his town. But Aerity . . . he'd never planned for her. She'd made her way under his skin, winding her delicate, strong hands around his heart, and he had to stop it. He had to run from her for both their sakes. He'd been a fool to think he could kill the beast and marry a princess, hiding his true self forever.

"Please, Pax."

"Don't," Paxton warned. "You will do well, with or without me."

"What will I tell everyone?"

Though Paxton owed the other hunters nothing, it felt wrong to leave without saying good-bye. Paxton shrugged, not stopping. "Tell them I left without a word, or that I'm ill with what the Zandalee had. Tell them I've grown tired of the hunt. Whatever you'd like."

Tiern let out a ragged breath of frustration. "They'll never believe you've quit."

"Stop making a scene," Paxton warned him. "Go back to the tent with Mum and Papa, and don't utter a word of this."

"But—"

Laughing voices bounded out from the tents up ahead. Three Ascomannians stumbled out, carrying brown bottles. Volgan took one look at Paxton with all his belongings and smirked.

Of all the bloody rotten luck, Paxton thought. He walked past the men without a word.

"I must admit, I'm surprised," Volgan said loudly. "I thought it'd be the scrawny one who went home first. Unless he's got his big brother carrying his belongings for him." The men sent up raucous laughs.

Paxton gritted his teeth, stopped, dropped his belongings, and turned. He would make time to take care of one last thing before he left.

Volgan's icy eyes went wide just before Paxton's fist connected with his nose. There was a loud, wet crunch. The sting of his knuckles and the sudden sounds of shouts disappeared as the two men locked eyes, a battle rage building between them. Paxton braced as the brawny Ascomannian threw himself forward.

Paxton never stopped moving, throwing punches, releasing all the anger he'd held. He barely felt the pain of the blows, his blood so filled with fire. Both grunted and shouted, beating each other senseless. He felt himself yanked down by the tunic when Volgan stumbled to the ground. They rolled, and Paxton caught the flash of something glint from the corner of his eye.

"Knife!" Tiern shouted.

Paxton brought the crown of his head down against Volgan's already-smashed nose. As the Ascomannian howled, Paxton reached for the man's wrist, which held a curved blade. But before he could get a good grip, Volgan lurched to the side and pulled his arm in, slicing through Paxton's palm. He yelled as a violent sting wrenched through him, and he clasped his hand closed around the injury.

Paxton hovered above the man, raising his fist, and before

he could swing, his arms were grabbed and pulled from behind. He kicked out and caught Volgan's hip with his boot as he was yanked backward. Volgan rolled away, wincing with pain. It took four guards to pull Paxton off and hold him. Once he calmed, they lifted him to his feet. Lord Lief Alvi stood beside them with his arms crossed over his wide, bare chest.

"Finally had it out? Good. Took you both long enough." He gave Paxton a wink and turned, his men following as he walked away. Volgan sat up, glowering at Paxton through his purpled eyes, spitting blood onto the grass.

Paxton looked down the narrow path, thankful his parents weren't in sight. Paxton pulled himself from the grip of the guards. As his breathing settled, he became aware of the bruises and cuts across his flesh.

"You're bleeding," Tiern said to Paxton as one of the guards led Volgan away, toward the castle.

"I'll take you to the infirmary," a guard told him.

Paxton's hand was clenched around the cut, but blood seeped through. This was no small wound. He wished he had the power to heal himself, but the magic didn't work that way.

"I'll tend to it myself." He reached down for his bag with his good hand, but Tiern batted his arm back, making Paxton hiss.

"Don't be so damned stubborn!" Tiern lowered his voice and moved close. "You're bleeding everywhere. Just do this one last thing to ease my mind, and I swear I won't ask you to stay again. I can't let you leave here like this. You'll get a fever or something worse—"

"Fine." At this one word, Tiern seemed to relax.

Paxton's hand was throbbing. The lack of sleep and physical trials of the past day and a half were finally catching up with him. He felt as if he could sleep for days. Maybe he would once he found a safe destination for himself. Once this cut stopped stinging, he'd be ready to go. He looked at the nearest guard, and said, "May I be taken to Mrs. Rathbrook?"

The young guard lifted an eyebrow and leaned closer where no one could hear. "You sure you want the Rocato touch? The castle has a regular healer who can sew that up and give you herbs for the pain if you—"

"No." Paxton's chest flamed with anger as he bit out, "Mrs. Rathbrook healed me before, and as you can see I survived just fine. She's no one to fear. She's not Rocato."

The guard gave a "suit yourself" shrug, and Paxton's fists itched to punch again. He let himself be led to the one place in Eurona where he did not wish to be while his fingers were marked—the castle. The place where the one person in Lochlanach lived whom Paxton's mind and heart could not handle—the princess.

Chapter

32

 Princess Aerity heard the commotion through the closed window of her studies room. Her teacher frowned at the disruption. He was already grumpy after having to postpone their lesson to late afternoon. But it was hard to concentrate when the men were shouting outside. Her heartbeat quickened as she began scribbling the last lines of her Eurona trade composition. She pushed it hastily toward her teacher and stood.

"Here you are, Professor. I'm sorry again for the delay today." She grabbed her shoulder bag and rushed from the room.

When Aerity reached the great doorway to the outdoors, a guard held out his arm. "I'm sorry, Princess, but tensions are high among the hunters at the moment. I can't let you go out there."

"What's going on?" she asked, trying to peer past him.

"Just a scuffle. It's under control now."

"Hm." Aerity moved into the side study room, an old library with shelves upon shelves of rare editions only a scholar could appreciate. She went to the window and saw two hunters being led toward the castle, surrounded by guards. She could have sworn the bowed head among them was Paxton's. Aerity rushed back to the doorway of the study and peeked through the crack as the men were led in: one of the gruffer Ascomannians, bloodied and swollen, followed by Paxton, his hands in loose fists, his hair a mess of brown waves around his face.

A flash of vivid red covering Paxton's closed hand caught Aerity's eye, turning her stomach. Another injury. This one from a fight. She waited until the men had all passed, then followed them quickly down the hall. Droplets of blood trailed the floor in their wake. A maid was already at the entrance of the hall, rag in hand.

Around the first corner, Wyneth and Lady Ashley stood arm in arm as the men passed. Wyneth kissed her mother's cheek and then went straight to Aerity's side, taking her arm instead as her mother went toward High Hall.

"What happened?" Wyneth whispered.

"I believe Paxton and one of the Ascomannians had a fight."

Wyneth sighed and shook her head.

"Will you do me a favor?" Aerity asked. "Will you go to the men and find out what happened for me?"

Wyneth stiffened a bit. "You mean, outside? With the hunters?"

"Erm, yes." Aerity didn't understand her cousin's reluctance. She'd been around the men many times now. And then she remembered the way Lord Lief had watched Wyneth. "You know what? Never mind."

Wyneth cleared her throat. "No, it's not a problem. I'll go."

Wyneth began to turn away, but Aerity kept hold of her fingers. "No, Cousin. The details don't matter. Won't you talk to me?" She gave a gentle tug until Wyneth faced her and met her eyes, smiling gently. "Tell me what's on your mind?"

"Nothing at all." Wyneth squeezed her fingertips. "I'm feeling a bit off, perhaps coming down with something—"

Aerity shook her head. "Stay inside, rest in the warmth."

"No, the fresh air might be good for me. I will find out what's happened and return shortly."

"Wyn, wait."

Wyneth ignored this. "I'm fine. Go check on the skirt raiser." She kissed Aerity's cheek and walked away, unwrapping a shawl from her waist as she went and tossing it around her shoulders.

Aerity watched her cousin until she had gone. A wave of worry batted at her heart—it was unlike her cousin to keep her thoughts so guarded from Aerity. She wished they could talk about all of this, no matter how awkward the circumstances.

Aerity made her way to the infirmary wing where the guards had left the men in separate rooms. She went to Paxton's doorway. His back was to her, and he seemed to be looking down at his hands. A young, beautiful nurse bustled up beside her with a steaming bucket of water and clean rags.

"I'll take that," Aerity told her.

The nurse's eyes widened, looking from Aerity to Paxton. "But, Princess . . ."

Aerity gripped the edges of the bucket and gave the girl a reassuring smile. "It's fine, I assure you. If you could tend to the Ascomannian hunter I'd be much obliged." The girl glanced toward Paxton's still form again, and nodded, looking somewhat crestfallen.

Aerity waited for the nurse to disappear before entering Paxton's room, kicking the door shut behind her. She set the bucket on the table. If possible, he was even dirtier than he'd been when she found him that afternoon.

"You shouldn't be here," Paxton said morosely without looking at her.

The despondency in his voice filled her with worry.

"We should clean your hands so Mrs. Rathbrook can tend to your injuries better." She dunked a cloth into the hot water. "Come here, Paxton."

He stared at a blank point on the wall. "I will wash myself, Princess. You can go."

297

Aerity bristled. "Can you not set aside your asinine pride for one moment, Paxton Seabolt? Are you like this with every person? Every woman? Or only me?" Her emotions were rising. She'd tried over and over, driven by the chemistry between them and the few glimpses of warmth he'd shown, like fleeting gifts of golden flecks she couldn't keep hold of.

Still, he stared at the wall, unmoving, hands clasped tightly.

"Why did you even join this hunt if you hate me so thoroughly?" Aerity snapped, immediately regretting the question.

Without looking her way, Paxton said, "It was never about you, Princess."

She swallowed hard. She'd known that. Perhaps it was even one of the reasons she felt so drawn to him—he wasn't after the prize of promised wealth or a royal lass in his bed. Yet she swore there'd been a mutual attraction from the beginning. Had it all been wishful thinking? Girlish imaginings?

"Of course," Aerity said quietly. Her palms rested on the side of the bucket, her fingers dipping into the water as her heart sank, and she felt as young and foolish as Vixie. "Just . . . wash while the water is hot."

"I will. You can go."

Aerity nearly obliged, but he appeared so forlorn. "I should stay until Mrs. Rathbrook gets here. You look as if you're about to fall over." He finally looked at her, with hard eyes that made Aerity feel as if he'd struck her. Indignation burned through her. She was tired of this. "What cause have you to hate me so? It seems the more kindness I show, the more bullheaded you become!" Aerity threw the cloth back into the water with a smack. Paxton's jaw clenched.

"Why do you care?" he asked.

"I'm beginning to wonder that myself." Aerity frowned up at him.

"Well, you won't need to worry about my bullheadedness getting in your way another day, Your darling Highness. The moment my hand is healed, I'm leaving."

Aerity flinched. "Leaving?"

"Yes."

Their eyes searched each other, seeking something she couldn't explain.

"Why?" Aerity whispered.

"For reasons you wouldn't understand."

Aerity's eyes burned. He was right: she didn't understand this man or his reasons. She believed he was acting out of hurt, but she couldn't figure out what could possibly have hurt him so deeply, or what it had to do with her.

"I don't know what's happened to you, Paxton. I want to help you, but—"

"You wouldn't want to help me if you knew."

Aerity stared up at him. Did he have a criminal past? With his temperament, it was a possibility. Even so, he seemed the type to act out of a sense of honor and justice, not petty reasons.

Aerity stared into the depths of his dark eyes, searching for answers. "I think you underestimate me, hunter. But I cannot stop you if you choose to go. I can only tell you with all honesty that I wish you would stay."

As she moved closer, she swore she felt Paxton soften, though his face remained impassive. She moved closer still, fully expecting him to back away, but he didn't.

"I must leave today," he said in a low voice.

Aerity, knowing this could be the last time she saw him, went up on the tips of her toes and placed her lips against his. She watched as his eyes fluttered closed. When he didn't stop her or push her away, she brought her hands up around his neck and pulled herself higher, tasting the fullness of his salty lips, like the seas.

"Princess," he whispered in a guttural tone against her lips. "You don't know what you do."

"I do know, hunter. I know exactly what I do."

His head pulled back and his eyes bore into hers, filled with a mix of punishment, anger, and desire. "You've no clue who I am."

Her skin pebbled with gooseflesh at a sense of foreboding. "Then tell me. Who are you, Paxton Seabolt?"

He slowly took her wrist from around his neck with his good hand and moved his bloodied, dirtied hand to the edge of the bucket, nodding toward it. He watched her, inviting her to wash him now. Aerity, flustered by the intensity in his eyes, as if he were inexplicably daring her to do this, reached into the bucket with a shaking hand and began to wash his wrist and the top of his tightly fisted hand. She gently turned his hand and coaxed open his fingers, dunking his open palm into the water. He didn't flinch, but it had to hurt as she gingerly wiped away the grime to reveal a gaping slash in the middle of his palm. Blood seeped out, coloring the water in swirls of red.

Aerity wound the cloth around his palm and set to cleaning the caked-on dirt from his fingers with her bare hands. When Paxton tensed, Aerity glanced at him. His jaw was set in hard lines as he watched her work.

She gently continued, trying not to cause him further pain, using her small nails to scrape away the dirt edged into his cuticles. The bit at the very bottom was particularly difficult. She splashed more water on his fingers and rubbed again, staring, then scratched harder, pushing at the dirt, willing it to budge. But it was too straight, too uniform, too smooth.

Her stomach dropped. She looked at his next finger, and the next. All the same.

It wasn't dirt at all.

Aerity went stiff as she stared at the purpled lines. She stood still, but the room seemed to be moving. For a moment she forgot to breathe. She couldn't look at Paxton's face, but she could hear his quickened breaths close to her ear. In a moment of denial, Aerity scratched lastly at his thumbnail, only to reveal another line.

Almighty seas . . . Aerity felt a sob rising up inside her as the truth flooded her system.

"Paxton . . ." she whispered.

"Now you know." His voice was resigned. "Now you can let me be."

But she couldn't. She knew he had not received those lashings from hurting another person, unless perhaps it was self-defense. No matter his outer temper, she had always sensed the man underneath this secret—a secret massive enough to warrant his anger and hurt. Aerity knew in her gut that he would have only used his power as a last resort.

He remained so still beside her, allowing her to keep his hand in her own.

Truth and understanding continued to pour over Aerity in a heavy wash. Stories cartwheeled through her mind— Lashed being persecuted and abused, rounded up and killed out of fear. She had studied the history of the Lashed in great detail. The thought of anyone seeing his hands in this state, of anyone trying to kill him, filled her with a fierce protectiveness. She held his hand tighter.

He could have chosen not to reveal this to her. Aerity felt certain that Paxton did not share his true identity lightly. In fact, he'd probably done it to scare her away, and at great risk to himself. Well, it hadn't worked, because she wasn't scared of him. If he'd intended to put a greater gap between them, he'd only succeeded in making her feel closer. Her heart filled with empathy.

Words would not do at this moment.

Aerity turned and their eyes caught. He stared at her as if wading through thorns, searching, waiting for what harsh word or sharp accusation might come from her lips.

The princess rose to her toes again, circling his neck with her wet hands, and pressing her mouth against his. He jolted in surprise before reacting. This time, he did not remain still.

Paxton's free hand rounded her waist and pulled her body firmly against his. His mouth took over, his lips moving against hers in a heated rush of ownership that caused her entire body to react.

He growled against her lips. "Will you never cease to surprise me?"

Aerity was overwhelmed and could only cling to him, her eyes stinging with emotion as she soaked in all he'd held back, all he'd tried to keep hidden. She hadn't been a fool after all—he'd felt this thing between them as much as she had.

Distant footsteps and voices sounded down the stone hall, and Paxton stepped away, rubbing his stubbled jaw with his uninjured hand. Aerity felt cold as she dropped her arms to her sides, except her mouth, which still burned. Paxton moved closer to the bucket, over which his injured hand hovered, the cloth now stained red.

"You should go," he said.

"Please don't leave tonight," Aerity whispered. "Talk to Mrs. Rathbrook."

She could only hope the woman would have some sort of idea or advice for Paxton.

His expression was one of disappointed strain. "I can make no promises to you, Aerity."

She swallowed and nodded. This was about life and death for him. It was wrong that he should have to live this way, that he should have to give up his freedom. Aerity needed to speak to her father. Something had to be done in the kingdom. It was one thing to read about Lashed. To see this pain, to feel it up close, was wholly different. She felt ashamed at her past inaction. She could no longer be silent.

A quiet knock sounded on the door as it opened. Mrs. Rathbrook's gaze passed between Aerity and Paxton before she let out a knowing sigh.

"Go," Paxton whispered to Aerity.

The princess gave a nod and shared a meaningful look with Mrs. Rathbrook before she exited the room, leaving her to heal, and hopefully mentor, the magical man who had so ensnared her heart.

Chapter

33

Lady Wyneth held her skirts tightly in her hands as she walked over the cobblestones. This morning she had started to choose a pale yellow dress, a favorite of hers. But even touching the fabric made her feel traitorous to her love's memory. She chose gray again, though she knew Breckon would want her to be happy. He wouldn't want her to continue mourning, but her heart was not ready to let go of what they'd had. A part of her would always long for that sweet love. Wind whipped past and she grasped the shawl at her chest.

A great divide had taken up residence within her—the half that ached to see Lord Lief Alvi each day and the half that dreaded it, knowing it was wrong to feed this interest. She hated herself for having these torn feelings for one man, as she wore the bereavement color for another.

Her heart became a rapid drum as she approached the entrance gates. Thankfully, Harrison and Tiern were standing close by with their bows strung across their backs, talking in low tones.

"Oy, lads," she called to them. They raised their chins and smiled as she entered. From the corner of her eye she saw a group of men emerge from the tents, geared up. The tallest, broadest, blondest of their ranks stared in her direction.

Feeling his eyes on her, she was momentarily too distracted to speak.

"All right then?" asked Harrison.

"Oh, yes." She cleared her throat. "I came to see what happened this afternoon."

"Pax finally kicked that coldlandman's arse," Tiern said, grinning. "Been asking for it since day one."

Wyneth raised her eyebrows. "But they're both all right?"

Harrison shrugged, like people beating each other was commonplace, and perhaps it was. "They'll survive. Probably even be back for the hunt tonight."

"Well, all right then." Wyneth could see Lief moving in their direction now, and her stomach rattled with nerves. "Good. I'll just be going, I suppose." She gave them nervous smiles as she turned to leave.

"Are you all right, Wyn?" Harrison called, his voice tinged with worry.

"Aye, fine," she responded over her shoulder.

When she was nearly at the gates, his smooth, deep voice called out to her. "My lady."

Wyneth slowed, her stomach giving a massive stir of satisfaction, which quickly filled her with shame. Her hand clung to the gate, but she didn't turn. The guards watched, and when Wyneth looked at them they turned their faces away.

"Are you well?" Lief's concerned voice asked her.

Wyneth shut her eyes. "I'm ready for this cursed beast to be killed, and this hunt to be over." Come what may, she meant that with all her heart. She was ready for this sense of doom to lift from the kingdom so they could all seek a normal life again, though "normal" would likely have a completely different meaning once the hunt finished.

"Walk with me?" He held out a bare arm, and Wyneth looked toward the guards. The self-preserving part of herself hoped the guards would suggest against it, as they would with Aerity, but they only moved aside. Wyneth's heart flipped and then fell in a single swoop. Past Lord Alvi, she could see Harrison still watching her, a terse frown on his face. Guilt churned within her.

"My lady?" Lord Alvi was holding out his arm.

Wyneth tore her gaze from Harrison and hesitantly took the coldlandman's arm, her fingers curling over a small portion of the muscle there, and he led her away from the castle. He felt so nice, so masculine and safe. But her brief feeling of comfort quickly morphed into one of misgiving. He wasn't hers and he wasn't safe. Nobody was.

"Lord Alvi," she said as they turned the corner toward paths into the forest. "I should return to the castle. This—it's not proper."

"It's merely a walk. I'll have you back soon."

She pulled his arm to stop him and dropped her hands, a sense of resolve settling over her. "This has to stop. Please. I don't want to think about you anymore—"

"Have you been thinking of me?" His light blue eyes trapped her, and his white smile dazzled her senseless.

"I . . ." She cleared her throat. "I mean it, Lord Alvi. I can't see you alone anymore."

"Why won't you call me Lief?"

"Your wife may call you Lief. But I will never be your wife."

His head tilted downward. A brisk wind came up from the waters and rustled through the nearby trees, causing Wyneth to shiver. How could he stand there, half naked, and completely unfazed by the elements? He reached for her arms, as if to warm her with his broad hands, but she stepped back in a hurry.

"You can't do that." Her voice held a plea, and his eyes fell. "Doesn't it bother you at all that you might be married to my cousin soon?"

He blinked, his lips pursed. "In Ascomanni, as it used to be here in Lochlanach, royalty marry for purpose—land, ties, wealth, politics, carrying on the bloodlines. Our commoners marry for companionship. It is understood that I will marry for the reasons all my fathers before me have married, but that does not mean I cannot have a separate relationship with one I love."

Wyneth swallowed down a bout of bile, sickened by the bitterness. "I will not be your mistress. To even suggest such a thing is offensive. Here, in this time, it is a great dishonor to your spouse to love another. And I would *never* do that to my cousin. You should be warned that Lochlans would withhold their support of any prince who treated their princess in such a way."

The look of ease never left his face. "Lady Wyneth, surely your king and your kingdom understand by his proclamation that Princess Aerity's marriage is not likely to be one born of love. And if I kill this beast, which I fully intend to, it would be a great dishonor to refuse the king's offer. I will treat your cousin with the utmost respect, but I will not deny myself or her, of taking another. It's simply how it's done."

She gaped. "But you'll lie with your wife to carry on the bloodlines?"

He let out a breath. "Yes."

"Well, I will not be that *other* whom you take." Tears welled in Wyneth's eyes at the fact that Lord Alvi could be so cold. In that moment, it was no longer about herself or him, but about her cousin, who deserved so much better than the vision of union this Ascomannian was willing to offer. She couldn't stand the thought that her cousin was doomed to such a marriage.

"I am not a heartless man, my lady. This is how it has been for generations. It works well for our royals. You only have to get your mind past the barriers of social norms you've accustomed yourself to. It's a different path of thought. Different, not wrong."

Wyneth shook her head. Romantic delusions or not, she could not get past this. "It's my hope that your feelings for my cousin will grow so that you don't need another. This ends right now."

"Lady Wyneth . . ." His warm, strong fingers reached for her and slipped away from her arm as she walked off, hurrying out of his reach. She kept her head down, hiding the heartache that was undoubtedly etched across her face.

Chapter

34

The smart thing for Paxton would have been to stop the kiss. The smart thing would have been to ignore his feelings for Aerity, and the calming words of the Lashed healer, and to leave as planned. But all of Paxton's wisdom had filtered away like water through sand when Aerity's kiss of acceptance had seized his heart, claiming it as easily as if it'd never been guarded at all.

And then there was Mrs. Rathbrook. The Lashed woman had appeared unsurprised when she saw his marks. She'd healed him, then returned with a small jar of a milky substance. She dabbed a bit on each of his nails and Paxton had strained to hear her quiet words.

"This will act as a temporary paint that matches your

normal coloring. I've invented this mixture myself. You're not the first I've had to hide. If you scrub or scratch your nails, it will chip off. Be careful, lad." She patted the top of his hand when the paint dried and sent him on his way. As he exited he heard her call out. "Will you hunt tonight? I think you should."

He thought about it solemnly before giving a nod. "Aye. Perhaps I will."

The woman grinned and set to cleaning the table. "Very good, then." She began to whistle a tune. It took Paxton a moment to recognize the folk song as he left the hall. He could almost hear his grandmother's voice singing it in her old cottage . . . something about the winds of change blowin' o'er the loch—a sea of change a-brewin'.

⤳⤳

Paxton groaned when Tiern saw him gearing up for the hunt, because his brother looked as excited as a child at the fall carnival. Paxton wanted to tell him not to get his hopes up, that he might have to leave at any moment without notice, but he didn't bother. Tiern's hopes were already too high. So much so that they were unperturbed by the sharp glances being thrown their way by a swollen Volgan. Lord Lief Alvi met Paxton's eyes, and though he gave Paxton a nod, he seemed disturbed by something.

The Zandalee entered the commons, dressed in their hunting clothes.

"How are you feeling?" Tiern asked.

"Good enough to eat you." Zandora made a move to bite him, her white teeth clicking an inch from his nose, which she touched with her finger before smiling. Her sisters laughed.

"All better then," Tiern said, his back stiff. "Well done."

"Though I am not happy with your healer."

"Why?" Paxton asked.

"She gave us a potion to sleep and we missed all of the fun." She appeared indignant that she'd been held back from joining them in their freezing hike.

"You have the heart of a true hunter, Zandora," Harrison said.

"Of course I do." She strapped on her bow. "Now you will tell me every detail we missed."

As they set off with the Ascomannians and Zandalee, Paxton furtively checked his nails. Then he wondered what in the high seas he was thinking remaining in this hunt. It was foolhardy at best for him to stay. His mind felt like a sapling caught in a gale, leaning this way and that.

When he'd decided to reveal his true nature to Aerity, he'd been fairly certain she would keep his secret, yet thought for sure she would be disappointed enough to finally let him go. What he'd not expected was for her to kiss him with more passion than he'd ever felt before. It turns out that the princess, in all her riches and innocence, was as hot-blooded as he. Even now his blood heated, warming him against the chill in the air, imagining her soft lips and the island scents of coconuts and berries that lingered over her fresh skin.

Deep seas alive, that kiss . . .

But even if Aerity accepted him, the kingdom never would. Secrets had a way of revealing themselves. If the people found out there was a Lashed among their royals, Paxton imagined riots, looting, and uprisings. Worst of all, he imagined the people would take their fears out on innocent Lashed and their families. Paxton would be selfish to take such a chance. He couldn't see himself living in a castle, anyhow. Though he could imagine himself sharing a bedchamber with Aerity.

Cursed thoughts.

Paxton shook his head and made his way quietly through the fallen leaves to the same spot they'd hidden in last time. They would line the same river, and the watermen had agreed to help once more, their boats offshore. Their hope was to lure the beast down from the mountains or out from the water.

They waited hours, feeling the frost set in around them. Paxton crouched under the drooping branches of a persimmon tree, his frozen ears perked for any sound. From a distance he could see Tiern shivering, even in his fur-lined leathers, but Paxton wasn't worried. The temperature was cold, but not quite freezing like last time.

The Zandalee were as still and quiet as ever.

The night was silent. No horns. No beast. No hunters calling out. No fishermen throwing rocks toward shore. Paxton nodded to himself as the far sky began to lighten. The creature had probably taken the night off to tend its wounds. He clenched his teeth in frustration at another unsuccessful hunt.

As the hunters marched stiffly back to royal lands, tired and sullen, Tiern and Paxton kept toward the river, talking in low tones in case Harrison or the Zandalee caught up to them.

"How long will that last on your fingers, whatever she used?" Tiern whispered.

"Few days, maybe a week if I'm careful."

They walked in silence a few moments until Tiern looked around to make sure nobody had come near. "Listen, Pax. In no time at all those marks'll be gone, and nobody will ever know. If you kill the beast, you can marry the princess, and—"

"No. Tiern, get it through your mind. I cannot marry her. Lashed . . . we don't even live full lives."

"What do you mean, you don't live full lives?"

Paxton shrugged. "Lashed need to work magic to live longer. Haven't you seen how quickly they age?" His brother's eyebrows were drawn together. Of course he hadn't noticed. "I'll most likely die in my forties, as ragged as an old seafarer." He hadn't let himself dwell on this part, though it bothered him far more than he let on.

"Deep seas," Tiern mumbled. "But you could secretly use magic and just keep wearing that paint—"

"No. I can't live that way."

"Why are you so keen on having another marry her, Pax? I thought you wanted her for yourself."

Paxton could feel Tiern staring at him when he didn't respond, as if trying to work a puzzle. "I know you care for her, you bloody brute. At this point, I would only marry her so that I might take care of Mum and Papa."

Paxton gave a dry laugh. "How quickly your attitude has changed. You make marrying Princess Aerity sound like a chore."

"Not a chore. It just feels . . . wrong now. And perhaps I fancy another."

The little sister. Paxton chuckled for real now. "She has several years before the king will let you sniff around her, Brother. She's bound to fall in love with a dozen officers and lords between now and then. Long after the hunters' invitations have expired."

Tiern looked down at his feet, and Paxton immediately regretted what he'd said. Yes, it was known that the king wanted his children to marry whom they chose, but this hunt was a special circumstance. The royal children did not regularly interact with commoners in normal life.

Tiern glared at him. "Why are you bothering to hunt, then, if you don't even plan to marry her? For the glory? One last show of your mighty greatness before you disappear forever and the rest of us are left empty-handed?"

Tiern's huff of angry air made a cloud of steam as he stomped ahead, leaving Paxton on the sandy, leaf-ridden shore.

Paxton turned toward the water and crossed his arms. Why did he stay, if not to claim Aerity's hand? He stared down at the broken oyster shells and smooth stones gently batted by the moving water.

The truth hit Paxton's chest with powerful force, but he couldn't admit it to his brother. Yes, he wanted Aerity, but in reality he felt he could not have her. If he couldn't have her, he wanted none of these other hunters to claim her either. Perhaps it was selfish, but he didn't care. He couldn't stand the thought of any of these men, including his own brother, smelling her scented skin or tasting her soft lips as he had. If he killed the beast and forfeited his "prize," it would baffle everyone, and perhaps even bring the royal family a moment of shame, but it would leave Aerity free to choose of her own accord.

No, he could not explain that to Tiern. His brother might keel over from shock to find out Paxton was capable of such thoughts and feelings.

He turned at the sound of footsteps in the sand. Harrison and the three Zandalee joined him in the surf.

"If I do not kill something soon," Zandora said, "I will need to fight." She rubbed a fist into her palm.

Paxton held up his hands. "Don't look at me. I've had my brawl. You'll have to pummel Harrison here."

The lieutenant laughed. "Have the healer at the ready for me!"

Zandora punched Paxton's arm. "Who did you fight?"

"Volgan."

Her eyes gaped wide and she punched him again. "I miss all the fun! Did he bleed?"

"We both bled."

"Who shed more?" By the seas, her eyes were hungry for details.

"Paxton was declared the winner," Harrison told her.

A rustle sounded from the trees, a squirrel jumping from branch to branch, showering the ground with colorful foliage. Paxton heard a whiz and the squirrel was suddenly falling to the ground, a shining arrow through it.

Zandora lowered her bow. "I feel better. A little."

Paxton grinned as Zandora stomped away with her sisters, grabbing up the impaled rodent on her way.

Harrison shook his head. "Remind me to stay on her good side."

"Bloody right."

They walked in silence, a strange unspoken tension between them.

⤝⤞

Paxton was relieved to return to his tent, where Tiern had wound himself tightly in his blankets with his face to the wall. Paxton sighed quietly to himself and climbed onto his own cot. He looked at each of his fingers and thumbs—the paint was still intact, so for now he would stay. He would play it day-by-day, though it was more reckless than he cared to be.

He fell asleep, dreaming unwillingly of coconut and berry breezes.

Chapter

35

The view from Aerity's window showed the trees had lost half their leaves, though the temperature was unseasonably warm and sunny. The princess left off her shawl when Vixie came to her chamber, asking her to visit the stables for a ride. She donned her leather riding pants, the sturdy material exquisitely soft and thin, with boots and a cream-colored tunic. They found Wyneth in the hall in her riding outfit as well.

"You're joining us?" Aerity couldn't help the grin that stretched across her face when Wyneth nodded.

"I heard there were no beast sightings last night," Vixie said.

Aerity and Wyneth both nodded, quiet. The princess

feared what would come of Lochlanach if the creature wasn't destroyed soon.

Guards surrounded them as the girls came to the stables and mounted their saddled horses. Wyneth and Aerity trotted their girls around a ring, Aerity's legs still sore from their morning ride yesterday.

"Lean in and relax," called Vixie.

But she couldn't help it—she always felt so unsteady when the horses gathered speed . . . unless she was nestled against Paxton. She let the other girls move ahead without her.

"Brilliant riding," one of the guards called as Vixie blew past him.

Aerity and Wyneth finished after an hour and led their horses to the stables, where they found the Zandalee women readying their large steeds. The leader, Zandora, gave Aerity a nod.

"It is a fine day for riding," Aerity said in Zorfinan.

"*Jes*." Zandora mounted gracefully, along with the two others. She wondered what their hair looked like since they always kept it covered. It gave them a sense of mystery. "Your climate is strange. Hot one day. Cold the next."

Aerity laughed. "Aye. As temperamental as a redhead."

Now it was Zandora's turn to laugh. She looked out at the forest of maroons, oranges, and yellows, mixed with evergreens. "But your trees, they are very beautiful. We have nothing like that." Before Aerity could respond, Zandora dug her heels into her horse's side and was off, the others following.

"What did she say to you?" Wyneth was watching the women ride away in awe.

Aerity almost forgot they'd been speaking another language. "Commenting on our crazy weather."

"Aye, I'm sweating today." At the sound of heavy hooves and cheers from the show ring, Wyneth smiled. "Sounds like your sister is entertaining."

They sent their horses off with a couple stable hands and rushed to the show ring on the far side of the stables. Sure enough, Vixie had a crowd of hunters and royal workers watching and cheering as her white horse made clean, high jumps. Vixie's bright hair soared behind her, her face exhilarated. Aerity couldn't help but smile.

Vixie sped past Aerity and Wyneth on the far side, sending up a trail of dust that the girls waved from their faces. As the dust settled, the princess searched the hunters and felt a pang of worried disappointment at the absence of Paxton. Had he left? Her stomach dropped at the possibility, but then she saw Tiern, who was far too happy for a boy who'd been abandoned by his brother. Paxton must be around somewhere.

Tiern watched avidly, cheering with a wide smile as Vixie took to the far path of the ring and began her aerial routine. This part always made Aerity nervous.

Vixie's instructor called out careful praises as Vixie balanced herself on the moving horse, holding the saddle's special handles with her hands and angling her elbows to the center. She raised one leg, toe pointed perfectly, and then the other, until she was doing a handstand atop the cantering animal. Wyneth and the hunters clapped wildly while Aerity held her breath until her sister was safely seated in the saddle again.

Tiern whistled through his fingers.

"It'd be a bit awkward if that one kills the beast, wouldn't it?" Aerity mused. "Seeing as how he now fancies my sister so?"

When Wyneth didn't answer, Aerity looked at her. Wyneth seemed pale as she stared across the ring. She turned and gave Aerity a rather sad smile. "Aye. Indeed."

Aerity looked across to where her cousin had been staring and saw Lord Lief Alvi turn his head away.

"That one, too," Aerity said quietly.

"What?"

Aerity found Wyneth's worried eyes. "Nothing, love." She squeezed Wyneth's hand. "I'm going to take a walk."

"May I join you?" She sounded keen to get away.

"Of course."

They walked arm in arm up the sunny path past the commons, two guards close behind.

"I haven't seen Harrison today," Wyneth remarked.

The thought of their friend warmed her. "Probably napping in his tent. That lad can fall asleep anywhere at any time."

Wyneth giggled. "Aye."

As they approached the commons gates, Aerity stole a peek through the bars. Her stomach flipped at the sight of Paxton's strong back, pulling back his bow and releasing it in perfect measure, hitting the bull's-eye. He surely must have heard their approach, but he didn't turn, nor did Aerity call out. She was glad to see he was still present—for how long, she didn't know.

The fact that he avoided her should have surprised her after their kiss, but it didn't. Aerity now understood why he'd been so reluctant to let her in. She could even understand why he wouldn't want to marry her and be tied to the spotlight in which she lived.

Aerity felt herself slump with the emptiness of her future, her skin dampening with sweat under the heat of the sun. She moved away from the gates.

"Are you all right?" Wyneth asked quietly, pulling her closer.

Aerity shook her head, unable to lie to her cousin.

"What do you need?" Wyneth asked. "What can I do?"

"Nothing," she whispered. There was nothing anyone could do to ease the burning weight in her chest.

"Why don't we visit the bay tip? We haven't done that in ages."

"All right," Aerity said without much enthusiasm.

A nearby guard stepped up. "Your Highness, I'm very sorry, but you're not to enter the woods."

Aerity frowned. "We rode through woods yesterday, and these are within royal lands."

"His majesty only allowed yesterday's excursion because you were surrounded by soldiers and hunters."

Raging seas! Aerity wanted to curse everything. The bit

of woods they'd have to walk through to get to the bay tip was fairly short and had a wide path.

Beyond the guards, a group of hunters surrounding Vixie ambled up the path to enter the commons, their loud voices carrying. Vixie caught sight of them down the walk and called out, waving. She ran in their direction, followed by her guard and Tiern.

Wyneth turned to the guards. "Might we go if hunters escort us with their weapons?"

Aerity groaned. "Never mind. It's not necessary."

"I think it is. You're so tense I think you'll crack."

Wyneth was one to talk. What Aerity really wanted right now was time away from reality, but that could never happen. Being surrounded by hunters, guards, and her beautiful sister and cousin were only serving to remind her of her predicament.

"What say you?" Wyneth asked the guards.

The older and younger guard looked at each other, as the higher-ranked guard responded. "If several hunters will accompany us, that should be fine. But we'll need to send word to the castle."

Wyneth nodded.

Vixie slowed her run as she got closer, her cheeks red and her smile huge.

"What're you doing? Going for a walk? May we join you?" *We*, Aerity noted. Vixie was coupling herself with Tiern, and it made Aerity's neck tighten. This could end badly for her sister, and she didn't want to see that happen.

"We wish to go to the bay tip," Wyneth told Vixie.

"But Father requires us to have an entire army of guards and hunters surrounding us," Aerity added.

Vixie turned to Tiern. "You don't mind escorting us to the tip of the bay, do you?"

"Of course not. It'd be my pleasure." His boyish grin made Vixie positively glow. "I'll go get Pax and my bow."

Aerity opened her mouth to object, but he was already jogging away. She was on the verge of calling off this nonsense and turning back, maybe holing up inside her chambers with a book for the rest of the day. She'd only wanted a quiet stroll with Wyneth, but instead it was turning into an event. Moments later her eyes snagged on a brown head and firm shoulders. Paxton was walking toward them, accompanied by Tiern and Harrison, whose short hair managed to stick up on one side.

"Definitely napping," Wyneth said, making Aerity laugh.

But her mirth fell away when she found Paxton's serious eyes on her. A swarm of buzzing filled her belly.

Wyneth groaned under her breath, an almost imperceptible sound. Aerity looked up to see the broad Lord Alvi joining the other men.

"Yes, everyone join us!" Vixie called.

"Where to?" Lord Alvi asked.

"We're strolling down to the tip of the bay," Vixie said.

The hunters joined them, setting down the path—all except Harrison, who wore an uncharacteristically dark expression. Aerity and Wyneth both stopped.

"Won't you join us?" Wyneth asked.

Harrison stared at the backs of the other three hunters, lips pursed. "I think I'll stay."

Aerity reached for his hand. "Are you certain?"

He gave her fingers a quick squeeze and released them. "Aye. Just . . . be careful. Both of you." His eyes darted to the other men before landing on Wyneth.

Her cousin's cheeks bloomed with color as she broke from his gaze.

"We'll be careful," Aerity promised him.

Harrison ran a hand over his cropped hair and left them to return to the commons.

"What was that about?" Aerity asked. "Did he have a row with one of the other men?"

"Nay, he's grumpy when he's tired." But Wyneth appeared flustered. "Let's just relax. Okay?"

Aerity rushed to catch up as Wyneth jogged down the path toward the two guards, Paxton, Tiern, Lief, and Vixie. The elder princess felt the opposite of relaxed. Vixie and Tiern tramped ahead, while the rest of them followed in awkward silence.

Aerity mumbled to her cousin, "For someone who was so against this hunt, Vix certainly seems fine with it now."

Wyneth pursed her lips in worry as she gazed at Vixie's back.

Eventually Aerity let herself enjoy the peace of the forest

and warmth of the air, trying her hardest not to skim peeks at Paxton and the messy way he'd tied back his hair. Her hands itched to tidy it up for him. She also pretended not to notice how Lord Alvi continued to throw covert glances at Wyneth, who stared straight ahead, unflinching. When the Ascomannian lord caught Aerity watching, he jerked his head forward again as if he'd been scolded.

After fifteen minutes, the trees gave way to open land and skies, and an abundance of shimmering water stretching outward. Vixie began pointing. "This is the entrance to Lochlanach Creek. And see that bit of land out there? That's the tip of the peninsula, so all of that over there is the bay. And then those two—"

"Isle of Loch and Red Crab Island," Paxton finished for her.

He speaks, thought Aerity, *just not to me.*

They all stared out at the strips of barrier islands that protected their coast, along with hundreds of others farther out.

"I see a building on that one," Lord Alvi said, pointing at the Isle of Loch. "It's inhabited?"

The others shook their heads.

"It was used to store trade goods from the outer islands," Aerity explained. "But it was damaged in a hurricane ten years ago."

"I recall that gale," Lord Alvi mused. "It reached its hand clear up to our seaboard. Nasty one, that was."

Aerity remembered bits of being rushed down into the

cellars, Vixie a toddler, and her mother very pregnant with Donubhan. The entire royal family had packed in. Even through the stones, they could hear the howling winds. To Aerity and Wyneth it had felt like an adventure. But lives and businesses were lost while they sat on the cold, stone floor playing pick-up sticks.

Now Aerity watched Paxton's back as he crossed his arms and stared out at the waterways. Vixie and Tiern began to search for hermit crabs along the shoreline. Lord Alvi took off his vest and boots, walked into the water to his waist, and dived in. Wyneth kept her back to him. The guards ignored all of this, surveying the woods behind them warily.

When Lord Alvi came up, shaking his hair, Aerity wanted to ask if the water was cold, but she knew his idea of cold was much different from hers. She wanted to enjoy the outing and the weather, but she couldn't. All around her were the constant reminders of what each of them could not have.

She felt a sourness deep inside her, threatening to make her cry at any moment. She shuffled through the sand and pebbles, walking over soft mounds of seaweed, and eventually sat on a rock next to Wyneth.

"I need to lie down," Aerity said. "My head is splitting."

"Here, let me." Wyneth reached up as if to massage her neck, but Aerity moved away, laughing.

"Nay, Cousin, you pinch."

Wyneth giggled and lifted the hair from her own neck. "I can't believe how warm it is."

They stared out at small waves, the tide buffered by barrier islands.

Deep in the woods behind them came the sounds of movement—the crackle of twigs and rustle of leaves. Aerity and Wyneth stood at once, and five bows were swiftly drawn, arrows pointed at the tree line. The men spread, shielding the unarmed royal lasses. Aerity wished she had her own bow.

"Seas, no, please," Wyneth begged, grasping Aerity's hand with all her might. The princess's stomach had risen into her throat.

In seconds, a small figure came bursting from the trees, laid eyes on the hunters and guards, then gave a loud yelp and fell back, covering his face with an arm. It was a page boy from the castle.

One of the guards yanked him to his feet. "Deep's sake, son, you almost got yourself killed. Call out next time!"

"Aye," said the boy, looking around as the bows lowered. "The king sends message to remind the princesses and lady to be back by dusk."

Aerity rolled her eyes. As if they needed a reminder. As if they could forget the dangers for a moment—oh, how she craved that.

"We'll have them back," the guard promised, and shoved the lad gently back toward the woods. "Rush back now, don't dawdle in the forest."

Tiern and Lord Alvi both chuckled, and a sense of relief blew through their group.

Aerity felt even hotter now after the scare. She gazed longingly at the water.

"Remember when we used to race to the barrier islands?" Aerity mused.

Wyneth laughed. "We were well matched, weren't we? It's as if we took turns winning."

Truth be told, they'd never been competitive with each other. Those races were for fun, and she missed those days of childish wiles.

"You swam to those islands?" asked a deep voice beside them.

The girls looked up into the handsome face of Lord Alvi, his glistening skin on full display. Wyneth quickly averted her sight back to the water.

"Aye, it's not that far," Aerity said.

He nodded. "I could make that in a blink. It's just that most Ascomannian women don't swim, so you'll forgive me for finding it hard to imagine the two of you out there." His smile was so dashing that Aerity's breath caught, and then his words hit her.

"You don't think we can do it?"

His smile turned to a teasing grin. "Well, if you say you can, then I've no choice but to believe you. It's just that all I can picture is a bit of this." He flapped his hands wildly, like an amateur swimmer flailing to stay afloat.

Wyneth and Aerity had to laugh at his ridiculous antics. The others came over to see what was going on.

"I assure you we can swim as well as any men," Aerity said.

"Or better!" Vixie grinned.

The older guard stepped up. "We should get you back soon, Your Highnesses."

"Soon?" Wyneth asked. "But we've got a couple hours before dusk. Plenty of time for a swim." She shot a rather challenging glance toward Lord Alvi and his chest seemed to puff in pride that she'd acknowledged him.

Aerity looked at Paxton, whose eyes were trained on the trees behind her, as if lost in thought. "How about this?" she began. "Us three girls versus you three lads. We race to the Isle of Loch and you race to Red Crab Island—that's what Wyn and I used to do."

"Absolutely!" Tiern rubbed his hands together.

"We can't let you go alone," said the younger guard to Aerity. The older one frowned at him.

"Then come along," Aerity responded.

The two guards exchanged a glance and the younger one spoke up. "I'll swim with them and you keep watch from here."

"I'm not sure the king would approve—"

"Father won't mind!" Vixie said, already peeling off her riding boots. "He knows we've done this loads of times."

"Aye, Your Highness, but that was . . . before."

"The beast has never attacked in daylight, has it?" Vixie challenged. "And besides, it's probably still in the mountains."

The older one let out a huff as if all this silliness were an unnecessary waste of time. Aerity disagreed. Her spirits were already lifting as she bent to untie her boots. At Lord Alvi's side, Tiern took off his shirt. He was lanky but strong.

"Are you sure you want to swim in your riding clothes, Your Highnesses and lady?" asked the older guard. "Perhaps we should return another day when we've had time to prepare and speak with the king."

"Rest your mind," Aerity told him, pulling back her hair with a leather strip from her pocket and tying it tightly. "We'll be to the islands and back in less than an hour and return to the castle straight away. We'll dry a bit on the walk back, and all will be well." She gave him a reassuring smile, but his face remained creased with worry.

Aerity knew if they asked her father to swim to the barrier islands he would refuse. His overbearing rules of late were suffocating her, and she longed for one moment of freedom and peace. Rebellion, even. Plus, she wanted Lord Alvi to eat his words.

She turned to see if the lads were ready, and had to swallow hard. Paxton's back was to them as he pulled his brown tunic over his head and tossed it onto a rock. He turned and immediately locked eyes with Aerity. Under his shirt had been a diagonal strap from his shoulder to waist holding sheathed daggers. She didn't bother looking away. She'd seen his chest before in the healing room, but seeing him standing there at a distance, his trousers hung low and his hair escaping the messy knot . . . all of it made Aerity's body tighten.

She definitely required a cool down. "Right." Aerity cleared her throat and walked to the edge of the water. The others followed. Behind her, the younger guard had taken off his shirt, and was tightening his bow and quiver across his back.

"You're taking your weapon?" Aerity asked. It hardly seemed necessary, and it would surely slow him down. She hoped he didn't expect them to wait if he lagged behind. The hunters had all set their bows on the shore.

"Course, Your Highness. It'll be a challenge, but how else will I protect you from sea vermin?" His tone was joking.

Aerity felt guilty for making him do this. "You honestly don't have to accompany us."

"Aye, but it'll put my mind at ease. Plus, I've got to stay fit so I can race my little lad. He's only three years and already threatening to overtake me." He winked, and Aerity smiled.

Vixie bent and rolled her trousers up until they were snug above her knees. She did a series of squats and arm stretches that made Aerity smile.

"All right, then." Aerity looked down the row at all the swimmers, who watched her in return—the men with serious, competitive faces, Vixie grinning wickedly, and Wyneth appearing flushed with readiness. "Ready? And . . . go!"

The seven of them bolted forward with a resounding, running splash into the cold water.

Chapter 36

Aerity sliced through the water as quickly as her arms and legs would take her, marveling at the sensation of leaving everything behind. She pushed beyond herself, past the burn of her shoulders and thighs, past her stifling fears of the future, past the ache that constantly pressed on her chest.

Wyneth was at her side, keeping pace. Vixie swam ahead of them, the guard behind. Now and then Aerity would turn to stare at the three bodies getting smaller as they swam toward the other barrier island. So far, the lads and lasses seemed neck and neck, but it was hard to tell for certain.

"Come on!" Vixie called to the girls over her shoulder.

Wyneth let out a groan and the two of them pushed

harder, their torsos angling side to side with the movement. Three quarters of the way, as Wyneth began to slow, Aerity wondered if this had been a bad idea. Her cousin hadn't had much physical activity over the past few months.

"Do you need to slow and rest?" Aerity called out to her.

This question seemed to awaken Wyneth and she responded with a loud, "No," picking up a burst of speed. Aerity smiled. Then she had a fleeting, unwelcome thought about the great beast, how well it swam. Panic coursed into the pit of her belly. She scanned the waters, which were as smooth as glass. The fear left as quickly as it had come, and Aerity nearly laughed at herself.

She watched the Isle of Loch as it neared. Almost there. She could see the sand through the water again. Soon it was too shallow to swim, so they stood, struggling to move their numb legs through the surf. Vixie kept shooting looks over her shoulder at the nearby island. Her muscles buzzed with exertion.

"They're standing too! Hurry!"

The girls trudged as quickly as they could, lifting their knees high and making a racket with all the splashing. Wyneth collapsed onto the sand, waves lapping at her feet. Aerity and Vixie saw the hunters standing on the other shore, having turned at the same time as them. They appeared so small.

"A tie?" Vixie shouted. "A bloody tie?"

From afar, Tiern raised his arms and appeared to be pointing down at the men, as if they'd won. Vixie slashed her arms through the air. "Not quite, sir! It was a tie!"

It looked as if their small figures were laughing. Paxton, with his hands on his waist, walked away from the other lads, while Lord Alvi and Tiern talked animatedly. She couldn't hear their voices at all.

"What do you suppose they're saying?" Vixie asked. "Better not be saying they won."

Wyneth sat up, smoothing the wet hair back from her face. "I'm going to need a rest before I can make it back."

Aerity patted her cousin's wet head as the guard made it up onto the sand.

He checked his arrows, seeming pleased that they survived the trip. "Bit colder than I anticipated."

"Aye," Aerity agreed. She closed her eyes and raised her face to the warm sun, grateful for it. "Let's rest and get warm again before we head back."

A warm breeze blew, bringing with it a powerful scent of animal decay. Aerity covered her nose and Wyneth gagged.

"Something's dead." The guard laughed.

He wiped water from the wood of each bow, and then gazed up toward the old, abandoned structure. One corner of the building was partly crumpled, a pile of rubble on the ground and exposed deteriorating wood.

"I take it Your Highnesses will be safe here if I go check out the building? I've never been here."

"Go ahead," Aerity told him. "We're not going anywhere."

"I'll only be a minute. We need to head back straight away."

The girls nodded as he left them. Aerity sat in the sand beside Wyneth and stared with her across the stretch of sea. Tiern and Lord Alvi were lounging back on rocks, while Paxton walked among the wild bushes.

Vixie had walked a good ways down the shore, calling out, "Look at the size of this clam! Do you think it has a pearl?"

"Pry it open and see!" Aerity yelled. Vixie plopped down on the sand with the gray clam in her lap. That should keep her little sister busy. She glanced at Wyneth, who wore a sad expression. They sat quietly a moment. Aerity was tired of all the unspoken things between them. She chose her next words with care.

"Is there anything you'd like to talk about, Wyn?"

Her cousin's eyes were blurred as she continued to stare out, shaking her head slowly.

"Not even a certain handsome man from the coldlands?"

Wyneth peered at her, face tight. "Definitely not."

"All right, then." Aerity sighed and took Wyneth's hand. "Maybe if we don't acknowledge any of this, the breath of the sea will blow over the lands and right all of the wrongs that've come about."

Wyneth shut her eyes. Princess Aerity's heart constricted as a line of tears rushed down her cousin's pink cheeks.

Wyneth whispered, choking out, "I'm sorry, dearest Aerity. I didn't mean to . . . I've tried . . ."

"No." The princess squeezed her cousin's hand. "You've done nothing wrong. It's as if fate is an evil sorceress playing cruel tricks on the lot of us."

Wyneth brushed away another drip of tears and sniffed, then leaned her head against Aerity's shoulder. They sat like that together, their hearts heavy with burden.

From down the way, Vixie groaned. "Ugh, no pearl. What a rotter!" Aerity heard the heavy plunk of Vixie chucking the clam into the ocean. She and Wyneth both giggled.

Vixie jogged over and sat herself down cross-legged next to them. "What's wrong with you two?"

Aerity's first instinct was to put on a smile and protect her sister from unpleasant knowledge, but perhaps it was time she stopped.

"Vix, lots of things are going on in the kingdom."

"I know. Oh . . ." She looked back and forth between them, her face falling. "Were you talking about Breckon? I'm sorry."

Wyneth blinked at the sand.

"No," Aerity said. "I mean, Breckon, he's always there in our thoughts. Since the start of it all." She looked at Wyneth, who slowly nodded. "And I don't want to upset you, Vix, but I need you to be careful where Tiern is concerned."

Vixie shrugged, looking down at the sand. "He's my friend."

"I know. He's great fun, and he's been a nice distraction from all this mess, but just be cautious. Of your heart, I mean.

Sometimes friendship can lead to deeper feelings."

Vixie nudged a half shell with her toe. "Well, he is handsome, I suppose."

Aerity closed her eyes. "See, that's what I mean, Vix. But you must know, if he kills the beast, I will marry him. He will be mine, perhaps not his heart, but he'll be the father of my children, the father of this land's future rulers."

"I see." Vixie dug her toes hard into the sand, her face unreadable, then she stood. "I'll keep my distance. And from all the other hunters, as well, seeing as they're all yours."

Wyneth jumped to her feet, speaking sharply. "Obviously your sister does not want all these lads for herself, and she doesn't want to hold you back from fancying anyone, Vixie. It's time to grow up. This is about the kingdom, not you. Don't make this any harder on Aer than it has to be."

Vixie slumped. "I'm not trying to. Honestly, I wasn't thinking of him as her future husband. He's just the first lad I've ever been around who makes me feel like a normal girl."

Aerity stood now, too. "I understand, and I've enjoyed seeing you happy. I don't want you to end up heartbroken. That's all." She pushed unruly, salty red curls over Vixie's shoulder, thinking of all the festivals the younger princess would attend in the next year. If her sister could keep her heart from settling on Tiern for a bit longer, Aerity was certain she would be just fine.

Vixie crossed her arms and her disappointed eyes went to the expanse between islands, where the lads still rested. Her jaw set in frustration and she kicked the sand, splattering the water. "I wish I could kill this stupid beast myself."

"And then I'd have to marry you." The moment Aerity said it, all three girls began laughing. Aerity adored the beautiful smiles on their faces.

From behind them, a distant scrape and bang sounded, followed by a pained grunt, cutting their laughter short. All three lasses turned their heads. They could see nothing but the building with overgrown weeds and vines.

"What was that?" Vixie asked.

Aerity listened hard. "The guard must have tripped on a faulty board or something."

"Do you think he's okay?" Wyneth asked.

Aerity continued to listen. "I'm sure he's fine. . . ." An uneasy feeling of dread spread through her stomach.

"I'll call him." Vixie sucked in a breath to yell, but a strange sense of foreboding filled Aerity and she covered her sister's mouth.

"No, keep quiet. We'll have a look."

She led the way over small dunes with dense, tall patches of beach grass sprouting upward. "Watch out for stickers." Aerity pointed to a thorny tangle of brush growing close to the ground.

They neared the stone and wood building, which Aerity knew to have entrances on all sides, some open to the elements after the doors had been battered away by storm winds. Another burst of sea breeze brought an unpleasant whiff of death, and the girls covered their mouths and noses.

"Must be a dead gull," Aerity said.

"More like a hundred of them." Vixie waved the air in front of her face.

"I'll check the warehouse side and meet you around back," Wyneth said. Aerity nodded and took Vixie by the arm, keeping her close when she looked as if she wanted to dart ahead, her eyes alight with adventure.

Stepping carefully onto the stone entryway, Aerity peered up at the overhang, which seemed solid. Gazing into the dim entry sent Aerity into a tailspin of nostalgia—the desk that was once used to check-in trade goods, and the open area to the side for keeping files of data. The girls used to play here, pretending to be queens of different lands bringing their foreign goods to barter. It looked the very same, if not smaller.

There was no sign of their guard.

"He must be around back," Aerity whispered. At one time, all large shipments were brought to the back entrance with its wide, warehouse door.

"Why are we whispering?" Vixie whispered.

"I don't know. I'm . . . nervous or something."

Vixie mimicked Aerity's quiet footing around the side of the building. When they got to a pile of cut wood, Aerity stopped.

Why was there a neat pile of wood on this barren island?

Aerity's heart picked up speed. She wasn't afraid of traveling persons, like vagabonds or gypsies—their own mother had been one for sixteen years—but what if outlawed criminals had taken up residence here? They needed to find their guard and Wyneth and get out of there. They could send a group of soldiers out to check the premises later. Aerity pressed a finger to her lips and Vixie nodded, frowning down at the woodpile, then peering around suspiciously. The island was so quiet. Whoever had been there must have ventured away.

As they turned the corner to the side of the building, the scents of decay became so strong that both girls covered their mouths and noses. They approached an open doorway. Aerity pressed a hand back at Vixie to keep her sister there, while she slowly peeked into the dim room, heart hammering.

Tables lined the room, laden with . . . animals? Or, rather, animal parts. Aerity was appalled, a sickening feeling traveling through her. What was going on here? She saw no people, but one of the animals, something that looked like a crocodile's head attached to a bear's body, actually looked to be breathing, though it lay very still.

Aerity whipped her head back around and stood against the wall outside the door, fighting for breaths. A sense of danger blanketed her. When Vixie poked her arm, Aerity shook her head and hissed through her teeth. "We have to find Wyn and get out of here! Right now!"

She took Vixie's hand, trying to creep quickly past the gruesome room toward the corner that would take them to the back of the building. Vixie slowed to a stop, peering in with wide eyes. In a panic, Aerity yanked her sister with too much force. Vixie stumbled and cried out quietly as she fell hard into debris of cut stones and warped metal.

"Vixie!" Aerity bent over and pulled her sister back by the waist, helping her sit in the dirt. "I'm so sorry! I didn't mean to make you . . ." She lost her voice when she saw the gash down Vixie's shin and the blood that seeped down to her feet. Aerity's first flustered thought was to run for Mrs. Rathbrook. *Stupid*. They were on an island, alone!

"Perhaps if we roll your trousers down." Aerity pulled the tight material around her sister's knee, but as she unrolled it and the fabric touched the wound, Vixie shook her head and pushed her hands away.

"No, please!"

"It could help hinder the blood flow."

"It *hurts*."

"Okay." Aerity chewed her lip. "Do you think you can swim?"

"I can try." She winced sharply when she attempted to stand.

"Maybe you should stay here while I go back for help."

Vixie whimpered and glanced back at the doorway behind her. "I don't want to stay here. What's going on in that room?"

"I don't know," Aerity admitted. "We have to keep quiet until we find out. Let's get you up." Her sister whimpered as Aerity helped her to her feet, keeping an arm around her waist. "We'll find Wyneth and get out of here."

They hobbled forward, Vixie bending her injured leg to keep weight off it. When they neared the corner to the rear of the building, a shrill scream pierced the air, causing Aerity's stomach to sink. The sound of old wood sliding and creaking came next, like doors being forced closed. Aerity felt Vixie squeeze her shoulder as the sisters froze, listening to the low, pleading voice of their cousin inside the building. Another deeper feminine voice said something indecipherable in response.

Tremors threatened to overtake Aerity as she put a finger to her lips and pulled her sister silently to the edge. She was fighting to take tiny gasps into her lungs when she peeked slowly around the corner—nobody was in sight. They must have been inside. Again, Aerity moved them forward, both girls creeping along to the large warehouse door.

"I told you, he will not hurt you," came the accented female voice again, alluring and husky—perhaps Kalorian? "Now relax, girl, and tell me who you are."

Aerity slowed their approach. As she got closer she released her sister to lean against the wall, and she found a gap in the door's wood where she could look in. It took a moment for her eyes to adjust to the dimness of the cavernous room. What she finally saw made her slap a hand over her mouth. At the wide entrance area, just inside the rickety old sliding door, was their guard, lying in a thick pool of his own blood. His head was wrenched to the side at an unnatural angle, his stomach torn open.

Vixie leaned in toward the gap and gave a small gasp, her face horrified. Aerity tried to block her view, but she knew it was too late. Her sister had seen the grotesque sight for herself. Aerity got close to Vixie, taking her ashen face in her hands, meeting her eye to eye. "Stay calm," she mouthed. Vixie's eyes watered as she nodded.

Hearing Wyneth fumbling for her voice, Aerity peered in again.

"I . . . I'm . . . L-lady Wyneth, miss."

"Lady?" The woman's voice was calm, even happy sounding. "As in a royal lady?"

Don't tell her who you are! Aerity wanted to scream.

"Y-yes. Wyneth Wavecrest." Curses. Her cousin was rasping, terrified. From Aerity's angle she could see her cousin's profile through the gap, but not the other woman.

"Ah . . . it appears the luck of your seas is on my side," said the woman, delighted.

Aerity heard another sound now, like the snuffling of a giant hog.

"Please, miss," Wyneth begged, but the woman only chuckled.

"The winds have sent you right to me . . . exactly what I need."

At Wyneth's side, a giant creature with both hair and scales flopped itself down and curled up, bumping Wyneth's hip, causing her to scream again and cover her mouth as she stared at it, trembling. Aerity and Vixie both jumped.

What in Eurona was it? Aerity stared, immobilized by fear.

"I told you, girl, he won't hurt you. He's trained to feed only from those with the scent of a grown man like that one who interrupted its sleep."

This . . . oh, seas . . . this was the beast! And it had killed the guard, a good man with a family, a young son. Aerity, flooded with panic, swallowed back the urge to be sick. She had to help Wyneth. She had to get into that room, but this door was the only entrance into the warehouse area. Aerity looked up at the high roof. A weathered ladder was at the corner they'd passed, and sections of the roof were missing, caved in.

Aerity had to move fast. She held Vixie's waist tightly, moving them back to the corner. She spoke in barely a whisper. "I'm going in."

Vixie shook her head in panic. The girl's eyes went up the ladder. "It's not safe!"

"Hold it for me as best as you can while I climb. Then go to the shore and signal the hunters to come." Aerity looked down at her sister's leg. It was worse than she'd thought, gaping red muscle showing. A path of blood trailed where she'd walked. And the side of Vixie's foot was swollen and bruised with scratches. Her face appeared drained, like she might pass out. Aerity wanted to tend to her, but there was no time.

Her eyes skittered around, searching for something she could use as a weapon, but all the fallen branches were too brittle, too small. Finally, she saw a jagged rock the size of her fist. She quietly bent to pick it up and stood again, flattening herself to the wall. Vixie grabbed a nearby rock as well, following her sister's actions. They squeezed the rocks into their pockets.

Aerity took hold of the ladder, giving it a gentle shake. Dustings of particles showered down. Aerity wiped her face and began to climb, testing each rung in her hand before applying weight. A few had to be bypassed. She looked down once to see Vixie's frightened hazel eyes staring up at her as she held the ladder tightly, balanced on one foot. Good girl.

Aerity lifted herself gingerly onto the edge of the roof, which hadn't fared well. She crawled to the largest gap of warped wood and lowered her head. A series of beams ran along the ceiling, crisscrossing. It was a far drop. Across the space, at the back of the warehouse, was a pulley system of ropes that'd been used to lift and lower crates. If Aerity could get to that, she could climb down. Her heart raced as she reached down for a beam, grabbing hold with her fingers and swinging her legs around.

The woman's back was to Aerity; her hair was black and she wore a gown of the richest red. Wyneth was stock-still, continuing to stare down at the thing at her side. It seemed benign, harmless, but Wyneth's face appeared ready to crack, her voice like shaken shards. "It . . . he . . . what do you mean *trained*?"

Aerity still couldn't see the woman's face, but her voice

sounded pleased, as if she was smiling. "All my life I have pre-pared, royal girl, to take back what is mine—my family's, my peoples'. For years I watched my father create and fail, but he never gave up. He went to his grave, laughing with satisfac-tion when he had succeeded at last, not even caring that his own creation took his life. And then I began building on what he had started, allowing it to grow. Now . . . finally . . . I have succeeded." The woman paused, and Aerity let the horror of her words sink in.

She carefully lifted herself onto the beam, as wide as her hand's length, and began to move on her hands and knees. Her breaths felt so loud, but neither Wyneth nor the woman seemed to notice her. She hoped to the seas that if Wyn saw, she'd have sense not to bring attention to her.

"Why?" Wyneth rasped, her shoulders curling in. "Why would you make this thing? Do have any idea what your experiment has done?"

"Oh, yes. Our experiment has shown that my people still hold power, even when others tried to take it from us."

Aerity moved lithely, glancing at her cousin between movements. Wyneth shook her head, horrified, trembling in terror. "Who are you?"

"These hands," the woman mused, not answering. "They look harmless, no?"

Wyneth shook her head, took a step backward.

"Do not move," the woman snapped. "I don't need my beast to kill you. My own hands can do that easily enough."

So the woman was Lashed. And insane.

Aerity's mouth went dry. Her heart was wildly skipping beats, and her mind could hardly process what she was hearing. She had to act fast. With hesitation, Aerity looked down toward the guard, a sense of vertigo temporarily dazing her. This was higher than she'd ever climbed. Finally her senses righted and her eyes bypassed the guard's mutilated torso, locking on the bow sticking out from under his back, the arrows that had half slid from their quiver.

Aerity needed to get to that bow, but she'd have to get past the woman.

"Who are you?" Wyneth repeated.

"Ah, yes. Soon, everyone will know. Now that I have you for bargaining power. I am Rozaria Rocato."

Rocato? As in *the* Rocato? Aerity's hand slipped, and she gripped the beam hard, wobbling. Slivers of wood fell as she flattened herself downward. She swore she saw Wyneth's eyes go up, but her gaze dropped just as quickly.

"R-Rocato?" Wyneth gave a tiny sound of surprise from the back of her throat.

"You fear the name Rocato, do you?" asked the woman. "As you should. I am the granddaughter of Rodolpho Rocato, the greatest Lashed to ever live."

No. Wyneth gave a strangled gasp. Aerity wanted to stay still and listen, but she had to move. She arrived at a junction in the middle of the ceiling. A vertical beam stood in her path. Aerity rose, flat-footed with her toes splayed for balance. She had to crouch so as not to hit her head on the ceiling. She brought her arms around the beam and wound her leg around it until she felt the horizontal beam on the other side. Carefully, she slid her body around, shifting her weight.

The woman's voice filled with dark glee. "Our blood is not diluted. The past five generations of our family have all been Lashed. My great-grandfather helped all the people in his town, and they showered him with gifts. That is how it was meant to be—symbiotic. My great-grandfather was overjoyed when his only son was called upon to be a healer of the royals."

Again, Aerity lowered to her hands and knees to crawl. She wasn't too far from the ropes now.

"If your great-grandfather and grandfather were so well and happy"—Wyneth licked her lips—"then why did Rocato kill the king? You speak of him like a hero. He was a murderer."

"No! The government of Kalor was corrupt. Your books lie. The old king wanted to use the Lasheds' power for his own gain, like work mules. He wanted to tax villagers who were helped by the Lashed. His plan was to own us, to make us his slaves."

Aerity's mind whirred. Was her father aware that Rocato had a son and granddaughter? Surely if those in charge of the kingdoms knew, they would have taken his family into custody all those years ago. Rocato had been captured and put to death after he killed so many people and rallied a civil war of Lashed against Unlashed.

"I didn't know," Wyneth said quietly. "But as awful as that was, Rocato killed everyone who stood in his path. Surely you can see that was wrong as well?"

"My grandfather was . . . passionate. Justice requires sacrifices."

"Don't speak to me of sacrifice," Wyneth ground out, her voice getting stronger. Her shaky hands turned into fists and she glared from the woman to the creature sleeping at her side. "Your idea of justice was to kill the man I loved! I watched it happen!"

The woman sighed. "What you must understand, royal one, is that Unlashed men, with their fear and greed, are the root of evil in Eurona."

"Breckon was not evil. He was a good man. You're nothing but a murderer, just like your grandfather!"

Don't make her angry! Aerity tensed, waiting for the woman to attack, but the woman remained unnervingly calm. Aerity was close to the pulley now. She hoped it wasn't rotted.

"You have been sheltered from the truth. You cannot possibly understand the cost of civility. When the scales of a civilization have been so severely uneven, they must tip in the opposite direction in order to eventually right the weight again. For over one hundred years the Lashed have suffered. Now the Unlashed must suffer. They must gain understanding and respect the hard way. Only then can the scales be even once again. I will make clear to everyone in Eurona the things my grandfather failed to teach."

Wyneth shook her head. "No. No. Not like this. They were all innocent people." Her voice cracked as she shouted. "How can you do this?! How can you create such suffering? This is madness. Why did you come here? Why did you bring your hate to Lochlanach?"

The woman chuckled. "The hate is already here. And I chose Lochlanach because your king is soft where other kings are harsh."

"Our king is honorable," Wyneth insisted with passion.

Aerity couldn't believe what she was hearing. Her hands were trembling violently when she reached the pulley. The ropes were thick, but frayed by time.

"He allows his people to treat its Lashed with disdain," Rozaria said. "With injustice, worse than rubbish."

Wyneth breathed in loudly. "All of the kingdoms are like that. I know, that doesn't make it right—"

"Not all kingdoms, royal girl. Kalor has improved on its own. Naturally. Our people understand the benefits of Lashed. Over time, many villages began to allow magic for healing. Prince Kalieno knows our worth. Though he dared not share his views with other kingdoms, he has lifted the ban on magic already, but he is swift to punish those who use it wrongly. He is a smart man. He has done well to rule while his father ails."

At this, Aerity paused. Could it be true? Lashed were free to work magic in Kalor? Aerity fumbled for the rope, careful to keep her weight on the beam as she leaned. She gave the rope a tug, and to her shock, it slipped completely from the faulty pulley. She barely grasped it in her hands in time to keep it from falling. Her breaths were loud as she righted her weight. Now what was she to do? It was too far to jump.

Wyneth's voice and hands shook wildly as she spat, "I take it you don't murder for fun in your own kingdom, then." She took another step back.

"I'm warning you." The woman's voice took on a sinister edge. "One more move and I will wake my beast to stop you." *No!* Aerity stared down as the woman made a sound from the back of her throat, like three clicks, and the beast quickly raised its head.

Quickly, Aerity pulled the rope with all her might, tying it around the beam with a double knot. Her arms burned and her hands stung. She wiped sweat from her brow.

Wyneth had gone still below. Aerity, panicking, lay flat against the beam and wound the end of the rope around herself, pulling it up and yanking it into a tight, double knot. The rock was heavy in her pocket, the sharp points pressing into her hip.

Aerity slowed her breathing, garnering her strength and concentration. She slid the lower half of her body over the edge, pressing her stomach against the beam. Her feet wound around the rope. It was thicker and rougher than her silks, but the concept was the same. She winced and grasped the rope, lowering herself slowly, with ease and care. She glanced over her shoulder, certain she'd be noticed midair, but nobody looked her way. Wyneth must have spotted her by now, and Aerity was proud of her cousin's cool demeanor in not giving her away. Aerity blessedly arrived at the dirty floor. Without hesitation, she hastened through old cabinets and crates toward the front of the room until she was close enough. She crouched behind a broken crate and pulled the rock from her pocket.

The woman continued talking. "Let me tell you what we are going to do now, Lady Wavecrest. I will send a letter to the king, letting him know I have you. . . ."

Aerity had no plans to let her finish. She stepped out from behind the crate, her arm cocked back. Aerity felt momentarily stunned as she faced the black-haired beauty, whose bright blue eyes widened at the sight of the princess. Before the woman had a chance to wake the beast with her call, Aerity threw the rock with all her might. The rock flew, hitting hard, bashing the woman's collarbone.

All at once the woman fell to her knees with a shrill scream of pain and anger. Aerity scrambled to the ground, yanking at the bow. The beast snorted, its glassy eyes cracking open before drooping closed again. Wyneth gave a cry and rushed to help, pulling up the guard's shoulder so Aerity could withdraw the bow and snatch out an arrow. Still on her knees, the princess had the arrow nocked and the bow drawn straight at the woman, who stared at her from the floor, shock and hatred in her blazing, light eyes.

"Do not make a single sound," Aerity warned her. "Or I

swear I will pierce you without thought."

The woman's full, red lips pursed. One hand was raised across her chest, holding her wound as her eyes darted toward the snoozing beast.

"Not. One. Sound." Aerity's eyes were trained on the woman as she spoke to her cousin. "Wyn, open the door. Help will be here soon."

But when Wyneth wrenched the sliding door open, what they found was Vixie, sitting, her back against the outer wall. "She's passed out!" Wyneth said. Aerity's stomach sank.

Wyneth crouched at Vixie's side and cupped the girl's face. Her eyes fluttered open and Aerity let out a breath.

"Go," Aerity urged Wyneth. "Swim for help."

Wyneth's voice shook as she stood and glared at the woman. "Don't hesitate to shoot her, Aer."

"I won't."

At this, Wyneth ran. Aerity stared down the Kalorian beauty, whose ice-blue eyes darted around with calculated desperation.

Aerity had never been face-to-face with a killer. This woman, in her bright red dress, seemed like some harmless, exotic jewel. But it was she who was at the center of the kingdom's sorrow. At the heart of the evil they'd endured. The people of the land had feared and suffered—the king, Wyneth, Aerity herself . . . all because of this person . . . and this beast she and her father had created, with its strange matted hair and rows of scales. It didn't seem possible. But then Aerity recalled the room of animal carcasses, what seemed like dark experiments, of beasts being cut apart and pieced together with the wrong parts to make something bigger, stronger, unnatural. Oceans deep . . . it was disturbing.

The woman glowered on her knees, as the gigantic creature gave a loud huff. And then the Rocato woman opened her mouth to whisper.

"There are more, you know—"

As promised, Aerity let the arrow fly, filled with anger.

The woman howled in pain and fury as the arrow skimmed her upper arm, tearing through the fabric and gouging her with a deep cut. An injuring shot, dark blood staining her dress, just as Aerity had intended.

Vixie crawled into the room, weakened. She crouched next to the guard, grabbing the bunch of arrows from his quiver and thrusting them toward Aerity. She gave Vixie a grateful glance as she nocked the next arrow, pulling tightly on the bow. Her sister sat back on her haunches, keeping the injured limb straight in front of her.

The woman's words suddenly hit Aerity. More? More of these monsters? She must have meant the ones in the other room. Aerity swallowed hard, trying to think straight.

The Rocato woman . . . Rozaria . . . surveyed the wound on her arm, her face taut. She let out a wail of anger and the beast stirred, whimpering.

"Shut up," Aerity growled.

Aerity and Vixie both watched the beast with bated

breath, but it didn't rise or show any aggression. Its massive head lay on its paws. It was hard to believe how much destruction this sleepy creature had caused.

Aerity had so many questions, but she was afraid to allow Rozaria to speak, afraid she'd make that clicking sound again.

They sat in silence, Aerity's muscles twitching from holding her position, Rozaria staring, her mind obviously plotting.

The sounds of legs splashing through shallow waters drifted into the room. Aerity tensed and the woman's eyes grew large.

"The hunters!" Vixie exclaimed. This word made something click inside Rozaria. She looked around wildly, panicked, then let out another guttural sound of pain.

"Quiet!" Aerity shouted, but the woman continued crying out in garbled mutterings. The beast raised its head. Kalorian. Aerity realized Rozaria was speaking in Kalorian through her cries. She couldn't make them out.

"I said shut up!"

But the woman cried out again as Aerity's face went pale. "Rise and go!"

"Enough!" Aerity yelled, just as the woman shouted again, louder now. *"Aliment!"* she said.

Feed.

The woman dived to the floor as the beast reared up, stretching. Vixie screamed, and Aerity moved quickly in front of her sister, changing her aim from the woman to the beast. But it had no interest in her. It simply turned and trotted from the room on heavy paws, its nails scraping the floor, heading toward the far side of the building, away from the sounds of the hunters.

Aerity turned to the woman, who had scuttled behind an old table. "Where is it going?" she shrieked, pointing the arrow at her. The woman exhaled an exuberant laugh, grinning. "Tell me!" Aerity screamed, panic coursing through her.

The woman laughed louder, her eyes twinkling like gems.

The stomp of footsteps against dirt rang out. Vixie leaned out the door, waving her arms. "Over here!"

Moments later, Paxton, Lord Alvi, and Tiern came to a halt in the doorway, soaking wet, shirtless, breathing hard. Their eyes darted from the guard's body to Vixie's leg to the rest of the room, landing on the partially hidden woman.

"She's Lashed," Aerity warned, heart pounding. "The granddaughter of Rocato. She's the one. . . . She created the beast."

Their eyes filled with confusion until realization and horror set in.

"Great seas," Tiern muttered. He crouched next to Vixie, and whispered, "I'll be okay."

"Created it?" Lord Alvi asked, his forehead creased in disbelief.

"Where is it?" Paxton asked, urgent, eyeing Aerity.

"It's gone, and you don't have your bows, Pax," Aerity reminded him.

He moved forward and grasped Aerity's shoulder. "Where is the beast? Do you know?"

Vixie pointed. "He ran that way! The lady told him to feed!"

"Vix!" Aerity yelled.

The three men ran out to chase the beast, bare feet pounding the ground. The younger princess shrank away from her sister's glare. "They might be able to catch it—"

"And do what? They've no weapons!"

"Pax has knives," Vixie said lamely, her eyebrows lowered in regret.

Aerity's heart rate was out of control, her nerves on edge. She thought of how easily soothed the beast had been in the women's company, of the triple-click sound Rozaria had used to control it. Her idea was a long shot, but she had to try.

"Vix, can you get on your knees?" Her sister moved herself upward, nodding, face strained.

She quickly handed her surprised sister the bow. "Aim at her the entire time."

"You're leaving me?"

"You can do this, Vix. Listen. Do not be afraid to shoot her if she so much as moves a notch or opens her mouth. I let her cry out, and that was a mistake. Kill her if you must—do not hesitate. Wyneth will arrive at land soon and soldiers will be here to help. Do you understand?"

Vixie swallowed tensely, angling her body toward the woman and stretching the bow tight. "But where will you go?"

Aerity wet her lips. "To kill the great beast, once and for all."

The mad mocking laughter of Rozaria Rocato followed her as she ran from the building as fast as she could go, praying all the while that help would reach her sister before she passed out again. Or worse.

Chapter
37

 Vixie's arms were shaking. The harder she focused, the more the room seemed to blur. She'd never been hurt like this before, never felt so weak.

She didn't care for the way the woman stared at her with a deep, wicked hatred—as if she could soar across the room and kill her with her hands at any moment—as if Vixie wasn't in control of the situation, weapon or not. Even with the blood running down Rozaria's shiny dress, the bruise swelling at her collar, the woman had the nerve to smile cruelly at Vixie.

The young princess wanted to shout at her to stop smiling, but she was too frightened to utter a word. That sharp gaze made Vixie feel weak, when all she wanted to be was strong and brave, the way Aerity had been.

"What took you so long?" the woman murmured, never taking her cold eyes from Vixie. "I thought you'd be out fishing forever, missing all the excitement."

"What are you talking about?" Vixie asked, and then shook her head. "Just be quiet! You're not to speak." The woman was mad.

A quiet shuffle sounded from the doorway behind Vixie, and she realized Rozaria hadn't been talking to her at all. She swung her head around and found herself looking up at a young, dark-haired woman holding a wooden board above her head, a fierce expression in her eyes, a jagged scar running down her cheek. Vixie gasped in shock and made to move, but it was too late. The length of wood came soaring down on her with a hard *whoosh*. Vixie felt a blunt impact against the side of her head, which sent her toppling to the floor in a dark fog. Vixie recognized the language of Kalor from her intense studies.

"My apologies, Rozaria," said the new, softer voice. "I had to wait for the hunters to leave."

"Your patience is unmatched, my friend," Rozaria said in delight as the young princess's world went black.

Chapter
38

Paxton swam, his arms on fire, his brother and
Lief at his side. He never took his eyes from the
beast swimming ahead of them, nearing the shore.
As they chased the creature, faint splashing sounded from
behind them. Paxton gave a quick glance backward and could
not believe what he saw. A petite form with slick, strawberry
hair was cutting through the water at rapid speed. His heart
bobbed in his throat with a great bang. What the curses was
she thinking?

"Aerity, go back!" he shouted.

"Why is she following?" Tiern muttered, his breathing
labored.

"No bloody clue." Paxton kept swimming, determined

not to lose the beast this time. He would kill the thing this very day. He had to.

The sight of the mutilated guard resounded in his mind. He couldn't fathom what had happened in that warehouse room, but he'd felt the static charge of Lashed power even before he'd seen the beautiful woman crouched on the floor, menace in her eyes.

"I mean it, go back!" he shouted loudly. This only made her swim faster.

The closer she got, the more he panicked. He didn't want her anywhere near the beast.

Paxton cursed and moved ahead of his brother and Lief as the beast waded onto the rocky shore. It stopped in the gritty surf and shook its body, beads of water flying wide around it. The creature turned and sniffed the air with a snuffled grunt. It snorted loudly, stamping the ground with one front paw. It made no move to flee, only watched them, waiting.

They were on the far side of the tip of the bay, a good ways around the curve of the land where they'd originally set out. From here, they could not see the bay or the marina on the other side. If this is where the beast set out to feed each night, it was the perfect spot, too rocky and rough for boats or swimming.

Paxton slowed and let his lower body sink, finding his feet could touch bottom now. Slick seaweed tangled with his toes.

"Exactly how in Eurona do we plan to stop this thing?" Tiern asked, breathing hard as he stopped behind his brother. Worry filled his voice.

Lord Alvi also halted, weaving his hands back and forth through the ebb and flow of the moving water as he stared at the beast. "You and I will have to hinder it somehow, Tiern. Distract it. Your brother was smart enough to bring his daggers; he should go for the kill." Lief eyed Paxton, whose pounding heart sent vibrations through him. He locked eyes with the Ascomannian lord. Was Lief simply going to give Paxton the kill? The urgent understanding in his gaze gave him the answer he needed. Paxton nodded just as the beast let out a raging snarl, stomping in the surf.

Tiern gave a nervous laugh. "Hinder it. All right, then. Will do. Somehow . . ."

Small, even splashes came from behind them, reminding Paxton that the princess was hot on their trail. He gritted his teeth as she neared.

Lord Alvi grinned tightly. "What brings you out on this fine day, Princess?"

She managed to speak through heavy breaths as she swam. "I . . . can help."

Paxton shook his head in disbelief. If the beast wanted, it could charge into the water now and devour them. He couldn't believe Aerity would take such a foolish risk. She finally reached them and tried to stand, but the water was over her head. She went under and pushed back up with a gasp, batting her hair and water from her eyes. Paxton grabbed her around the waist to lift her.

"Go back," he whispered with urgency. "I'm begging you."

She put her hands on his shoulders to raise herself to his eye level. Her voice shook from the strain, from the cold water chilling her skin. She spoke urgently. "It won't attack women."

The men stared at her and then glanced at the beast that merely stood ashore, watching intently.

"The woman, its maker, she told us. It was created to hunt and kill and feed on men. She's trained it." Aerity gasped for breath. "It was completely harmless toward us in the warehouse. Gentle, even."

Deep seas . . . Paxton looked at Tiern and Lief, whose minds seemed to reel with this information as quickly as his did.

"I'll go ashore and calm it—" Aerity began.

"No, you won't." Paxton shook his head, remembering how the beast could slash a body open with a single swipe of its paw. He couldn't stand to think of Aerity that close to the beast, no matter what she said. "Be reasonable."

"You be reasonable," she shot back. "The beast has never attacked a woman or child. Think about it!"

"It killed one of the Zandalee, didn't it?" Lief asked.

Paxton's jaw set with a tangle of emotion as he realized

what Aerity said was true. "The beast swatted the Zandalee when she shot him. I saw it. He went after the man behind her instead."

"By the tides," Tiern whispered. "All those times in the towns . . . it only killed the men!"

"Even so, you must still be careful, Princess," said Lord Alvi, never taking his gaze from the beast. "It knows it's being hunted by us. It will react badly if it feels threatened, female or not."

"I will be careful," Aerity promised.

Under the water, Paxton felt her hands skim across his chest, and fought the urge to savor the sensation. Her fingers stopped when they reached his weapons. He let her unsheathe the small dagger and slip it in the waist of her leathers. His eyes bore into hers, and she stared back just as firmly. He would let her have the knife, for what small protection it might bring, but he had no intention of allowing the beast access to her. His hands tightened around her waist.

"We will all approach it," he said to her. "Together."

She bit her lip and exhaled through her nose. "All right, fine. Then we'll spread out a bit. But don't even think of trying to push me aside when we get close."

Paxton gave no response. He thought of Aerity standing in the warehouse, her arrow pointed at that woman. The deadly, capable look on her face had resonated deep inside him. "You should know," he told her, "the beast's weakness is the patch of skin at its neck."

Aerity spared him a look of surprise at his forthrightness before staring at the beast closely. "It has no neck."

"Exactly," Tiern whispered. "Damn near impossible to kill."

"It's there," Paxton assured her. "Under its mouth, but it tucks its head."

Lord Alvi nodded, looking from the beast to their group. He touched the four fingertips of his right hand to his forehead before raising them to the skies. "May the stars be with you."

"And the seas with you," Aerity said.

The four of them slowly moved forward through the rocky water. The beast prowled back and forth over the shore, watching and waiting. Paxton had never known the beast to behave this way. Almost thoughtful. He'd also never seen it in the light of the sun, which was now setting. This watchful version of the beast made him even more nervous than the animalistic one he'd encountered before.

They were hip deep in the water, a mere twenty steps from the feared creature.

"Lief and Tiern, take the sides," Paxton said.

"Surround it," Lord Alvi agreed.

Tiern's eyes were wild as he nodded. They silently moved wide to either side, the beast swinging his head toward each of them, snorting.

Aerity moved forward, garnering the beast's attention again. Paxton grabbed her arm, and the beast let out a ferocious growl that split the air. It forged forward, splashing one paw into the water. Aerity raised her palm toward it and let out a series of three clear clicks with her tongue, causing the beast to stop abruptly.

The massive creature watched her with loud breaths, and then it sat down.

All three men stared, astonished. Paxton even dropped the princess's arm in surprise.

"It worked," Aerity whispered.

Paxton's heart, which had nearly stopped, was now hammering. He couldn't believe it was possible that anyone could control the beast, much less the soft and gentle female by his side. He felt humbled to his core, but as Aerity took a cautious step forward, fear surged again. He withheld the urge to grasp her once more.

"Slowly, Aerity," he whispered.

She had locked eyes with the creature, and gave a slight nod.

"Keep the knife poised in your hand," Paxton told the princess. He watched as her hand clutched the handle of the small, sharp blade.

Slowly, so slowly, with movements barely discernible, the four of them began to form a circle around the beast. Time stretched on. The skies dimmed. The beast remained sitting, tense, its hackles of neck fur shooting upward, watching Aerity as she spoke to it in low, firm tones. Paxton tried to make out the soothing words, but he was certain they were a different language.

He had never been so ill at ease. Aerity was far too close to the beast now, and too far from Paxton, whose gut filled with fear. Though Aerity never shrank away, a mere seven paces from the beast now, he could see the sheer terror in her bracing stance. One of her palms was stretched out toward the monster, while the other was at her side, clutching the dagger.

The beast seemed agitated, turning its head slightly to the left and right, as if trying to catch sight of where the hunters had gone. Only Aerity's voice and commands seemed to be keeping it from turning to attack. Aerity took two small steps forward. The beast seemed to relax the closer she got, so she moved again toward it. She was nearly close enough to touch it now. He could see her chest rise and fall faster. Paxton held his breath and readied his body to sprint forward as she closed the distance and allowed the beast to snort against the palm of her hand.

Her voice shook and thickened, as if she might cry. Paxton's chest seized, overwhelmed by his lack of power. He could see Lief at the other end of the shore, and Tiern near the tree line behind the beast, both ready to charge forward at a moment's notice. He could only pray to the seas that it wouldn't be too late.

Aerity's trembling hand moved up, trailing the wiry jawline, past the giant tusks, to scratch near the beast's ear. She murmured under her breath, and her other arm seemed to tense. As she scratched harder, the beast raised its paunchy chin just a touch. An expression of dismay and sadness seemed to cross Aerity's face.

No, Paxton thought. *Don't feel sorry for it—*

In a flash so quick it shocked Paxton, Aerity struck, jamming the blade straight up into the beast's neck. The creature reacted, kicking out, sending Aerity flying backward, landing hard in the rocky water.

Oh, seas . . .

Paxton bolted forward, splashing into the surf and crouching at her side. To his relief, she was breathing, but knocked out cold. He grasped Aerity under the shoulders and knees, and carried her ashore. At his back, the beast let out a vicious wail.

Tiern was the first to reach it, jumping on its back as the raging creature attempted to turn. Tiern's legs flung out as he hung on tight, pulling its head upward to expose the dark, red wound. Lief reached it second, sending a strong punch straight at the beast's throat. As Paxton neared, the beast bent with a quick downward snap of its body, sending Tiern flying, landing on Lief with a grunt.

Before Paxton could stop it, he watched as if in slow motion as the beast reached down, claws flashing, and slashed Tiern deep across the abdomen.

Paxton barely heard Tiern's strangled cry through the *whooshing* in his ears. Tiern's lifeblood poured from his wounds as Lief pulled himself out from under the lad's body, yelling. Tiern's head fell to the side, a look of innocent dismay on his pallid face.

"Paxton, kill the beast!" Lief bellowed.

The creature had stumbled to the side, disoriented, but Paxton had seen it injured before. It would be up and running in less than a breath's moment. He had to choose. If he could simply get his hands on the beast for a solid couple of moments, he could use his magic to stop its heart. Then he would focus on Tiern.

Paxton grasped the handle of his wicked dagger and yanked it from its sheathe on his chest. He charged, preparing to jump, but the beast swiped outward with shockingly fast reflexes, batting Paxton's chest. He landed on his arse in the surf. He jumped to his feet and ran again, this time with Lief attacking from the other side. Paxton leaped up, his hands seizing the back of the creature's scales, but, curses, he was flying to the side again, this time with a face full of sand.

As he pulled himself up, his eyes landed on his brother's still form. The blood glistening. "Tiern . . ."

"He's gone, Pax!" Lief yelled. "Kill the beast!" The creature roared, swatting at its injured neck and stomping the ground in a fit. Panic flared through Paxton's chest, panic that had nothing to do with the beast. He threw his dagger into the sand by Lief's side. "The kill is yours."

The lord shot him an incredulous look before snatching up the blade and jumping to his feet.

Paxton barely registered what was happening around him as he fell to his knees at his brother's side. So much blood. Tiern no longer breathed. His light brown irises were dull, empty. Paxton pressed his hands tightly against the seeping wounds and shut his eyes.

He felt Tiern's blood and skin heat as the burn of life force flowed from his fingers and palms.

"C'mon, Tiern," Paxton murmured through gritted teeth. Heal, mend, fuse, revive, *live.* He felt that extra sense of his seeking, trying to make sense of the mess created by those claws. The rest of the world ceased to exist. He imagined blood moving back to the places it belonged, the walls of organs sealing themselves, muscles rebinding, flesh stitching as if by an invisible seamstress. *Please.* He focused again, pleading, urging Tiern's wounds to heal. And then he imagined Tiern's lifeless heart zapped with a jolt of power.

Under Paxton's hands, Tiern's chest rose with a sudden heave and he turned on his side, gasping, coughing out blood. Thank the seas! Paxton breathed out, fisted his hands, and pressed them into the sand, his heavy eyes falling closed, even as a bolt of energy filled him like the purest, sweetest bliss. But his mind knew better than to enjoy it.

"Pax . . ." Tiern whispered.

Paxton let out a dry laugh of relief at the sound of his brother's voice. He stretched out his hands to touch his Tiern's face, but halted, staring down at the thick purple lines on several fingernails where the paint had chipped off.

He blearily turned his head to the scene beside him on the shore, blinking as it sank in. Lief stood over top of the beast, breathing hard. The hilt of the dagger stuck out of the beast's hairy throat, where it had been deeply lodged. It was unmoving. Their foe was dead, killed by the Ascomannian lord.

Lief turned his head and froze when he saw Paxton watching. He shook his head. "You could have been a prince."

Aye. He could have been a prince with a dead brother. But Aerity . . . deep seas. She would be Lief's wife. Paxton's gut clenched with lost hope.

Lief's eyes went to Tiern, who pushed up onto his elbows, and the lord's mouth fell open. He gawked back and forth between Paxton and Tiern, then his mouth clamped shut, and he chuckled without humor, shaking his head.

"Pax . . . ?" Tiern took in the situation, glancing down at the blood surrounding him, and at Lord Alvi standing over the beast. "What have you done? You . . . you shouldn't have . . ."

"Quiet." Pax got to his feet and brushed the sand from his body as best as he could. His heart raced. His stomach rolled. He looked over at Princess Aerity's passed-out form on the shore. He'd made his choice. What's done was done and now he had to live with it.

"Princess. Princess Aerity . . . can you hear me?"

The deep masculine voice seemed to come to her from afar, like a soft dream of foreign lands she'd read about in books. She tried to move, and a shooting pain sang out from her ribs, urging a moan to rise from her throat. She'd only felt this sort of pain when the horse had broken her arm all those years ago.

"Sh, Princess," said the deep voice again. But it wasn't the voice she sought. "The beast is dead. Boats are coming. Be still for now."

Dead? Boats? Aerity blinked her eyes, feeling the grit of sand and salt covering her body. She tried to sit up, but gasped against the pain and grabbed the spot under her breast. Definitely broken ribs.

Slowly, the horrific events came back to her—the beast's dull, trusting eyes; the feel of tough flesh as she'd shoved the knife into its neck. Her stomach turned, remembering. And then she'd watched it react in pain, recalled its great hind leg rising, and felt the crack of her ribs, the wind at her back, the water filling her ears.

She blinked again at the dark gray sky, stars just beginning to sparkle to life. And then a shudder violently overtook Aerity's body. She nearly retched as realization dawned. She'd left her little sister, weakened, in the building with that madwoman. Had help arrived? Was she safe? And, oh, seas . . . the beast . . . who had killed it?

Aerity turned her head and saw Tiern sitting at the edge of the shore, his knees pulled up. But it had been Lord Alvi's voice she heard upon awakening. . . . *The beast is dead* . . . and here sat Tiern, alone and upset. Where was Paxton? Ignoring the pain, Aerity's head whipped to the side. There was the beast, truly dead by the water, with Lief standing over it. Paxton was nowhere. Aerity felt bewildered as bits of reality shook her. She was afraid to speak, to learn what had happened.

Tiern stared down at the water that splashed over his bare feet. She'd never seen him look forlorn like this, as if lost in dark thoughts.

Fear seized her. Her eyes adjusted as she peered around. A boat was being rowed rapidly around the bend toward them.

Farther behind it, great flames rose from the distant Isle of Loch, thick smoke licking the sky.

"Vixie . . ." Carefully, Aerity rolled and pushed up on her elbow, one hand in the sand to anchor herself. Down the shore, Lord Alvi was still leaning over the beast's stiff form, doing something that she couldn't figure out. Her eyes darted around, panic pumping through her.

"Vixie," she whispered. It hurt to talk. "They need to get Vixie." But nobody could hear her.

As the boat neared, and an anchor was thrown out, Aerity heard a guard shout, "Has the great beast been slain? Is it finally done?"

Lord Alvi, stood, in all his glory, holding the beast's massive head in his hand. His face was fearsome. Aerity's breath caught as he shouted, "The beast will no longer ravish the lands of Lochlanach! I have killed it this very night!"

Cursed seas . . .

The boat full of men roared a unified cheer, in direct opposition to the feelings raging inside Aerity. Tiern's head hung. Men jumped out, splashing, running ashore to congratulate Lord Alvi and thank him.

"Tiern!" the princess shouted, crying out in pain, but he couldn't hear her over the men. Surely they wouldn't be celebrating if something had happened to the younger princess. Aerity pushed to her knees and yelled again, "Where! Is! Vixie?" One soldier turned, blanching at the sight of her, then jogged over.

"Are you okay, Princess Aerity? I'm so sorry, I didn't notice you—"

"Never mind me. Where is my sister?"

He nodded. "Princess Vixie was rushed by boat to the castle docks."

"Thank you," Aerity breathed painfully. Having seen that she was now awake, Tiern stood and rushed over, lowering himself to her side.

"It's all right," he told the soldier. "I've got her."

"Another boat is coming," the man told Aerity. "We'll have you back to the castle and fixed up in no time." She nodded, and the man left them.

Aerity pressed a hand against her ribs. "Tiern?"

He faced her, his long hair hanging limp. "Aye?" he whispered.

She could barely force the words out. "Where . . . where is Pax?"

He dropped his eyes, ashamed. "Gone. He has left."

Aerity's mind spun. "He's alive?"

Tiern nodded. Aerity's heart plumped with relief, only to sink again as she realized he'd truly left, just as he promised. Tiern glanced over at the celebrating men, and shook his head. "I'm sorry, Princess. It's my fault. Pax should have had the kill. It was his, but he gave it to Lief. . . . He should have let me die."

A chill of realization tingled down Aerity's spine as she took in Tiern's blood-soaked skin and trousers. Her head snapped up to Lord Alvi, midshore. Amid the animated talking, his blond head turned to her and met her eyes. His face was firm—the face of her husband to be. He gave her a nod of acknowledgment and turned his attention back to the men.

"No," Aerity whispered. A deep longing for Paxton expanded within her. "Seas, no. Please." Her stomach knotted so hard that it sent another shooting pain through her ribs.

Tiern pressed his face into his hands.

Just then voices from a second boat cast across the waters. Aerity heard her name being called. She looked up to see the Ascomannian hunters, the Zandalee, Harrison, and Wyneth. Her cousin was waving, her forehead scrunched with concern. The men on the boat burst into cheers and Wyneth followed their gazes to Lord Alvi, still holding the beast's head high. The lord was watching the boat as it neared, but his eyes were hardly on his men. He slowly lowered the beast's head. Wyneth tore her sight from him, focusing on Aerity instead. Harrison stared at Lief with a set jaw.

The princess allowed one pair of tears to fall before she wiped them away with the back of her sandy hand and swallowed hard. She had to be strong. This was a good thing for the people of their lands. She would keep telling herself that, and perhaps someday this feeling of dire regret would dissipate. Perhaps someday her own bitter disappointment would be swallowed up by all the good that would come from today's events.

But for now, those things were still wholly present and alive within her.

When Wyneth's boat touched shore, guards leaped out and were surrounding Aerity within seconds, gently lifting her, wrapping her in a blanket. And then her cousin's beautiful face, flushed with splotches of cream and rose.

"Did they catch Rozaria?" Aerity asked.

"Aer . . . she's gone. That Rocato woman somehow knocked out Vixie and fled—"

"Knocked her out?" Aerity shouted in fury, grabbing her chest.

"How badly is she hurt?" Tiern asked, jumping to his feet at the mention of Vixie.

"She's fine," Wyneth quickly amended. Aerity nearly collapsed into her cousin's arms. "Vixie's safe, and they'll catch that woman. Everything will be all right. In time, it truly will."

"I should have been here," came a low voice beside them. Harrison was still staring at Lief.

"Harrison." Aerity touched his arm. He turned to her, and his eyes cleared.

"You shouldn't be walking, Aer." He bent and gently lifted her into his arms, cradling her. Under his breath he asked, "Where is Paxton?"

"He's gone," she whispered back.

"I'm sorry."

Aerity pressed her face into his shoulder.

"Let's get the princess back to the castle," ordered a guard.

"We'll be at the boat in a moment," Aerity told him. "Wait for us there." The guard left as the Zandalee jogged over. Zandora's eyes scanned Tiern from top to bottom.

"Your brother is gone?"

He nodded, looked down. Zandora crouched at his side. "Whose blood covers you, Tiern Seabolt, if you did not slay the beast?"

His mouth opened, then shut as he stared at her. His eyes lifted, searching, as he turned toward Harrison, Aerity, and Wyneth. He shook his head.

"Wade into the water," Zandora told him. "Wash as much of your blood away as you can before the men notice."

She knows. Aerity's heart rate picked up speed. Tiern obeyed, moving out to the water to wash. Zandora turned and bowed her head at Aerity. The other two Zandalee did the same.

"It was an honor to serve your kingdom. Now we must go."

Aerity nodded, realizing the hunt was truly over. "Thank you," she said quietly.

"What's going on?" Harrison asked. He watched Tiern washing in the water. Wyneth met Aerity's eyes. She could trust them.

"The beast nearly killed Tiern. But Paxton . . . he's Lashed. He saved Tiern, and Lief took the kill."

Wyneth's eyes bulged. Harrison's arms slackened, and

Aerity yelped as she felt herself slip. He quickly flexed and lifted her again. "Sorry . . . I just . . . deep seas. I had no idea." He kissed the top of Aerity's head, and she pressed her face into his shoulder.

"Oh, my seas," she heard Wyneth breathe.

A sense of finality lay inside Aerity. It was over. Paxton was gone. She would marry a man who felt more for her cousin than he did for her, a man who cared more for his glory than anything else. And possibly worst of all, a madwoman was on the loose again.

"Take me to the boat," Aerity whispered. Harrison obliged.

The sounds of celebration—Ascomannian chants and Lochlan praises—were so out of place in Aerity's sluggish mind. She could not bring herself to cheer for the death of this beast, when it felt as if her troubles were merely beginning. But the kingdom was safe, and that's what mattered.

A cold wind blew across Aerity's face as Harrison settled her into a seat, her hair whipping against her skin, and all traces of warmth from earlier that day disappeared.

Chapter

40

 South.

Paxton headed south along the coast of Loch-lanach.

He regretted that he couldn't return to royal lands to retrieve his few belongings, especially his bow. A shirt and boots at the very least. But that was the only regret he would allow himself to contemplate. He kept thoughts of Aerity, Lief, and Tiern at bay. If he did not acknowledge such things, they would eventually fade from his heart. Surely that was how it worked.

These feelings. They were all different for him. He was accustomed to a low burn of anger in his life, always anger. But these other things, he didn't know how to deal with them.

They threatened to stop his breath. To make him behave foolishly. So it was best not to contemplate them. Those people, they were now his past. He could not linger. He would build a new life. One in which he kept to himself and let nobody in, as he should have done all along.

In the childhood summer he'd spent with his grandmother, he'd asked her if there was anywhere in all of Eurona where people like them did not have to hide. His question had seemed to surprise her.

"My dear boy," she'd said, "people in all the lands fear the Lashed after the uprising of Rocato. But it's said there are tribes of Lashed hidden in the jungles of Kalor where they still revere our kind—where Lashed can gather and work their magic in peace."

"Where in Kalor?" he'd asked, fascinated.

His grandmother had chuckled. "Oh, Pax. It could be folklore for all I know. It was just something I heard a neighbor woman say to my mother in passing when she thought I was too young to understand, but she said it like it was a frightening place. Something about Rainiard Lake in the hotlands. If it were true, it could be overtaken by now."

Paxton had always held tight to those words. Keeping them in his pocket as a plan he thought he'd never have to use.

Now, he was Rainiard Lake bound. And from what he'd learned about the area, it was remote. He would have to travel through thick jungle rumored to be inhabited by wild people and fierce animals. Even Rainiard Lake itself was said to be riddled with giant biting fish and bugs that could kill with a single sting.

He'd also contemplated finding the Zandalee tribe down in southern Zorfina, but that would mean traveling through deserts, a thought that troubled him more than stinging bugs.

Both were places of possible freedom, and neither would be easy to get to. He wasn't holding his breath about any of it. He would travel south and take this journey day-by-day. Certain death awaited Paxton around every corner, even in his seemingly safe homeland of Lashed fearers. He wasn't afraid anymore. It was only a matter of time before death took him. Paxton mused about which one of the many forms would be the one to steal his last breath.

He became accustomed to solitude as he hiked. His first night he slept in the mossy space of a fallen tree, blanketed by leaves. He woke dirty and itching the next morning, still bare of chest and feet. He muddied himself in patches, careful to press mud into the cuticles and base of his fingernails. His second night he found an abandoned barn with bug-ridden hay.

His third day he wandered onto the outskirts of a small fishing village with two men tending their oyster beds. They looked him up and down, suspicious.

"My apologies, sirs," Paxton began. "My boat was overturned during the night and I had to swim ashore." He looked down at himself, feeling guilty for the lie. "I'm a bit worse for wear after sleeping in the woods. I'll work for a pair of boots and shirt, if you require a hand."

The younger man looked down at Paxton's feet, as if to gauge the size, and nodded.

But the older man frowned. "Ye sound northern, ye do."

"Aye," Paxton said. "Indeed, I am."

"Should 'ave been fishing yer own waters, then."

Paxton nodded, and the younger man gave a roll of his eyes. "Sure then, don't mind him," he said, hitching a finger at the older man, who grumbled and poked a bag of oysters with his long stick. "Ever farmed an oyster bed?"

Only his whole childhood. "Aye, sir. I can do anything seas related that you need."

The man pointed out at the cove. "This here is all our land. You'll have to work from now until sundown to earn a pair of boots, though."

Paxton nodded. "I can do that. I give you both many thanks."

"We don't have boots to spare!" the older man shouted.

"Aw, come now, Papa. We could use the help. Didn't you say just this morn you wish you was fishing instead?" He patted the stooped man on the shoulder to lead him away, giving Paxton a few last bits of information over his shoulder as he went.

Paxton nodded and set to work immediately. He turned the bunches of oysters in their beds to smooth out the calcified edges and create deeper grooves for the growing flesh inside. His body numbed to the chill of the water and breeze, and he soaked in the moments when the clouds dispersed, allowing sun to shine down on his back and shoulders.

As the sun began to set, Paxton heard a single set of foot-steps rustling along the path. He quickly muddied his hands, which had been cleaned by the water. He stood, his muscles sore, and faced the younger man who looked around the marshy cove before giving a satisfied nod.

Paxton came ashore and the man held out a used long-sleeved brown tunic and a worn pair of boots with sturdy soles.

"These were my brother-in-law's. They might be a tad big, but they're all I could find."

"Thank you." Paxton took them, grateful.

"Would you care to stay for supper?"

He longed to accept their hospitality, but he knew it would come with an array of questions.

"I appreciate your kindness, but I need to head back before my family worries."

The man nodded and pulled a cloth from his deep hip pocket. "I thought you might say that. Here is a bit of food. I wish you safe travels. Blessings of the seas."

Paxton gave a small bow of his head just as his stomach growled. They both laughed. "Blessings to you and yours, as well."

The man left him to dress, and Paxton ate the slice of grainy bread; sharp cheese; and dried, salted fish as he walked. He was famished but forced himself to eat slowly. He would sleep outdoors again, drinking from fresh springs. And each day he would work to try and earn food and money to buy a bow and new daggers. He couldn't face the foreign lands without protection.

But unfortunately there was no protection against the things that hurt him the most—the things inside his heart that left his chest vastly empty, hollowing him with a sense of loss, forcing him to remember when all he wanted to do was forget.

⌒⌒⌒

Paxton was fast asleep on a bed of leaves when a snap awoke him. He rose to his knees, grabbing the makeshift spear he'd made. Clouds covered the sliver of moon. Paxton squinted into the darkness. A low, feminine chuckle sounded from the depths of the night. He pulled back his arm as a form solidified through the trees.

Paxton exhaled and sank back on his heels. "Zandora, I nearly pierced you through."

"With what? That stick? Men . . . always with the dramatics."

Paxton grinned, despite his racing heart. "What are you doing here?"

"Tracking you, of course."

"Why?" A moment of apprehension went through him. Had the king asked her to find him? Did they know he'd worked magic? But no, this was Zandora. He shook away his worries.

"Would you prefer to hunt with that stick and sleep on

the ground forever, Paxton Seabolt? Or join us on our return journey to Zorfina?"

Relief and the promise of companionship settled over him. "I will join you."

"I had no doubt, Lashed One."

He stilled, though there was no threat or judgment in her voice. He wasn't certain how she'd found out—if it was common knowledge now, or if Tiern had confided in her—but he supposed it didn't matter.

Zandora whistled, and moments later her two sisters appeared, two on horseback, one leading Zandora's horse. She said something to them in Zorfinan, and the older sister tossed Paxton his pack.

"Ah, bless you." He'd never been happier to see his material things.

"Now. Move over and share your leaves."

Paxton obliged. As the sisters joined him on the ground, he wondered what Zandora would have chosen in his position: to kill the beast or save one of her sisters. Did she think him a fool, like Lord Alvi, the future prince of these lands? Paxton cursed himself for the trivial thoughts. It was all inconsequential.

He could not allow himself to look back, to wonder what was happening at the castle, to imagine Lief and Aerity . . . no.

He could only move forward.

Chapter 41

Aerity stood before her chamber mirror in a gown of the purest, softest white—her betrothal dress for the engagement ceremony. Her gut clenched at the merry sounds of voices outside the castle walls. It had been one week since the beast was slain. Rozaria Rocato had not been found, but neither had there been any new attacks.

In a meeting with her father that morning, the king told her he hoped all of Rozaria's experiments had been burned on the island, but Aerity wasn't holding her breath. Soldiers were out searching for the Lashed woman to punish her for her crimes. In the meantime, word had been sent to Kalor of their murderous citizen, and King Charles awaited Prince Kalieno's response.

"She could have lied about being an heir of Rocato," the king told Aerity in his office. "She could be lying about all of it." King Charles had seemed especially appalled by the thought that Prince Kalieno might be going against the mutual laws of all Eurona by openly allowing magic.

"I don't think so, Father." Aerity pressed a hand against her abdomen, which had been corsetted tightly under her dress.

"Rocato was killed during the uprising. No one has ever spoken of him having a family."

"Perhaps they did not know he had one," Aerity said. "If he always had a rebellious heart, maybe he kept his family hidden for their safety."

The king leaned against his desk, running a hand over his short beard. "Aye. It could be. We shall speak of her crimes to no one. Only the royal family and my elite advisers shall know this beast was created at the hands of a Lashed."

Aerity shivered and nodded, understanding. The people could not find out or there'd be an uprising against innocent Lashed.

"We will find her, Aerity. It's a blessing from the sea that you girls are safe and the beast is dead. Lord Alvi will make a fine husband—your mother and I are glad for such a handsome match. Our ties to Ascomanni have been strained over the years. This arrangement will greatly help. A win-win for all." Aerity's stomach clenched at his happy assurance. He had no idea how much she and Lord Alvi were *not* a fine match. She gave a curt nod and left her father's office.

The royal lands had been opened to the public for the betrothal ceremony. Today, the king would publicly announce Aerity's engagement to the foreign lord. Normally, the people of Lochlanach were not keen on change—Lochlans tended to be distrustful, traditional people. Lord Lief Alvi, however, was a special exception. Not only were the women swooning over his handsome, regal airs but every person felt indebted and grateful to him for killing the beast that had terrorized them. The curfew had been lifted. People celebrated with bonfires into the night and revelries grander than any holiday.

But within the castle there were no raised spirits. The Lochsons, Baycreeks, and Wavecrests could sense sadness emanating from Princess Aerity and Lady Wyneth. Though they did not know all the reasons for the darkness surrounding the girls, each family felt it.

"They're traumatized by what happened on that island. . . ." Aerity had heard Lady Ashley whisper to Queen Leighlane as the women tried to make sense of the castle's mood.

"Aye," the queen had answered. "All three of them facing the beast . . . My own Aerity playing a part in its death! Can you imagine? I've been on my knees, thanking the seas each day that they are still alive."

"Perhaps they weren't killed," Lady Ashley whispered, "but I daresay a great damage has been done. They haven't spoken more than a few words this week."

"Indeed . . . but that shall pass with time. They will heal."

Aerity's mother had sounded so certain. Yet the queen knew only half the story.

Aerity closed her eyes against the reflected image of herself, the intricate braid winding around her head and falling over her shoulder. A bejeweled circlet draped around her head. Across her forehead, a round diamond hung heavily on her brow. She certainly looked the part, though she didn't feel it.

She and Wyneth had scarcely made eye contact all week. Even when they sat side by side at meals. One of them would reach beneath the table and take the other's hand, squeezing tightly, but they did not speak or meet each others' gaze.

The last thing the princess wanted was to marry Lord Alvi next month at the winter gala.

Lost in her thoughts, the knock at her chamber door made Aerity jump. Everyone should have been in High Hall by now.

Aerity crept to the door and opened it a crack. Her breath caught at the sight of Lord Alvi himself, blond locks tucked behind his ears, and the finest rabbit furs lining his vest and boots. Aerity opened the door further and peeked around him—not a soul in sight. Still, it wasn't proper for him to come to her chambers, or the women's hall at all. Behind him, Aerity saw Caitrin poke her head around the corner, her eyebrows raised and a questioning, guilty look on her face.

Aerity sighed and nodded, stepping aside to let him in. She kept the door open a crack.

Lord Alvi took one of her hands between both of his warm ones. His light blue eyes were like cool, melting ice. "You look lovely, Princess."

His presence made her heart race with nervousness. If it weren't for the complication of Wyneth, or the fact that her heart was with Paxton, she might have been able to feel something for this brave, powerful, handsome man. But as it was, she could not see him as her own.

Her throat was dry, making her voice a raspy whisper. "Thank you."

"I know it's not me you prefer to see before you."

Aerity dropped her eyes to his large hands, saying nothing.

"Did you speak to Tiern about what happened that night?" he asked gently. Aerity said nothing. "Do you know how I came to slay the beast when the one you loved possessed the weapon?"

Aerity looked up, her throat closing. "I don't want to speak of it."

He continued, carefully, as if he hadn't heard. "The beast nearly killed Tiern—actually, I think he had taken his final breath. Paxton Seabolt chose to save his life. He gave me the knife. He is Lashed, Princess."

Aerity stared into his eyes, a fiery passion rising up in her at the judgment in his voice. "I know who he is." She pulled her hand away.

"You knew he was Lashed?" His voice sounded accusatory.

She felt her lips purse in anger. "I knew, aye."

He wore a bewildered expression. "And you believed your people would tolerate it?"

"I believe my people need to gain a better understanding of the Lashed. Many changes need to be made in this kingdom." She lifted her chin.

"A revolutionary, are you? All right then, Princess, perhaps you are not afraid of his magic. But does it not bother you that he gave you away so easily?"

Aerity felt as if she'd been kicked by the beast all over again. *Gave you away . . .* "No. He didn't give me away, he saved his brother." If Aerity had had to choose between Vixie's life and marrying the man of her choice, she would choose her sister. She could not fault Paxton for his decision, no matter how it saddened her.

"Do you have brothers, Lord Alvi?"

"I do."

"Would you not have saved any one of them in that situation?"

His eyebrows smoothed in confidence. "I was bound by my duty to kill the beast. Any one of my brothers would have understood that and wanted me to forsake his life to claim the slay. For the honor of our family."

Aerity had heard tell of the honor-bound attitudes of the coldlands people. She'd always thought it a romantic ideal, to be so sacrificial for one's family and land, that is, until now.

"I respect our differences, Lord Alvi, and I hope you can, as well. Here in Lochlanach we choose to honor individual lives over family glory."

Lord Alvi gave a small nod. "So I've gathered."

Aerity swallowed and stepped back.

"Very well," Lord Alvi said quietly. "I shall leave you until the betrothal ceremony." He watched her curiously a moment longer.

Aerity gave a curtsy as he left. She stood there, alone, and suddenly cold as stone at the thought of entering High Hall. It would be filled with smiling faces—hunters and royals that had traveled down from the coldlands, all of her family and Lochlanach's elite. Aerity pressed a hand over her mouth, afraid she might be sick. With her other hand she gathered the bottom of her dress and ran from the room toward the only person in the castle she could stomach seeing at that moment—the only person she felt would understand what she'd lost.

She ran, her slippered feet sliding on the smooth stone. She took the spiraled steps up two at a time, panting when she reached the top. The guard stepped aside. When she knocked on the wooden door, her knuckles were numb from holding her skirts so tightly.

Mrs. Rathbrook opened the door, her eyes wide. "Princess Aerity! What in Eurona is the matter? Shouldn't you be at the ceremony now?"

"I—I don't . . ." Aerity lowered her voice to a whisper.

"Paxton Seabolt . . ." They both glanced at the guard, who stared straight ahead at the staircase.

Mrs. Rathbrook grasped her by the elbow and gently pulled her in, closing the door tightly behind her. "Come and sit."

"I'm sorry," Aerity said. Her heart was beating too hard, and her breaths were coming too fast. She sat and bent forward, wrapping her arms around her middle. "It's just that . . . he's Lashed, and he's run away, and I don't know what to do. I—"

"Try for deep breaths, dear," Mrs. Rathbrook said. "You're in a panic."

Aerity tried, feeling her heart slow.

"Where would he go?" Aerity mused, tears burning her eyelids. "Why does it have to be like this? He shouldn't have to hide! He hasn't done anything wrong!"

"Sh, love." The woman rubbed her back.

Aerity looked up into Mrs. Rathbrook's pained eyes. She looked as upset as Aerity felt.

"What can be done?" the princess asked. She'd never felt so small. So powerless. The beast was nothing compared to the notions of hatred, fear, and prejudice against Lashed throughout the lands. "If we could only show people, and explain that Lashed are not dangerous . . ." Mrs. Rathbrook looked upon her pityingly.

And then Aerity remembered Rozaria Rocato, the essence of danger, and she shut her eyes.

A strange noise came from the quiet halls below. Faint at first, then growing louder. Shouting. Aerity stood. She and Mrs. Rathbrook grabbed each other's arms, listening. Next came terrified screams and stomping feet.

"Great seas," Mrs. Rathbrook whispered. "We must hide you, Princess."

But Aerity was already swinging the door open. The guard was gone.

"Princess Aerity!" Mrs. Rathbrook reached out for her.

"Stay here," she told the woman. "Lock this door!" Aerity shut it and ran down the stairs. Officer Vest was at the bottom, watching the chaos with confusion.

People ran into the castle with expressions of terror, screaming, some dressed in finery, some in common clothes.

"Princess, you mustn't go out there," Officer Vest told her.

Aerity grabbed her skirts. "Please go back up and guard her with care." She darted away, pushing through the people.

"It's out there!" a commoner shouted.

"Shut the doors!" Aerity heard a familiar voice call down the hall. Harrison!

Aerity's heart was banging. She ran with the crowd. People stopped, jostling into one another, trying to decide where to go.

"To the left!" Aerity yelled over the crowd, pushing her way through. "High Hall!"

People around her gasped and began to murmur.

"The princess!"

"It's Princess Aerity!"

They let her through and she led the people to High Hall. Her silks no longer hung in the room, which had been transformed for the grand celebration. Her mother and father stood at their throne, surrounded by guards, demanding to know what was happening as people poured in. Aerity ushered townsfolk in, and when the last person had squeezed through, she shut the doors.

"Bar them!" she ordered a guard.

"What is happening?" King Charles shouted.

"A beast!" The commoner's voice trembled. *Seas, no.* Aerity pushed through the people and found the townsman, not much older than her own father.

"Please, sir," she said. "Come forward and speak to the king." He appeared dazed with fright, but allowed Aerity to lead him forward.

"Quiet!" yelled a guard to the restless crowd.

When Aerity and the man stopped in front of her parents, she noticed Lord Alvi and his family for the first time. They were each wearing furs, their hair like spun gold, their faces fierce and warriorlike. One of the men had hair to his waist, an extraordinarily broad chest, and the most massive gold crown Aerity had ever seen—King Dagur of Ascomanni, and uncle of her betrothed. Lord Alvi moved closer to hear, his eyebrows furrowed.

"Tell us what you saw outside the castle," Queen Leigh-lane said to the commoner.

The man fell to a knee and lowered his head. "A—a creature, Your Highness. Larger than the grandest horse you've ever seen, but . . . but . . . its body was like . . ." He fought for composure, shaking his head against the image.

"Go on," the king said. His face was deathly pale.

"Its neck and head were like a swamp lizard, Your Majesty. Its teeth so large. It moved fast, like a racing horse, tearing at men with its teeth as it passed, taking whole heads in its mouth!"

Great seas.

Murmurs of disbelief and fear filled the room. The king grabbed his forehead while the queen covered her mouth. Lady Ashley wrapped an arm around Wyneth, crushing her to her chest.

"You are certain of what you saw?" The king asked.

"It's true." Harrison stepped up, bowing at the waist. "I saw it from afar, Your Majesty."

"It was unnatural!" shouted a woman. "I saw it, too!"

Others called out their tales. Aerity felt a heavy, sour weight fill her stomach as she met Lord Alvi's eyes. His fists flexed, causing his arms to ripple with a need to go—to hunt and kill this new foe.

A series of echoing bangs came from the arched wooden doors.

"A soldier with a message!" called the door guard. The

king gave a nod for him to open it. The guard did so, taking a scroll and reclosing the door.

"He says there are more of these notices," the guard said from the entrance, holding up the scroll. "Messages posted throughout the land."

Donubhan dashed from the queen's side. He weaved through the crowd, taking the scroll, and rushed back through, handing it to his father.

The king scanned the parchment. His eyelids fluttered closed and back open. His jaw set. The room went silent as the king poised to speak.

"In this time of sorrow, we must not panic. I beg you."

"What does it say?" someone behind Aerity whispered.

The king looked to his wife. "If these parchments have been posted, word will spread."

"Aye," the queen said quietly. "Be forthright with the people. We must maintain order with truth and fact."

The king took several labored breaths before composing himself. "It seems that, unbeknown to all, Rocato had a son who had a daughter."

Voices and gasps rose up. Harrison called out, "Quiet!"

Aerity wanted to scream at her father not to read it, though she knew it was no use if the notices were all over the kingdom. King Charles raised his voice. "Rozaria Rocato is her name, and she has left us a message."

Horrified murmurs of "Rocato!" rippled through the crowd.

"What does it say?" a man called out boldly.

"Again, I beg you to remain calm," the king said, shushing the murmurs. "It reads: 'For each week that passes, my pets will devour seven men, one for each day. . . .'" The king stopped to swallow. "'I created them. I control them. This punishment will only cease if the laws of your land are changed, beginning with a public burning of your Lashed lists. Each kingdom will face these same requirements and same consequences. Lashed must be given equal rights and allowed to use their power without punishment, or all the lands will suffer.'"

A beat of stunned silence fell, and then a commoner woman screamed, "Never!"

A blast of voices filled the room.

"You cannot bargain with this madwoman!" bellowed the king of Ascomanni. "Do not bow to her threats, Charles. Find and kill her!"

King Charles raised his hands to quiet the crowd. He turned toward the king of Ascomanni with a steely expression. "I will do what is right for my lands. I have no intention of bowing to Rocato's heir. She must be found and dealt with immediately—"

"Your people have proven they cannot manage to hunt or kill—"

The queen stepped forward. "How dare you!" But the king held up a hand to calm her, his steely gaze never breaking from the coldlands king.

"According to this message, ours is not the only land that

must deal with such a threat. Perhaps we should consider calling off today's ceremony so that we may each focus on the perils at hand."

"Don't even think of trying to worm your way out of this marriage arrangement." Queen Agnetha lay a hand on her husband's arm to calm him, but he flung it off, staring coldly at Aerity's father.

"I have no plan to end our arrangement," King Charles stated calmly. "My daughter will marry your nephew, as promised. However, given the circumstances, today's betrothal ceremony no longer takes precedence. You may remain in my home as long as you please, but I beg your leave as I now have urgent matters to attend." He looked out at the crowd. "To my guests, I ask you to please remain calm, in this room, until it is deemed safe for you to leave the premises. I will send message to the kitchen to bring the feast now."

King Charles swept down the steps, eyes straight forward. Queen Leighlane cast a glare at the visiting king before following her husband. The crowd pressed together, making an aisle for them. The royal family followed suit, all of Aerity's aunts, uncles, cousins, and siblings. Wyneth grasped her hand and gave it a firm squeeze as she passed. But Aerity could not move. She was rooted to that spot, her heart in her throat. Lord Alvi sent her a look of deep regret as his uncle began to grumble to his unhappy advisers.

Aerity could not believe it had come to this. Her entire world—every small detail—was crumbling.

The Ascomannian king clearly could not wait to get his hands on anything the Lochlan partnership would offer him, free trade, no doubt. And Lord Alvi would be honor bound to do and give whatever his uncle deemed his. Aerity's father had swallowed his pride so often she didn't know how he could possibly keep his chin up. Lochlanach now had a new beast, which presented itself in daylight, and a powerful, elusive madwoman to deal with. Paxton was gone, and Rozaria's notices to the lands would no doubt stir up friction against all Lashed.

Behind her, Aerity heard women crying. Questions and demands rose to a crescendo in the room. Two men began to argue, shoving each other, and guards rushed to break it up. This is how it would be throughout the land. Ordinary people would be at odds. Chaos would ensue if something wasn't done. Quickly.

Aerity took Harrison's arm and whispered, "Get Wyn out of here if you can." He eyed her and nodded.

Aerity's feet moved her forward. She mounted the steps and reached out for Lord Alvi's hand. He took it, with silent question in his eyes. The grumbling coldlands king quieted as he looked upon her. Aerity turned to the hall full of people, and her voice rang out above them.

"Good people of Lochlanach!"

Heads turned. Voices quieted. All eyes were suddenly upon her. Aerity stood tall.

"There has never been a time in my father's rule when it

has been more necessary for us all to come together." Lord Alvi moved closer to her side. "I understand your fear. I understand your worries. And I make you this promise. Together with the brave people of Ascomanni, we shall overcome those who wish to hurt us. We must all do our part, and the most important thing each of you can do is to stay calm and act within the law. Do not rise up in fear against the unknown. That is what Rozaria Rocato wants. She seeks chaos, and we must not let her have it. We must band together and show unity, now more than ever. We are seeking the heir of Rocato and her accomplice, not the entire Lashed community, most of whom are as innocent as you and I."

Some muttered, shaking their heads, and Aerity raised her voice. "If we act out of fear and hatred, then our enemy has won. Will you let your hearts be so easily betrayed by darkness?" She felt herself getting choked up. "Do not seek enemies of your neighbors, Lashed or Unlashed. I beg you, please, pass this word of encouragement throughout the lands. Let everyone you see know that the Lochsons and Alvis, the Lochlans and Ascomannians, will unite together to beat this enemy, just as my betrothed, your future prince, slew the great beast."

The crowd broke into cheer and Aerity let out a breath of relief. She looked up at Lord Alvi, who watched her with warmth.

"Spoken like a true queen," he said to her.

Aerity let a genuine smile grace her lips for the first time in a week. Still holding his hand, her eyes crossed the room to the two bright red heads by the door. Wyneth stood there holding Donubhan by the arm. Aerity's hand went clammy within Lord Alvi's. Her smile was wiped away as her stomach dropped. Harrison stood at the door, holding it open. Wyneth's jaw trembled as she gave Aerity a nod and then pulled Donny from the room. Harrison sent her an apologetic last look before following them out.

High Hall seemed to spin as kitchen staff began bringing in platters, filled to overflowing with the finest seafare, breads, and roasted root vegetables. Aerity dropped Lord Alvi's hand as the people's attention stirred away from her.

"Please, excuse me," she whispered to her betrothed, who nodded.

Princess Aerity slipped through the room, allowing people to take her hand and kiss her fingers. She gave them each smiles and blessings, wanting more than anything to fill them with the one thing she herself no longer had.

Hope.

But she now had purpose, and that would have to do.

Acknowledgments

I've started lots of stories in my life only to abandon them. I nearly cut the rope on this one, because, frankly, high fantasy is intimidating. I have a whole new outlook and appreciation for the genre. I'm so happy we moved forward, forcing me to face all my writerly fears and push myself to new limits. I'd like to thank my first readers, Morgan Shamy, Nyrae Dawn, and my agent, Jill Corcoran, for their genuine excitement in those early days of Eurona's sprouting world when I needed it most.

I'm the type of writer who requires lots of eyes on my books and lots of revising/layering. I rely so much on my beta readers to help me shape a story and show me where it's lacking. Thank you, Evie J. Burdette (beta reader and blog caretaker!), Elizabeth May, Meredith Crowley, Jill Wilson, Carolee Noury, Malissa Jayne Coy, and Jen Fisher for your valuable feedback. Many thanks to graphic artist Jennifer Munswami for her time and expertise in designing bookmarks and extraordinary graphics every time I need them (I'm very needy). I also owe so much to authors Gena Showalter and Jennifer L. Armentrout for always being there with encouragement.

I must thank my editor, Alyson Day, and HarperTeen in a *big* way, for saying, "Let's do it," once again taking my dream-come-true career to new heights, and for letting me add that additional scene so late in the game—you're the best!

A huge thanks to Jon Howard and my copy-editing team for picking up the messy pieces of this manuscript and making it shine. Thank you to Amy Ryan and Katie Fitch in design for their hard work on the cover. As for the map artist, I'm still in awe that Jonathan Roberts was able to take my terrible sketches and turn them into something amazing! Much gratitude to Jenna Lisanti, Megan Barlog, Abbe Goldberg, and Stephanie Hoover for their marketing/publicity work, always with such kindness.

Big squeezy hugs to my husband, children, parents, siblings, and friends for your constant love. And an extra thanks to my kids for coming up with the names Aerity and Rocato. "[Love] always protects, always trusts, always hopes, always perseveres" (Corinthians 13:7).

To my readers—I adore you. Blessed beyond measure. Thank you.

TURN THE PAGE FOR A SNEAK PEEK AT

The GREAT PURSUIT

Chapter

1

A new beast roamed the kingdom of Lochlanach, killing at will. A second unnatural monster created by the hands of Rozaria Rocato, granddaughter of the most infamous and hated Lashed One of all time.

Princess Aerity Lochson's mind was a blur of piled-up worries as she rushed from High Hall of the castle, away from the frightened commoners and guests who'd come for her betrothal ceremony, and toward the office of her father, King Charles. She turned at the sound of heavy footsteps behind her and found both her childhood friend Lieutenant Harrison Gillfin and her betrothed, Lord Lief Alvi, following. Lord Alvi looked every bit the hero—his broad stature striking, with elk furs about his shoulders and a black kilt to his knees above leather boots. His blue eyes were filled with bright passion and hunger, but those emotions were not for her. They were for the beast. The new hunt.

He had killed the first creature, thereby earning her hand in marriage. The thought twisted Aerity's stomach with discomfort and turned her mind to the man who'd disappeared weeks before when the beast was killed—the Lashed man who'd taken her heart with him and would likely never return. She clenched her jaw. This was no time to think of Paxton Seabolt or her drowned desires. The kingdom was suffering again—rendering everything she'd sacrificed to have been in vain.

Her eyes shifted from Lord Alvi's to Harrison's and found a fierce, protective comfort there. Harrison stood tall, lean, and capable. Never faltering. The thought of her noble friend fighting yet another beast filled her with sharp fear. So many lives had already been lost, including Harrison's cousin Breckon, who'd been the true love of Aerity's cousin Wyneth. Half a year was all it had taken to trample the dreams and futures of so many.

Aerity gave the men a nod to follow her. She lifted her long white skirts and moved quickly down the tapestry-lined hallway to her father's office. Guards and soldiers ran past, shouting orders, fully armed with bows, swords, and lines of throwing daggers strapped across their uniformed tunics.

She opened the door without knocking. No fewer than twenty faces shot toward her. She recognized the burgundy red hair of her mother, along with her aunts and uncles, military elite, and royal advisers. Her father invited them in with a quick flick of his fingers.

When the door closed he asked her, "What is the state of things in High Hall?"

"The people seemed to have calmed for the moment, Father," Aerity said. "And supper is being served."

"Your daughter gave a rousing speech," Lord Alvi proclaimed in his rumbling voice. "She is to thank for the calm."

Aerity's face flushed with heat at the unexpected compliment. Then he put a heavy hand on her shoulder and pulled her close. Aerity fought the urge to shrug away. For the sake of the kingdom, she had made a commitment to become his bride, and she would follow through regardless of what her heart wanted, and regardless of the fact that she was certain feelings had grown between Lief and Wyneth.

"Did she?" The king's eyes softened with pride, and her mother, Queen Leighlane, smiled at Aerity and Lief, no doubt thinking what a lovely couple they were. If she only knew.

Behind them Harrison cleared his throat. "Are we to begin hunting the creature, Your Majesty?"

King Charles nodded, his face lined with anxiety. "Aye. But most of the hunters have dispersed." *Or been killed*, Aerity thought with sorrow, remembering the men who'd come from all over Eurona and even a huntress who'd lost her life.

"I can have a message sent to Tiern Seabolt," Harrison said. "I'm certain he would return with haste."

Aerity's abdomen tightened. Tiern was Paxton's younger brother. He'd nearly been killed by the first beast and had been saved by Paxton's Lashed magic. It was the very reason Pax had fled the kingdom—using magic was illegal, even to heal. Aerity didn't want Tiern to hunt again. She didn't want Paxton's sacrifice to have been a waste.

"And his older brother?" the king asked.

"Nay." Harrison paused. "He disappeared after the hunt. We don't know his whereabouts."

"Must you call Tiern back?" Aerity asked. When her father's eyebrows drew together she emended, "He's . . . so young."

"He's the same age as you, Daughter," the king reminded her. "Seventeen. A man who's already proven himself in the hunt." Aerity pressed her lips together and nodded. She could not keep Tiern safe any more than she could force Harrison to stay out of harm's reach. Their heroic hearts would urge them forward.

"Can we send word to the Zandalee?" Aerity's uncle Lord Wavecrest asked.

The king shook his head. "I'm afraid not this time. The letter from the Rocato woman stated that her creatures have now been released in all the lands of Eurona. The Zandalee will be needed to fight in their own drylands of Zorfina."

A fearful silence fell over the room. Each kingdom was on its own with its own beasts to battle now. Lochlanach was a quaint kingdom of fishermen and crop villagers, farmers,

4

that had enjoyed many years of peace. The people had risen together to fight the first beast, but how much more could the king expect from them? It was too much. To imagine this kind of horror inflicted on innocent people all over Eurona sickened Aerity.

"Perhaps another proclamation?" Lord Wavecrest suggested carefully. At this proposal from Aerity's uncle, the men in the room glanced around at one another, and the hairs rose on the princess's arms. The queen caught her daughter's eyes, and they both went still.

The last proclamation had offered Aerity's hand in marriage to whoever killed the beast. The only thing left to give was the second princess, Aerity's fifteen-year-old sister, Vixie. Her father stared down at his desk.

"No." Aerity stepped forward, out of Lord Alvi's embrace, her body trembling. "You cannot offer Vixie's hand."

The king's hazel eyes, filled with regret, rose to hers. "I have nothing left to give." With Vixie's hand would come her dowry of lands. Using Vixie as a prize would surely smother her soul. Aerity wouldn't stand for it.

"And why should you oppose it?" her uncle Preston asked haughtily. "The first proclamation provided you with a fine match. It can do the same for Vixie."

Aerity stilled, forcing back the torrent of words that flooded her mind: *unfair, poor match, confinement, no joy, no love.* She was to endure those things for her kingdom, but the thought of Vixie losing her freedom to choose her future . . .

it gutted Aerity. She knew how it appeared to the world—that she'd landed a handsome, noble, brave lord—but the heart didn't care about appearances. It wanted who it wanted.

"And then what?" Aerity asked. "Who shall we offer for the next beast, and the one after that? Your own Wyneth? Or perhaps six-year-old Merity?"

Lord Wavecrest scowled.

"Enough, Aerity," Queen Leighlane said quietly. Aerity met her mother's eyes and felt an understanding there. No one knew better than the two of them how this would crush Vixie's spirit. These men couldn't possibly understand.

"Vixie's nearly sixteen," Lord Wavecrest pressed. Aerity wanted to claw out his eyes and force him to stop speaking.

"A proclamation offering Vixie's hand will be my very last resort," King Charles said, standing taller. "It is my hope that the people will rise of their own free will to protect their families and lands as they did in the last hunt. I will not hinder them with further curfews."

Lord Wavecrest shook his head and crossed his arms. Aerity breathed a temporary sigh of relief.

"Sire, we should address the *other* part of the Rocato woman's letter." This was from the king's oldest adviser, Duke Gulfton. This duke had been the closest adviser to Aerity's grandfather King Leon. His views on the Lashed were legendarily conservative and strict, and he was a proponent of keeping the Lashed lists up to date. All persons with Lashed capabilities and their families were notated in the records and checked regularly for markings.

The stooped man wore a sea-green robe around his shoulders and a perpetual serious frown on his face. He leaned on his cane. "We cannot do as the Rocato woman demands. We cannot burn our records of Lashed Ones in these lands, or give them rein to take over our kingdom."

A few of the other older men murmured their agreement.

Harrison stepped forward. "What if we made a copy of the list? Then it wouldn't matter if one was destroyed."

"I've got scribes copying pages as we speak," the king responded. "But the Rocato woman has called for the records to be burned by sundown. The copy won't be complete. There are thousands of names."

Thousands of persons with Lashed blood in Lochlanach. *Amazing*, Aerity thought. Only a small percentage of those on the list actually had magic, though. Paxton's family was not on the list. Aerity wondered how many others of magical blood had been able to elude the system.

"How will the madwoman know the difference?" Duke Gulfton asked. "Burn papers to appease her, then kill her and her monsters once and for all. End of story."

"Here, here!" a few men shouted, as if it were that simple. As if they wouldn't have done it by now if they could.

The king's jaw was set. "I have a terrible feeling this woman has eyes and ears everywhere."

The room quieted and a sense of unease spread as heads turned and everyone eyed the others present. Her father's council was a small group of family and a mere handful of wise advisers, all landowners, who'd been loyal to the kingdom since her grandfather ruled. She couldn't imagine this group being compromised.

"With all due respect, gentlemen," Lord Alvi said to the room, "we will find every beast and even Rocato herself, but we cannot guarantee immediate success. The last hunt took two months."

"Aye," Harrison added. "And she's threatening to kill seven men each week."

"You'll have to work faster this time," Duke Gulfton told them.

The room tensed. During the last hunt they'd had a hundred men. They'd sought the monster nearly ten hours a night and spent the days scouting and preparing. The lands of Lochlanach stretched far and wide. Yet people like Duke Gulfton were expecting a miracle of the sea.

Queen Leighlane cleared her throat. "The fact of the matter is that we're going to have to at least put on a show of honoring her wishes. We need to buy time as we plan."

Another elder, Duke Streamson, asked, "What are you proposing, Your Highness? Rocato is demanding that all Lashed be allowed to freely work magic."

Magic that wasn't all bad, Aerity thought. Magic that had saved Tiern and could save others. If only she could get them to embrace that.

"I have an idea." Aerity's brain whirred as all eyes turned

to her. "What if we set up a public area just outside the royal lands and invited Lashed from throughout the kingdom to come, and any Unlashed who wishes to seek their healing can receive it?"

Duke Streamson made a choking sound. "Round up the people of Rocato to turn against us in one place? That's precisely what she wants!"

Aerity rushed on. "I don't believe all Lashed are 'her people.' The entire area would be heavily guarded so that if any Lashed got out of line, they could be dealt with immediately." The old dukes scoffed at her.

One of the military advisers stepped forward. "Our numbers are not as large as they once were. Our troop sizes have been modest in the past fifty years. I've got to keep men patrolling the seas and borders, and we've lost many in the past months. I worry that a large-scale showing of the Lashed will bring crowds."

The room broke out into fervent debate. Those who were against Aerity's idea were adamant, passionate in their fears. Those in favor seemed on weak, shaky ground.

"Given permission to put their hands on innocent people, it could be a massacre!"

"What if the Lashed overwhelm our guards?"

"They'll rise up throughout the lands!"

". . . commoner revolts . . . war . . ."

Aerity felt a hand on her shoulder and turned to see Harrison, his light brown eyes showing the never-faltering respect he seemed to hold for her. She gave his hand a quick squeeze of gratitude before he released her. Aerity caught Lord Alvi watching the exchange with curiosity, so she turned her gaze forward again—she would let him think what he wanted.

"Enough!" King Charles's voice silenced the room. "I will think on it. I must put safety first. I'm not ready to overturn our laws—" Aerity opened her mouth to argue that she wasn't suggesting a complete overturn, but a one-time, enclosed, secure circumstance. Her father held up a hand to stop her. "This blasted parchment from Rozaria Rocato is bound to have our people in terror. If I take the stability of our rules away, it will cause chaos. Tonight on the lawn we will burn whatever pages my scribes have managed to copy, to keep Rozaria satisfied, but the original lists remain with us. I pray to the sea this works."

He looked at the hunters. "Lord Alvi. Lieutenant Gillfin. Gather as many hunters as you can and begin hunting this new beast immediately." They nodded and took their leave. Aerity watched them go, swallowing a dry lump in her throat. The king looked to his military advisers. "I want every soldier on duty, and round-the-clock patrolling of royal lands. I want Rozaria Rocato, dead or alive." He turned to his top castle guard. "Send messengers to the other four lands to let them know of our new foe and to find out their circumstances."

Without another word, the king swept from the room with Queen Leighlane and a line of advisers close behind.

Aerity felt the brush of velvet on her arm and peered

down at the old man beside her. It was Duke Gulfton, his eyes glistening. "I mean no disrespect, Princess, only a piece of advice. In times of fear and upheaval, absolute routine and stability in the law are called for. Any slight change can set the people off."

"As I recall," Aerity said steadily, "Mrs. Rathbrook healed your ailing heart last year." Mrs. Rathbrook was the royal healer—the only Lashed allowed to work magic.

He grasped the top of his cane with both hands. "Aye."

"Should we not allow the people of this land to benefit from magic as you have?"

He looked down at his hands, nodding solemnly. "Not all Lashed are as trustworthy as Mrs. Rathbrook. You saw the Rocato woman face-to-face. You know the evil of which she is capable."

"I suppose everyone is capable of evil, Duke Gulfton. None of us is immune, Lashed or not. But I choose to believe the best in people until they show me otherwise."

Duke Streamson, waiting in the doorway, cleared his throat. Duke Gulfton peered up at Aerity and patted her hand. "Once they show you otherwise, it is often too late. As a rule, it is not safe to take such chances. Seas help Lochlanach in our time of need."

As Duke Gulfton shuffled away, Aerity whispered in return. "Seas help us, indeed."

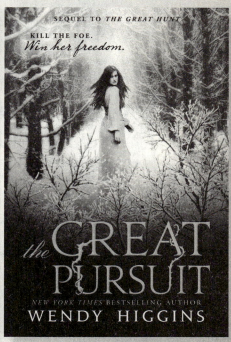

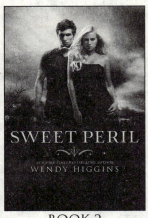

JOIN THE

Epic Reads
COMMUNITY

 THE ULTIMATE YA DESTINATION

◀ **DISCOVER** ▶
your next favorite read

◀ **MEET** ▶
new authors to love

◀ **WIN** ▶
free books

◀ **SHARE** ▶
infographics, playlists, quizzes, and more

◀ **WATCH** ▶
the latest videos